WHAT THE CRITICS ARE SAYING

✶ ✶ ✶

✶ **WORLD** magazine says *The Last Days* is "dramatic . . . good entertainment . . . a *New York Times* best seller with the gospel tucked inside."

✶ The **New York Times** calls Rosenberg "a Washington success story."

✶ **Rush Limbaugh** says *The Last Jihad* is "amazing. . . . I could not put this book down. . . . You have to read this."

✶ **Sean Hannity** calls *The Last Days* "riveting to the point you can't put it down—a heart-pounding, edge-of-your-seat roller-coaster ride."

✶ **Joe Scarborough, MSNBC,** says, "Joel Rosenberg is almost a prophet. . . . I would recommend you read these books. This is a guy who understands what is going on in the Middle East."

✶ **The Jerusalem Post** calls *The Last Days* "a fast-paced thriller, packed with the authentic details and behind-the-scenes tidbits that only a Washington insider such as Rosenberg could know. . . . Screams 'possible' from every page."

✶ **U.S. News & World Report** says Rosenberg's novels are so close to reality he seems like a "modern Nostradamus."

✶ **CNN Headline News** says, "J.K. Rowling may be the writer of the moment for the young and the young at heart. But for many adults Joel Rosenberg is the '*it author*' right now. Inside and outside the Beltway in Washington, people are snatching up copies of his almost lifelike terrorist suspense novels."

✶ **Michael Reagan** says, "*The Last Days* is a gutsy new breed of political thriller— almost prophetically forecasting what you'll read in tomorrow's headlines. . . . Rosenberg is a rising new star on the American fiction scene."

✶ **The Tampa Tribune** says, "Predicting the future can be risky business unless perhaps your name is Nostradamus. But Joel Rosenberg hit it in his first political thriller, *The Last Jihad*, written in 2001, in which he predicted a war between the United States and Iraq over weapons of mass destruction."

✯ **Steve Forbes** says, "What a timely tale. Rosenberg has written, à la Clancy, one of those rare novels that is riveting to read because it seems too real. A tingling triumph."

✯ **Vincent Flynn**, *New York Times* best-selling author of *Separation of Power*, says, "A wild, rocketing read, *The Last Jihad* is Tom Clancy writ large."

✯ *Publishers Weekly* calls *The Last Days* "an action-packed Clancyesque political thriller."

✯ *Forbes* magazine says *The Last Days* is "a rip-roaring, heart-pounding, page-turning, high-octane geopolitical thriller . . . the action never stops from the first sentence to the last."

✯ **FaithfulReader.com** says, "Rosenberg creates the narrative vortex that sucks you in by warping the timeline and populating his story with real people in imaginary places."

THE LAST JIHAD

★ ★
★

THE LAST JIHAD

★ ★ ★

JOEL C. ROSENBERG

★ ★ ★

TYNDALE HOUSE PUBLISHERS, INC.,
CAROL STREAM, ILLINOIS

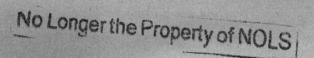

Visit Tyndale's exciting Web site at www.tyndale.com.

TYNDALE and Tyndale's quill logo are registered trademarks of Tyndale House Publishers, Inc.

The Last Jihad

Copyright © 2002 by Joel C. Rosenberg. All rights reserved.

Cover photo copyright © by Chris Dyball/Innerlight/Getty Images. All rights reserved.

Author photo copyright © 2005 by Joel Rosenberg. All rights reserved.

Designed by Dean H. Renninger

Previously published in 2002 by Tom Doherty Associates, LLC, under ISBN 0-765-30715-4.

First printing by Tyndale House Publishers, Inc., in 2006.

Library of Congress Cataloging-in-Publication Data

Rosenberg, Joel., date.
  The last jihad : a novel / by Joel C. Rosenberg.
    p. cm.
    ISBN 978-1-4143-1272-9 (pbk.)
    1. Petroleum industry and trade—Fiction. 2. Terrorism—Prevention—Fiction.
3. International relations—Fiction. 4. Middle East—Fiction. 5. Political fiction. I. Title.
  PS3618.O832L37 2006
  813'.54—dc22   2006014982

Printed in the United States of America

16   15   14   13   12   11
14   13   12   11   10   9

To Lynn—
Thank you for loving me, believing in me, encouraging me,
and running the race with me—
Next year in Jerusalem

AUTHOR'S NOTE TO THE 9/11 ANNIVERSARY EDITION

★   ★   ★

Few will ever forget what they were doing on September 11, 2001, when they first heard the news that the United States was under attack by radical Islamic jihadists using jet planes on kamikaze missions. I certainly never will.

On that beautiful, sunny, crystal clear Tuesday morning, I was putting the finishing touches on my first novel, a political thriller called *The Last Jihad*, which, as you are about to read, opens with radical Islamic terrorists hijacking a jet plane and flying an attack mission into an American city. What's more, I was doing so in a town house barely fifteen minutes from Washington Dulles Airport, where at that very moment American Airlines Flight 77 was being seized and flown right over our home toward the Pentagon.

At the time, I had no idea anything unusual was under way. I had begun writing *Jihad* in January 2001. A literary agent in Manhattan had read the first three chapters that spring. He was convinced that he could get it published, and urged me to finish it as quickly as possible. I took the advice seriously, working feverishly to get the book done before my savings account ran dry.

As had become my morning ritual, I had breakfast that fateful morning with my wife, Lynn, and our kids, threw on jeans and a T-shirt, and settled down to work on the novel's second-to-last chapter. I didn't have radio or television on. I was simply typing away on my laptop when, about an hour later, Lynn burst into the house and said, "You will not believe what's going on." She quickly explained that after dropping off two of our kids at school, she had turned on the radio and heard that the World Trade Center had been hit by two planes. We immediately turned the television on and saw the horror begin to unfold for ourselves. We saw the smoke pouring out of the North Tower. We saw the constant replays of United Airlines Flight 175 plowing into the South Tower and erupting into a massive ball of fire. And then, before we could fully process it all, we saw the World Trade Center towers collapse.

Wherever I speak around the world, people ask me what my first reaction was, but I don't recall thinking that my novel was coming true. I simply remember the feeling of shock. I remember calling friends at the White House and on Capitol Hill, and my agent, Scott Miller, in New York, hoping for word that they were safe but unable to get through, with so many phone lines jammed.

Lynn and I got our boys back from school, and several friends came over to spend the day with us. We tracked events on television, e-mailed other family and friends around the country and around the world with updates from Washington, and prayed for those directly affected by the crisis, and for our president to have the wisdom to know what to do next. Were more attacks coming? Would there be a 9/12, a 9/13, a 9/14? Would there be a series of terrorist attacks, one after another, as Israel experienced for so many years?

It was not until sometime in late November or early December that events began to settle down enough for my thoughts to turn back to *The Last Jihad*. What was I supposed to do with it? No one wanted to read a novel that opened with a kamikaze attack against an American city. It was no longer entertainment. It was too raw, too real. So I stuck it in a drawer and tried to forget about it.

But then something curious happened. Lynn and I were watching the State of the Union address in January of 2002 when President Bush delivered his now-famous "axis of evil" line, warning all Americans that the next war we might have to face could be with Saddam Hussein over terrorism and weapons of mass destruction.

Lynn and I just looked at each other as if we were living in an episode of *The Twilight Zone*. After all, it was one thing to write a novel that opened with a kamikaze attack against America. It was another thing to write a novel in which such an event triggers a global war on terror and then leads the president of the United States and his senior advisors into a showdown with Saddam Hussein over terrorism and weapons of mass destruction. But that's exactly what happens in the novel you now hold in your hands.

Scott Miller called me the next day.

"Do you work for the CIA?" he asked.

"No, of course not," I assured him.

"Sure, sure," he replied. "That's what you'd have to say if you *did* work for the CIA and just couldn't tell me."

Scott believed that the dynamic had just changed dramatically and that publishers would now be very interested in *The Last Jihad*. The country had largely recovered from the initial shock of the 9/11 attacks. We were now on offense against the Taliban in Afghanistan. People were reading everything they could get their hands on regarding the threat of radical Islam. And there were no other novels in print or on the horizon that could take readers inside the Oval Office and White House Situation Room as an American president and his war council wrestled over the morality of launching a preemptive war against the regime of Saddam Hussein. As such, Scott wanted to move quickly.

Jihad needed a few tweaks—acknowledging, for example, that 9/11 had happened and thus setting my fictional story a few years into the future—but other than that it was essentially ready to go. A publisher quickly agreed to take a risk on this unknown author and give the book a chance to find an audience. *The Last Jihad* was rushed through the publishing process and released on November 23, 2002, just as the international debate over Iraq, terrorism, and WMD reached a fever pitch.

The novel caught fire immediately. *Jihad* sold out in many stores in less than twenty-four hours and prompted nine reprintings before Christmas. In less than sixty days, I was interviewed on more than 160 radio and TV talk shows, including Rush Limbaugh, Sean Hannity, FOX, and MSNBC. The questions were as much about the novel itself as about the story behind the novel. How could I possibly have written a book that seemed to foreshadow coming events so closely? Was it a fluke? Did I get lucky? Or was there something else going on? More importantly, what did I think was coming next?

As you will see in the pages ahead, there are a number of significant differences between my fictional scenario and what really happened. But people kept asking me about the striking parallels to real life. During such interviews, I tried to focus people on the bigger picture, summing up the theme of the novel with this line: *"To misunderstand the nature and threat of evil is to risk being blindsided by it."* The truth is, America was blindsided on 9/11 by an evil few saw coming. What's more, those attacks were just the beginning of a long war against the forces of radical Islam. The most crucial question we face in the post-9/11 world is whether we have learned anything as a result of that terrible Tuesday. Do we truly understand that the forces of evil are preparing to strike us again when we least expect it? Do we truly grasp that the ultimate goal of the jihadists is not to terrorize us but to annihilate us? Are we willing to take any actions necessary to defend Western civilization from extinction? Or are we going to elevate peace over victory, retreat from the world, and simply hope for the best?

It has now been almost four years since *The Last Jihad* was first published. During this time, three more of my novels—*The Last Days*, *The Ezekiel Option*, and *The Copper Scroll*—have been published. Each continues the story and the themes that I began in *Jihad*, and each has had an uncanny, sometimes unnerving way of coming true as well. This led Tyndale House Publishers to ask me to write a nonfiction book, *Epicenter*, to explain the process I use to write books that feel "eerily prophetic" and to explain the next war that will shake our world and shape our future.

Together, these books have sold more than one million copies and have spent months on the national best-seller lists. *Jihad* alone spent eleven weeks on the *New York Times* hardcover fiction best-seller list. Such broad interest is, I believe, an indication of the anxious times in which we live. Ours, after all, is an age of kamikazes and snipers, anthrax and suicide bombers, ballistic missiles and nuclear warheads. And while we no longer face Saddam Hussein, now we face a new Iranian regime threatening to wipe the U.S. and Israel off the map. All of this raises troubling new questions: What is coming next? How bad will it be? Where will I be when it happens? And am I ready to meet my Maker if, God forbid, I'm in the wrong place at the wrong time when evil strikes again?

Such questions lie at the heart of *The Last Jihad*, and they explain, I think, why it has captured the curiosity of so many.

Perhaps you have picked up *Jihad* with these very questions in mind. Or maybe you're simply looking for a high-speed adventure ride to sweep you away from your everyday world. Either way, thank you for reading this 9/11 Anniversary Edition. Nothing has been added to the original story. No factual mistakes have been corrected. No dates or details or characters have been changed as a result of events in the actual Iraq war, or for any other reason. All we've done is a bit of copyediting to clean up a manuscript that was rushed to print so quickly in the fall of 2002.

May you enjoy reading this edition of my first novel as much as I enjoyed writing it, and may God bless you as you do.

Joel C. Rosenberg
WASHINGTON, D.C.
MAY 2006

For more about Joel's books—or to read his weblog—please visit

www.joelrosenberg.com.

Before your eyes I will repay Babylon and all who live in Babylonia for all the wrong they have done in Zion, declares the LORD. Babylon will be a heap of ruins, a haunt of jackals, an object of horror and scorn, a place where no one lives.

JEREMIAH 51:24, 37

The real test of a man is not when he plays the role that he wants for himself, but when he plays the role destiny has for him.

VACLAV HAVEL

I

★ ★
★

A PRESIDENTIAL MOTORCADE is a fascinating sight, particularly at night, and particularly from the air.

Even from twenty miles out and ten thousand feet up—on approach to Denver International Airport's runway 17R—both pilots of the Gulfstream IV could clearly see the red-and-blue flashing lights of the entourage on the ground at about one o'clock, beginning to snake westward down Pena Boulevard.

The late November air was cool, crisp, and cloudless. A full moon bathed the flat plains below and the Rockies jutting heavenward to the right with a bluish tint and remarkable visibility.

A phalanx of two dozen police motorcycles led the way toward downtown Denver, forming a V, with the captain of the motorcycle force riding point. Then came a dozen Colorado State Patrol squad cars, four rows of three each, spread out and taking up all three lanes of westbound highway with more lights and more sirens. Two jet-black Lincoln Town Cars followed immediately, carrying the White House advance team. These were followed by two black Chevy Suburbans, each carrying teams of plainclothes agents from the United States Secret Service.

Next—one after the other—came two identical limousines, both black, bulletproof Cadillacs built to precise Secret Service specifications. The first was code-named Dodgeball. The second, Stagecoach. To the untrained eye it was impossible to know the difference, or to know which vehicle the president was in.

The limousines were tailed closely by six more government-owned

Suburbans, most carrying fully locked-and-loaded Secret Service assault teams. A mobile-communications vehicle followed, along with two ambulances, a half dozen white vans carrying staffers, and two buses carrying national and local press, baggage, and equipment. Bringing up the rear were a half dozen TV-network satellite trucks, more squad cars, and another phalanx of police motorcycles.

Overhead, two Denver Metro Police helicopters flanked the motorcade—one on the right, the other on the left—and led it by at least half a mile. All in all, the caravan lit up the night sky and made a terrible racket. But it was certainly impressive—and intimidating—for anyone who cared to watch.

A local FOX reporter estimated that more than three thousand Coloradoans had just packed a DIA hangar and tarmac to see their former governor—now president of the United States—come home for Thanksgiving, his last stop on a multistate "victory tour" after the midterm elections. Some had stood in the crosswinds for more than six hours. They'd held American flags and hand-painted signs and sipped thermoses of hot chocolate. They'd waited patiently to clear through incredibly tight security and get a good spot to see the president step off *Air Force One*, flash his warm trademark smile, and deliver one simple, Reaganesque sound bite: "You ain't seen nothin' yet."

The crowd absolutely thundered with approval. They'd seen his televised Thanksgiving-week address to the nation from the Oval Office. They knew the daunting task he'd faced stepping in after Bush. And they knew the score.

America's economy was stronger than ever. Housing sales were at a record high. Small businesses were being launched at a healthy clip. Unemployment was dropping fast. The Dow and NASDAQ were reaching new heights. Homeland security had been firmly reestablished. The long war on terrorism had been an unqualified success. Al-Qaeda and the Taliban had been obliterated. Osama bin Laden had finally been found—dead, not alive.

Forty-three terrorist training camps throughout the Middle East and North Africa had been destroyed by the U.S. Delta Force and British SAS commandos. Not a single domestic hijacking had occurred in the past several years—not since a U.S. air marshal put three bullets in the heart of a

Sudanese man who single-handedly tried to take over a U.S. Airways shuttle from Washington Dulles to New York. And thousands of cell members and associates of various terrorist groups and factions had been arrested, convicted, and imprisoned in the United States, Canada, and Mexico.

Overseas, however, the news wasn't quite as good. The global economy still struggled. Car bombs and assassinations continued to occur sporadically throughout Europe and Asia as remaining terrorist networks—unable to penetrate the U.S.—tried to find new ways to lash out against the allies of the "Great Satan." One newspaper editorial said the U.S. seemed to be playing "terrorist whack-a-mole," crushing the heads of some cells at home only to see others pop up around the world. This was true. Many Americans still felt unsafe traveling overseas, and global trade, though improving, remained somewhat sluggish.

But within the U.S. there was now a restored sense of economic optimism and national security. Domestically, at least, recessions were a thing of the past and terrorism seemed to have been quashed. Presidential promises made were promises kept. And the sense of relief was palpable.

As a result, the president's job-approval ratings now stood steady at a remarkable 71 percent. At this rate he'd win reelection in a landslide, probably pick up even more House seats and very likely a solid Senate majority as well.

Then the challenge would be to move to the next level, to bolster the U.S. and international economies with his sweeping new tax cut and simplification plan. Could he really get a single-rate, 17 percent flat tax through Congress? That remained to be seen. But he could probably get the country back just to low tax rates, say 10 percent and 20 percent. And that might be good enough. Especially if he abolished the capital-gains tax and allowed immediate write-offs for investment in new plants, buildings, equipment, high-tech hardware, and computer software, instead of long, complicated, Jurassic Park–era depreciation schedules.

But all that was a headache for another day. For now, it was time for the president to head to the Brown Palace Hotel in downtown Denver and get some rest. Wednesday night he'd attend a Thanksgiving-eve party and raise $4.2 million for the Republican National Committee, then join his family already up at their palatial lodge, nestled on the slope of the Rockies in Beaver Creek, for a cozy, intimate weekend of skiing and turkey and chess. He could smell the fireplace and taste the sweet potatoes and marshmallows even now.

* * *

The motorcade cleared the airport grounds at 12:14 Wednesday morning.

Special Agent Charlie McKittrick of the U.S. Secret Service put down his high-powered night-vision binoculars and looked north, scanning the night sky from high atop the DIA control tower. In the distance, he could see the lights of the Gulfstream IV, a private jet chartered by some oil-company executives that was now the first aircraft in the holding pattern and waiting to land. Whenever the president, vice president, or other world leader flew into an airport, all other aircraft were prevented from landing or taking off, and the agency tasked with maintaining complete security put an agent in the tower to keep control of the airspace over and around the protectee. In this case, until Gambit—the code name assigned to the president—was secure at the Brown Palace, McKittrick would maintain his vigil in the tower and work with the local air-traffic controllers.

The holding pattern was now approaching five hours in length, and McKittrick had heard the G4 pilots repeat four times that they were running low on fuel. He hardly wanted to be responsible for a foul-up. It wasn't his fault the flight crew hadn't topped their tanks in Chicago rather than flying straight from Toronto. But it would certainly be his fault if something went wrong now. He glanced down at the radar screen beside him and saw thirteen other flights behind the Gulfstream. They were a potpourri of private and commercial aircraft whose pilots undoubtedly couldn't care less about the White House victory lap or the Secret Service. They just wanted their landing instructions and a good night's rest.

"All right, open 17R," McKittrick told the senior air-traffic controller, his voice suggesting an unhealthy combination of fatigue and fatalism. "Let's get the G4 down and go from there."

He cracked his knuckles, rubbed his neck, and swallowed the last of his umpteenth cup of coffee.

"TRACON, this is Tower. Over," the senior controller immediately barked into his headset. Exhausted, he just wanted to get these planes on the ground, go home, and call in sick the next day. He desperately needed a vacation, and he needed it now.

Linked by state-of-the-art fiber optics to the FAA's Terminal Radar Approach Control facility three miles south of the airport, the reply came instantaneously.

"Tower, this is TRACON. Over."

"TRACON, we're bringing in the Gulfstream on 17 Romeo. Put all other aircraft on notice. It won't be long now. Over."

"Roger that and hallelujah, Tower. Over."

The senior controller immediately switched frequencies to one-three-three-point-three-zero, and began putting the Gulfstream into an immediate landing pattern. Then he grabbed the last slice of cold pepperoni-and-sausage pizza from the box behind McKittrick and stuffed half of it in his mouth.

"Tower, this is Foxtrot Delta Lima, Niner Four Niner, on approach for 17 Romeo," said the Gulfstream. "We are going to increase speed and get on the ground as quickly as possible. Roger that?"

His mouth full, the senior controller thrust his finger at a junior controller by the window, who immediately jumped into action, used to finishing his bosses' sentences.

The young man grabbed a headset, and patched himself in. "Roger that, Foxtrot. You're cleared for landing. Bring her down."

Special Agent McKittrick didn't want to be here any more than these guys wanted him to be. But they'd better get used to it—all of them. If Gambit won his reelection campaign, he might as well open up his own bed-and-breakfast.

* * *

On board the Gulfstream, the pilot focused on the white strobe lights guiding him in and the green lamps imbedded down both sides of the runway.

He didn't have to worry about any other planes around him, because there weren't any. He didn't have to worry about any planes taxiing on the ground, because they were still in the Secret Service's holding pattern. He increased speed, lowered the landing gear, and tilted the nose down, taking the plane down from ten thousand feet to just a few hundred feet in a matter of moments.

A few minutes more and the long night would be over.

✦ ✦ ✦

Marcus Jackson munched on peanut M&M's and tapped away quietly on his Sony VAIO notebook computer as the motorcade sped along at well over seventy miles an hour.

As the *New York Times* White House correspondent, Jackson was permanently assigned Seat 1 on Press Bus 1. That put him just over the right shoulder of the driver, able to see and hear everything. But having awoken at 4:45 a.m. for baggage call in Miami—and having visited twelve states in the past four days on the president's Thanksgiving Tour—Jackson couldn't care less what could be seen or heard from his coveted seat. All he wanted to do now was get to the hotel and shut down for the night.

Behind Jackson sat two dozen veteran newspaper and magazine reporters, TV correspondents, network news producers, and "big foot" columnists—the big, brand-name pundits who not only wrote their political analyses for the *Times* and the *Post* and the *Journal* but also loved to engage each other on *Hannity & Colmes* and *Hardball*, O'Reilly and King, *Crossfire* and *Capital Gang*. All of them had wanted to see the president's victory lap up close and personal. Now all of them wanted it to be over so they, too, could get home for Thanksgiving.

Some dozed off. Some updated their Palm Pilots. Others talked on cell phones with their editors or their spouses. A junior press aide offered them sandwiches, snacks, and fresh, hot coffee from Starbucks. This was the A team, everyone from ABC News and the Associated Press to the *Washington Post* and the *Washington Times*. Together, what the journalists on this bus alone wrote and spoke could be read, watched, or listened to by upward of 50 million Americans by 9 a.m.

So they were handled with care by a White House press operation that wanted to make sure the A team didn't add to their generally ingrained bias against conservative Republicans by also being hungry, cold, or in any other way uncomfortable. Sleep was something national political reporters learned to do without. Starbucks wasn't.

A former *Army Times* correspondent who covered the Gulf War, then moved back to his hometown to work for the *Denver Post*, Jackson had joined the *New York Times* less than ten days before Gambit announced his campaign for the GOP nomination. What a roller coaster since then, and he was getting tired. Maybe he needed a new assignment. Did the *Times* have a bureau in Bermuda? Maybe he should open one. *Just get through today,* Jackson thought to himself. *There'll be plenty of time for vacation soon enough.* He glanced up to ask a question about the president's weekend schedule.

Across the aisle and leaning against the window sat Chuck Murray, the White House press secretary. Jackson noticed that for the first time since he'd met Murray a dozen years ago, "Answer Man" actually looked peaceful. His tie was off. His eyes were closed. His hands were folded gently across his chest, holding his walkie-talkie with a tiny black wire running up to an earpiece in his right ear. This allowed him to hear any critical internal communications without being overheard by the reporters on the bus. On the empty seat beside Murray lay a fresh yellow legal pad. No to-do list. No phone calls to return. Nothing. This little PR campaign was just about over. Do or die, there was nothing else Murray or his press team could do to get the president's approval ratings higher than they already were, and he knew it. So he relaxed.

Jackson made a mental note: *This guy's good. Let him rest.*

☆　☆　☆

Special Agent McKittrick was tired.

He walked over to the Mr. Coffee machine near the western windows of the control tower, out of everyone's way, itching to head home. He ripped open a tiny packet of creamer and sprinkled it into his latest cup. Then two packets of sugar, a little red stirrer, and *voilà*—a new man. Hardly. He took a sip—ouch, too hot—then turned back to the rest of the group.

For an instant, McKittrick's brain didn't register what his eyes were seeing. The Gulfstream was coming in too fast, too high. Of course it was in a hurry to get on the ground. But get it right, for crying out loud. McKittrick knew each DIA runway was twelve thousand feet long. From his younger days as a navy pilot, he figured the G4 needed only about three thousand feet to make a safe landing. But at this rate, the idiots were actually going to miss—or crash. No, that wasn't it. The landing gear was going back up. The plane was actually *increasing* its speed and pulling up.

"*What's going on, Foxtrot?*" screamed the senior controller into his headset.

When McKittrick saw the Gulfstream bank right toward the mountains, he knew.

"*Avalanche. Avalanche,*" McKittrick shouted into his secure digital cell phone.

★ ★ ★

Marcus Jackson saw the bus driver's head snap to attention.

A split second later, Chuck Murray bolted upright in his seat. His face was ashen.

"What is it?" asked Jackson.

Murray didn't respond. He seemed momentarily paralyzed. Jackson turned to the front windshield and saw the two ambulances and the mobile-communications van pulling off on either side of the road. Their own bus began slowing and moving to the right shoulder. Up ahead, the rest of the motorcade began rapidly pulling away from them. Though he couldn't see the limousines, he could see the Secret Service Suburbans now moving at what he guessed had to be at least a hundred miles an hour, maybe more.

Jackson's combat instincts took over. He grabbed for his leather carry-on bag on the floor, fished through it frantically, and pulled out a pair of sports binoculars he'd found handy during the campaign when the press was kept far from the candidate. He trained on the Suburbans and quietly gasped. The tinted rear windows of all four specially designed Suburbans were now open. In the back of each of the first four vehicles were sharpshooters wearing black masks, black helmets, steel gray jumpsuits, and thick Kevlar bulletproof vests. What sent a chill down Jackson's spine, however, wasn't their uniforms, or their high-powered rifles. It was the two agents in the last two vehicles, the ones holding the Stinger surface-to-air missile launchers.

★ ★ ★

"*Talk to me, McKittrick.*"

Special Agent-in-Charge John Moore—head of the president's protective detail—shouted into his secure cellular phone as he sat in the front seat of Gambit's limousine, his head craning to see what was happening behind him.

Just hearing McKittrick yell, "Avalanche"—the Secret Service's code for a possible airborne attack—had already triggered an entire series of preset, well-trained, and now instinctual reactions from Moore's entire team. Now he needed real information, and he needed it fast.

"You've got a possible bogey on your tail," said McKittrick from the control tower, his binoculars trained on the lights of the Gulfstream. "He's not responding to his radio, but we know it's working."

"*Intent?*"

"What's that?" McKittrick asked, garbled by a flash of static.

"*Intent? What's his intent? Is he hostile?*" shouted Moore.

"Don't know, John. We're warning him over and over—he's just not responding."

Gambit lay on the floor, his body covered by two agents. The agents had no idea what threats they faced. But they were trained to react first and ask questions later. Moore scrambled over them all to get a better look through the tiny back window. For a moment he could see the lights of the Gulfstream bearing down on them. Suddenly the plane's lights went out, and Moore lost visual contact.

Glancing to his right, he could see Dodgeball—the decoy limousine—pulling up to his side as Pena Boulevard ended and the motorcade poured onto I-70 West. Both cars were moving at close to 130 miles an hour.

The question facing both drivers was whether or not they could get off the open and exposed stretch of highway they were now on and get under the interwoven combination of concrete bridges and overpasses that lay just ahead at the interchange of I-70 and I-25. This would make an overhead attack more difficult, though not impossible. The challenge would be driving fast enough to get there and then being able to stop fast enough—or stop and back up fast enough—to get and stay under the bridges and out of the potential line of fire.

But what if the bridges were booby-trapped with explosives? What if the Denver Metro Police and Colorado State Patrol securing the bridges were compromised? Were they escaping an enemy, or being driven into the enemy's hands?

Moore reacquired the Gulfstream in his high-powered night-vision binoculars. It was gaining fast.

"Nighthawk Four, Nighthawk Five, this is Stagecoach. Where are you guys?" Moore shouted into his wrist-mounted microphone.

"Stagecoach, this is Nighthawk Five. We'll be airborne in one minute," came the reply.

"Nighthawk Four. Same thing, Stagecoach."

Moore cursed. The pair of AH-64 Apaches were state-of-the-art combat helicopters. Both could fly at a maximum speed of 186 miles per hour, and both carried sixteen Hellfire laser-guided missiles and 30 mm front-mounted machine guns. But both—on loan from the army's Fort Hood in Texas—might actually end up being useless to him.

After the suicide airplane attacks against the Twin Towers and the Pentagon, the Secret Service had decided that motorcades should be tailed by Apaches. "Just in case" was, after all, the Service's unofficial motto. But the White House political team went nuts. It was one thing to keep the president secure. It was another thing to have military helicopters flying CAP—combat air patrols—over city streets and civilian populations year after year after year. A compromise was reached. The Apaches would be pre-positioned and on standby at each airport the president or vice president was flying into, but wouldn't actually fly over the motorcades. It seemed reasonable at the time. Not anymore.

But it didn't matter now. Moore's mind scrambled for options.

Nikon One. Nikon Two. This is Stagecoach. Turn around and get in front of this guy.

"Nikon One, roger that."

"Nikon Two, roger."

The two Denver Metro Police helicopters weren't attack helicopters. They certainly weren't Apaches. They were basically reconnaissance aircraft using night-vision video equipment to look for signs of trouble on the ground—not the air. But they immediately peeled off the formation and banked hard to get behind Gambit's limousine. The question was, could they make the maneuver fast enough? And what then?

☆　☆　☆

The Gulfstream pilot ripped his headphones off and tossed them behind him.

The tower was screaming at him in vain to change course immediately or risk being fired upon. Why be distracted?

He could see the police helicopters beginning to break right and left, respectively, so he increased his speed, lowered the nose and began bearing down on the two limousines, now side by side.

* * *

"Tommy, you got an exit coming up?" Moore shouted back to his driver.

"Sure do, boss. Coming up fast on the right—270 West."

"Good. Stagecoach to Dodgeball."

"Dodgeball—go."

"Pull ahead and break right at the 270 West exit. 270 West—go, go, go."

Agent Tomas Rodriguez imperceptibly eased his foot off the gas, just enough to let the decoy limousine roar ahead, pull in front of him, and then peel off to the right—just barely making the exit ramp.

* * *

For the first time, the Gulfstream pilot let out a string of obscenities.

With one limousine peeling off to the right and two Chevy Suburbans going with it, he suddenly doubted the intelligence he'd been given. Which limousine was he after? Which had the president? He was pretty sure it was not the one that had just peeled off. But now he hesitated.

His heart was racing. His palms were sweaty. His breathing was rapid and he was scared. Yes, he was ready to die for this mission. But he'd better take someone with him—and the right someone at that.

* * *

"Tommy, how far to the interchange?" Moore demanded.

"Don't know, sir—five miles, maybe eight."

It felt like they were moving at light speed, but Moore didn't like his odds. After all, they were rapidly approaching the outskirts of Denver. He could clearly see the city skyline and the bright blue Qwest logo, high atop the city's tallest building. All around him, industrial buildings and restaurants and hotels and strip malls were blurring past on each side of the highway. In his race to escape, he was drawing the G4 into the city and putting thousands of innocent civilians in danger.

"Cupid, Gabriel, this is Stagecoach. Do you copy?" Moore sure hoped they did.

"Stagecoach, this is Cupid. Copy you loud and clear, sir."

"Roger that, Stagecoach. This is Gabriel. Copy you five by five."

"You guys got a shot?"

"Yes, sir," said Cupid. "Ten miles out—2,500 feet up."

Both Cupid's and Gabriel's eyesight was 20/20 uncorrected. Their night-vision goggles made the G4 impossible to lose against the night sky. Both voices were steady and calm. A former CIA special-ops guy, Cupid was extremely well trained, having lived in Afghanistan for years, training *mujahedin* how to use portable, shoulder-mounted, heat-seeking Stinger missiles in the war against the Soviets in the eighties. Gabriel was nearly as good, having been Cupid's understudy for the past six years.

Moore gripped the backseat of the limousine. He didn't have time to consult Washington. He barely had enough time to give an order to shoot. What if he was wrong? What if he was misreading the situation? If the United States Secret Service shot down a bunch of businessmen in cold blood . . .

✱ ✱ ✱

"Sir, it's Home Plate—line one," Agent Rodriguez shouted from the driver's seat.

Moore grabbed the digital phone lying on the seat beside him. "Stagecoach to Home Plate, go secure."

"Secure, go. John, it's Bud. What've you got?"

Bud Norris was the gray, stocky, balding director of the U.S. Secret Service, a twenty-nine-year veteran of the Service and a Vietnam veteran who'd driven for U.S. generals and VIPs in Saigon until it fell. In 1981, he'd been President Reagan's limousine driver the day John Hinckley Jr. tried to assassinate the president in a vain attempt to impress actress Jodie Foster. In fact, within the Service, Norris was widely credited with helping save Reagan's life that day. At first, Reagan's agents hadn't realized he'd been shot—until he began coughing up bright red blood on the way to the White House. Told to divert immediately to GW Hospital, Norris slammed on the brakes, did a 180-degree turn into oncoming traffic on Pennsylvania Avenue, and made it to the hospital just moments before Reagan collapsed and slipped into unconsciousness from massive internal bleeding.

Norris was a pro. His agents knew it. And having worked his way up through the ranks from one promotion to another to the top spot just three years ago, Norris commanded enormous respect from his team.

"Sir, we've got a G4 bearing down on us. Broke out of a landing pattern, pulled up its gear, and cut its lights. We're racing for cover but right now we're in the open. Dodgeball broke right but the G4 is sticking with us," Moore told his boss, surprised by the relative steadiness in his voice.

"Range?"

"Twenty-five hundred feet up, ten miles out, closing fast."

"Contact?"

"Not anymore. Tower's been talking to him all night. But now McKittrick's screaming at them to change course and he's getting nothing back."

"Who's on board?"

"I don't know. Charter from Toronto. Supposed to be oil execs, but I don't really know."

"What's your gut tell you, John?"

Moore hesitated for a moment. The full weight of responsibility for protecting the president of the United States sent an involuntary shudder through his body. He suddenly felt cold and clammy. His wrinkled, rumpled suit was now soaked with sweat. Whatever he said next would seal the G4's fate—and his.

"I don't know, sir."

"Make a call, John."

Moore took a deep breath—the first he actually remembered taking in the last several minutes. "I think we've got another kamikaze, sir, and he's coming after Gambit."

"Take him out," Norris commanded instantly.

"We don't know a hundred percent for sure who's on board that plane, sir," Moore reminded his boss, for the record, for the audiotapes being recorded in the basement of the Treasury Building in Washington.

"Take him out."

"Yes, sir."

Moore tossed the phone aside and grabbed his wrist-mounted microphone. "Nikon One, Nikon Two—this is Stagecoach. Abort. Abort. Abort."

"Roger that, Stagecoach."

Both police helicopters banked hard right and left respectively and raced for cover.

"Cupid, Gabriel, this is Stagecoach. You got tone?"

The November air and whipping winds caused by speeds upward of 140 miles per hour created a windchill in the back of the black Chevy Suburbans somewhere south of zero. It also made it almost impossible for any normal person to hear anything. But the agents code-named Cupid and Gabriel wore black ski masks and gloves to protect their faces and hands from arctic temperatures and wore the same brand and model of headphones worn by NASCAR's Jeff Gordon at the Daytona 500. Moore's voice was, therefore, crystal clear.

"Stand by, Stagecoach," Cupid said calmly.

The G4 was now only seven miles from Gambit's limousine and coming in white-hot.

First, Cupid "interrogated" the Gulfstream, pressing the IFF challenge switch on his Stinger missile launcher. This immediately sent a signal to the aircraft's transponder asking whether it was a friend or foe. The answer didn't actually matter at this point. But the procedure did.

Beep, beep, beep, beep, beep, beep.

The rapid-fire beeping meant the answer was "unknown." Cupid sniffed in disgust, turned off the safety, and pushed the actuator button forward and downward. This warmed up the BCU—the battery coolant unit—hooked to Cupid's belt and made the weapon go live. Though it took only five seconds, it felt like a lifetime.

Next, Cupid triggered an infrared signal at the G4 to determine its range and acquire the heat emanating from the plane's jet engines. Instantly hearing a strong, clear, high-pitched tone, he quickly pressed the weapon's uncaging switch with his right thumb and held it in, and the tone got louder. He now had a lock on the G4, just three miles away and down to a mere one thousand feet.

"I have tone. I have a lock," Cupid shouted into the whipping wind and the microphone attached to his headphones. The G4 was now just two miles back.

"Me, too, sir," Gabriel echoed.

Moore was not normally a religious man. But he was today.

"Oh, God, have mercy," he whispered, then crossed himself for the first time since graduating from St. Jude's Catholic High School.

"Fire, fire, fire," Moore shouted.

"Roger that. Hold your breath, hold your breath," Cupid shouted.

Moore and all his agents immediately responded, gulping as much oxygen as they possibly could. But Cupid wasn't actually talking to them. Per his intensive training, he was reminding himself and his driver that they were about to be trapped inside a live, mobile missile silo, and it wasn't going to be pretty. Cupid's driver quickly lowered every other window in the vehicle and threw another switch turning on a small, portable air pump as well. The G4 was now less than a mile back.

"Three, two, one, fire."

Cupid squeezed the trigger.

Nothing happened.

Moore waited, his heart racing, his eyes desperately scanning the sky.

"Cupid, what's the problem?"

"Don't know, sir. Malfunction. Hold on."

"I don't have time to—Gabriel, talk to me."

"Got it, sir. Don't worry. Hold your breath, hold your breath. Three, two, one . . ."

The Stinger missile exploded from its fiberglass tube and streaked into the night sky. The Suburban filled with a flash of blinding fire and hot, toxic, deadly fumes. For a moment, the driver began to lose control of the vehicle. Moore could see the Suburban rock and swerve. But within seconds the smoke and fumes were sucked out of the vehicle and into the atmosphere. The driver could see again. Gabriel could breathe again if he wanted to—but he didn't. Not until he was sure.

☆　☆　☆

McKittrick knew combat firsthand.

He'd been in the Gulf War. He'd seen gunfire and death. But he'd never seen anything like this. Nor would he again. As he watched through his high-powered binoculars from the control tower, he saw the Stinger missile tear the G4 in half. The plane then erupted in a massive fireball. McKittrick fell to the ground, screaming in pain. The explosion

was magnified so intensely by his night-vision binoculars that it had
burned holes in his retinas, leaving him permanently blinded.

*　*　*

Moore was horrified.

Despite all of his training, he was suddenly completely unprepared for
what was happening. This was no ordinary charter plane falling from the
sky. It was a death machine, packed with explosives for maximum impact.
The roar of the explosion was deafening, heard as far away as Castle Rock.
The sky was now on fire. Night turned to day. The flash of heat was un-
bearable. Molten metal rained down on the motorcade.

Cupid's Chevy Suburban swerved hard and barely escaped being landed upon by the disintegrating G4. Gabriel was not so lucky. Moore saw
one of the G4's engines slam into the young agent's vehicle and explode
into yet another blinding fireball. But what Moore saw next terrified him
more than anything else. The fuselage of the G4 was hurtling at him like
a flaming meteor, propelled forward by the force of the blast.

"Tommy!" Moore screamed.

Agent Rodriguez began swerving right, heading for an off-ramp and
praying desperately the car wouldn't overturn. But it was too late. The
G4's burning fuselage crashed into the pavement just behind them and
slammed into the back of the limousine, sending Stagecoach careening
into the concrete dividers in the center of the superhighway in a series of
360-degree spins. The car rolled over and over again in a fury of sparks
and flames and smoke, eventually grinding to a halt upside down below
the overpass for which Rodriguez had been racing. Inside Stagecoach—
from the moment of impact—airbags exploded from the steering wheel
and dashboard, from each car door and even from the roof, a feature designed exclusively for Secret Service vehicles, particularly since no one
inside ever wore seat belts.

*　*　*

I-70 was ablaze.

The wreckage of the G4 and whatever was inside it was strewn
everywhere, on fire and scorching hot. The surviving Suburbans screeched
to a halt. Secret Service assault teams immediately jumped out, armed with

M16 rifles and fire-suppression equipment. Cupid regained his bearings and quickly began to check his weapon for the malfunction. He'd personally failed his mission. He had no idea what else might transpire. And he wasn't about to take any chances.

Dodgeball and its security package now reversed course and raced to rejoin Stagecoach. Weaving carefully through the wreckage, the backup vehicles arrived to find assault teams taking up positions in a perimeter around Gambit's car. Two more assault teams quickly joined their colleagues while three agents hauled a large metal box from the back of one of the Suburbans and hurried it to Stagecoach's side. They rapidly removed a specially designed Jaws of Life kit and began trying desperately to get Gambit out of the wreckage.

Colorado State Patrol cars and local fire trucks, along with the motorcycle units, raced to the scene. Overhead, the two police helicopters hovered nosily, each shining powerful search lamps onto the ground below to help the rescuers do their jobs.

☆ ☆ ☆

"John. John. This is Bud. What's your status?"

Bud Norris heard the explosion and the screaming through John Moore's digital cell phone on the backseat of Gambit's car. But now the line was pure static and he feared the worst. Norris grabbed a secure digital phone from the bank of phones in front of him and speed-dialed the lead Apache pilot.

"Nighthawk Four, this is Home Plate. Do you copy?" Norris barked.

"Home Plate, this is Nighthawk Four—we have a Code Red in progress. Repeat, we have a Code Red in progress. Please advise. I repeat, please advise."

"Nighthawk, you've got video capability, right?"

"Affirmative, Home Plate. We've got three systems on board. What do you need?" the lead pilot responded.

"What've you got?" Norris asked, his mind suddenly scrambling to remember the details he needed.

"Sir, we've got the TADS FLIR system, which is thermal imaging. But, sir, you've got two police helicopters here lighting the whole scene with spotlights. It's basically a TV studio down there, sir. If you'd like, we can use our Day TV system with black-and-white video imaging, or the DVO system with full color and magnification. It's your call, sir."

"Can you get it to me through a secure satellite, son?"

"We can get it to the Pentagon, sir. I think they can patch you in, sir, but don't quote me. You gotta check with Ops to be sure."

"I'll do it. Start transmitting, son. I'll take care of the rest."

Norris picked up another phone and speed-dialed the other Apache. "Nighthawk Five, this is Home Plate. You there? Over."

"Nighthawk Five, standing by, sir."

"Set up a perimeter around the crash site and tell the news helicopters they're grounded immediately. I'm scrambling an F-15 fighter squadron to join you in the next few minutes, and I want a no-fly zone over the state of Colorado. Got that?"

"Roger that, Home Plate."

Next, Norris sent out a Code Red on all Secret Service frequencies and gave the word for the vice president, the Speaker of the House, and all cabinet members—spread out all over the country for the holidays—to be evacuated to secure underground facilities immediately. Moments later Norris was on the phone with the secretary of defense and the Pentagon watch commander. The air force scrambled aircraft to secure the skies over Denver.

Now a live, color, digital video feed from the hovering Nighthawk Four began streaming into the National Military Command Center, the nuclear-missile-proof war room deep underground, below the Pentagon. It was then cross-linked via secure fiber-optic lines to the Secret Service command center in the bombproof basement of the Treasury Department in Washington, the White House Situation Room, the FBI Op Center, and the CIA's Global Operations Center at Langley. Norris could finally see the grisly scene unfolding on one of the five large-screen TVs. His top staff worked the phones around him, gathering intelligence from the ground, alerting other security details and opening a direct line to FBI Director Scott Harris.

"My God," Norris said quietly.

The terrorists had struck again.

2

★ ★
★

JON BENNETT nervously sipped his Turkish coffee.

He looked out at the morning sun warming the golden stones of Jerusalem's Old City. But, though he now sat in a restaurant within the King David Hotel—where the British army once maintained its head-quarters, where Winston Churchill once dined, where the Rothschilds once cut investment deals, where Israel's late prime minister Yitzhak Rabin and Jordan's late King Hussein once signed a peace treaty—Bennett had little interest in the hotel's history.

He had little interest in its $25 million face-lift, or its exquisitely polished marble floors, or its plush Moroccan upholstery. He had little interest in the huge vases of fresh-cut Israeli roses and huge baskets of crusty French breads on the tables behind him. Or in the cantankerous elderly French couple beside him, as crusty as the breads, hunched over their travel books and already muttering complaints on the first day of their tour.

Bennett's first trip to Israel was no vacation. He'd arrived at four in the afternoon the day before. He was leaving in less than three hours. He needed no travel books. He'd do no sightseeing. He was here for one purpose, and one purpose only—to get a signature, get it quickly, and get out.

The fiftyish, balding Russian in the ill-fitting suit and thick, wire-rimmed spectacles sat hunched across the table from Bennett, chain-smoking cigarettes as he carefully read the documents before him. Only minor changes had been made from the night before. They were the precise changes on which the Russian had insisted, to which Bennett had agreed, and for which Bennett had gotten up before dawn to enter them into his laptop, print the documents out, and bring them to this morning's brief and final meeting. But neither this Russian nor any other had exactly been raised in a culture of trust. So the man pored over every jot and tittle, every comma and semicolon, as the minutes ticked by.

Just sign the thing, be done with it, and be rich, Bennett thought. Yet the more anxious he grew internally, the more it seemed his dear Russian friend would slow down and reread some paragraph again and again and again.

☆   ☆   ☆

At forty, Bennett was one of the youngest and most successful investment strategists on Wall Street.

Single, six feet tall, and an obsessive runner, Bennett had wavy dark hair, grayish green eyes, and rakish good looks. He was, more important in his mind, smart and sharp and rich—in part because he was stealthy.

Unlike his colleagues ten to twenty years his senior—the chief investment strategists for the powerhouse firms like Merrill Lynch and Goldman Sachs and UBS Paine Webber—Bennett didn't appear on CNBC, or kibitz with Maria Bartiromo, or speak at Fortune 500 conferences, or get himself profiled in the *Wall Street Journal*. Run a LexisNexis search on him and you'd come up empty-handed. To most he was unknown. To the few who knew him outside his own company, he was underestimated. To those who underestimated him, he was considered unimportant. And this gave him precisely the element of surprise he needed to stay one step ahead of the vicious competition.

Bennett wasn't a stockbroker, or a bond trader, or a mutual-fund manager. In fact, he didn't trade money at all. His trade was information.

"Foreknowledge cannot be elicited from ghosts and spirits," wrote Sun Tzu, the Chinese war strategist. "It cannot be inferred from comparison of previous events, or from the calculations of the heavens, but must be obtained from people who have knowledge of the enemy's situation."

This was Bennett's life verse. Beyond Wall Street, he seemed to know everyone, though few seemed to know him. He spent nearly every day on the phone with junior staffers and doormen and secretaries and drivers and flight crews and bank tellers and temps from Silicon Valley to the Jordan Valley, from Hong Kong to obscure oil-drilling equipment manufacturers in Waco, Texas.

He trolled for seemingly meaningless tips. Properly analyzed, he believed such tips could unlock important truths. Such truths could foretell emerging trends. And such trends, he knew from personal experience, could beget unspeakable treasures. "Get the facts, get them right, and get them first," Bennett told his elite team of researchers over and over again. "Yes, make the most of charts and graphs and statistical analysis. But don't stop there. Build personal relationships with people who don't even realize they know the world's most important secrets, and you'll quietly enter the world of people whose secrets they hold."

Bennett's currency, his stock-in-trade, was precious little nuggets of information about the future of companies and countries and the leaders who ran them. He knew how to pan for such nuggets. He knew how to melt them down and extract the precious from the worthless. He knew what to do with the gold he found, and how to sell it for large fees, rather than give it away to lazy reporters, or worse, blab about it to day traders on CNNfn. That was why he was in Jerusalem today, while his colleagues were back in New York. The big-name strategists-turned-stars of Wall Street—and their fast-talking, high-priced PR pitchmen—were fanning out to talk with the worldwide media about what the successful U.S. war against terrorism and rising consumer confidence would mean to the markets. Not Bennett. He knew something his colleagues didn't, and it was big. Very big.

☆　☆　☆

Bennett took another sip of his coffee.

He checked his watch, obsessively tapped his foot, and discreetly scanned the room. It was still fairly early, and nearly empty. But not for long. He glanced again at his Russian friend. Three more pages to go.

For crying out loud, just sign the stupid thing, Bennett silently screamed. *Sign it before someone sees us hiding in plain sight.*

☆　☆　☆

No question, this was the biggest deal Bennett had ever worked on.

By the end of the year—possibly by the end of the month—he would be named the new president and CEO of his company. Thus, the financial rewards of the Russian across the table putting his Ivan Hancock on the dotted line in the next five minutes were something beyond even Bennett's most vivid imagination. Within five years, possibly less, he could actually be a member of the Nine Zeroes Club, a billionaire on the Forbes 400 list. His cover would be blown. He would no longer be obscure, operating in the shadows. But it wouldn't matter. The world would know he had discovered buried treasure, and before he was fifty, he would know a measure of wealth once inconceivable.

Finding something of value in a seemingly worthless field was something of a gift for Bennett. Persuading clients to buy an entire "worthless" field in order to quietly, stealthily capture the hidden gems within it was something of an art form, and though his countenance rarely showed it, he loved every minute of the game. It wasn't the primal thrill of an African safari, of lying in wait and going for the big kill, though some of his colleagues seemed to love that metaphor. It was more like the quiet, private thrill an offensive coach experiences when—after watching hour after hour of an upcoming competitor's game films—he suddenly, unexpectedly, sees something no else has: a chink in his opponent's armor, a tiny, nearly imperceptible weakness that—properly analyzed—could be exploited to major advantage. He stops the videotape, rewinds it, and looks at it again and again and again. Then, convinced he's right, he faces the challenge of convincing his head coach not only that he's right, but that he's also got a strategy to seize the moment. Victory is found in the tiny details, Bennett believed, and he had an uncanny track record for being right.

* * *

Sometimes it still amazed Bennett how he'd gotten here.

He'd graduated from high school at seventeen, and locked down an undergraduate degree from Georgetown and an MBA degree from Harvard in near-record time. He'd worked for a summer as a junior reporter for the *Wall Street Journal* in New York, covering the oh-so-thrilling world of variable annuities and long-term life insurance products. Bored stiff and making peanuts, he knew he needed a change of attitude—and *altitude*.

Good-bye, Wall Street. Hello, Denver.

It took a few months—during which he busied himself with back-packing and mountain biking—but he finally landed a job as a research assistant to James MacPherson, something of a legend in the financial-services industry. A decorated navy fighter pilot in Vietnam, MacPherson came back from the war ready to make serious money—and ski. He'd worked his way up Wall Street's greasy pole as a bond trader in the mid-1970s, then jumped ship in 1980 to Fidelity to help launch new mutual funds, eventually managing one of the largest himself. A millionaire several times over by 1988, MacPherson then made his own move from Wall Street to Denver, in this case to launch his own aggressive global growth fund—the Joshua Fund—and be closer to his beloved Rocky Mountains, the mountains of his youth.

Simultaneously, MacPherson founded Global Strategix, Inc., known by insiders as GSX. One part strategic-research firm, one part venture-capital fund, GSX advised multibillion-dollar mutual-fund and pension-fund managers—including MacPherson's own Joshua Fund—on the strengths and weaknesses of individual companies; market sectors; the U.S. and foreign economies; currencies; stock exchanges; regulatory, tax, and political developments; and anything else that could affect the value of a client's assets. Both companies caught the wave and became phenomenally successful, creating MacPherson's legend of building two multibillion-dollar companies at the same time. But Jon Bennett, his young protégé, knew the truth was a little less dramatic. MacPherson once told him on a late-night flight from Rio that he'd never been entirely sure the Joshua Fund would actually succeed and had created GSX to fall back on if necessary.

Over the years, GSX developed the reputation among fund managers as the industry's AWACS—its airborne warning and control system, refer-ring to the U.S. military's premier air battle command-and-control plane that warned friendly forces of incoming trouble long before it arrived. GSX seemed to have an uncanny ability to forecast financial trouble and chart a consistently impressive path to safer, sunnier skies.

GSX also developed a reputation for finding "sure things," early investments in fledgling, start-up companies that hit the jackpot and paid off big, both in terms of profits and stock prices. In fact, whenever

MacPherson and his team found a sure thing, they not only advised their clients to play big, but invested heavily themselves as well. Indeed, it was rumored they weren't above actually "forgetting" to mention the occasional sure thing to even their best clients and instead investing only their own venture-capital funds. Asked by reporters about such rumors, however, MacPherson never tipped his hand. He would simply smile.

Early on, MacPherson snagged the help of one of the most prescient of global economic wise men, a man widely regarded as something of a master at seeing around corners and over the horizons, be they east or west. He hired a man named Stuart Iverson, the blunt-talking, pipe-smoking, French-cuff wearing, never-married, newly retired U.S. ambassador to Russia, to be president and CEO of Global Strategix and vice chairman of the Joshua Fund.

"I want you to make GSX the financial industry's equivalent of the CIA," insisted MacPherson at their seal-the-deal luncheon at Ruth's Chris Steak House in LoDo.

"You'd better hope I do a heck of a lot better than the boys at Langley," Iverson laughed. "They thought the Soviet Union was an economic superpower. Until the day it went out of business."

In fact, it was Iverson—not the CIA—who had accurately predicted the Soviet Union's imminent demise during the 1980s and, as ambassador, fed Langley remarkably accurate forecasts of the economic and political upheavals that were on the way. Unfortunately, no one listened to him quite as carefully as they should have.

His instincts telling him that both MacPherson and his two companies were poised for dramatic growth, Ambassador Iverson took the job. In turn, Iverson hired young Jon Bennett and assigned him to work for MacPherson. Bennett's father, Sol, had been the *New York Times* bureau chief in Moscow during the 1970s when he met Iverson, who was then serving as an economic attaché at the U.S. Embassy in Moscow. It was all just further proof to Bennett that Sun Tzu was right: success is as much who you know as what you know.

In early 1992, Bennett found himself in a private meeting with the CEO he had come to admire and even like. He'd been summoned into the inner sanctum, MacPherson's private corner office. Two walls of floor-to-ceiling windows, each with a breathtaking view of the snowcapped

Rocky Mountains. A sparse desk sporting a state-of-the-art laptop computer. Big leather couches. A grainy photo of MacPherson in his F-4 flight gear on the deck of an aircraft carrier, somewhere off the coast of South Vietnam. A huge chunk of the Berlin Wall in a Plexiglas case, next to a photo of MacPherson at the White House, with President Reagan on one side and British Prime Minister Margaret Thatcher on the other.

On this bright blue, dazzling morning, MacPherson wanted to know whether he should make a major investment in interactive, high-definition TV, which, rumor had it, was going to be big. He tasked Bennett to get the answer. Bennett's voraciousness and high energy made a big impression. He sunk his teeth into the project, crunched the numbers, and talked to everyone he could find, including the secretaries, drivers, and associates at a slew of major high-tech venture-capital firms. He also quickly and very ambitiously commissioned focus groups at a dozen junior high schools across the country to see if interactive TV had a future. Bennett concluded it didn't. It would cost too much and take too long. More to the point, kids didn't want it.

On a weird hunch, however, Bennett began sniffing down another trail. In doing his focus groups at all those junior high schools, he met not only with students but also with their moms, who came to pick them up after school. Time after time one mom after another brought with her bottles of spring water and sipped them casually during the focus groups. Curious, he asked them why they weren't drinking soda. *Too much sugar. Too much caffeine. Slows me down. Makes me fat.* And so on. What about the cost? he would ask. *I'm doing this for me, to be healthy, to lose weight, to clear my system, to be natural,* he heard over and over again. Unbelievable, thought Bennett. These middle-class suburban homemakers were paying nearly two bucks a bottle for water—during a recession. He did the math and almost choked on his Big Mac. That was nearly eight bucks a gallon—which at that time was nearly seven times the cost of gasoline.

Working feverishly for the next several days while his boss was speaking at an economic conference in London, Bennett concluded that aging, weight- and health-conscious Baby Boomers—beginning with women— were shifting from soda to bottled water in the U.S. and Europe. That gave the two bottled-water industry leaders—Perrier and Evian—huge upside potential. Both were French-owned, both were fast-growing, and both were ripe for takeovers by companies with much larger distribution networks. Bennett concluded that the two major U.S. soft-drink companies—Coke and Pepsi—would soon wake up to this phenomenon, and either buy these French brands, or launch their own. This could dramatically boost their profitability, even as U.S. soft-drink sales were slowly beginning to flatten.

The day MacPherson returned from London, Bennett presented his case: Forget interactive TV. Buy major positions in bottled-water companies—and buy now before anyone else realizes that they're cash-cows-to-be.

MacPherson nearly choked on *his* Big Mac. What kind of idiot had Iverson hired? He nearly fired Bennett on the spot—and invested heavily in interactive TV anyway. Bad move. Interactive TV went nowhere. A few months later, however, Nestle stunned the markets by buying Perrier. Its stock shot through the roof.

The CEO called Bennett back into his office and got right to the point. "I may be dumb, but I'm not stupid. Let's buy water."

He immediately bought huge blocks of shares in the Danone Group, owner of Evian, and took major positions in Coca-Cola and Pepsi-Cola. Sure enough, the rebounding U.S. economy and rapidly expanding foreign markets boosted the stock of all three companies dramatically. Even more interesting, in December of 1995, Pepsi entered the bottled water market with its Aquafina brand. It quickly became the number one bottled-water retailer in U.S. convenience stores and gas stations. In 1996, Coke launched its own bottled-water brand, Dasani, also gobbling up a huge market share. By 1999, when MacPherson finally sold a boatload of holdings to begin financing his political ambitions, the value of his Pepsi stock had doubled. The value of his Evian stock had nearly doubled (to $191 a share). And the value of his Coca-Cola stock had nearly tripled.

But Bennett's career wasn't built on bottled water. It was built on MacPherson's growing confidence that this young whippersnapper was developing a real strategic vision, great sources, and great instincts. Bennett's friendship with a young programmer at Netscape led him to advise the Joshua Fund to buy into the Web browser company's IPO at $20 and sell at $160 five years later. Likewise, Bennett advised the Joshua Fund to buy Microsoft at $20 in the early 1990s and sell at $100 when his friends in the Clinton Justice Department convinced him over lunch at the Willard that their antitrust case could be a company-killer. It wasn't, but the tip helped the Joshua Fund sell high and not get burned during the tech crash to follow.

During the summer of 1997, a college friend of Bennett's called collect from a short-term missions trip in Chiang Mai, Thailand. The local currency, the Thai *baht*, was beginning to crash and a whiff of panic was in the air. Bennett sensed this might be big. He jumped on the next plane from Denver to Bangkok and confirmed the extent of the currency troubles. Bennett immediately called Iverson—skiing in the Swiss Alps—on his satellite phone and suggested Iverson and MacPherson dump all of the Joshua Fund's Asian holdings. This was a full-blown currency crisis, the young analyst insisted, and it was going to get worse. It would spread through Asia like the economic equivalent of Ebola.

Iverson was skeptical. The Thai *baht?* Dump all their holdings in Asia? This kid was working too hard. He needed a vacation. At 14,053 feet, sweating in his ski garb, Iverson put the phone down for a moment, looked out over a breathtaking Alpine mountain range, took a swig of Evian—and swallowed hard. Suddenly, he hung up with Bennett, speed-dialed his team back in Denver, and issued the command: "Dump all of our Asian holdings— *immediately.*" By October, sure enough, the Thai currency troubles had erupted into a full-blown Asian economic crisis that swept the globe and for a while put a number of U.S. companies at severe risk. The Dow dropped more than five hundred points in one day. But the Joshua Fund didn't lose a dime.

Jonathan Meyers Bennett's mission in life was to read the tea leaves— then tell James Michael MacPherson and Stuart Morris Iverson when to buy the tea company. As a result, MacPherson and Iverson had become very rich, very happy men.

Bennett wasn't doing too badly himself. Now Global Strategix's senior vice president and chief investment strategist, Bennett ran the company's New York office from the thirty-eighth floor of a skyscraper overlooking Central Park. It wasn't exactly Colorado's Front Range, but it would do. For now. Six months before, Iverson had been nominated to be the next U.S. treasury secretary and subsequently confirmed by the Senate by a vote of ninety-eight to nothing, with two senators absent. Iverson was now in Washington, and Bennett would soon be moving back to Denver to assume control of GSX. The gorgeous office looking out at the magnificent Rocky Mountains was about to be his.

* * *

Bennett's parents were retired now and living just outside of Orlando.

Sol and his wife, Ruth, still didn't exactly understand what their son did every day. Sol had never earned more than $60,000 a year as a reporter, and for most of his career much, much less. They'd never worried about money, but they'd never sought it either. Sol preferred tracking the CIA to CNBC, covering the IRA to opening an IRA, and reporting the fall of the Berlin Wall to reporting the rise of Wall Street.

The Bennetts were proud of their son, but they were also concerned. Jon had lost a number of his colleagues and associates in the attacks on the World Trade Center. But he refused to talk about any of it. He'd gone back to work the very next day and refused to take any personal time off, except to attend funerals. He'd given his staff flexible leave time to deal with their grieving, but didn't seem to deal with his own. They weren't even sure if he was grieving. He must have been, but he absolutely refused to entertain the subject when they tried to bring it up.

Their son was a young man in a hurry. But was that what he really wanted—to move at a million miles an hour while life sped past by him in a gray, murky, colorless blur? Was that what they'd brought him up to do, to be, to cling to? It didn't seem right. His mother worried that he seemed hollow, distant, and short-tempered.

But it wasn't hard to see that their son had become successful beyond their dreams. He owned a penthouse apartment in the Village near NYU, for which he had paid cash, though he was rarely home, except to sleep. He had a massive walk-in closet filled with Zegna suits and expensive Italian handcrafted shoes. He earned a generous six-figure salary, a rapidly growing seven-figure personal portfolio, and an even larger seven-figure retirement portfolio. Not bad. Not bad at all. Now all they needed was a daughter-in-law and some grandchildren.

* * *

Bennett set down his Turkish coffee.

He glanced at his Rolex, compulsively twisted his cloth napkin, and peered across the table. He needed that signature, and he needed it now. A car would be arriving to pick him up for Ben Gurion International Airport in twelve minutes. He'd be in London by midday and New York by evening. If he was lucky, he might even have time to catch a show by himself and celebrate this incredible deal.

As Dmitri Galishnikov, the man whose signature he so urgently wanted, pored over the contract's final page, Bennett found himself intrigued by this riddle wrapped in a mystery surrounded by an enigma. Galishnikov was a careful man, a cautious man, and to be fair, Bennett reminded himself, these were no character flaws. They were traits conceived in persecution, born in suffering, and refined in the gulag. This was a man who had survived three years in Lefortovo, the KGB interrogation prison in Moscow. Some night, late at night, over *chai* and black bread and beef Stroganoff, he would ask this quiet, careful, cautious man to tell him his story in far greater detail, to describe his journey as a Jewish petroleum engineer from Stalin's Siberia through a long, dark, lonely night and into the pinkish dawn of a Jerusalem sunrise at the King David Hotel. No doubt it would take more than one night for Galishnikov to do the story justice. No matter. Bennett would stay as long as it took.

☆ ☆ ☆

Bennett's journey to this rare breed of Russian had begun with a newspaper story.

On a British Airways red-eye from London to New York many moons before, he'd been restless and unable to sleep. Finished with all the Sunday papers he had with him, he'd begun glancing through the Friday morning *New York Times* he'd uncharacteristically been too busy to read all weekend. He distinctly remembered the date of that paper—September 15, 2000—because it would change his life forever.

Bennett began in the back of the Business section, circling intriguing little stories that caught his eye with a thick, new Montblanc pen his dad had given him for his birthday. He always read the Business section in reverse order, from the last page to the first, believing the good stuff—the precious nuggets for which he panned—were rarely useful once they'd reached the front page for all the world to see.

It wasn't, however, until he finished the Business section and the A section that Bennett came upon a front-page story that stopped him dead in his tracks. "Gas Deposits Off Israel and Gaza Opening Visions of Joint Ventures" read the headline. Natural gas in the Mediterranean? Bennett felt a surge of adrenaline and read on.

"Drilling deep below the seas off Israel and the Gaza Strip, foreign energy companies are discovering gas reserves that could lift the Palestinian economy and give Israel its first taste of energy independence," reporter William A. Orme Jr. began. "Industry experts, including those on this giant platform, say the Palestinians and Israelis will both profit if they can work together in a high-stakes partnership. They need each other for the efficient development of these offshore reserves, since neither side alone can fully afford the billion-dollar investment in pipelines and pumping facilities that is being sketched out, the experts say."

The article went on to say an Israeli government official estimated his country had "some three to five trillion cubic feet of proven gas reserves," an astonishing figure that could fuel Israel's electricity network for a quarter of a century.

"And there may be more," the official added.

Even now, the phrase kept ringing in Bennett's ears. *"There may be more."* Even now he could remember the urgency he had felt to call his GSX colleagues to brainstorm their next move. But it had been four in the morning in New York, and only two in the morning in Denver, and everyone he knew had been asleep.

Well, not everyone.

In Israel, it was eleven o'clock in the morning as Bennett sat in first class at thirty thousand feet, staring at his copy of the *Times*. GSX had an office in Israel—in Tel Aviv, actually. He'd never been there. He couldn't even remember the name of the director there. But he'd be awake. And now was as good a time as any to get acquainted.

"*Shalom,*" said a young secretary with a thick Israeli accent and a thicker trace of attitude.

"*Shalom* . . . uh, yes . . . uh, who's your director there?" Bennett asked, his mind racing.

"And you would be . . . ?"

"Yeah, my name is Jon Bennett, I'm . . ."

"From New York? *That* Mr. Bennett?" the young woman asked, suddenly humble, suddenly alert.

"Yeah. I'm on a flight to New York right now and I've got an urgent question for your office, but, I'm sorry, I just can't remember the—"

"Roni," came the interruption. "Roni Barshevsky. I'll put you right through, Mr. Bennett."

He was about to say thank you but the line was already ringing in Barshevsky's office.

"Mr. Bennett?" Barshevsky said with a heavy Russian accent.

"Please, call me Jon."

"Okay, Jon. Good to meet you, finally. What can I do for you?"

"Roni, I need to know everything you know about gas reserves off your coast," Bennett nearly whispered.

"Uh, nothing. Why?"

"Nothing?"

"*Nyet.* What's this about?"

"Buried treasure, Roni. Go grab your copy of Friday's *Times.*"

"Which *Times?*"

"The *New York Times*, Roni, the *New York Times*. Grab the paper, Roni. Get the front page. Come back to the phone."

"Okay, boss."

Bennett was tired and wired and ready to unleash on this guy. But with everyone else on the plane around him sleeping like babies, screaming wasn't exactly an option.

As he waited on hold, Bennett cursed himself that he hadn't read the story earlier, hadn't known about the story days or weeks in advance, that no one in his entire company had the brains to bring it to his attention. This thing was white-hot, and his Israel director had no idea what he was talking about.

"Hmm. This is very interesting," Barshevsky mumbled, coming back on the line. "What do we do?"

"Who should I talk to? Who can I call to get us into this thing?"

"Let's see . . . hmm . . . ah yes. I know just the guy. Dmitri Galishnikov. He's Russian. Runs an amazing company called Medexco. Pipes, drilling, pumping—you name it, he does it. Mostly they work in Central Asia. But he's probably the one working with these guys. *Da*, call Dmitri."

"I need a number, Roni, and I need it now."

"Okay, boss. One minute."

It actually took two, but to Bennett it felt like an hour.

"You're a saint, Roni. Stay alert. I'll call you soon."

Bennett hung up, slid his credit card through the GTE air phone again, and dialed Medexco. The number was busy. He tried again. Same thing. Bennett started to curse, then thought better of it. Discussing a billion dollars in venture capital sight unseen—on an unsecured line, over the Atlantic Ocean, no less—wasn't exactly the model of shrewd, stealthy, strategic savvy on which Bennett prided himself and for which he'd so often been promoted. He'd have to wait until landing at Kennedy, then race back to the office and . . . and what? What was he really going to try to accomplish over the phone? Who knew how many calls this Galish-nikov guy had already received over the weekend, much less in the months leading up to this story? People might already be jetting to Israel to see him. Deals might already be under way. For that matter, they might even be done.

Slow down, Bennett told himself, *slow down. Focus.* He took a deep breath and reached for the call button above him. He needed a drink, and he needed it now. Even if it was four-thirty in the morning. A flight attendant emerged on cue. He ordered a tiny airplane bottle of Absolut—and some coffee. Then he picked the air phone back up, slid his credit card through again, and called Barshevsky back.

"Get Galishnikov on a plane," Bennett commanded, albeit in a whisper. "I want him in my office in New York by dinner."

Sure enough, Galishnikov took the bait, came for dinner, and bared his soul. The fact was, he'd gotten a few other calls. But no one seemed interested in making a billion-dollar bet on the bloody Middle East. Gas and oil were risky enough. Nobody wanted a bunch of Hamas and Hezbollah and Islamic Jihad terrorists blowing up their investments with a smile on their faces as some gift to Allah. They'd rather drill in Siberia or the Arctic Circle than get in the middle of the Israelis and the Palestin-ians. But Bennett was ready. And he said so. Galishnikov agreed to go back and talk to his partner, a gentle, soft-spoken Arab by the name of Ibrahim Sa'id—head of a new, privately held company called the Palestinian Petroleum Group, or PPG—to see what could be done.

By September 28, there was a new headline in the *New York Times*: "Arafat Hails Big Gas Find off the Coast of Gaza Strip." In fact, *Times* reporter Bill Orme wrote Arafat was "celebrating the multibillion-dollar discovery of what industry officials confirmed is a major gas deposit" and telling people it would provide "a strong foundation for a Palestinian state."

"This is a gift from our god to our people," Arafat told Orme, "to our children, to our women, to our people inside and outside, to our refugees and those who are living here on our land."

So began a seemingly never-ending chain of meetings with the principals in New York, London, Jerusalem, and Ramallah. Staffers began constantly shuttling back and forth from the U.S. to Israel, Gaza, and the West Bank. Then came the blizzard of business plans, background checks, geological surveys, cost-benefit analyses, insurance assessments, credit checks, and financial negotiations. It seemed to go on forever. But everyone involved knew it would be worth it, and they could barely contain their excitement.

Until September 11, 2001. The day Islamic terrorists attacked New York and Washington. The day the Twin Towers fell and the Pentagon burned. The day three thousand Americans lost their lives. The day Palestinians began dancing in the streets. The day Osama bin Laden became a household name around the globe and brought cheers throughout the Muslim world. The day President Bush declared a "war on terrorism." The day any prospect for Arab-Israeli peace and prosperity was mothballed, yet again.

But time heals all wounds. Almost a decade later, Bennett now believed there were once again signs of hope. The war on terrorism had been a huge success. Not only were Al-Qaeda and the Taliban destroyed. Key Palestinian terrorist networks such as Hamas, Hezbollah, and Islamic Jihad had also been effectively ripped up and wiped out by the Israelis, with tacit approval from Washington. And several moderate Arab countries like Jordan, Egypt, and Morocco were clamping down on terrorist cells within their borders or just passing through. It wasn't perfect. But it was progress. Overall, the good guys were winning.

In the meantime, not only natural-gas reserves had been discovered off the Israeli-Palestinian coastlines. Medexco and PPG geologists and engineers had recently, quietly, and unexpectedly discovered massive tracts of oil reserves as well. The Israelis and Palestinians were sitting on a gold mine, and it was time to move decisively. Every light looked green. All systems seemed go. They'd better be. So much hung in the balance.

☆ ☆ ☆

Barshevsky popped his head in the door of the restaurant.

He caught Bennett's eye. The car was ready. It was time to go.

Bennett looked at Galishnikov. "Well?"

Galishnikov straightened up, took off his glasses for a moment and rubbed his eyes. Then he cleaned his glasses with a white cloth napkin and carefully repositioned them on his pale, gaunt face. "*Tov,*" he said quietly, in his newly acquired Hebrew. Then he picked up Bennett's Montblanc pen and signed his name.

"Good," said Bennett, looking Galishnikov square in the eyes. "It's a pleasure doing business with you."

"You too, my friend."

Bennett slipped the papers into his briefcase and slipped quietly out the door and into the waiting black Mercedes. This was no time for celebrating. Not now. Not in public. The deal of the century had just been signed. It was going to change everything. Not more than two dozen people in the entire world had any idea, and Bennett's job was to keep it that way for a little while longer.

Galishnikov watched his young friend leave, sighed, then stared down at his plate of cold, untouched breakfast. He'd awoken with no appetite whatsoever. Now he felt famished.

☆ ☆ ☆

Bennett leaned back into the leather seat of the black Mercedes.

He rolled down the tinted window beside him to get some fresh, cool air. The drive to Ben Gurion airport wouldn't take long. But the flights ahead of him would feel like a lifetime. Why hadn't he simply taken the company's private jet? He closed his eyes and tried to imagine MacPherson's and Iverson's faces when he told them the good news.

Suddenly, his digital cell phone rang.

"Bennett."

"Mr. Bennett. This is the White House operator. I have Treasury Secretary Iverson on the line. I remind you, it is not a secure line. Stand by one."

A crackle of static, and then . . .

"Jon, it's Stu."

"Hey, Stu—er, Mr. Secretary—I've got good news."

"I don't."

"Why? What's going on?"

"Mac may be dead."

"What?" Bennett sat bolt upright.

"His motorcade was attacked a few minutes ago."

"What?"

"I don't know. A plane. A kamikaze. Something. I don't know."

"I don't . . . how?"

"I don't know anything yet. The Secret Service just woke me up."

"Where are you?"

"The Brown Palace . . . we've got a dinner tonight . . . later tonight."

"Who's with you?"

"Everybody. Bob just walked in. He came on an earlier flight to schmooze some donors. It's a nightmare, Jon. We don't know any details. Not yet."

"I can't believe this."

"I know. I know. It's 9/11 all over again. Look, where are you right now?"

"Uh, I'm, uh . . . I'm in a car on the way to the airport."

"New York?"

"No, no—Jerusalem."

"Right, well, just get here as fast as you can."

The line went dead.

Bennett's mind went numb.

James "Mac" MacPherson—the Vietnam vet turned Wall Street wizard turned two-term governor of Colorado turned president of the United States—was poised to be *Time*'s "Man of the Year," the chief architect of America's dazzling economic comeback.

Now . . . he might be dead.

3

★ ★
★

THE ACRID STENCH of blazing jet fuel and thick, black smoke overwhelmed him.

Three deafening helicopters hovered overhead, beaming their spotlights onto the carnage below. A fourth could be seen circling a larger perimeter, and now a squadron of F-15s streaked overhead, flying CAP. Despite the chilly night breeze, he could feel the intense heat of the roaring flames. Close his eyes and he could easily be back with the *Army Times*, back in the Gulf War, back on Iraq's "highway of death," picking his way through the putrefying bodies and smoldering hulks of anks, trucks, and other scorched remnants of Saddam Hussein's Republican Guard.

It had been almost two decades since Marcus Jackson, now with the *New York Times*, had covered a hot war. It had been at least six or seven years since he stopped waking up in the wee hours of the morning, drenched with sweat from yet another nightmare, his wife holding his shaking body. Like many men his age, he had signed up for military service in the early eighties not truly believing he'd ever see combat. And for the sake of his twin girls—who had just turned five the previous weekend in another slumber party he had missed—he prayed every night that he'd never have to witness the horrors of combat again. The White House beat was more than enough for him now, especially over the last few years. But, in an instant, it all came rushing back.

Jackson was several miles back from the wreckage of Stagecoach and the G4. Prevented from exiting Press Bus 1, he could see a wall of police officers surrounding his bus and the others behind him, guns drawn. But with a front-row seat, high-powered binoculars hanging from his neck, and a digital wireless phone in each hand, he was now one of the most valuable witnesses in the world.

With one phone, Jackson repeatedly speed-dialed his assignment desk back in New York. Busy. Again. Busy. Again. No luck. With the other phone, he quickly speed-dialed CNN in Atlanta, connecting immediately. Some kind of party was going on in the control room. Jackson could hear the night crew singing happy birthday to someone.

Jackson shouted into the phone. "Josh, it's Marcus. I'm . . . everything's on fire. I'm with the pres—"

"What? I can't hear you. Hold on— *everybody shut up.*"

Jackson could hear the party in the control room die instantly as Josh Simon, CNN's overnight producer, shocked everybody with his uncharacteristic outburst.

"All right, Marcus, what is it?"

"I saw it all, Josh—the thing just came screaming down out of the sky and erupted into a fireball. . . ."

"What? Whoa, whoa. What are you talking about?"

"Some kind of kamikaze just attacked MacPherson's motorcade."

"Holy . . ."

"It's total chaos."

"Not again . . ."

"It's bad, Josh; it's bad."

"Where are you?"

"We just left DIA. The whole road's on fire."

"Unbelievable. You're the first to call in. Nothing's on the wires."

"I know, I know. It literally just happened."

"What about MacPherson?"

"I don't know. I can't tell. I'm looking at his car right now through binoculars. Cops are everywhere. The thing's upside down. They're trying to get the doors open. There's fire everywhere."

"Marcus, we've got to get you on the air. Hold on—can you hold on?"

"Absolutely."

Simon quickly explained to his team what they were about to report. He checked again, but the story still wasn't on the AP or Reuters wires.

It would be soon. Jackson could hear over his left shoulder as the Associated Press's Tom Perkins dictated an urgent bulletin to a night editor in Washington. He could also hear the gasps in the CNN control room back in Atlanta as Simon spoke.

Just twenty-nine, Josh Simon was young but sharp, intense, and already losing his hair. Too much stress, too many graveyard shifts, too many Marlboros. His superiors weren't yet convinced of his full potential. But to Jackson—who'd known him for years—Simon seemed to have a gift. He truly understood the power of live, breaking television news. He'd grown up with it. Gone to school for it. Sacrificed his marriage for it. He understood its style, its rhythm, its cadence. He knew how to tell a story visually and—when pictures weren't available—he knew how to capture a viewer through music and graphics and the tone of an anchor's voice.

Now Jackson heard his friend on the other end of the line prepare his team to be the first to break this story to the entire world.

"Josh—can you hear me?"

"Hold on, Marcus. Bill, we're cutting in—breaking news—I'll cue you as we go. It's huge—stand by.

"Camera two, stand by . . . we're going to breaking news . . . ready graphics . . . cue music. . . . Dirk—get me a map of Colorado. Okay, everybody, this is it. . . . Let's get it right. . . . Going live . . . stand by . . . three . . . two . . . one . . . go."

Simon's voice was calm and steady and professional. Jackson could hear a roundup of the day's financial news suddenly interrupted by the distinctive music. Then: "This is CNN Breaking News." Even as a hardened, cynical, battle-weary reporter, that very sound sent shivers down his spine. Simon dictated a lead-in as anchor Bill Blake flawlessly repeated every jarring word.

"Marcus, stand by one. . . ."

For a moment, a hiss of static made it sound as though the phone had gone dead. But Jackson could tell he'd actually been patched through and was live on the air.

Blake was already introducing him. ". . . on the line now from I-70, just outside of Denver . . . Mr. Jackson, can you hear me?"

"Yes, Bill, I can."

"CNN is now reporting that the president's motorcade has just been attacked, apparently by a kamikaze, on the road leaving Denver International Airport. I understand you've witnessed the whole thing. What can you tell us?"

* * *

Bennett stared out the window.

Roni Barshevsky maneuvered the aging Mercedes through morning traffic and raced to the airport. But Bennett's mind was elsewhere. He needed information. What was happening? Was it true? How could it be? President MacPherson couldn't be dead. He couldn't be.

James MacPherson was practically Bennett's godfather. More than any other man in Bennett's life—except his own father—MacPherson had taken a personal interest in his skills, his career, and his life, teaching him the tricks of the financial trade and treating him as much like a son as a protégé. Back in the early nineties, when he'd first been hired by GSX and before MacPherson was elected governor, the young Bennett had often been surprised to be a regular guest in his boss's gorgeous Cherry Creek home, sometimes working deep into the night on some proposal or another, sometimes devouring Mrs. MacPherson's incredible chocolate-chip cookies, or shooting hoops with the girls in the driveway, or helping plot the CEO's political future.

When MacPherson began planning his first run for governor, Bennett was one of a dozen people in the room—despite the fact that the governor called him his resident Democrat—taking notes and helping draft policy papers and campaign speeches. When MacPherson won his reelection campaign overwhelmingly, Bennett was one of only six other men in the Denver hotel suite on election night, mapping out the road from Denver to Iowa to New Hampshire to the GOP convention. For some strange, inexplicable reason, he'd been invited into the inner circle, the inner sanctum—the "circle of trust," as the MacPhersons liked to joke. He'd become family in the process, not to mention a multimillionaire.

Bennett closed his eyes and let himself sink into the rich, thick leather in the backseat of the Mercedes. He rubbed his eyes, now aching from the early stages of what felt like a sinus headache. He took a swig of water and could feel his throat getting worse. He reached for the window and opened it wide, his dark brown hair now whipping around in the incoming wind. The thrill of the Medexco deal was gone.

He felt tired, achy, sluggish, his brain on mental overload. He soon found his thoughts drifting back a few years, to the MacPhersons' breathtaking lodge, nestled high up in Beaver Creek on the slope of the Rockies. He'd been invited to go skiing with the governor, his family, and Iverson.

Instead, he'd found himself with an excruciating case of strep throat. Mrs. MacPherson—he'd never quite felt right calling her Julie, though she'd always insisted—wrapped him up under heaps of wool blankets, gave him a steaming pot of Earl Grey tea, and left him to rest in the huge, quiet house, staring out a massive plate-glass window, overlooking some of the most beautiful mountains he'd ever seen.

He could still see the snowy, cold white peaks, and the thick, sturdy evergreens, and the hazy orange sunset, and the long, dark shadows in the valley, and the twinkling white lights of the family Christmas tree. He could still hear the howl of the bitter winds outside, the roaring crackle of the fire inside, and the gentle carols rising from tiny speakers hidden all over the house. Perhaps for the first time since hopping onto the Wall Street bullet train, he'd felt safe.

The weight of the world—the weight of the massive deals and the anticipation of the next global economic or financial crisis—slowly slipped off his shoulders and he'd slept and slept and slept.

☆　☆　☆

It was never built to be a fortress.

The elegant three-story, white-brick, nineteenth-century Victorian house on the southeast corner of Thirty-fourth Street and Massachusetts Avenue in Washington, D.C., may have been built by and for the military, but it was not impregnable.

Set on a lovely, hilly knoll, surrounded by towering trees and within the gates of a calm and grassy compound, the Queen Anne–style structure completed in April of 1893 began as the home of the various superintendents of the U.S. Naval Observatory, until 1928, when it became the official home of the chief of U.S. Naval Operations.

In 1974, Congress designated the home the official residence for the vice president of the United States. Nelson Rockefeller and his family entertained there, but it wasn't until 1977 that Walter Mondale and his family actually became the first "Second Family" to take up full-time residence. Now it was the home of Vice President William Harvard Oaks, and the stillness of the historic grounds was about to be shattered.

Special Agent-in-Charge Steve Sinclair sat behind his desk at Checkpoint One, just inside the front doors of the residence. He'd just finished editing his oldest son's tenth-grade term paper on Lincoln's address at Gettysburg and was settling down with a steaming cup of coffee, a fresh blueberry muffin, and the early edition of the *Washington Post* Sports section when all three of his secure phones began ringing almost simultaneously. All six of the agents on post in the living room and dining room snapped to attention.

Sinclair grabbed the red phone first. "Sinclair, go."

"Code Red. Code Red," shouted the watch commander beside Bud Norris at the Secret Service headquarters at Treasury. "Fire up the chopper and get Checkmate out of there *now.*"

"Copy that—hold one."

Sinclair grabbed his wrist-mounted microphone and shouted, "Code Red. Code Red. Evacuate. Evacuate. *Marine Two*—scramble, scramble, scramble."

All six agents now had Uzis drawn and four blew past Sinclair up the stairs. One took up his position guarding the front door while another moved to open the side kitchen door. Ten other agents now poured in through the kitchen from a guard station immediately adjacent to the residence, taking up positions at the windows throughout the first floor. Sinclair meanwhile hit two buttons—one white, one red—on the panel behind him. One instantly lit up the entire compound with blinding searchlights. The other set off a succession of deafening air-horn blasts declaring the compound at war.

Sinclair quickly scanned all twelve television monitors in front of him and could see no immediate incoming threat. He did see two Marine pilots race from their guardhouse to the lead helicopter in the courtyard, jump inside, and plow through emergency procedures to get the chopper airborne-ready in the next few seconds.

"Home Plate, what've you got?" Sinclair shouted into his secure line to the Secret Service op center.

"Gambit's motorcade is under fire—I repeat, motorcade under fire. Execute Deep Gopher. I repeat, execute Deep Gopher. Air support is on the way."

* * *

Bolling Air Force Base in Washington, D.C., sprang to life.

Emergency sirens and air horns suddenly jolted everyone awake. In an instant, night turned to day as huge spotlights flooded the elite base along the Potomac River. Moments later, Humvees were moving to block every entrance. Combat-ready Marines grabbed M16s as they bolted out of their barracks and to their posts. Above them, ten crack pilots—all part of the Executive Flight Detail—were lifting three Apache helicopter gunships and two forest green Marine transport helicopters off the ground and into a rescue formation. In the blink of an eye, they disappeared.

* * *

They had only a few seconds.

Upstairs at the vice president's residence, agents turned the corner and shot down the hallway, past the VP's study, past his den, past the empty kids' bedroom on the left to the master bedroom on the right at the end. Agents Chuck Kroll and Mike Martin burst in without knocking.

"Sir, you need to come with us immediately."

The flannel-pajama-clad vice president was barely awake, but it didn't matter. The two agents quickly hauled him out of bed and out of the room, leaving behind his terrified and disoriented wife. A third agent grabbed the VP's always-packed emergency suitcase and briefcase and raced to follow the other two agents back down the stairs. The fourth agent stayed with the VP's wife to calm her down and explain that a helicopter would be coming to evacuate her momentarily.

Marine Two was now fully powered as the VP and his agents burst out a side door just thirty yards from the howling chopper, the VP's feet barely touching the ground. Twenty agents brandishing Uzis and Marines in full battle gear carrying locked and loaded M16s made a secure human corridor through which the agents dragged their protectee and literally threw him through the side door of the chopper. Kroll followed and jumped in.

Martin jumped in as well, slammed the door shut, and furiously slapped the pilots on the back. *"Go, go, go,"* he screamed.

Marine Two lifted off into a formation with the three Apache helicopter gunships hovering overhead, and in a moment they were gone. From the instant Agent Sinclair's phone had first rung with news of the Code Red, less than three minutes had elapsed.

* * *

Now the whole world was about to know almost as much as he did.

Back at the Secret Service command center in Washington, Director Bud Norris saw the CNN feed appear on one of five large-screen video monitors before him and slammed his fist down on the console beside him.

Norris held two phones to his head. One was a secure line to the FBI Operations Center. It was patched through to Director Scott Harris's bulletproof Chevy Tahoe, racing him back to his office at the Robert F. Kennedy Building on E Street, northwest. The other was an encrypted satellite link to Secret Service Special Agent Jackie Sanchez on the scene in Denver, now in command of the rescue operation and trying desperately to break into the badly mangled, inverted limousine.

As Norris quickly briefed Harris, his eyes fixed on another of the video monitors before him. This brought him images neither CNN nor anyone else had—a live feed from the Apache helicopter over the crash site. He could see the image of a specially designed Jaws of Life saw now piercing the bulletproof door of Stagecoach. He could see heavily armed agents surrounding the vehicle. He could see firefighters battling the blazing G4. And he could see Sanchez directing the action.

"Jackie," Norris barked.

"Yes, sir," Sanchez replied immediately.

"How much longer?"

"Almost there, sir. Stand by."

* * *

His briefcase beeped.

He was getting an e-mail. Bennett grabbed his leather briefcase and fished out his BlackBerry. A breaking news alert from AP. He scrolled down rapidly. *"MacPherson Motorcade Attacked by Kamikaze."* Details were sketchy.

A few minutes later, another beep. An update. The Secret Service had just evacuated the vice president from the Naval Observatory. The Speaker of the House had just been awakened by his security detail in Chicago, evacuated in an air force helicopter, and was now being taken to an undisclosed military base. Cabinet members were being taken to secure, undisclosed locations as a *"precaution against any possible further attacks,"* according to an unnamed U.S. Secret Service official.

Another beep. Another update. CNN was now reporting the Secret Service was *"taking bodies out of the president's limousine."*

Bodies? Bennett's throat burned. He suddenly felt nauseated.

☆ ☆ ☆

"Bob, I've got a feeding frenzy here."

Press Secretary Chuck Murray pressed his earpiece closer and stepped off Press Bus 1 for a moment—away from the carnivores within—desperate for something real, something solid from White House Chief of Staff Bob Corsetti. But with the wind, the choppers, and the sirens of emergency vehicles arriving from every direction, he could barely hear a thing.

"What about the president? . . . What? . . . Bob, we don't have a few minutes. I've got a bus full of cell phones about to report he might be dead. . . . I know what he's saying. . . . I was right next to him. . . . What? . . . Well, I'm seeing the exact same thing . . . two . . . What? . . . Yes—two bodies so far . . . here comes the third right now. . . . Who? . . . Okay, fine, I'll talk to him."

Murray suddenly realized he'd left his coat on the bus. Drenched with sweat, he was now shivering uncontrollably.

"Hello? Who's this? Agent Parker, this is Chuck Murray. What've we got? I need to know right now—is he dead or alive?"

☆ ☆ ☆

Bennett's BlackBerry beeped again—e-mail from London.

```
jon—just heard the news . . . watching cnn . . . what
do you know? . . . I keep calling your cell phone but
can't get through . . . call me—erin.
```

Erin McCoy was Global Strategix's international communications director, based in London.

At thirty-one, she was North Carolina–born and raised and the great-granddaughter of a former U.S. secretary of state, a fact she took pride in and liked to remind Bennett of every now and then. A UNC Chapel Hill grad in economics with an MBA from Wharton, she was feisty, gorgeous, yet also inexplicably single, a fact Bennett liked to remind *her* of every now and then.

Not that she had much time to date, much less marry. These days she was working around the clock on the Israeli Medexco deal and had fast become one of the most valuable members of Bennett's team. He punched one button on his phone, and got her on the first ring.

"McCoy."

"Erin, it's Jon."

"You watching this?"

"No—I'm with Roni on the way to the airport. What've you got?"

"Not much. Just what's on TV. We can't get anybody back in Denver and no one in New York knows anything. You talked to Stu yet?"

"Just for a moment."

"And?"

Bennett paused. Should he tell her? "And it's bad—the president may be dead."

Not that she wasn't already fearing the worst, but Bennett's words seemed to knock the breath out of her. Silence. Then, suddenly, she reengaged. "Wait—hold on."

"What?"

"FOX has pictures—hold on. . . ."

Bennett had been to McCoy's penthouse office several times and nick-named it NORAD. High atop London, overlooking the Thames and Big Ben, McCoy and her team had created a high-tech financial war room, wired up with the world's state-of-the-art communications equipment—from shortwave radios and satellite dishes to high-speed Internet access and fiber-optic cables capable of transmitting 30 million phone calls across the Atlantic in a single second.

All of it allowed McCoy and her team to receive instantaneous reports from news services, financial markets, GSX staff, and other sources all over the planet. "Know well the condition of thy flocks," read the tiny ceramic plaque beside her phones and computer and always-stocked jar of lollypops, all neatly arranged on her massive cherry desk, a desk once used by Churchill when he was a parliamentary backbencher and self-designated rabble-rouser.

Bennett could picture McCoy and her staff, piled into her office in the early hours of the British morning, simultaneously watching ten wall-mounted TV screens and working the phones.

"Erin? What've you got?"

"All right . . . hold on . . . uh . . . they're zooming in. . . . Come on, guys, get it in focus. . . . Wait . . . oh . . . oh no . . . oh no . . ."

"What? Erin, what is it?"

★ ★ ★

Norris didn't want the world to see anything, least of all these pictures.

He guessed a FOX cameraman had somehow climbed atop his satellite truck or somehow scrambled atop one of the press buses. Either way, using a high-powered zoom lens, the image he was capturing and beaming to the entire world was now zeroed in on the newly created hole in the side of Stagecoach.

Secret Service agents could be seen beginning to carefully lift another lifeless body—strapped to a wooden stretcher—out of the car. Billowing smoke occasionally obscured the image. But no doubt, this was powerful television—and thus far, an exclusive.

"Sanchez—stop everything—I repeat, stop your evacuation *immediately.*" Norris was screaming into his phone.

Stunned, everyone in the Secret Service op center stared at him in horror.

"Nikon One, Nikon One, this is Home Plate—land in front of Stagecoach now. Get on the ground—now. Go, go, go—get on the ground, now."

Around the world, viewers suddenly found the gripping FOX and Sky News image completely obscured by a rapidly descending Denver police helicopter. The cameraman zoomed out, but to no avail. No camera, no reporter, no one could now see what was unfolding. No one except Bud Norris and his colleagues at the White House, Pentagon, FBI, and CIA, that is. The secure images streaming in from the front-mounted video camera on the Apache helicopter still hovering above the scene once again provided them exclusive command of the situation.

Norris finally gave the word and the extraction effort resumed, quickly but carefully. More agents with M16s moved in to surround the rescue crew. Another ambulance now backed carefully into position, along with Dodgeball, flanked by plainclothes agents brandishing Uzis.

"Sanchez, what've you got?"

"Thomas and Stevens are bad," she told him, referring to Gambit's two "body men," the two agents directly assigned to protecting the president's life. "Both unconscious, massive internal bleeding. We're about to medevac them out."

Norris's stomach tightened.

"Burdett and Rodriguez just came out. Burdett's unconscious, but stable. Rodriguez is a mess, sir, very bad," Sanchez relayed, referring to Terry Burdett, the president's personal assistant, and Tommy Rodriguez, the limousine driver.

Norris found himself getting angry. Yes, he cared about his own men. Yes, he cared about the president's staff. But none were his prime concern right now.

"Sanchez, what about Gambit?"

"We'll know in a moment, sir."

* * *

Marine Two dropped fast and hard onto the South Lawn of the White House.

On the way down, the vice president—code-named Checkmate by his protective detail—could see batteries of surface-to-air missiles out of their casings and ready for action on the roof of the White House and the Old Executive Office Building. He could also see Secret Service SWAT teams in black battle gear swarming the grounds.

The instant the chopper touched ground, a bulletproof black Suburban raced to its side, the chopper door flew open, and Checkmate was thrown into one of the Suburban's side doors. Agents piled in on top of him and the Suburban peeled out, heading for the Oval Office.

There, a platoon of agents surrounded the vehicle, Uzis drawn. They dragged Checkmate through the Oval Office, down the main hallway of the West Wing, through the doors of a secure stairway, down two flights of stairs, through a password-protected doorway guarded by two armed Marines, down a long corridor, and into the PEOC, the nuclear-blast-proof Presidential Emergency Operations Center.

Already waiting for him were National Security Advisor Marsha Kirkpatrick, Secretary of State Tucker Paine, and their top aides. All had landed minutes earlier at Andrews Air Force Base from a trip to Moscow. When their security details got the word of the mushrooming crisis, they immediately rushed the high-level diplomatic team to the White House.

The massive, three-foot-thick steel vault door slammed shut behind them. Only then did Kroll send out the word through his wrist-mounted microphone: "Checkmate is secure. I repeat—Checkmate is secure."

☆　☆　☆

"Director, it's Mr. Norris on line one."

By 3:27 a.m. eastern, FBI Director Scott Harris was back in his seventh-floor executive suite, joined by top aides crackling with nervous energy.

"Bud, it's Scott. How's Gambit?"

"I don't know yet. I'll know more in a minute. What've you got?"

"Full metal jacket. We've lit up our whole network. Pressing informants all over the globe. I've got the field team in Toronto headed to the airport and two more teams heading there from Buffalo and Boston. We just got off the phone with the Canadians. They're offering us their full assistance."

"Lot of good it does us now. What's our tactical situation?"

"You've got me. I don't think we can assume this thing is over."

"I agree."

"But I don't have anything hard yet."

"They knew the timing, the car, the best moment to strike."

"They had to have people on the ground."

"To calibrate a flight from Toronto to be in the right place at the right time? Absolutely. It's a nightmare. You bet there's more of them. The question is, where?"

"I can flood Denver with agents."

"Do it. Send 'em into Colorado Springs and have 'em drive up. I'm keeping DIA shut down for now."

"Good. We'll do it. How are you gonna move Gambit? I heard *Marine One* had mechanical trouble."

"It does. That's why we did the motorcade in the first place."

"You can't risk the roads now. You don't know who you can trust out there."

"I'm going to put him in one of the choppers. Sanchez will fly it out, flanked by the Apaches."

"And go where?"

"Crystal Palace."

"Not back to *Air Force One?*"

"I'm not taking him back there until I know it's secure."

"All right. What do you need from us?"

"Just find out who did this."

★　★　★

"Home Plate, I've got Moore," Sanchez told Norris over her satellite phone.

On the video screen, Norris watched Sanchez move quickly, direct her team, reposition her men, and commandeer the police helicopter. Now he saw Sanchez hand her phone inside Stagecoach.

"John? John, it's Bud."

"Hey, boss . . . ," Moore said, groggy and in pain.

"Talk to me, John."

"Gambit's safe."

"Thank God."

"He's got a lot of cuts, bruises, mild concussion. He's pretty freaked out. We've got him on sedatives, and oxygen. We've got him immobilized. But we've checked him over pretty good, and he's gonna be okay. Thank goodness for air bags."

Five thousand agents and billions of dollars' worth of the latest high-tech equipment and a president's life could actually be saved or lost during a terrorist attack by air bags? After two years off nicotine, Norris suddenly found himself craving a cigarette.

"John, I can't even tell you—"

"Bud? Bud, it's Mac—is this . . . is this another one of your . . . your exercises?"

At first, Norris was taken aback at hearing MacPherson's voice. Then he began laughing—more from pent-up nervous energy than the president's lame but noble attempt at humor. The man's voice faltered, but his spirit seemed strong.

"Yes, sir. Didn't you get the memo?"

MacPherson laughed weakly, then began to cough.

"Sir, are you—?"

But now it was Moore back on the line. "Are we cleared to move him, sir?"

"Absolutely, do it."

Norris and his team watched the Apache video feed as the agents on the ground now quickly, carefully, professionally extracted Gambit's stretcher from Stagecoach and positioned him in the back of the police helicopter. Sanchez positioned herself in the pilot's seat, beside another agent, once an army reserve helicopter pilot. Agents carefully helped Moore climb into the chopper, along with two other plainclothes agents from Dodgeball, one a specially trained medic.

As the chopper began to lift off, it was flanked by the two Apaches, led by the other police helicopter, flown by and packed with agents, and covered by a squadron of F-15s. On the ground, Secret Service vehicles and police cars began peeling away from the scene, going back to the airport to guard *Air Force One*. A few minutes later, a dozen more police and National Guard helicopters landed to carry away agents and top White House staff.

Back in Washington, Norris turned to his team and looked each one in the eye. "Gambit is alive."

The op center erupted with applause. People began to breathe for the first time in hours.

"Put me on all frequencies," Norris told his deputy. "Ball Players, this is Home Plate. We've got good news. Gambit is alive. I repeat: Gambit is alive."

He paused—just for a moment—to let his words sink in, then quickly continued.

"Checkmate is also secure. As is Megaphone. We haven't lost any principal—not yet. But it was close. And I, for one, don't think this thing is over. Not by a long shot. So listen up. We're now at ThreatCon Delta. We don't know what's out there. You may have your suspicions about who did this. But remember, that's not our mission. Not tonight. Our mission is to make sure the inmates don't rule the asylum. Our mission is vigilance, not vengeance. Everyone got that? So stay on your toes. Stay alert out there. And may God help us."

4

***

RONI BARSHEVSKY was almost there.

He pulled his Mercedes onto the jam-packed access road leading to Ben Gurion International Airport near Tel Aviv. As news of the attack on the American president began to spread, an already busy travel season got dramatically busier. Tourists and businesspeople headed to the airport in droves, worried once again that being in Israel might not be safe, and slowing traffic to a crawl in the process.

Unusually, however, Bennett didn't seem to mind. He was glued to the unfolding drama and grateful not to be getting out of the car anytime soon. As the car inched forward, Erin McCoy in London translated the play-by-play coverage from the TV correspondents in Denver, Atlanta, New York, and Washington to Bennett in Israel.

"Jon, they've just airlifted the president away from the scene."

"Is he alive?"

"They're not saying."

"Where are they headed?"

"Don't know. They're not saying."

"What *are* they saying?"

"They've just got video from some local station. . . . Hold on. . . . This is unbelievable. . . . Jon, they've got video of the kamikaze plane heading for the motorcade—for the president's limousine—and then something, I don't know, something like a rocket or a missile or something comes shooting out of the back of one of the Secret Service trucks and hits the plane, and this thing erupts in a fireball like you've never seen before."

"What?"

"The whole sky explodes."

"Wait, wait—I thought the plane came down and exploded onto the motorcade."

"I thought so too. But I'm telling you—some kind of rocket or missile came shooting out of the back of one of those black cars and blew up the plane first. Then it all comes raining down on the motorcade and you can see the president's car slam into the concrete dividers on I-70 and the whole thing goes up in flames—just keeps flipping over and over and over."

Bennett began to feel hot and nauseated. He quickly grabbed a bottle of water and began drinking.

"Jon? . . . Jon—you still there?"

"Yeah . . . yeah . . . I'm . . . I just . . . I don't know. . . ."

"I know . . . it's horrible. . . ."

"Have you been able to break through to Iverson?"

"No, not yet. All the lines in the Denver area are jammed. We're paging him but we've got nothing yet."

"Okay, look, get someone on the line to Brooks in New York."

"Okay."

"Tell him to dump everything at the opening bell."

"Everything?"

"Everything—go to cash."

"Cash? Jon, what are you talking about?"

"What are *you* talking about? It's going to be a freaking meltdown. Somebody just tried to kill the president of the United States—they may have succeeded."

"I know, but . . ."

"But what? Erin, the Dow's going to drop a couple thousand points in a few hours. NASDAQ's going to tank. What's the Nikkei doing right now?"

"Hold on, let's see—just starting to react, down three percent."

"There you go. What about the Hang Seng?"

"Down two and a half percent."

"I'm telling you, they'll both be down ten percent or worse by the end of the day. You watch."

"Jon . . ."

"What? You think I'm wrong."

"I don't know. . . . I'm just . . ."

"Just what? Erin, are you kidding? Come on, think. Think. What if the president is dead? Or what if he's alive but doesn't pull through? Then what?"

McCoy was silent.

"You think anyone's going to get on an airplane again? You think they're going to go out and buy a house next week? You think they're going to go start their own business?"

"No."

"You better believe it's no. Consumer confidence is going to tank. The market's going to collapse. You know what that means?"

"We're going to get killed."

"It means we're not going to have enough to do this deal. Then what?"

"How can we even go through with the Galishnikov deal now?"

"No. No. I'm not going to let it die. Absolutely not. You get Brooks on the phone and you tell him to dump *everything. Everything.* You got that?" Bennett was now screaming into his phone.

"Okay, okay—I got it. . . . I got it. . . . I got it. . . ."

The two were silent for a moment, McCoy rattled by Bennett's anger, Bennett rattled by the fear rising rapidly within him. As Bennett listened in, McCoy now awakened Tom Brooks—the Joshua Fund's head trader— at his home in Greenwich Village. She carefully explained to him over her speakerphone what was happening, told him to page everyone and get them into the office immediately, and to prepare to liquidate all of the Fund's holdings and go to cash.

Bennett was struck by McCoy's calmness, her patience as Brooks fumbled around his apartment for his remote control to turn on his TV and watch the ghastly coverage on CNN and then FOX and then MSNBC. There was a genuineness, a sweetness to her he'd never paid much attention to, and it just made him feel worse.

Barshevsky pulled up to the terminal without saying a word, popped the trunk, and got out quickly to get the luggage. Bennett hung up his phone, tossed it into his briefcase, and got out. The two shook hands, but said nothing. Then Bennett grabbed his bags and raced into the airport for a flight he was now almost certain to have missed.

✯ ✯ ✯

"Get me the president."

At least the VP was secure deep underneath the White House.

"Sir, Bud Norris at Secret Service just told me the president is fading in and out of consciousness," said NSC Advisor Marsha Kirkpatrick, the fifty-three-year-old Georgetown University Russian history professor turned senior White House advisor, seated at the huge conference table and trying to open a secure satellite phone link to the president and his security team.

"Where is he right now?"

"He's on his way to Crystal Palace, flanked by two Apaches. A team of agents is trailing in another helicopter, and two more choppers are picking up the rest of the agents at the crash site as we speak."

"How long till they get to Crystal Palace?"

"Not sure. One second."

Just then, Kirkpatrick finally connected with the commandeered Denver Metro Police helicopter whose call sign was now Eagle One, flying low and without lights southward along the foothills of the Rockies.

"Eagle One—go."

"Eagle One this is Prairie Ranch—secure code Matrix Delta Tango."

"Copy that—Matrix Delta Tango. We are secure."

"Eagle One, this is the national security advisor. Whom do I have on the line?"

"Ma'am, this is Special Agent Jackie Sanchez."

"Do you have Gambit?"

"We do, ma'am. We're inbound for Crystal Palace."

"Agent Sanchez, I've got Checkmate with me. Stand by one."

The vice president grabbed the black phone on the console before him as a military aide punched in his secure code.

"Sir, you've got Agent Jackie Sanchez on the line. She's in flight with the president."

"Agent, this is Checkmate. How is he?" the VP asked calmly.

"Sir, Gambit is alive. He's in pretty good shape, considering. He asked me to tell you to activate Operation Irish X-Ray immediately."

"Really?"

"That's what he said."

"Fine. Tell him we'll do it. What else?"

"Vital signs are fine. He's stable. We're about to touch down at Crystal Palace and we've got a medic team waiting for us. Can I give you a full report once we're secure inside?"

"Absolutely—but keep this line open, Agent."

"Yes, sir."

The vice president hit the mute button and looked back at Kirkpatrick. "Two things. First, Gambit wants us to execute Operation Irish X-Ray. Can you make that happen?"

Kirkpatrick was taken aback for a moment. "That quickly?"

"Apparently."

"Okay. I'll do it right now."

"Good. Second, how soon till you can get me the Counterterrorism Task Force on line?"

"Almost done, sir."

☆   ☆   ☆

It was just after eleven in the morning Israel time.

Four in the morning in Washington.

Two in the morning back in Colorado.

Sure enough, Bennett had missed his flight. It wasn't actually going to leave the gate for another ten minutes. But it would take him at least an hour to get through the long lines and clear through Israeli airport security, and he knew he'd never make it.

His phone rang.

"Jon, is that you?"

It was Secretary Iverson.

"Stu? Yeah, it's me. Where are you?"

"I'm in a helicopter with Corsetti. We're headed to see the president. But there's a storm breaking over us right now, so I can barely hear you."

"Is the president all right? The networks aren't saying, but it doesn't sound good."

"I can't say much on an open line. But I think he's going to make it."

"Thank God," said Bennett.

"What's that, Jon? You're breaking up." Iverson was shouting at the top of his lungs as his helicopter shook and rocked in the intensifying storm.

Bennett ducked into a corner of the airport and tried to talk as loudly as possible without attracting attention, but it wasn't easy. "Can you hear me now?"

"Barely—look, Bob talked to the president a few minutes ago. He wants you out here tonight. He actually wants both of us. That's why Bob sent an agent to grab me and throw me onto this chopper. He's gonna get us both killed."

"Where is he right now?" asked Bennett.

"The president?"

"Yeah."

"Can't say," Iverson told him. "It's don't ask, don't tell right now."

"What should I do?"

Between the crashing thunder, the pelting rain, and the roar of the rotors, it was a wonder Bennett could hear Iverson at all. He plugged his right ear with his finger and pressed the phone tight against his left ear, straining to hear every word.

"I think the best thing is to get yourself to New York before they close the airports. The Learjet is out here with me—but it's locked down at DIA. They're not letting anything take off or land."

"Okay."

"So charter a plane out of New York and get yourself to Colorado Springs. Don't worry about the cost. I'll leave further instructions on your home answering machine. That ought to be pretty secure for now. If you need me, leave me messages on my home phone. You'll never get me by cell."

"Okay, I'll do that."

"And, Jon . . ."

"Yeah?"

"Bring the papers with you."

"Okay. Why? What are you thinking?"

"Just do it."

"You don't think any of this is connected to the Medexco deal, do you?"

"I have no idea—but, Jon . . ."

"Yeah, Stu?"

"You remember what the president said to us before you left?"

"The 'oath'?"

"Right."

"Of course."

"Jon, I can't stress this enough. You can't say anything to anyone about this deal. You understand that, right?"

"Don't worry."

"Jon, I'm telling you . . ."

"Stu, I said I get it."

"I'm dead serious. Nothing, to no one. That's an order from the president."

"Stu . . ."

"I know. I know. I'm just saying—no misunderstandings."

"Don't worry."

"Okay—look, I've got to go."

"Okay—oh, and Stu?"

"Jon, I've got to go."

"One more thing."

"What?"

"I told Brooks to dump everything at the bell—go to cash."

"I know. Tom already told me. Smart move, kiddo. But remember, I can't really talk to you about that kind of stuff anymore. Just get out here fast—tonight. The president's counting on you. Got it?"

"Got it. Take care of yourself."

The line went dead. Bennett went numb.

⋆　⋆　⋆

Security was incredibly tight.

Lt. Col. Nick Calloway, an air force medical-trauma specialist, had never seen it like this. Battle-ready Marines surrounded the perimeter as

F-15s circled overhead and three Apaches hovered just a few hundred feet off the ground. The two helicopters carrying the president of the United States and his security team now prepared to set down. Deafening thunder, blinding lightning, howling winds, and driving rain made flight conditions perilous at best, and everyone on the ground was soaked to the bone and terrified that one or more of the choppers would crash.

Suddenly, *Marine One* slammed down on the helipad and its side door ripped open. Calloway rushed in.

"You John Moore?" Calloway shouted above the whipping winds of all the choppers.

"Yeah," Moore shouted back.

"Lt. Col. Nick Calloway—welcome to the Mountain."

"You guys ready for us?"

"We sure are. Is the president okay?"

"He's stable, but we need to get him into the medical bay on the double. Let's move."

"Yes, sir." Calloway turned back to his medical and security teams standing just behind him. *"Okay, let's move."*

The agents—led by Moore and Jackie Sanchez—scrambled out of the two choppers and worked with the Crystal Palace teams to get the president onto a stretcher and into a caravan of one ambulance, two Chevy Suburbans, and seven Humvees. Four minutes later, the caravan was racing down a long, dark tunnel into the heart of the Mountain, through two sets of six-foot-thick steel blast doors, which closed behind them with a bone-rattling shudder.

This was Crystal Palace, code name for the North American Air Defense command—NORAD—located deep inside Cheyenne Mountain in southern Colorado. The Mountain was now sealed. The president was safe.

☆   ☆   ☆

The principals were ready.

The Counterterrorism Task Force videoconference was now in session, linking all the major players in the federal government to the vice president in the PEOC, code-named Prairie Ranch.

National Security Advisor Marsha Kirkpatrick quickly settled the room down and got things moving. "Okay, gentlemen, if you'd take your seats . . . and, Mr. Secretary, if you'd sit in that seat to your right . . . great . . . Okay, we're a go," said Kirkpatrick as everyone in the room looked up at a wall of large-screen video monitors and digital clocks showing the time in major cities all over the world.

"Take the roll call," the vice president directed.

"Yes, sir. Gentlemen, this is National Security Advisor Marsha Kirkpatrick at Prairie Ranch. With me are Vice President Oaks and Secretary of State Tucker Paine. SecDef, are you with us?"

"I'm here, and I've got almost all the chiefs with me—navy is still on the way," said Defense Secretary Burt Trainor, the sixty-four-year-old Vietnam vet and recent General Motors CEO, once named one of *Black Enterprise* magazine's top ten CEOs of the twenty-first century.

"Good. Treasury Secretary Iverson is out in Colorado with Bob Corsetti, en route to Crystal Palace. Is the deputy secretary with us?"

"Yes, Marsha, I'm here, and I've got Fed Chairman Allen with me," said the sixty-three-year-old deputy treasury secretary, Michael Forrester. "The chairman and I are in the communications center underneath the U.S. Embassy in Tokyo. We were supposed to meet with the prime minister later today, and the heads of the Asian central banks."

"That's off," said Kirkpatrick.

"Right, we're getting on an air force jet in about an hour to head back to Washington," replied Forrester.

"Mr. Chairman? It's Bill," interjected the vice president.

"Yes, Mr. Vice President," responded George Allen, seventy-one, in his first term as chairman after nearly two decades on the Federal Reserve Board.

"Got anything?"

"As a matter of fact, I do, sir. At 6:45 a.m. eastern the Fed will announce a significant cut in the Fed funds rate."

"How much are we looking at, George? Off the record, of course."

"Off the record? Fifty basis points."

"Half a point? That's great, George. Thanks. I'll tell the president."

"Yes, sir. How is he?"

"He'll be fine, incredibly. It's a miracle. Have you seen the video of the attack yet?"

"No, sir, not yet," said Allen.

"Horrifying. How anyone could have walked out alive is, well . . ."

"The grace of God, sir," noted the Fed chairman.

"Certainly is. The sad thing is the agents. We've lost three for sure. The others . . . well . . . some of them are in pretty bad shape. I don't know if some of these guys are going to make it."

"We're praying for all of them, and the president, and you, sir," Chairman Allen added.

"Thanks, George, that's very gracious of you."

"My pleasure."

"Do we have the AG?" asked Kirkpatrick.

"I'm here, Marsha. And I've got my senior team with me," said Attorney General Neil Wittimore, the fifty-six-year-old former New York State attorney general, at the Justice Department.

"And the DCI?"

"Yes, ma'am," said Jack Mitchell, fifty-one, the colorful, Houston-born Director of Central Intelligence and a twenty-two-year veteran of the intelligence community. "I've got the DDO with me. The DDI is downstairs, but I've got an open line to him."

"Is he alone, in a secure room?" Kirkpatrick asked.

"Yes, ma'am. We're all set."

"Great. Thanks. FBI?"

"I'm here," said Bureau Director Scott Harris.

"Secret Service?"

"It's Bud. I'm here, Marsha, and I concur with the vice president's comments," said Bud Norris. "The president is really hanging in there. But my boys are fighting—they're fighting for their lives right now and, Mr. Chairman, they'll take all the prayers they can get. Thank you very much, sir."

"You're welcome, Bud," Chairman Allen said softy. "You hang in there."

"Will do, sir. Will do."

"Okay, we're all present and accounted for, Mr. Vice President. It's all yours," Kirkpatrick said, sifting through a series of cables and intel reports just set before her.

* * *

"Jim—thank God you're alive."

First Lady Julie MacPherson, surrounded by heavily armed Secret Service agents in the family's Beaver Creek lodge, was already on heavy medication to calm her shattered nerves. Hearing her husband's voice for the first time since the attack, she immediately welled up with tears.

"Hey, sweetie. . . . How are you? . . . How are the girls?" he responded, his voice weak, his blood coursing with narcotics.

Julie MacPherson tried to fight back her emotions, to be strong for her husband, to be there for him in spirit if not in person. "We're all good, sweetheart. It's so good to hear your voice. We've been praying for you nonstop."

"Thanks . . . I just keep . . . I just keep thinking . . . what did . . . what did Reagan say that time? . . . 'Honey, I forgot to duck' . . ."

The First Lady began to laugh, but it quickly disintegrated into sobbing, her body heaving with emotion. All she could think of was how blessed she was, and how devastated the wives of the slain agents must be. And for the moment, it was more than she could bear.

* * *

The room was a meat locker.

It couldn't have been more than sixty degrees in there. The vice president—now wearing jeans, a thick navy blue wool sweater, and a navy blue fleece jacket with the vice presidential seal on it—leaned forward and held court.

"Okay. The president is safe and secure at Crystal Palace. They've buttoned up the Mountain and he's got a team of medics working on him as we speak. Burt, where are we with airspace and military status right now?"

"Mr. Vice President, as you know we've moved to ThreatCon Delta. With your permission, we'd like to go to DefCon Three."

"Do it."

"Thank you, sir. As you also know, we've scrambled three F-15 squadrons to fly CAP over Colorado at the moment. The state is under a full ground stop. No flights can take off or land in the state until further notice. We've also instituted a full ground stop over the Washington, D.C., Virginia and Maryland area and have F-15s and F-16s flying CAP here, as well. We've also scrambled F-16s to guard the coastlines and the borders with Canada and Mexico."

"Mr. Vice President, this is Scott at FBI."

"Yes, Scott."

"Shouldn't we shut down everything?"

"Burt, what do you guys think?" the VP asked, turning to the defense secretary.

"Mr. Vice President, I don't think we have any indication that this is another 9/11. Not yet, anyway. I think what we've got is an attempt to take out the president, not a general series of attacks."

"Marsha, how about you?"

"I think the secretary is probably right. You're secure. The Speaker is secure. All of the cabinet secretaries are secure. We're going to keep monitoring everything. But let's keep in mind what we know. This wasn't a commercial jetliner. It was a private jet—a Gulfstream IV—chartered out of Toronto, apparently by some oil executives. That, of course, may just be a cover story. It may not have been a hijacking at all. And despite some twenty-five thousand flights each and every day, we haven't had a single hijacking over U.S. airspace in quite some time. Again, we'll shut down everything if we have to. But I just want us to be careful not to overreact here."

"Overreact?" interjected Harris. "Someone just tried to take out the president and decapitate the U.S. government."

"Scott, I don't disagree with you. I'm saying the airline industry is finally back on its feet. We've got millions of Thanksgiving passengers headed to the airports later today. Let's just stay cool before we shut the thing down again."

"You've got to be kidding, Marsha," Harris sniffed in disgust. "That's precisely why we need to shut everything down. We could have a nightmare scenario on our hands. Look, when I woke up this morning—yesterday morning, whatever—I would have told you unequivocally that we're doing a pretty good job protecting U.S. air travel. I'd have put my wife and kids on any commercial flight in the country. Right now, I'm not so sure."

"How many air marshals have we got up tonight, Scott?" the VP asked.

"I don't know off the top of my head, sir."

"Ballpark."

"Ballpark? Probably about three hundred—mostly on international flights coming into the U.S. and on all flights that are headed—*were* headed—in and out of Washington. But private aviation is totally unmonitored. No security checks. No metal detectors or X-ray machines or anything. You can just get on any private plane at any time of the day or night and there's absolutely no security. At the minimum, we should ground all private aviation until we get to the bottom of this thing."

The VP sat back for a moment and scanned the bank of video screens before him. "All right. I'm going to talk to the president. But I want the FAA on notice that we may shut everything down on a moment's notice. Marsha, you got that?"

"Yes, sir."

"What about y'alls engagement orders over D.C. and Colorado?" asked Jack Mitchell at Langley.

Defense Secretary Trainor took that one. "Per the president's executive order several years ago, any full ground stop combined with a CAP triggers immediate presidential authorization to shoot down any aircraft noncompliant with the order."

"Neil, are we in any constitutional problems with the president under so much sedation?" Kirkpatrick asked the attorney general.

"We could be soon. My team is working up the papers to put the VP in charge, should that become necessary. We really need an update on his progress."

"Shouldn't be long," Kirkpatrick told Wittimore, then turned to the VP. "Sir, once we know for sure the president's status, I think you should make a statement in the pressroom."

"I agree."

The VP turned and directed an aide to begin gathering the White House press corps—at least, those not traveling with the president and thus stranded out on I-70 in Denver—to begin assembling for a briefing.

"Mr. Vice President, just a few things from my shop," said Secretary of State Tucker Paine, as the immediate security issues were finished.

"Yes, Tuck, what've you got?"

"I just got off the phone with the Kremlin a moment ago. As you know, Marsha and I just returned from Moscow."

"Right. What are they saying?"

"The trip itself was productive. They appreciated the emergency aid package very much, and they've been remarkably cooperative on the intelligence-sharing front. But they are very concerned about this latest attack, and they don't believe there's any Al-Qaeda involvement. Not this time. Not with all the success we've all had in ripping up their network."

"Who are they looking at?"

"They're reluctant to say. But their first instinct is that it smells like Iraq."

"Why?"

"I think they're working on something. We should have more later this morning."

"Okay, let me know first thing."

"Mr. Vice President?"

"Yes, Jack?"

Jack Mitchell—Texas born and bred—was a close friend of the VP, as well as the president, having met MacPherson in the jungles of Vietnam as a junior field agent with the CIA. When MacPherson returned to the States and headed for Wall Street, Mitchell asked for and received a transfer to the Middle East, rotating through a number of Gulf states. He eventually worked his way up to become the CIA station chief in Baghdad, shadowing the operatives of *Mukhabbarat*—the Iraqi intelligence service—tracking the influx of Soviet and East German weapons, advisors, and scientists, and trying to keep tabs on activities at such places as Salman Pak, a terrorist training camp and biological-weapons factory located south of Baghdad along the Tigris River.

Mitchell returned to the U.S. in 1989 to head up the Near East Operations Division at Langley, directing the agency's Scud-hunting efforts during the Gulf War in 1991. He was also instrumental in helping secure the defection of two of Iraq's top nuclear scientists during the 1990s, two of the most dramatic yet publicly unheralded modern successes of the beleaguered American spy network.

But for all his experience, Mitchell now shifted uncomfortably in his seat and stuffed some fresh tobacco chew between his cheek and gum. "This thing's going from bad to worse, fast."

"How so?" the VP asked.

"We're not the only ones getting hit."

Mitchell whispered to an assistant to begin rolling some newly acquired videotape from various CIA stations around the globe. Then he began narrating.

Though obviously taken by amateurs, the images were surreal. The Canadian Embassy in Paris was on fire. Every building in the compound was completely ablaze. Somehow the photographer—a Canadian tourist filming his fiancée in front of the embassy just moments before the attack began—had captured three car-bomb explosions, one after another, inside the gates, followed by mortar fire coming in over the couple's heads. Everyone in the room, including the vice president, was visibly shaken.

"This footage just came in," said Mitchell.

"Casualties?" asked the VP.

"No word yet, sir. We're still trying to gather more information. We've got two field agents on the scene right now and more on the way."

"The Canadian Embassy, Jack? What for?" asked Trainor.

"It's the new embassy. Just completed. Canadian president Jean Luc was there to dedicate it. They've been having a huge party there all night."

The room fell silent.

"I'm afraid that's not all, sir."

Mitchell now directed everyone's attention to a second video screen. It was worse than the first.

"This is a live feed. Buckingham Palace in London is also on fire, apparently hit by a barrage of mortars and RPGs less than ten minutes ago."

Everyone in the room gasped.

"London Station reports machine-gun fire can presently be heard in the streets around the palace. I'm trying to get more on that right now, sir."

"Is the queen there?" asked FBI Director Harris.

"It seems she is," said Mitchell. "Our embassy reports she's okay, but she's being airlifted to a military hospital as a precaution."

On the video screen, an aide could now be seen handing Mitchell a note.

"What've you got now, Jack?" asked the VP.

"Holy . . . is this confirmed? . . . Are you sure? . . . Mr. Vice President, I've just been handed a report that a 747 has just crashed into the Royal Palace in Saudi Arabia."

"What?"

"One of my guys was actually driving to the palace when it happened. Saw the whole thing. Just sent a flash traffic e-mail to the U.S. Embassy in Riyadh, which was immediately forwarded here to Langley. Our agent started taking high-eight video footage. We should be getting that uplinked to us momentarily."

"Sir, this is Burt at the Pentagon."

"Yes, Burt?"

"Sir, I have to say, I now think we're looking at a coordinated global attack on our allied leaders. We need to go to DefCon Two immediately, not Three. And, I'm sorry, I think now we've got to shut down the air-traffic control system."

"A full ground stop—no planes up or down—on the day before Thanksgiving?" asked the deputy treasury secretary from Japan.

"I don't think we have any choice, sir," Trainor replied, directing his remarks to the vice president.

"Jack, do we have any reason to believe we're going to see attacks on civilians? Or is Burt right—this is a series of assassination attempts designed to decapitate governments friendly to us?"

"Well, Bill, I can't rightly say for sure. I can't go on record about what else might be coming. You got a bunch of lunatics out there right now trying to undo Western civilization. But, yes, for the moment, the initial evidence suggests a concerted campaign of assassinations, targeted at friendly governments—mostly NATO governments—rather than widespread civilian terrorism. But, sir, you know as well as I do that could change very fast."

The vice president took a deep breath and took a sip of fresh coffee, just poured and prepared to his liking—heavy cream, three sugar cubes—by a Filipino navy steward.

"All right. Look, here's what we're going to do. Marsha, put a full ground stop on private planes immediately. But hold off a bit on a full commercial ground stop. At least until I can talk to the president. I'll get you an answer soon. Burt, take us to DefCon Two. The president will definitely concur on that, and I'll get it written out at Crystal Palace in the next few minutes. Tuck, send out a flash traffic alert to all of our embassies worldwide. Explain what's happening. Tell them to be in immediate contact with the leadership of their host countries that a wave of assassination attempts is under way. Then you get a conference call set up immediately with the foreign ministers of the G8. Find out what they know and what they're doing about it."

"From here, or State?"

"Good question. I don't know. Bud?"

"Sir, I don't think any of you should leave that bunker right now, not with what we're seeing unfold," said Norris.

"I think he's right, sir," Kirkpatrick agreed. "We've got the facilities in the next room over. Tuck, you can run your diplomatic track from Conference Room Two while we coordinate with the president and the task force from here."

"Good, do it," said the VP. "Jack, anything else? Tell me some good news."

"Sorry, sir," said Mitchell. "I'm afraid I don't have any."

5

⋆ ⋆
⋆

BENNETT SLIPPED his U.S. passport and American Express Gold
Card to the Delta ticket agent behind the bulletproof glass.

He'd already been in line for nearly half an hour, and the line behind
him now stretched out the door. He began to think he'd never get out.
But membership does have its privileges. Nine minutes later he got
lucky—the last seat on the last flight that could get him to New York
before the day's end, and it just happened to be first class.

The attractive young Israeli woman with the slicked-back dark hair
and smoky dark eyes smiled seductively and slid him his passport, credit
card, and a nonstop ticket. Delta Flight 97, leaving Tel Aviv at 1:30 p.m.
local time and landing at Kennedy at 6:45 p.m. eastern. That would be
the easy part. Getting to Colorado would be the headache.

DIA, of course, was shut down indefinitely. The last flight from Kennedy to Colorado Springs—via American through Dallas–Fort Worth—
left at 6:10 p.m. eastern, more than a half hour before he'd even be on the
ground in New York, much less cleared through customs and able to get
to the domestic terminals. And even if the American flight left late, it was
completely booked anyhow. The next commercial flight to Colorado
Springs didn't leave until 5:50 the next morning. But that wasn't the worst
of it. The FAA had just ordered a full ground stop in Colorado—nothing
was flying in or out of the state—so all of this was now moot anyway.

Bennett picked up his bags and glanced back at the Delta agent, who
caught his eye and winked. He lingered for a moment, then finally

convinced himself to go stand in another endless line, this one through security on the way to the passengers-only lounge. As he waited, he fished his cell phone out of his briefcase, speed-dialed McCoy in London, and told her about Iverson's call. Next, he instructed her to track down the Signature flight-support center at LaGuardia and charter a private jet to Cheyenne, Wyoming. Get it big and fast and don't worry about the cost, Bennett told her. And have Carey Limo waiting for him at Kennedy when he arrived. He would be signing all the expense vouchers from now on, and this one would be the least of his worries.

Assuming he could clear customs and get picked up by the car service between eight and eighty-thirty, Bennett figured he could get to LaGuardia and meet the jet on the tarmac—engines running, flight plan cleared— sometime between nine and nine-thirty, depending on weather and traffic. He could then be in the air no later than ten o'clock New York time. With a good pilot and a tailwind, he could be on the ground in Cheyenne by midnight local time, maybe twelve-thirty. If he had to rent a car, McCoy told him the drive was about a hundred and eighty miles, or about three hours. If the Colorado State Patrol or the Secret Service could put him in a chopper, he might be able to get to the Springs—or wherever he was going—by one, maybe two in the morning at the latest.

Bennett felt suffocated—unable to think, unable to react, and half a world out of position. But there wasn't anything more he could do. *One step at a time*, he told himself. *One step at a time.*

* * *

His name was General Khalid Azziz.

He had served as head of the Iraqi Republican Guard—Saddam Hussein's elite military machine—since the end of the Gulf War, and no one was more trusted with the president's personal security or the stability of the regime than he.

As head of Saddam's intelligence services during the war with Iran in the 1980s, it was Azziz who pressed successfully for funding to build an elaborate and sophisticated maze of steel-and-concrete-hardened, bomb-proof bunkers underneath Baghdad in case such hiding places would ever be needed for the leaders of the regime during war or revolution. Construction began in late 1986 amid various and conflicting public reports that Saddam was launching a massive archeological excavation, building a world-class subway system to rival any such system in the West, or renovating downtown Baghdad and building a huge new office and shopping complex. By the time U.S. smart bombs began falling from the Baghdad sky like rain on Seattle, the construction was largely complete. But no archeological site, subway system, or commercial complex was ever officially announced, much less opened. And Saddam Hussein had almost effortlessly survived one of the most aggressive bombing campaigns in the history of modern warfare. It didn't take a rocket scientist for the CIA or Saddam himself to figure out why. And General Azziz emerged as a national hero as a result.

The general was also the man almost singularly responsible for kicking UNSCOM—the United Nations Special Commission for finding and destroying all of Saddam Hussein's weapons of mass destruction—out of Iraq forever. It had been years since UNSCOM inspectors set foot in the country. It was the general's job to keep it that way. And to the amazement of his boss—and most of the world—he'd been spectacularly successful.

The most perilous moment of the general's long career came in the early 1990s, when two top Iraqi nuclear scientists escaped the country and defected to the United States. Operations Purse Snatcher and Glowing Thunder were both spearheaded by Azziz's archenemy, Jack Mitchell, and these disasters nearly cost Azziz his life.

Fortunately for the general, one of his lieutenants was able to locate one of the scientists—still in Jordan—and persuade him to come back without harm to see his family. According to the story picked up by the Jordanian intelligence services, when the scientist was finally brought to Azziz, an elaborate feast was prepared, and his wife, seven children, and close relatives were brought to see him.

Everyone was assembled, including President Hussein. It was quite an affair. General Azziz hugged the man, kissed him on both cheeks, and forgave him.

Then—without warning—he drew a pistol and shot the scientist in the face.

Each immediate family member was then individually beheaded in full view of the others by Azziz personally, with a gleaming Persian saber dating back to the fourteenth century.

The screaming and hysterical wife was forced to watch, and was beheaded last. Hussein and Azziz then sat down for the meal of roasted lamb, couscous, and baklava as the scientist's numb relatives were forced to mop up. This redeemed the general in the eyes of the nation's supreme leader, and he had once again become Iraq's most glorious son.

Now, however, Khalid Azziz was again in grave danger. Through careful tracking of Western trade publications and a series of e-mails from a mole burrowed deep inside the MacPherson administration, *Mukhabbarat* agents had recently picked up the scent of the enormous petroleum deal being hammered out by Galishnikov, Sa'id, and the American president's alma mater, GSX and the Joshua Fund. Azziz was stunned when he learned the unprecedented magnitude of the deal. His boss went ballistic.

Enraged by the prospect of unprecedented Israeli oil wealth, the destabilizing of OPEC, the obvious sellout by some moderate Palestinians in creating a joint venture with the Israelis, and the intensive involvement of the Americans—both in funding the project and working behind the scenes to persuade the Palestinian leadership to offer their blessings—Saddam Hussein's instructions were crystal clear: *Shut it down*. There were scores to be settled, and now was the time.

Azziz had been given an operational plan, handcrafted by Saddam himself. It was as brazen as it was barbaric. Assassinating President MacPherson was just the beginning. The crown jewel would be unleashing the fury of Allah on Tel Aviv and New York to send the world a message and to finish the job Osama bin Laden had set into motion on September 11, 2001.

The plan was stark—it was all or nothing, kill or be killed, wipe out the Americans and the Israelis or be wiped out forever.

The plan was simple—not easy, but clear, concise, uncomplicated, and straightforward.

And the plan was fully funded—immediately.

The best men and the best weapons were being made available for the cause. The critical elements of the plan's success, of course, were stealth, speed, and surprise.

Now, however, events were already spinning out of control. Azziz's boss would not be happy. And he was due to brief the Iraqi president in just ten minutes. It was time to set Plan B into motion.

* * *

It took Bennett thirty-five minutes to get up to the front of the line.

But it never dawned on him what was coming next.

A single man traveling on a one-way ticket from Israel to New York and seeking information on flights to Colorado mere hours after an airborne assassination attempt against the president of the United States in Colorado—most likely at the hands of Middle Easterners—set off red flares worthy of the Fourth of July long before Bennett actually handed over his passport, ticket, and boarding pass for inspection.

Even as Bennett was trying to buy his ticket, the Delta agent had typed an *alef* alert—priority one—into her computer and stepped on a small button beside her left foot. This triggered immediate video-camera surveillance on Bennett, which the agent could see in the top left-hand corner of her computer screen.

As she seemed to be typing in his passport information, the young woman was actually typing instructions to the video camera behind her to center Bennett in its frame, zoom in, focus, and then "paint" him with an infrared code.

This would now allow him to be tracked by every video camera in the airport, including a highly sophisticated, Israeli-made X-ray camera that could scan his body and his luggage for weapons. It would also allow him to be tracked by every hidden laser-guided microphone in the airport as he made his way through the crowds. All this, in turn, would allow the staff in the central security office deep under the airport to see and hear him at all times.

But that was only the start. The silent alarm also rapidly summoned three undercover security agents to surround Bennett and shadow him without his knowledge. The *alef* alert, meanwhile, began a high-speed computer search for every detail of Jonathan Meyers Bennett's life through the massive Israeli database, cross-linked with Interpol and the FBI.

The attractive young Israeli woman behind the Delta ticket counter was no typical airline employee. She was actually a counterterrorism specialist for the Shin Bet, Israel's counterintelligence and internal security agency, roughly equivalent to the U.S. FBI.

When his check-in security interview lasted for more than forty-five frustrating minutes, Bennett began losing his patience. His briefcase and garment bags were X-rayed and searched by hand. His toothpaste was squeezed out of its tube to check for plastic explosives. His shaving cream was shaken and sprayed to see if any kind of toxin could be found inside. His cell phone was quickly dismantled and then reassembled, as was his BlackBerry. His laptop computer was carefully scrutinized and his papers rifled through.

The real trouble began, however, when one of the security guards leafed through his address book—under Bennett's intense protest—and noticed he had the home phone numbers and direct office numbers for all of President MacPherson's most senior advisors.

This now attracted the attention of an American official, who Bennett guessed probably worked for the FBI or the U.S. air marshal program. Bennett was taken out of line, down a hallway, around a corner, out of the sight of other passengers, and down five flights of stairs. There he passed through a series of security doors and into one of several interrogation rooms at the far end of a dark, shadowy corridor.

It was a small room. No windows. Pale green–painted brick walls. No clock. No furniture at all, except for one rickety wooden chair in the middle of the filthy white tile floor where a small, used, red-plastic syringe lay in the corner. A single dusty green metal lamp hung from an incredibly long, bare cord from far above him—so far above him that Bennett couldn't actually see the ceiling.

The room, in fact, appeared to be a tower of some kind. The green paint on the walls ended about eight or nine feet up, and from there Bennett could see only thick stones reminiscent of a medieval castle or some ancient Roman ruin. But the shadows and the darkness above made it impossible to see any higher. Bennett was also immediately struck by the temperature. It was hot and steamy, a good twenty to thirty degrees hotter than the already stifling passenger terminal, and the whole place stank of stale cigarettes. Bennett was a long way from the King David Hotel, and his anger was rising.

Two stocky, muscular Israeli men in blue jeans and blue blazers slammed Bennett down into the chair and forced his hands into metal handcuffs that dug sharply into his skin and cut off the circulation to his hands.

"What is this for?" demanded Bennett.

The two men said nothing. Instead, they took up positions by the locked door.

"Hey, hello. I'm an American citizen. I have rights. Now would someone tell me what is going on?"

No one said a word. A third Israeli—shorter, thinner, wearing an impressive charcoal gray Italian-made suit but no tie and thin, square, gold-rimmed glasses—moved to the far corner of the room opposite the door and lit up a cigarette, but said nothing.

The American agent, meanwhile, paced quietly, playing obsessively with a bright red yo-yo. "Mr. Bennett, why exactly are you so eager to get to Colorado tonight?" he asked, lighting up a cigarette.

"Look, I've answered this question nineteen times already."

The man with the yo-yo stopped behind Bennett, lowered his face behind Bennett's left ear, and whispered, "Answer it again."

Bennett could feel the blood rising through the back of his neck. His ears were getting hot and red. All four armed men could see his reaction, and it did nothing to calm their nerves or cool their suspicions. The mood was darkening quickly, and Bennett struggled to stay calm and navigate a way out.

"You say you know the president?"

"Yes, I told you—I'm a personal friend of the president. I'm the senior vice president of the investment house he used to run out of Denver, Global Strategix. I'm here on business. I've been asked to go out and see him as quickly as I possibly can."

"And you spoke with him this morning?"

"No, I told these gentlemen already—I spoke with Stuart Iverson."

"The treasury secretary?"

"Exactly, and the former chairman of GSX."

"And who'd you say he's with right now?"

"He and Bob Corsetti are on their way to see the president. I just spoke to them an hour or two ago."

"Bob Corsetti, the White House chief of staff?"

"Right."

"And you're supposed to meet up with them?"

"That's right."

"Where again?"

"Colorado Springs."

"Where in Colorado Springs?"

"Like I said, I don't know. I'm supposed to get there and wait for instructions."

"From whom?"

"From Stu or Bob, I guess—I don't know yet."

"I see. That's interesting."

The room fell eerily silent. The man just played with his yo-yo. He certainly didn't identify himself, though two identification badges hung over his neck by a thin metal chain. One was clearly a U.S. government ID of some kind, probably from the FBI, though it was hard for Bennett to get a good look since the man stood behind him most of the time. The other ID was some kind of Israeli airport-security pass, but again, Bennett couldn't really tell. All he knew was that nothing he said was getting through. The man behind him clearly didn't believe a single word Bennett was saying. But why not? A few quick phone calls could check out Bennett's story and be done with it. What was wrong with this guy?

At least five minutes passed, though it might have been more. Bennett wasn't sure what to do. The more he pled his innocence, the quieter the man became. The more angry he got, the more suspicious the man became. The problem was these questions. The more Bennett thought about it, the more he realized that the questions weren't designed to elicit answers, facts. They held implications, insinuations. They were accusations. Bennett had heard a million stories about Israeli airport security. But not like this. This was no longer an interview. It was an interrogation. And it wasn't being conducted by an Israeli. It was being conducted by an American. And it wasn't any American. It was an American with an ax to grind, an American whose president had just been viciously attacked by men on a plane, maybe men who had come from the Middle East.

Bennett fought to control his anger, simmer it, check it, and wall it off from his logic. He was an analyst, a strategist. *So analyze this.* He winced at the sharp metal now digging into his wrists. But he refocused and tried to clear his thoughts.

The man who stood behind him was a loner, single, probably had never been married. He wore no wedding ring. He wore no rings of any kind. He was a solitary man, a man who lived not off the warmth of family and friendships but off the cold adrenaline of fear and doubt and danger.

He was a driven man, a man with a mission and a purpose. But he was a frustrated man, a man whose job was impossible, really—to know the mind and intentions and imminent actions of evil men determined to do his country great harm. His sole purpose in life was to outfox men from an alien mind-set, men who lived in a hellish, ghoulish world of death and deception—educated and moderately wealthy men with wives and children and futures who would willingly decapitate a pilot with a box cutter and their bare hands and steer a 757 loaded with jet fuel into a 110-story monument of steel and glass and concrete and somehow enjoy being incinerated in an 1,800-degree fireball, believing they were on the way to glory at the right hand of Mohammed.

The man who stood behind Bennett with the yo-yo was a man with a job. His job was to stop planes from being hijacked, to stop planes from being turned into human missiles, weapons of mass destruction. And he had just failed. Not just him, of course. He and his colleagues had failed. Again. The system had failed. The world had failed. But this man was taking it personally. And now this man was a bubbling cauldron of suspicions. He believed he had a suspect and circumstantial evidence, a man with means if not yet an evident motive. And now this man was considering his options.

He said nothing. He just sucked on one cigarette after another and slowly circled Bennett again and again, first one way, then the other, like a shark circling a wounded, bloody fish. The man clearly held seniority in this room. The others stayed pressed against the wall, giving him room to play with his yo-yo, and with the mind of his intended victim. As the minutes ticked by, Bennett could sense the man's rage. It was real. It was rising. And it was palpable.

He wore brown slacks, a wrinkled white shirt with a worn collar, a thin brown tie, an old navy blue sports coat, and shiny new black dress shoes. His hair was black and thin and cut short, though it was not quite a crew cut. He wore a thick mustache that partially covered a large, jagged scar that started beside his left eye and went down to his mouth. He was taller than Bennett, about six foot two, maybe two hundred pounds, and his eyes were small and black and fierce. No, it was more than that. They seemed hollow. They seemed glassy, lifeless. It was then that Bennett's anger began turning to fear.

"Okay, get started," the man calmly told the agent with the gold-rimmed glasses.

This agent quickly complied, stepping behind Bennett, removing the cuff link on Bennett's left wrist and rolling up his sleeve. From inside his jacket he pulled out a small piece of cotton and dabbed it against a tiny flask of a clear liquid, probably rubbing alcohol, Bennett figured. He cleaned a section of Bennett's left arm, just below the elbow, and straightened, standing before Bennett.

Next he removed from his other jacket pocket three plastic syringes—one green, one yellow, one red. He removed the caps from all three, exposing two-inch needles. Bennett's heart raced. Beads of sweat were now dripping down his face, and he suddenly realized his shirt was almost completely soaked. The agent held the syringes in front of Bennett's eyes for ten or fifteen seconds.

"You have a choice, Mr. Bennett," the man with the jagged scar began.

Bennett tried to swallow, but his mouth was completely dry.

"Life, or death."

Bennett's mind reeled. This could not be happening. There had to be something he could say, something he could do.

"Needle one, the green needle? Sodium Pentothal."

Bennett's stomach tightened.

"We call it truth serum."

Bennett struggled to maintain his composure.

"You talk. I listen. You live."

The two guards by the door shifted nervously.

"Needle two, the yellow one? Sodium thiopental."

One of the guards slowly wiped drops of sweat from his nose and chin.

"That was Rickey Ray Rector's favorite. You remember him? Rickey Ray Rector. Arkansas mental patient. Murderer. Arrested. Tried. Convicted. Then denied clemency by good ole Bill Clinton during the '92 election. Remember that? Executed by—what?—oh, that's right—lethal injection. I heard it took the doctors forty-five minutes to find a good, clear vein. But they did it. Oh, they did it all right. Rickey Ray Rector. Put him right in a nice, long, deep sleep with the yellow needle. But that wasn't the end. The end is needle three. That's the red one. You know what that one's called?"

Bennett sat motionless, frozen, unable to speak.

"Potassium chloride. You know what that one does?"

The room was silent.

"Stops your heart. Shuts you down. Does you in."

The man with the jagged scar began to play with his yo-yo again. "Now, Mr. Bennett, you're gonna get the first one, the green one. That's nonnegotiable. Done deal. The question . . . well, I'll just let you figure that one out for yourself. You're a pretty bright man, Mr. Bennett. Working on Wall Street. Hey, you're a friend of the president, and what are friends for?"

The man with the gold-rimmed glasses handed the green needle over Bennett's head. Bennett suddenly stiffened—and waited. What would happen? What did Sodium Pentothal do?

That's when he felt the needle drive deep into his vein. Bennett screamed and shook uncontrollably. And then, in an instant, he felt drowsy and weak. His heart rate slowed. Every muscle relaxed. He could feel himself losing control. He could feel a warm sensation passing through him. He could feel himself drifting, lingering on the edge of unconsciousness. His eyes closed, his breathing slowed, and he felt safe.

"Now, let me get this straight," the man began, quietly, almost in a whisper.

"Okay," Bennett replied softly, wearily, almost in some kind of hypnotic state.

"Jonathan Meyers Bennett."

"Right."

"Forty. Multimillionaire."

"Right."

"Gonna be a billionaire."

"Maybe . . . hopefully."

The man now began to circle Bennett slowly, twirling his yo-yo around his fingers. "Grew up in Moscow."

"For a while."

"You speak Russian."

"A little."

"Dad worked for the *Times.*"

"Right."

"Sources in the KGB."

"Sure."

"Worked for the KGB?"

"No."

"Maybe?"

"No . . . no . . . I don't think so . . . no."

"Do you like your father, Mr. Bennett?"

"Well, sure, I . . ."

"Don't you resent him?"

"No."

"Never spent much time with you. Always working. Always too busy."

"Well, yeah . . . but I . . ."

"You don't talk to him much."

"Right."

"You don't call him."

"Not often."

"He doesn't call you."

"Not that much, no."

"Are you married?"

"No."

"Why not?"

"I don't know—too busy, I guess."

"Seeing someone?"

"No."

"Close friends?"

"Some . . . a few . . . not really."

"Why not?"

Bennett took a deep breath. "I . . . I just don't."

"You religious?"

"No."

"Believe in God?"

"Well . . . no . . . I don't know."

"You don't believe in God?"

"I . . . I don't know. . . . I just . . . I don't think about it much."

"What do you believe in?"

Bennett was silent. Drugged and drowsy, drifting in a murky fog of semiconsciousness, the question seemed to confuse him all the more.

"You must believe in something, Mr. Bennett. What is it?"

"I don't know."

"In your gut, in your heart, in your soul—isn't there something you live for?"

Bennett hesitated, grasping for something slippery and elusive. "I don't know . . . I want to . . . make a difference somehow."

"Have you?"

Bennett thought about that for a moment, didn't like his answer, and kept quiet.

"Pathetic. So, you say you know the president personally."

"I do."

"Know where he lives?"

"Yep."

"Been to his house?"

"Yep."

"Been up to the lodge?"

"Yep."

"Slept in his beds?"

"Yeah."

"Played with his daughters?"

"Yeah."

"Helped them pick out colleges?"

"Yeah."

"Attractive?"

"Yeah."

"Flirtatious?"

"A little."

"Ever gone out with them?"

"No."

"Ever wanted to?"

Bennett was silent.

"Really . . ." The man stopped and stared at Bennett, whose eyes were now closed and who was nearly asleep. He reversed course and began slowly walking in the opposite direction. "You know the agents around the president?"

"Yes."

"They know you by sight?"

"Yes."

"Been in the Oval Office?"

"Yes."

"Hung out in the chief of staff's office?"

"Yes."

"Know all the corridors of the West Wing?"

"Pretty much."

"Knew when the president was flying to Denver?"

"Yes."

"Knew what time he'd land?"

"I guess."

"Knew which car he'd be in?"

"Probably."

"But you weren't there."

"No."

Again, the man stopped, right behind Bennett. "Now you listen closely, you understand?" he whispered. "You come to Israel for a day. One day. You have dinner with a Palestinian Muslim and a Russian Jew, both of whom work on some oil-and-gas project. Gonna make you all rich, right?"

How did he know all this? thought Bennett.

The man grew louder. "Then you just happen to meet with this Russian again—for breakfast. Just so happens to be at the same exact moment that someone is trying to kill the president of the United States. But you don't take your original flight back home through London. Oh no. Because London's under attack. Buckingham Palace is being blown back to the Stone Age. No. Instead, you buy a one-way ticket back to the U.S. and try to figure out some way to get to Colorado Springs. Why?"

Silence. Bennett's head began to lean forward, his eyes still closed, his mind still swimming.

The man with the scar paced quickly as his voice grew louder, angrier.

"Why? Why? Oh, I know why. Because you're supposed to see the president. Because he wants to see you right away. ASAP. Pronto. Yesterday. Right?"

"That's the truth."

"Shut up."

Bennett was scared—suddenly, distantly aware of the man's rising anger and frustration.

"But you have no idea where, or when, or why. You're just supposed to 'wait for instructions.' That's interesting—'wait for instructions.' Some mysterious instructions."

Blood started rushing back to Bennett's head. His eyes suddenly snapped open. He tried to refocus.

"And now, now you want me to clear you to board this American aircraft so you can go see the president. So you can go meet the president. So you can go kill the president. Isn't that right?"

"No," Bennett insisted.

Either the sedative was beginning to wear off or it was being overridden by Bennett's own growing anger. The agent was in Bennett's face, blowing a mouthful of smoke into his eyes, causing him to begin to wince and choke.

"Look, you've got it all wrong."

"Who are you working with?"

"I don't know. I don't know what you're talking about."

"Who's the woman in London?"

"What?"

"Who'd you call to charter you a plane?"

Bennett was completely awake now, but disoriented and confused. "How do you know that?"

The question was a mistake.

The agent recoiled. He now stood behind Bennett holding the bright red yo-yo over Bennett's head, slowly dangling it in front of his face like a dead man in a noose. He gritted his teeth and practically spat his next sentence.

"Bennett, I don't like you. You're hiding something. I can smell it. I can feel it. And if you don't start telling me the truth—" he pulled all the string out of the yo-yo, held it taut at both ends, and slowly began pressing it against Bennett's neck—"I'm either gonna have to squeeze it out of you . . . or give you the yellow needle."

Bennett's breathing quickened. Clarity was coming back to him, but so was fear. "I want a lawyer. You can't . . . this is wrong."

"It's your choice, Bennett."

"How hard is it to verify what I'm saying?"

"Life or death?"

"I got Secret Service clearance during the campaign. Look it up. Call the White House. They'll tell you who I am."

No one said a word. No one made a call. No one even twitched. For the first time, Bennett realized he was in a soundproof room. He couldn't hear anything outside these four walls—if he screamed, or died, no one would know.

"Call the White House. Call Corsetti's office. They'll tell you who I am."

No reply from the scar-faced agent. But the yo-yo string grew tighter around Bennett's neck.

"Mohammed Jibril."

The name just hung in the air for at least a minute.

"Who's that?" asked Bennett.

"You don't know?"

"No."

Bennett was now gagging.

"Mohammed Jibril is a terrorist, Mr. Bennett. He lives in Moscow these days, working with various Islamic terrorist cells."

"What does that have to do with me?"

"You just met with his brother."

"What? What are you talking about? I did not."

Bennett felt sick to his stomach. He'd run extensive background checks on Ibrahim Sa'id, the head of the PPG, and his top staff. But there'd been no evidence of links to terrorist groups. None.

Until now, Bennett had refused to talk to this guy about the details of his oil deal. It was none of their business, and he was under strict orders by the president of the United States to brief him—and him alone—before talking to anyone else on the planet about the substance of this deal. Bennett struggled to breathe. The urge to tell these men everything he knew was overpowering. Was it the truth serum, or just pure survival instinct?

But he couldn't. He couldn't. He'd given the president his word. He'd given Iverson his word. Who were these guys? What if they were linked to the men who'd just tried to kill the president? But how could they be? They'd just scooped him out of the Israeli airport. But did that really matter? Couldn't they be double agents? Couldn't they be paid off by the enemy? What enemy? Whose side were these guys on? Then again, what if he was now holding back crucial information? What if somehow he'd made a mistake? What if somehow his oil deal had gotten mixed up with the very people who'd just tried to assassinate the president? What if he was actually financing such evil?

Bennett winced in fear and pain. He didn't know what to do. And his interrogator could tell. The man tightened the yo-yo string. Sweat poured down Bennett's face.

"Galishnikov."

"What about him?" Bennett tried to swallow, but he couldn't.

"Do you know who he is?"

Bennett was about to throw up. "He's—he's a friend."

The man tightened the string.

"Four years ago, Dmitri Galishnikov helped mastermind a terrorist explosion that destroyed one of the largest refineries in the former Soviet Union. Cost the Russian government half a billion dollars. Not that they needed the money, mind you. They're such a rich, wealthy country. But they did get a little ticked off by the fact that two hundred and twelve Russian citizens died in the explosion."

"I don't know what you're talking about. I don't . . . I . . . please . . . call the White House. . . ."

The agent suddenly exploded. He unwound the yo-yo string from Bennett's throat, grabbed him by the shirt and his hair, and threw him against the wall. Cuffed and unable to protect himself, Bennett hit the wall headfirst, then slumped to the floor and curled into a fetal position, bracing himself for the blows he knew were coming.

The man was shaking with rage and seemed about to lose it completely. He grabbed the wooden chair and smashed it against the wall, shattering it in pieces and sending splinters flying everywhere. Bennett knew it was a show, knew it was designed to frighten him. But knowing did nothing to lessen the impact. Bennett was terrified. He wasn't used to not being in charge. He wasn't used to being ordered around. And now he feared for his life.

"You want yellow, Mr. Bennett? You want red?"

There was nothing for Bennett to say.

"No. God, no."

Bennett felt the needle go in.

"You've got two minutes, Bennett. Are you a terrorist?"

"No."

"Do you fund terrorists?"

"No."

"Is Sa'id a terrorist?"

"No—I don't know."

"Is Galishnikov a terrorist?"

"I don't know."

"Did you help conspire against the president of the United States? *Did you?*"

"*No, no, no . . .*"

"Tell me what I want to hear. Tell me what you know."

"God, please, no."

The man grabbed him again and pulled him to his knees. "*Forget you, Bennett.*"

When Bennett's eyes focused, the man showed him the red needle, dropped it to the ground, and crushed it with his foot.

Bennett sucked in as much oxygen as he could. He felt the man grab his sweaty hair and jerk his face upward. He stared into the eyes above him for a split second and he saw no mercy. This wasn't a pardon. It was an execution.

The man pulled out a Beretta 9 mm and pressed it hard against Bennett's forehead. Then he drew it back, walked behind Bennett, and drove the gun into the back of his head while pushing his body and face to the floor. Just inches away, Bennett could see a dark brown liquid oozing from the crushed red syringe. His body was now shaking uncontrollably.

"You sick little monster," the man screamed in his ear. "You think I'm going to let you get away with this? Do you? I'm going to count to three.

And you're going to tell me why you're paying terrorists to kill the president—or I'm going to splatter your worthless stinking brains all over this room. I'm going to annihilate you and no one will ever even know you're dead. You hear me? *Do you hear me?*"

"It's not true—you're wrong—please—I don't know anything—please."

"One."

"No—I don't know anything—please—I beg you—please."

"Two."

"Oh, God, help me. Please help me."

"*Three.*"

"Oh, God. I don't want to die. *Please.*"

The deafening explosion from the Beretta rocked the room, echoing up and down the tall, dark tower.

Then all was silent.

The Israelis stood aghast, not believing what they'd just seen. All three quickly exited the room. A moment later, the man with the jagged scar holstered his weapon, picked up his yo-yo, and followed them out, locking the door behind him.

Bennett's body lay on the filthy white tile floor—crumpled and still.

6

★ ★
★

IT WAS THE LAST TIME the four men would be in the West.

They knew it. And they didn't care. Extraordinary events had been set into motion, and now it was time for them to get their final instructions and play their part.

The *Wall Street Journal Europe* had a front-page profile of the new treasury secretary, Stuart Iverson. High-ranking but unnamed administration officials said the president now had someone he, the nation, and the world could trust to lead the global economy to new heights. Iverson seemed to fit the bill, and even Democrats on the Senate Finance Committee were singing his praises.

The four could only smile at their good fortune. They certainly couldn't talk about it. Not here, at least. Not sitting in separate pews at St. Stephan's Cathedral—*Stephansdom*—in Vienna. One never knew who was lurking in the shadows, or hiding in plain sight.

Built originally as a Romanesque basilica in the twelfth century, and then rebuilt in the fourteenth century as a cathedral in the classic Gothic style, St. Stephan's was an icon in the heart of Vienna, covered with the black, filthy soot of some six hundred years of wars and fires and industrial development. Vienna, of course, was not only the capital and largest city of Austria but itself an icon in the heart of Europe, a city long known as the gateway to the Eastern powers and Moscow. Here Germans and Russians and the Allies once battled for control. Here the external walls of the cathedral were pockmarked with the bullet holes of Nazi soldiers, whose jackboots once clip-clopped along the cobblestones, instilling fear in the hearts of all who could see or hear them.

Today, the icon within an icon was a great draw for tourists, and no one on this gentle, snowy morning could suspect such monsters in their midst.

Never glancing at one another, the four casually watched the visitors come in, one by one, minute by minute. Mostly old women. Very few men. Almost no children, except for an occasional screaming infant who invariably echoed throughout the cavernous sanctuary and high up into the great tower and steeple. Eventually, a woman in a black dress and matching black hat with a white ribbon pinned to her lapel came in, knelt down, and began to pray.

Slowly, one by one, each of the four men gathered his belongings and casually made his way out of the cathedral. It was time.

None acted as though they knew each other, and each headed in a separate direction. But twenty minutes later, convinced they were not being followed, they converged on the *Graben*—Ditch Street, in English—at the place known as the Plague Monument. Built in remembrance of the end of the bubonic plague, which raged through Europe in the sixth, fourteenth, and seventeenth centuries and killed more than 137 million people, it was now the point of rendezvous for four men, once dubbed by analysts at the CIA—and their British counterparts at MI6—as "the four horsemen of the apocalypse."

One of the men unlocked and entered a white rented Volvo parked nearby. Another took pictures like a tourist, while his partner flipped through a Fodor's guide to Austria and talked about finding an inexpensive restaurant for lunch. The fourth discreetly slipped his gloved hand into a nearby trash can and fished out the unmarked envelope within a discarded German newspaper. He peeked inside. Four train tickets. Four new passports. Four visas. And forty thousand euros in small bills. The team now jumped into the waiting, running Volvo and headed for *Südbahnhof,* Vienna's South Train Station.

On their way, all but the driver passed the *Journal* story around, as well as a copy of the *International Herald-Tribune*, the newspaper published jointly in Europe by the *New York Times* and the *Washington Post*.

The story that attracted their greatest interest this morning was a front-page profile of Russian President Vadim, his remarkable new strategic partnership with the U.S. and NATO, as well as his intensifying political troubles with hard-line nationalists within the *Duma*, the Russian parliament.

New polls inside Russia put Vadim's approval ratings south of Stalin's, and with a cold, bitter winter settling in over Moscow, people's frustration over the rapidly deteriorating economic conditions inside the country—and growing fears of a new wave of hyperinflation—were running deeper every day. Being a friend of the West was doing the shrewd and savvy Russian leader little good at home, and various Western analysts quoted in the story worried that Vadim's days in office might be numbered. Even the country's oil industry—which accounted for nearly half of its entire gross domestic product—was falling on hard times. The price of oil hovered between twenty-two and twenty-five dollars a barrel. If it dropped too low, Russia would be in very serious trouble indeed. The *Herald-Tribune* writer wrote that "growing concerns in Washington over the future of the Russian economy suggest an old Russia hand like Iverson could be the right man for the moment."

At precisely nine-thirty, the four parked, entered the train station, and headed for the *Ost* Section—the East Section—where they arrived on the platform and waited. The terminal was dark and dingy, yet somehow classic and impressive, with a high, arched roof of steel and glass, suggestive of a World War II airplane hangar. Trains from all over Europe arrived and departed here, and tens of thousands of passengers crisscrossed these platforms every day. But not these passengers. Not one of them had ever been to Vienna before, and the longer they waited, the more nervous they got.

Their eastbound train to Bratislava was supposed to leave at 10:05 a.m. sharp. But, in fact, it was late, and all four would end up waiting for another two full hours. Each cursed the gray skies and freezing temperatures and lit up his American-made cigarettes, unaware that, from three separate angles, two men and one woman—each in a separate rental car—were furiously snapping dozens of 35 mm photographs with powerful zoom lenses while radioing a team of other agents loitering inside the terminal that the four horsemen were in the corral.

* * *

The two calls came almost simultaneously.

One from the Pentagon. One from Langley. Both were top priority, and within minutes, the U.S. Counterterrorism Task Force was reassembled via secure videoconference link.

"Mr. Vice President, this is Jack at CIA."

"Go ahead, Jack."

"Sir, we just got word from one of our teams in Vienna. They've positively identified the Iraqi cell as the four horsemen. They're at the train station, and the Iraqis have tickets that take them to Moscow, sir. My team wants permission to take them down and interrogate them for what they know about the attack on the president."

The VP considered that for a moment, then shifted gears. "No. Not yet. Have your team trail them. Intercept any calls they make. Monitor any contacts they make. Have them check in on the hour. I want to know where these guys are going and why, and I want to know before anyone knows we're watching them."

"Sir, you sure? We've been hunting these guys for six years. Now we've got them."

"And they just happen to be moving the same day somebody's attacked the president."

"Exactly, sir. That's why we need to take them down—now."

"No. That's why we need to shadow them until we find out what they're up to—or until I say to take them down. Got it?"

"Yes, sir."

"Good. Who's next?"

"Mr. Vice President, this is Burt at the Pentagon," began the secretary of defense, his eyes weary and red.

"Yes, Burt, what've you got?"

"Sir, we just got this report. Three of our reconnaissance jets have just been shot down over southern Iraq. We've got F-15s going in right now to take out the SAM sites. But it doesn't look good."

"Are you kidding me?"

"No, sir—and there's more."

"I'm listening."

"Our satellites are picking up indications that the Iraqi Republican Guard may be in the process of being mobilized. There's activity around three mechanized units southeast of Baghdad—and we just got word from our forward command post near the border inside Kuwait. Radar is picking up several small blips—could be recon units. We're trying to verify that right now, sir."

"You're right—that's not good."

"No, sir, it isn't. We'll know more over the next few hours, sir, but given all the rest of what's going on, I'm concerned Iraq may be preparing to make a major military move of some sort."

Trainor didn't complete the thought. But he didn't have to.

Suddenly, CIA Director Jack Mitchell broke in. "Mr. Vice President?"

"Yes, Jack."

"DDI just called from downstairs. He's on the phone with Brigadier General Yoni Barak, head of Aman, Israeli military intelligence."

"Sure, I know Yoni—what's he got?"

"Sir, he's got a team—I think you've met with these guys—the *Sayeret* . . ."

"*Sayeret Matkal.*"

"Yes, sir."

"One of their deep recon units."

"That's right, sir."

"What are they telling him?"

"The unit is picking up intercepts of heavy military radio traffic in and around Baghdad. . . . Hold on. . . . Okay . . . he says that agents on the ground are reporting air-raid sirens are going off throughout the city. . . . Apparently, there are no civilians on the streets. . . . State radio and TV are off the air. . . . The Republican Guard appears to be mobilizing and there are already some advance recon units heading east toward Kuwait and south toward Saudi Arabia. . . . It's all pretty chaotic, sir—but that's the latest."

"Any Iraqi units heading toward Israel?"

"Not that they have picked up."

"What's their sense of it all right now?"

"Prime Minister Doron doesn't want to wait. He's convening an emergency Security Cabinet session any moment. The thinking is he'll put the IDF on high alert and call up their reserves within the hour."

"Full or partial?"

"He couldn't say. Not yet."

"What's your gut tell you, Burt?"

"Full."

"Jack?"

"Y'all know what I think. The Israelis are going full—and we should get started too. Calling up our reserves and moving our forces back into the region immediately."

"Marsha?"

"Sir, I think they'll go full. Given what's been going on all night, this does have all the makings of a move by Saddam and may be a prelude to Iraq seizing control of the oil fields in Kuwait and Saudi Arabia. I agree with Jack. We need to move fast on our own reserves and we need to talk to the Saudis about putting boots on the ground there immediately. That's all going to take time—a lot more time than for the Israelis. But we don't have much choice."

"If it is a move by Saddam, who's he most likely to go after first—Kuwait or the Saudis?" pressed the VP.

"Both. Either. I don't know yet," admitted Kirkpatrick. "Either way it's extremely serious."

"Mr. Vice President?"

Everyone turned toward Secretary of State Tucker Paine.

"Yes, Tuck?"

"Sir, I just got off the phone with the Saudi prince to express our condolences. They're safe, but pretty shook up."

"Do they have any clue as to who did this?"

"Not yet. Everything's happening too fast. But they promised to call me the minute they had something."

"What about Moscow? Heard anything from them yet?"

"No, sir. Not yet. I'll keep checking."

"So we don't know what we're looking at yet."

"Not exactly," the secretary of state replied. "I just think we need to be very careful not to jump the gun here."

"Jump the gun?" asked Mitchell. "Mr. Secretary, the president and the leaders of several of our major allies have just been the subjects of an incredibly well-planned, well-financed, and almost flawlessly executed conspiracy to kill them. It's early, I agree. But as we've just said, there is strong circumstantial evidence that this may all be the work of Saddam Hussein in a new play to dominate the Gulf and disrupt the formation of a Western coalition that could stop him. How exactly is calling up the reserves and deploying our forces to the region jumping the gun?"

"Sir, I am just saying that we need to stay focused on our diplomatic options—not go off half-cocked," said Paine.

"Half-cocked?" asked Mitchell. "How about locked and loaded? We're at war, Mr. Secretary. We all know there ain't no diplomatic options with the Butcher of Baghdad. We all know we should've dealt with Iraq earlier. Not just arming and training the anti-Saddam forces. Not just playing games at the U.N., but really taking out this monster once and for all. We didn't. Fair enough. But now it's coming back to haunt us."

"Mr. Vice President, with all due respect, we are not at war, not yet, not unless you and the president listen to the yahoos," warned Paine, the pasty-white, silver-haired former U.S. ambassador to the United Nations. "We need to consult with our allies and come up with a game plan."

"Yahoos?" laughed Mitchell. "Glad to know State has it all figured out. Why don't ya'll just invite Saddam over for a barbeque and, you know, just hammer out this little disagreement once and for all—like nice, civilized U.N. choirboys. In fact, why not just pass another worthless resolution."

Paine sniffed with disgust.

The VP moved to regain control of the discussion. "Gentlemen, please. Settle down. Marsha, what's your sense of things? What would you recommend the president do?"

"Sir, I'm afraid we've crossed the Rubicon. We don't have any choice. I recommend a full ground stop immediately on all planes in the U.S. and no aircraft entering the country. Combat air patrols over both coasts and the borders. Shut down the borders with Canada and Mexico—at least until we get a handle on things. The last thing we need is suicide bombers coming over in eighteen-wheelers or freight trains."

"What else?"

"Then, sir, I believe we need to execute Operation Imminent Cyclone as quickly as possible. That will move the Nimitz battle group back into the Gulf and park the *Roosevelt* and *Reagan* battle groups off the coast of Israel. We'll move out the 82nd Airborne and Delta Force and get them on the way to Saudi Arabia this morning. The key is to get as many troops and mechanized units and air units in place as we can ASAP."

She was right. Events were beginning to spiral out of control. Even the graying sixty-seven-year-old vice president—a former Naval Intelligence officer, onetime Virginia governor, four-term U.S. senator, and longtime chairman of the Senate Armed Services Committee, a solid Washington hand if there ever was one—was beginning to get edgy.

"I agree with all of your recommendations, and so will the president," the VP began. "But you guys know as well as I do, this isn't going to be enough. It's a start. But, look, if Saddam Hussein has decided to go back after Kuwait, or after the Saudis, or after all the Gulf states, Imminent Cyclone isn't going to stop him. And all of you know it."

He scanned the room and the video screens on the wall in front of him. No one seemed to disagree.

"We don't have the forces in place to shut him down quickly. Not if he launches a full-fledged invasion. We can mobilize NATO to come with us—we'll definitely get the British. Who knows about the French and the Germans? But even if we do get NATO to go with us, we certainly don't have six or eight months to build up. Saddam could have half the world's oil supply under his control by the end of the week."

The team was silent, each principal contemplating the past few hours.

"I am going to go ahead and recommend to the president that we go to a full ground stop. That we immediately call up fifty thousand reservists. And that we execute Imminent Cyclone. But, Tuck, first get back on the phone with the Saudis and get them to ask us."

"Sir, I . . ."

"Right now, Mr. Secretary."

"Sir, obviously I will comply. But I must say for the record that we need to get the president on the line here soon and convene an official meeting of the National Security Council before we proceed much further."

"We will," assured the vice president. "You just make sure the Saudis are with us one hundred percent. They've been edgy in the past about us being there. And I don't need to tell you all there have been a lot of strains in our relationship over the past few years. They don't like U.S. troops—especially women and Christians—anywhere near the holy cities of Mecca and Medina. But they need us and we need them. We need to make sure we're all on the same page, fighting the same war. And they need to know we're not going to abandon them to the likes of Saddam Hussein. We're not going to undermine their regime like Carter did to the shah of Iran. And we're not going to waffle and hedge and run feckless, photo-op foreign policy like Clinton did. We're dead serious about shutting Saddam Hussein down—and we're in this for as long as it takes. It's your job to make that crystal clear, Tuck. You got it?"

"Yes, sir."

"Okay. Now, that said, ladies and gentlemen—" the vice president again scanned the faces of everyone in the room with him, and every face on the video screens on the wall before him—"I'm going to say it again. This isn't good enough. The president and I can't tell the world we *were* winning the war on terrorism and then lose the Gulf, for crying out loud. We need new options—and we need them fast."

The vice president sat and stared for a moment at the communications console in front of him. No one knew whether he was done. No one knew quite what to do.

"So much for the victory lap."

☆   ☆   ☆

Delays were not uncommon.

They happened all the time, in and out of the two major Vienna railway stations. But this was no typical day. By the time this particular train finally pulled in, twenty U.S. agents—fifteen men and five women, each Arabic- and Russian-speaking—had arrived, been briefed, had taken up positions in each of the train cars most likely to be occupied by the four horsemen.

These Iraqis were professionals. Though they didn't yet know they were being followed, they certainly had no intention of mingling out in the open to be observed and overheard if they were being shadowed. No sooner were they on board with their tickets punched by a conductor than they slipped into their reserved, four-person sleeper compartment and locked the door.

The best the lead CIA agent could do was put a few of his team in the two sleeping berths on either side and have them attach highly sensitive listening equipment to the walls, connected to digital recording equipment. The rest of his team would assume the roles of waiters, tourists, and baggage handlers while he took up his own command-and-control position with the engineers at the front of the train. The only good news on this leg of the assignment: the four weren't going anywhere the agents couldn't go as well . . . at least not for the next two and a half days.

They all might as well settle in for a long winter's night.

*　*　*

The American and Israeli agents regrouped.

They walked quietly down an empty corridor. When they reached the end, the man with the gold-rimmed glasses punched a nine-digit passcode into a plastic box on the wall, unlocked a massive steel door, and entered. Everyone moved briskly down three flights of stairs. There they showed their IDs to two armed sentries, put their thumbs on a fingerprint-identification pad, were cleared, and stepped into a huge, soundproof, blastproof, wood-paneled office packed with TV monitors and computer screens, military aides, and bodyguards—the office of Israeli airport security chief Yitzhak Galit.

Galit didn't look up as the four men entered and quickly shut the door behind them. He was huddled around a TV screen behind his desk with three other men. One was Yossi Ben Ramon, the head of Shin Bet—Israel's internal security service—nervously chain-smoking Winstons. The second was Avi Zadok, head of the Mossad—Israel's renowned foreign-intelligence service—calmly puffing on a thick Cuban cigar. The third was a quiet man named Dietrich Black, head of the FBI counterterrorism team based in Israel, who now poured a Diet Coke into a glass mug filled with ice.

"Well?" said the American who'd just walked in the room.

All eyes looked to Black. But Black—wearing jeans, casual brown shoes, a black T-shirt, and a .45 caliber sidearm in a shoulder holster—just stared into his glass and waited for the fizz to subside. Secondhand smoke filled the room with a bluish haze, but no one seemed to mind.

"You know why I drink Diet Coke?" Black asked the room of high-powered spooks as he continued to watch the fizz in his glass go down.

No one had any idea what he was talking about.

"I always hated Diet Coke—stuff tastes like dishwater," Black continued. "But I had lunch once in Washington with the director of the bureau at the time. It was in the fall of 1991 and we were having lunch at the Four Seasons with Henry Kissinger."

Zadok glanced at Ben Ramon. Was this guy losing it?

"Kissinger ordered a Diet Coke. And then the director ordered a Diet Coke. And I figured, 'Well, I guess martinis are out.' So I ordered a Diet Coke. 'Cause, you know, Kissinger's a pretty smart guy. If he drinks Diet Coke, then I probably should, too. And I've been drinking them ever since."

Black looked up, picked up his glass, and raised it in the air. "Cheers."

The Israelis in the room burst out laughing—partly out of nervous tension and partly because they had never known quite what to make of Black. As an operative, he impressed them. But as a human being, he amused them no end.

Zadok was the first to catch his breath and light up a new cigar. "You're a moron, Black," he told him, with a thick Israeli accent.

"Yeah, but I'm thin."

"Fine, you're a thin moron."

Even Black had to laugh at that.

Six foot three, trim, completely bald—his wife once told him she couldn't decide if he looked more like Lex Luthor or Mr. Clean—and about to turn fifty, Dietrich Peter Black was a twenty-five-year veteran of the Federal Bureau of Investigation. Recruited fresh out of Harvard Business School at a time when none of his classmates would ever have even considered a career in law enforcement over one on Wall Street, he loved his job and had never thought twice about having taken it.

After hopscotching the world for most of the 1980s, he'd spent most of the 1990s based in Washington, working on high-profile terrorism cases like the World Trade Center bombing in 1993, the Oklahoma City bombing in 1994, the Atlanta Olympics bombing in 1996, and, of course, the attacks on the World Trade Center and the Pentagon in 2001.

He was cool, methodical, and virtually devoid of the kind of passion and emotion that can cloud the judgment of a successful investigator. That wasn't to say he wasn't moved with compassion by the deaths of fellow citizens and colleagues. He certainly was. But he seemed to have an instinctual ability to channel that passion into a laserlike focus. He focused on the details and anomalies and idiosyncrasies and discrepancies that turn up in every case and often turn into determinative leads—leads that can turn into fibers that become threads that emanate from finely woven fabric and that can end up unraveling even the most complicated of cases.

"So, Deek, you know, we're all really intrigued about how you pick soft drinks," said the man with the yo-yo. "But what's the deal here? What's the verdict?"

Black took another sip of the cold, bubbly soda, then turned to the others. "Avi? How 'bout you?"

Avi Zadok leaned back in his chair and took another puff on his cigar, savoring the taste and the moment. Finally, he broke the suspense. "To tell you the truth, I believed him," declared the aging Mossad leader.

Black picked up a half-eaten falafel sandwich sitting on a paper plate beside his Diet Coke and took a huge bite. "Yossi?" he asked, his mouth full of pita and hummus.

"Honestly, Deek?" Ben Ramon replied, his accent just as thick as Zadok's but betraying his Sephardic Moroccan roots. "I'm afraid I have to agree with Avi."

Black looked him straight in the eye, and Ben Ramon finished his thought. "He didn't know anything."

"No, it was more than that," interjected Galit, the airport security chief, suddenly capturing everyone's attention. "He was actually good. Very good. He was honest."

"And loyal," added Ben Ramon.

"Anyone else?" Black asked, eyebrows raised, scanning the room, thick again with nervous tension. No one said a word. Especially not the man with the yo-yo.

Black paced the room, thinking, chewing, assessing the turn of events. He stepped over to the TV on Galit's desk, picked up the remote, and rewound the tape—then played it again without the sound, just watching the face in the center of the screen. He slowly finished his sandwich and his Diet Coke, then wiped his mouth with a tiny, thin paper napkin and turned back to the rest of the group.

"I agree," Black finally admitted. "He didn't know."

Everyone looked down, quiet and smoking.

Then Galit broke the silence. "You Americans should have recruited him," he said, nervously looking around the room for agreement.

Then Black smiled.

"We just did."

* * *

The black phone marked "FBI" rang just before 10:30 a.m. eastern.

The national security advisor picked it up on the first digital ring. "Kirkpatrick."

"Prairie Ranch, stand by for Black Ops."

"Orange Grove?"

"Yes, ma'am."

"Secure?"

"Yes, ma'am."

"Put him through."

"Thank you, ma'am. Hold one."

Kirkpatrick grabbed a nearby yellow legal pad and a black Sharpie. She pulled the cap off and prepared to take down the message. "What's the word?"

"It's done."

"And?" she asked.

There was a pause. Then she nodded. "Thanks. Now clean up and get back here now. Bring everything. You'll get instructions in the air."

Kirkpatrick hung up the phone and looked over at the vice president. Everyone else in the room was consumed with other activities. The VP waited for the answer. Kirkpatrick wrote one word on the last page of the yellow legal pad and slid it over to him.

He looked down, discreetly peeked at the last page, and nodded.

"Clean," it read.

The vice president picked up the blue phone in the console before him, the one marked "NORAD."

"Get me the president."

* * *

Black placed a secure phone call from Galit's office.

"Seventh floor, may I help you?"

"I need to talk to Esther. It's urgent."

"One moment please."

As Black waited, he asked one of the Israeli staffers to pack up everything he'd need for the trip back—including Bennett's body.

"Ambassador's office. Esther speaking."

"Esther, it's Deek."

"Hey, Deek, you okay?"

"I need the DCM."

"He's on a call."

"*Now*, Esther."

"All right. Hold on."

Black opened a new Diet Coke. On one TV, he watched the Sky News replays of the attack on the presidential motorcade and the attacks in London and Paris and Saudi Arabia. On another TV, he watched CNN replay excerpts from a press conference with White House Press Secretary Chuck Murray at Peterson Air Force Base in Colorado.

"I need Bennett's cell phone and BlackBerry," he told Galit. "And I need your guys to crack the passcodes fast."

Galit nodded. One of his men scrambled off to make it happen.

Just then, Tom Ramsey—the deputy chief of mission at the U.S. Embassy in Tel Aviv—came on the line. "Deek?"

"Hey, Tom, it's me."

"You need the ambassador's plane."

"How'd you know?"

"Checkmate just called."

"What about Paine? You need his clearance?" asked Black.

"Are you kidding?"

"I'm just asking."

"Deek, don't you know the facts of life yet, son?"

"I'm just saying . . ."

"I know what you're saying. And I'm saying that asking Secretary Paine to sign off on a covert ops mission using a State Department plane would be like asking Pat Robertson to sign off on a nudist convention on the *700 Club*. It ain't gonna happen."

Black chuckled.

"Get it?"

"Got it."

"Good. How soon you leaving?"

"Soon as it's ready."

"They're warming it up now—oh, and I just sent Jane over with a little surprise."

"Tom, I don't need any more surprises."

"Don't worry. It's from the ambassador himself. Just take care of yourself."

"Thanks, but what did I do to deserve anything from you guys?"

"Nothing."

"Right."

"Be good."

"I'll try."

☆ ☆ ☆

An hour later, Yitzhak Galit's security office was nearly empty.

Zadok and Ben Ramon shut down the airport until further notice and rushed back to meet with the prime minister and the Security Cabinet. Most of Galit's men were clearing the buildings above and setting up a heavily armed perimeter around Israel's only international airport.

As he waited for his flight back to the U.S. to be ready, Black began scanning Bennett's e-mails, a combination of urgent pleas from his staff all over the world to fill them in on what he knew about the president's condition, news bulletins from AP, and one little e-mail from Erin McCoy in London. Black took a deep breath. She'd sent him all the details on his charter flight, including tail number, two phone numbers for the Signature operations desk, the cell numbers of his flight crew, and even direct numbers for the tower, followed by a little reminder: *Don't panic. :)*

Black made a mental note to have that flight canceled, then scrolled through the AP updates.

- ☆ Sources: President Alive; Location Unknown
- ☆ VP Takes Command at White House
- ☆ Queen Safe despite London Attacks
- ☆ Canadian Prime Minister Wounded in Paris Bombings
- ☆ 747 Destroys Saudi Palace; King, Family Barely Escape
- ☆ Three Secret Service Agents Dead
- ☆ Breaking: White House Says President Secure at NORAD

* ☆ Nation Awakes to Terrifying TV Images
* ☆ Fed Cuts Interest Rates by Half Percent
* ☆ World Reacts in Horror to Attack on U.S. President
* ☆ Market Plunges 11 in Japan, 13 in Hong Kong
* ☆ FAA Orders No=-Fly Zone over Entire U.S.
* ☆ Fourth Secret Service Agent Dies of Head Trauma
* ☆ Vice President Consoles Secret Service Widows
* ☆ Russian President Vadim Offers U.S. Help in Tracking Down Terrorists
* ☆ FBI Briefing Describes Gulfstream's Final Minutes
* ☆ Murray: "Evil Has Reared Its Ugly Face Again"
* ☆ President "Doing Better," Will Address Nation at 9pm
* ☆ Dow Plunges 9, NASDAQ Down 12 at Opening Bell
* ☆ Breaking: CIA Sources Say Iraq May Be "Preparing for War"
* ☆ White House: Memorial Service to Be Planned for Saturday

With the help of a technical expert on Galit's team, Black finally broke through Bennett's cell-phone password protection and began listening to his voice-mail messages. Most were calls from the GSX team scattered across the globe. Two were from McCoy, repeating all the flight details she'd e-mailed to him. One was from his executive assistant about his luggage. Two were from his parents, checking on him.

Black now called Bennett's home answering machine. Again, Galit's technical people broke through and Black listened to the messages. The eeriest was from Secretary Iverson. Black winced and replayed it twice:

"Hey, Jon, it's Stu. Quick update. Things have settled down a bit. The president's doing okay. Wants to meet with you about the deal ASAP. You can reach me at 303-555-9697. Again, 303-555-9697. And use a landline—not a cell phone. I'll figure out a way to get you to us. If you get in any trouble, let me know. See ya, kid."

Black took a deep breath. It was going to be a long flight.

☆   ☆   ☆

It was now 10 p.m. Israel time.

Black finally received the clearance he needed to get back to the U.S. The November night air was brisk and breezy, but after so many hours cooped up in Galit's smoke-filled bunker, it felt refreshing. Black walked across the tarmac, stood for a moment, and stretched his legs. He felt exhausted and light-headed. He suddenly wanted to retire, move to Vail or Aspen, buy a little ski lodge, and sit under a peaceful, quiet canopy of moon and sky and stars, far away from cell phones and pagers and crises. He was getting too old for this.

"Good evening, Mr. Black," said a fit, rugged black man in a crisp blue air force uniform. "I'll be your pilot tonight. Colonel Frank Oakland. Good to meet you."

The two shook hands. Three heavily armed American agents with plastic wires running into their ears stood nearby, as six more Israeli security agents with Uzis at the ready surrounded the plane at Galit's directive. The plane was fully loaded and fully fueled, just waiting for its final passengers to board.

"Good to meet you, Colonel. Let's get this show on the road."

"You got it, sir. We'll be wheels up in eight minutes. And you just let us know if there's anything we can do for you—anything at all. All right?"

"Thanks. Let's do it."

Black walked a few feet over to the steps of the plane, then stopped abruptly. "It's a G4, isn't it?"

The pilot hesitated. "Yes, sir, she is," he said quietly.

Black stood for a moment, sizing up the aircraft, then began to walk around the nose of the plane. "She's big."

"Eighty-eight feet, four inches long," Oakland agreed as he followed Black around the plane. "Got a wingspan of almost seventy-eight feet, and she's nearly two and a half stories high."

"How heavy?"

"Maximum?"

"Yeah."

"About seventy-five thousand pounds. She can carry a boatload of fuel and go more than four thousand two hundred nautical miles in one flight."

Black said nothing, then stopped beside one of the two engines.

"Rolls Royce," offered the pilot, unprompted. "The best money can buy. Fourteen thousand pounds of takeoff thrust. She can almost hit Mach 1."

Black shook his head in disbelief. "How high can she go?"

"Forty-five thousand feet—about nine miles, give or take."

Black slipped under the tail, careful not to get behind the engines, walked slowly back over to the steps, and turned to the pilot. He stared at the man for a moment, without saying a word. Then, almost in a whisper, "If you were flying from Toronto to Denver . . ."

He paused for a second, then took a deep breath. ". . . would you—would you be in danger of running out of gas?"

The pilot looked him straight in the eye. "No, sir. Not a chance."

Black stared into his eyes for a moment, then looked away, checked his watch, turned, and headed up the steps. His security detail and the pilot followed right behind him, and the ground crew scrambled quickly to secure the aircraft for takeoff.

On board, Black leaned into the cockpit, quickly scanned the instrumentation panels, and shook hands with the copilot, completing his final preflight checklist. As he turned back to the cabin, he was greeted by a flight attendant who couldn't have been more than twenty-five.

With short black hair and warm brown eyes, Maria Perez had a sweet, gentle smile. But best of all, she was holding some fresh, hot coffee in a dark maroon mug with a gold seal that read "American Embassy Tel Aviv" on the side and a small white-china plate of warm, gooey, chocolate-chip cookies baked fresh and brought over by the security team.

Black gratefully took the mug and the plate of cookies and carefully set them both on a small, low table to his right. A larger table to his left held a huge, dark blue porcelain vase of fresh-cut pink roses and a giant platter of luscious fresh fruit—Jaffa oranges, watermelon, strawberries, kiwi, red grapes, Red Delicious apples, and plump, juicy pears to die for.

On another side table farther back there were crystal dishes of mixed nuts and silver dishes of Christmas M&M's—green and red, plain and peanut, along with small bottles of springwater, Perrier, fruit juices, and sodas of every kind. This was the surprise Ramsey had been talking about— a nice little spread from the ambassador and his wife—and Black appreciated it. His job didn't come with many perks and he savored each one.

Black had never been on the U.S. ambassador's plane, but he was impressed, and he quickly settled into one of eight white-leather swivel chairs. Next, he fastened his seat belt quickly as the plane began to taxi almost immediately. The G4's interior was absolutely gorgeous and far roomier than the aging, stripped-down Learjet the FBI usually used to send him around in the U.S. Thick, rich carpet. A long, white-leather couch. A beautiful, polished mahogany conference table with a collection of the *New York Times*, the *Wall Street Journal*, *Time*, *Newsweek*, and *Forbes*. A built-in combination TV and DVD player. And a stereo system with a six-disk CD player, from which Mozart's *Turkish March* softly filled the cabin.

Black leaned back in his chair and stared out the window, watching four Israeli army jeeps with soldiers in full battle gear escort the G4 to the runway. An involuntary chill shuddered through his body. He closed two air-conditioning vents nearby, retrieved his coffee mug and a cookie, checked to see that the coffee wasn't too hot, and then took a long sip.

Perez—the daughter of the air force chief of staff, he later learned— quickly unbuckled herself from her seat in the back of the plane and brought him a thick wool blanket and a large soft pillow. Black accepted both gratefully, setting aside his coffee and cookie. Then he slid off his shoes and put his feet up on the low table in front of him as the flight attendant dimmed the lights and settled back in her seat.

It had been a long day, and it wasn't over yet. But by the time the G4 lifted off, Dietrich Black was out.

☆　☆　☆

The plane was halfway across the Atlantic.

Oakland came over the intercom and told Black he had a secure call from Washington.

Black quickly rubbed his eyes, took a swig of cold coffee, grabbed the air phone beside him, and punched line one. "Black."

"Do it."

"Now?"

"Now."

"Roger that."

And the line went dead.

Black gathered his thoughts for a moment, got up, walked over to the table of drinks, opened a tiny bottle of springwater, poured some on his hands, and splashed it on his face. Next he chugged down the rest of the bottle and wiped his face with a nearby hand towel.

"Okay," he announced to his team somberly. "It's time."

One of the three members of his security detail unbuckled himself and got up. He was not just a skilled marksman. He was also a physician on loan from the CIA. He got out his medical bag and knelt by the couch. It was there that the lifeless body of Jonathan Meyers Bennett lay covered with a navy blue wool blanket.

The CIA doctor quickly rolled up Bennett's left sleeve, swabbed the skin below his elbow with cotton dabbed in rubbing alcohol, and pulled out a white plastic syringe. Next, he pulled off the cap, squirted out some fluid, and tapped the syringe to remove any remaining air bubbles. Then he stabbed Bennett's arm and waited.

Seconds later, Bennett's eyes flickered to life, and everyone began to breathe again.

Black sat in a swivel chair across from Bennett. Once the doctor was done with his work, he and everyone else moved to the front of the plane, out of Bennett's immediate line of sight. It took a few moments, but the young man came to and slowly sat up.

Black just swiveled slowly, back and forth, back and forth.

Bennett looked out the windows on both sides of the plane and saw two F-16s flying escort. "Where am I?" he asked, groggy and disoriented.

"Thirty-nine thousand feet over the Atlantic," said Black.

"I'm not dead."

It wasn't a question. It was a statement of disbelief.

"No, Mr. Bennett. You're not dead. In fact, welcome back."

A few moments passed. Bennett tried mentally to grab hold of something—anything—that would root him in some reality he could understand. "Where was I?"

"On a mission, Mr. Bennett."

"What—doing what?"

"Proving your loyalty to the president."

Bennett tried to swallow. His mouth was completely dry.

Black handed him an opened bottle of water.

Bennett took a small sip, but still had trouble swallowing. "Who are you?"

"My name is Dietrich Black. I'm a counterterrorism specialist with the FBI."

"Oh," said Bennett, blankly. "You the guy that tried to kill me?"

"No."

"Where's he?"

"Nobody tried to kill you, Mr. Bennett."

Bennett wasn't amused, but he said nothing. "We call this Operation Irish X-Ray. It's a way we can shake a person down and test him in a moment of crisis to see if he's what we call 'Irish spring'—you know, clean as a whistle. Let's just say it's faster and more effective than a three- to six-month FBI background check."

"You're saying you've done this to other people, friends of the president?"

"I can't really say more than I have."

"But the idea is that I'm supposed to think I'm about to be killed so I'll spill my guts—if not my bladder—if I've got anything to hide?"

"Pretty much."

"Well, it worked."

"It did. And you passed. With flying colors."

"So you believe me?"

"I do."

Bennett tried to take another sip of water, but began coughing. Black handed him the small hand towel, and Bennett wiped his mouth. He was still very drowsy and not fully there. "Did you before?"

"Did I believe you? Before our little test?"

"Yeah, whatever."

"Honestly, Mr. Bennett? I wasn't sure."

"Was anyone?"

"Let's just say you have some good friends in high places."

Bennett stared at Black for a moment, then turned and noticed the rest of Black's team anxiously staring at him. "Who are they?"

"The good guys."

"Oh." Bennett nodded and tried to take another few sips of water. The flight attendant slowly, cautiously, gently came over and offered him a small, cold dish of applesauce and some saltine crackers. Bennett looked up at her. He felt completely drained, but peaceful and calm. He guessed it was the narcotics, or whatever they'd shot him up with. Apparently, it hadn't been lethal. He smiled at Perez, and she smiled back.

"Sa'id . . . ," Bennett said, turning back to Black. "Is he really . . . you know . . . a terrorist?"

"No."

Bennett nodded and tried to take a spoonful of applesauce. "That's nice. . . . And Galish . . . Galishnikov?"

"No," Black said. "He really is your friend."

Bennett coughed, then took another small spoonful of applesauce. "Was all this really necessary?"

The FBI agent hesitated. "That's not my call," Black said, honestly glad that was true.

"I just want to know who to sue," Bennett said, his face betraying neither anger nor amusement. "Were they really about to give me a lethal injection?"

"No. It was a mild sedative. A liquefied version of a sleeping pill. The whole thing was designed to act like an accelerated truth detector—to find out what you know and how loyal to the president you really are."

Bennett set the bowl of applesauce and the little plate of crackers down on the table beside him and pulled the blanket up over most of his body. He was cold, and lonely, and spent. "So now you know," he said quietly. "Now what?"

Black reclined in his leather seat, folded his hands behind his head, and smiled. "You're going to see the president."

Bennett nodded, closed his eyes, and slowly drifted back to sleep.

Dietrich Black knew the young man might not remember this conversation. Indeed, they might have to have it several times before they finally got to Colorado, or at least before they were actually cleared to go in and see the president. But at least his target was alive, breathing, clean . . . and in the hands of the U.S. government, not Islamic terrorists.

Operation Irish X-Ray—the arguably unethical if not illegal capture and interrogation of Jonathan Meyers Bennett by direct order of the president of the United States—had been an enormous risk. And it could still backfire. But it also just might have been worth it.

Black chewed on that, then pulled a blanket over himself and closed his own eyes. The Secret Service didn't call this president Gambit for nothing.

Now he knew why.

7

"LADIES AND GENTLEMEN, please buckle up—we're making our final approach."

Colonel Oakland clicked off the intercom at just before nine o'clock in the morning Colorado time. The refueling stop at Andrews Air Force Base outside of Washington had taken longer than expected. But the FBI-commandeered Gulfstream IV was finally arriving at its destination—Peterson Air Force Base—still flanked by two F-16s at the direct order of the president.

Bennett was just beginning to awaken. He checked his seat belt and found it still fastened snugly at his waist. He discreetly glanced over at Black, who seemed to be typing up a report of some kind on his laptop—a report, no doubt, on his state-sponsored torture and near execution of a personal friend of the president—and at Maria Perez, the attractive flight attendant he wouldn't mind seeing again.

As he slowly emerged from his drug-induced hypnotic state through-out the night, Bennett had talked at length with Black about the way he had been treated and why. But oddly enough, even after a few more hours of sleep, he couldn't seem to muster the anger he wanted to feel.

In his head, he wanted to crucify Black. The concept of an American citizen being subject not just to a fake lethal injection but also to a fake gunshot to the back of the head at the hands of his own government sick-ened him.

But in his gut, though he cursed the means, Bennett understood the motive and couldn't find it within himself to condemn the man or his team. It might have been easier to turn his resentment into rage if the man with the scar and the yo-yo were on board. But he wasn't. That guy was a thug, a scrap of human debris hired to do the dirty work.

But Black was different. Bennett couldn't help but like him. There was something intriguing about this guy—something real and genuine and reassuring.

For one thing, Black was a guy's guy. He carried a badge and a gun and stole planes from the State Department. For another thing, Black had a mission, a purpose in life. He traveled the world hunting down scum and eliminating them from the face of the earth. Good work if you could get it, and a world away from what Bennett did for a living.

Sure, he could buy and sell this guy. Black probably made somewhere around $65,000, maybe $70,000 a year. Three weeks of vacation, which he probably never took. And he was married—he could tell that by the ring on Black's left hand. But how often could he be home to enjoy married life?

Bennett, on the other hand, made nearly a million dollars a year—$975,000 and change to be more precise—plus another $2 to $3 million a year in stock options and profit sharing and other assorted benefits, depending on the ups and downs of the market. It was *great* work if you could get it. And he'd gotten it. And that was just the beginning.

He also had a forest green Jaguar XJR he used for business and a little red turbo-powered Porsche he used for dates and weekends in the country. He traveled all over the world. He schmoozed the most powerful CEOs and VCs in business.

He could pick up a phone and within a few minutes—never any longer than a few hours—get the president of the United States on the phone. He'd flown on *Air Force One* and slept over at Camp David. He'd dined at the Kremlin and toasted in Tiananmen Square. He'd once bought a gorgeous two-carat diamond engagement ring on a business trip to Johannesburg, South Africa, for someday. He just hadn't met "Mrs. Someday." Not yet.

He was smart and respected and rich. But he was also hot-tempered and lonely and a workaholic. He had a huge office with an incredible view overlooking the wealthiest section of the wealthiest city in the most powerful country on the face of the planet in the history of mankind. But it was a restless existence.

Life on the bullet train was about trade-offs, about little deals he made with himself to get ahead. He had only so much emotional capital to invest, and he'd chosen a long time ago not to diversify. He'd invested everything he had in his career, and his professional account was paying off in spades. The problem was he seemed to have real trouble maintaining a minimum daily balance in his other accounts—personal, emotional, and spiritual.

He didn't really have any close guy friends, guys he could call up and hang out with and really talk with outside of work, away from the office, away from the deals. He couldn't seem to keep a steady girlfriend—much less a fiancée or wife—a soul mate who knew him deeply and loved him unconditionally and wanted him to know her and love her the same way. So what was the point if he didn't have anyone to share his success with?

Maybe he who dies with the most toys doesn't win, thought Bennett. *Maybe he's just dead.*

Bennett stared out the window at the F-16 on his wing and the lights of the air force base quickly approaching. It suddenly hit Bennett how rapidly and radically life could change. Twenty-four hours ago, he'd woken up with visions of becoming a billionaire. Now he was just grateful to be alive. Twenty-four hours ago, a new world had seemed possible—a world where Arabs and Israelis jointly drilled for oil, a world where two nations could become wealthy beyond belief, a world of prosperity leading to peace, of hope transcending hate, of freedom conquering fear. And now it was all gone. The ugly, evil face of terrorism was back. Men and women lay dead and dying.

Today the world was teetering on the edge of war and recession, and tomorrow could be worse.

* * *

Jackie Sanchez was now the Secret Service agent-in-charge.

The entire presidential security detail reported to her now that John Moore was in the intensive-care unit, fighting for his life. After helping get Gambit to safety inside Crystal Palace, Moore had collapsed walking down a hallway and begun coughing up blood. He'd been hurried back to the base hospital at Peterson and rushed into emergency surgery. But at this point, the prognosis looked grim.

"You're absolutely sure?" pressed Sanchez over a secure landline.

It was a few minutes after noon as she stood inside a small, top-secret conference room down the hall from the massive NORAD operations center made famous—if not quite precisely represented—by *War Games*, the hit movie in the eighties about a couple of young computer hackers who accidentally bring the world to the brink of nuclear war. Two Secret Service agents—one with a bomb-sniffing canine unit, another from the technical division, checking for eavesdropping bugs—finished sweeping the room.

"One hundred percent," replied her boss, Bud Norris.

"Okay," said Sanchez. "It just makes me nervous, given what's happened."

"I know. But believe me, I just read the report Black e-mailed in from the plane."

"And?"

"He'll send it to you in a few moments. But believe me, it's convincing."

"They really worked him over, huh?"

"Brutally."

"And Black's guys were good?"

"Oscar-winning."

Another female agent popped her head in the conference room door and gave Sanchez the thumbs-up.

"All right, boss. I'll take your word for it. Hey, about this memorial service the president wants for Saturday. What's happening with that?"

"Don't worry about it. I've put together a team to get it done. It'll be Saturday at two o'clock at the National Cathedral. The guys over at White House Public Liaison are putting all the details together. We're mapping out the security and making sure the families all get here safely and are taken care of."

"Great. Let me know. Hey, look, I've got company."

"Fair enough. But, Sanchez?"

"Yes, sir?"

"When Bennett gets there, take good care of him. If he can survive the CIA and the FBI, we don't want to lose him on our watch."

"You got it, sir."

"Take care, Sanchez."

"I will, sir. Thanks."

Sanchez hung up the phone and closed her eyes for a moment to catch her breath and gather her thoughts. Suddenly, the phone rang again.

"Sanchez. Absolutely. Send them in."

☆   ☆   ☆

Ten minutes later, the conference table was set for Thanksgiving.

Freshly squeezed orange juice with thick bits of pulp was poured into crystal glasses. Freshly brewed Colombian coffee was poured into white Syracuse China cups, and on a side counter sat a bucket of ice, a selection of sodas, and a row of NORAD-embossed glasses. Two metal carts were wheeled in from the NORAD commander's personal kitchen with heated platters of steaming slices of golden roasted turkey and honey-baked ham, buttery mounds of mashed potatoes, bowls of stuffing, tangy cranberry sauce, piping-hot sweet potatoes, boats of thick gravy, little plates of carrots and celery and sweet pickles and olives, and cloth-napkin-covered baskets filled with corn bread and warm potato rolls, all lightly buttered and smelling like heaven.

Bob Corsetti was the first to enter, followed by Secretary Iverson. Two Secret Service agents were already in place in the back corners of the room. Corsetti and Iverson wasted no time in serving themselves, then welcomed Dietrich Black, freshly showered, shaved, and now wearing a business suit—his own Beretta having been left with security back at the air force base.

"Deek, Bob Corsetti," said the White House chief of staff, vigorously shaking Black's hand.

"Hey, Bob, good to see you again."

"It's been a while. Wasn't sure if you'd remember me."

"Oh, well, hey, how could I forget?"

"Sorry it's always on such difficult occasions."

Black nodded.

"I don't think you know Stu Iverson, the new treasury secretary," offered Corsetti.

"No—good to meet you, sir."

"Pleasure's mine," said Iverson, reaching for Black's outstretched hand and shaking it vigorously. "How was your flight?"

"Uneventful."

"We should all be so lucky," said Corsetti. "You must be starved. Please, have some dinner."

"It hardly seems right, sir."

"I know. But we have a lot to be thankful for. The president's alive— and you guys did quite a job with Bennett. Now eat."

"Yes, sir. Thank you, sir." Black reluctantly but gratefully helped himself, then grabbed a NORAD coffee mug, some ice, and a Diet Coke—of course—and joined the two men at the table, silently bowing his head to say grace.

"Stu, what do you expect at the bell on Monday?" Corsetti asked.

"Hellfire and brimstone," Iverson said bluntly, stirring some heavy cream into his coffee. "Asia and Europe both crashed overnight. S&P futures are down sharply. NASDAQ's been acting like a whipped dog."

"Meltdown?"

"The China Syndrome." Iverson cut his turkey with his knife and fork, took a bite, then carefully wiped his mouth with his freshly ironed white cloth napkin. "Bob, we need some good news, and we need it fast."

"And what happens if we don't get it?"

Iverson pondered that a moment, then set his knife and fork down. "Look. It was a rough time after the Twin Towers went down. The markets struggled for quite some time. But they eventually got back on their feet. People finally got their confidence back. They started flying again. They began to take vacations again. Companies began to hire again. Okay? Now, they wake up after all these new attacks—fearful more is on the way—and you've got a serious confidence problem on your hands. Companies around the world lost trillions of dollars of market value yesterday. Trillions. In one day."

"And?"

"And it's going to get worse. People aren't going to spend—again."

"And?"

"You've got huge layoffs coming—again."

"And?"

"And what, Bob? That's it. Econ 101. Nobody buys. Nobody produces. People get laid off. They spend less. They produce less. It's a vicious cycle—and it's tough to get out."

"Worst-case scenario?"

"Look, Bob, I don't want to . . ."

"Recession?"

Iverson shook his head. "Bob, a recession is the least of your troubles right now."

"Spell it out for me, Stu."

Iverson set his coffee down and took a deep breath. "Look, the only thing that matters right now is what the president does this weekend. That's it. Period. You mess this up and you've got a global economic meltdown on your hands. And I've got to tell you, Bob, arresting somebody isn't going to help. You can arrest a thousand terrorists—a million—and no one's going to care. No one. Even if they're all guilty. *Especially* if they're all guilty. People don't want arrests. They don't want to hear about frozen assets and economic sanctions and funding the Iraqi National Congress and pinpricks and surgical strikes and all that."

"You're saying we screwed up?"

Corsetti was getting a little defensive.

"Apparently."

"We did the best we could, Stu. This hasn't exactly been easy."

"I know," said Iverson. "I'm just saying, it wasn't enough, Bob. It just wasn't."

"You think we should have gone harder after Iraq—taken out Saddam somehow. Regime change?"

"Isn't that what CIA recommended?"

"You think we backed off from a full-court press against Saddam because we were scoring big against other terrorist groups, smaller groups?"

"It was a good show. And we certainly vacuumed up a lot of bad guys, but . . ."

"But not enough?"

"Obviously not. Bob, this isn't a criminal investigation. It's a war."

"What's that supposed to mean?"

"It means fight it like a war, not an episode of *Cops*."

"Well, aren't you Mr. Sound Bite," Corsetti sniffed. "What about all those Delta Force raids? the SAS raids? all that video of our forces wiping out terrorist-training camps—forty-three of them, to be exact?"

"What about it?"

Corsetti's voice dripped with cynicism. "Well, that's easy for you to say, Stu—sorry your portfolio might take a beating this year."

"Bob, this isn't about me and you know it. If all that Rambo stuff had worked, you and I wouldn't be sitting in a missileproof mountain eating Thanksgiving dinner from a cafeteria. You'd better wake up and smell the Starbucks, son. People aren't going to sit back and let the president and the queen of England get attacked and have the White House tell everybody, 'Hey, we're handling it.' "

"They want someone to pay."

"Big-time."

"And if they don't get the vengeance they're looking for?"

"It's not vengeance, it's—"

"Yeah, whatever—if people don't get the Hollywood ending they're looking for?"

"Bob, look, you asked me what the markets were going to do. I'm just saying that's what markets are for. They're one giant fortune cookie. They're a giant daily tracking poll. They tell us what people think about the future of the world. Are they waking up filled with fear or faith? Do they think things are going to get better or worse? They're tea leaves, Bob. They're oracles. And they're sending a pretty powerful message to the president right now, whether you guys want to listen or not."

"Action."

"Big action—or a big meltdown—come Monday."

Corsetti said nothing. He wasn't a CEO, a business and economic strategist like MacPherson. He wasn't a Wall Street wizard, an investment strategist like Bennett. He wasn't an ambassador or diplomat, a global-affairs strategist like Iverson.

He was a political operative, a savvy tactician more than a big-picture guy. He took polls and counted votes. He greased squeaky wheels before they made too much noise and put out brush fires before they became raging forest fires. He didn't think in ten- or twenty- or fifty-year increments of history. He thought in terms of twenty-four-hour news cycles and two-year election cycles.

Iverson respected him for it. But it also made him nervous. For this was no longer about red states and blue states on some electoral college map.

"Bob, someone's going to pay the piper," Iverson concluded. "It's either going to be the good guys or the bad guys. And it's your call. You guys had better make it right, or a lot of innocent people are going to suffer."

Corsetti just stared at the turkey sitting uneaten on his plate and growing cold. Black kept his head down and quietly played with the mashed potatoes on his plate with his fork. The phone rang and Corsetti answered it. A moment later he had excused himself to go meet with the president.

Iverson and Black were left to eat alone.

★ ★ ★

FBI Director Scott Harris wasn't alone.

He was sitting at a small conference table in his office having lunch with a couple of deputies when the phone rang. He'd just taken a huge bite of a Jersey Mike's sub number nine—the Club Supreme with roast beef, turkey, Swiss cheese, lettuce, tomato, mayo, and bacon—brought in fresh by a field agent who'd just flown down from Trenton for a meeting.

But Harris answered anyway, on the second ring. "Harris," he mumbled, trying to chew at the same time.

"Scott? That you? It's the president."

Harris eyes went wide. His deputies watched him freeze for a moment, his eyes darting every which way.

"Scott? You there?" the president asked again.

Harris had no place to go—and no choice. He grabbed the trash basket by his desk and spit out the entire mouthful of the mouthwatering sub. "Yes, Mr. President. What can I do for you, sir? And how are you, sir?"

"Under the circumstances, I was pretty lucky. You okay?"

"Yes, sir. Fine, sir."

Harris's deputies were now laughing openly as their director turned his back on them and looked out his window at Pennsylvania Avenue and the brightly lit Capitol Building down the street.

"What've you got so far, Scott?"

"Sir, we've got a full-court press on. We've got some interesting leads. But nothing I can really give you yet. Soon. Hang in there."

"That's fine. I appreciate it. But look, here's my concern. How many people could possibly have known which limousine I'd be in?"

"Sixty-three, not including your wife and daughters. We just nailed that number down, sir."

"You know where I'm going with this then."

"I think so, sir. A mole in our ranks. Perhaps even a sleeper agent."

"Is that possible?"

"Honestly, sir, I wouldn't have thought so. But there's too much circumstantial evidence in terms of the precision of the attack against you. The problem is, there's not a lot of people I can talk to about this. If there is someone—or several people—inside the U.S. government working with terrorists on the outside, or with a terrorist state like Iraq or Iran or North Korea or whomever, then it's going to be very tough to find them without letting them know we're hunting them down."

"That's precisely what worries me, Scott. So you do whatever it takes. Within the law, obviously. But pull out all the stops. Redo background checks. Do surveillance. Tap phones. Intercept e-mails. I don't care. I want to know who's been leaking, and I want to know why. If you need an executive order from me, draft it and I'll sign it. Just get your best people on it—fast. And don't breathe a word to anyone on my team that you're doing it. You got it?"

"Got it, sir."

"Scott, I'm counting on you. These people aren't sending me a message. They want me dead. And they're not going to take no for an answer. If they've got someone working with them on the inside, then I'm in a race for my life. We've got to hunt them down and take them out before they do the same to me."

"You got it, sir."

* * *

Stuart Iverson thought back to election night two years back.

It had been MacPherson's first presidential campaign. He remembered the black-and-red digital countdown clock hanging over the reception desk, the one that read 00:00:00. Election day—the zero hour—had arrived. It was all over but the counting.

The campaign headquarters had been located on the fifth and sixth floors of a huge, renovated warehouse in downtown Denver, overlooking Coors Field. Table after table of phones and computers and fax machines and copiers on both floors were manned by dozens of paid staffers, volunteers, and interns.

Phones rang constantly, and though everyone seemed to have at least one, if not two, phones to his or her ears, the ringing never seemed to stop. The amazing thing was that any of the senior staff on the sixth floor could get any work done with the sound of a Ricky Martin CD—belting out the World Cup theme song—rising from the bull pen of college interns on the fifth floor.

The tattered, coffee-stained carpet was littered with old newspapers, empty pizza and Chinese food boxes, and used pink phone-message slips. Massive red, white, and blue banners covered the walls, along with scores of editorial cartoons and campaign fact sheets and internal phone lists. Five televisions—each tuned to a different network—hung overhead.

Young kids—barely out of adolescence—scurried about in ripped jeans and college sweatshirts, each on some urgent task or another. The whole place was surreal, a cross between a big-city TV newsroom and a college fraternity house on a Saturday morning.

It wasn't pretty, but it was here that the campaign's get-out-the-vote operation had been in overdrive throughout the day.

Iverson, the campaign's national chairman, had watched as Bob Corsetti—immaculately dressed in a charcoal gray pin-striped Italian suit, with his jet-black hair slicked back like a Wall Street tycoon—moved quietly through the rows of twentysomethings manning the phone banks, like a panther moving through a jungle.

As his right hand obsessively twirled an unlit cigar, Corsetti's eyes scanned every computer screen, every open notebook. His ears tuned in to every conversation, while tracking all five networks above him. He said nothing, but you could actually see people stiffen as he walked by them— each suddenly, perceptibly working a little harder, talking a little faster. Corsetti was the mastermind behind the MacPherson miracle, and everyone in the room knew it.

Back in the nineties, when Clinton was in office, it had been Corsetti—then the executive director of the Colorado State Republican Party—who quietly approached MacPherson about running for governor.

It was eventually Corsetti who—upon being hired as MacPherson's campaign manager—persuaded this never-elected-before CEO to partially finance his own campaign, and shake down his venture capitalist buddies to raise another $15 million.

It was Corsetti who mapped out the game plan for MacPherson to win not only the governor's residence but also a majority of the state legislature that year. It was Corsetti—now the newly elected governor's chief political strategist—who helped the novice push through an aggressive, conservative agenda of tax cuts, welfare reform, and abolishing parole for repeat violent thugs. This set up MacPherson to win a landslide reelection and positioned him beautifully to run for the GOP nomination and the presidency.

Indeed, it was Corsetti—not MacPherson—to whom everyone looked to make the math work, to put their man in the White House, to redeem all the eighteen-hour days they'd put in over the past eighteen months when they could've been making real money or going to the bars every night.

The odd thing about a presidential campaign is that staffers often get more attached to the campaign manager than to the candidate. The candidate, after all, is an illusion, a fantasy, a projection of everything you hope for in the next leader of the country. But you never see him. He's never in the headquarters. You're never in a meeting with him. You never get to ask him questions, or hang out with him, or ride in the motorcade or travel on the bus with him. He's simply a face on a campaign poster, a name on a flyer, a position, a poll number, a sound bite on the evening news.

The manager, on the other hand, is real. He's the one who hires you. He holds the staff meetings. He approves the requisition orders. He signs the checks. He chews you out one minute and decides you're staffer of the week the next, rewarding you with a little jar of thermonuclear Southwestern salsa as a present. If you work harder, fight harder, stay longer, sacrifice more of your personal time for the sake of the campaign, odds are you're doing it more for the manager than the candidate. Because he's your leader. In a way, the candidate is just a slogan.

Corsetti intuitively seemed to understand the psychology and rhythms and moods of a campaign. He knew when to strike and when to be silent. He knew when to let his money ride and when to cut his losses. He certainly preferred to be feared than liked, but to his own team he was both.

At forty-nine, he was more of a father to these kids than a boss, and more godfather than father. The *New York Times* had once described him as the "the Colorado consigliere." *Newsweek* dubbed him "the Denver Don." The Democratic National Committee called him "Don Corleone in a Donald Trump suit." But no one inside the campaign dared repeat such monikers . . . not in his presence, at least. Bob Corsetti suffered no fools and brooked no foolishness. He was all business, all the time, and his business was winning.

Iverson remembered that as Corsetti had finished his final rounds for that election night, he had given no reminders to his team of California's importance. He didn't tell them the California polls were open for only one more hour. He didn't give anyone a pat on the back or rip anyone's head off.

He simply walked through the room, surveyed the battlefield, and left the building without saying a word. He didn't need to. Everyone knew what they needed to do, and everyone knew the stakes. And no victory ever tasted sweeter than the one they got that night.

If they had only known what lay ahead.

★　★　★

At precisely 4:00 p.m., Bennett entered the conference room.

Corsetti, now done with his meeting with the president, glanced up from a phone call and nodded, as did Iverson. Black stood up and greeted him, shaking his hand and asking him if he'd like something to eat. But they could all tell Bennett's mind was elsewhere.

Agent Sanchez popped her head in again and pointed at Bennett. "Sir?"

"Yes?"

"The president would like to see you now."

Bennett took a quick swig of orange juice from the place setting marked for him and wiped his mouth with the cloth napkin waiting on his empty plate.

"Hey, Stu," he said as he slid past his old boss.

"Hey, Jon," Iverson said, still numb from the whole experience.

Bennett followed Sanchez and closed the door behind him. He was now standing in the dimly lit private study of the NORAD commander, its walls lined with bookshelves sagging from the weight of great tomes by Churchill and Clausewitz, Kissinger and Kearns Goodwin. It was a long room, somewhat narrow, and permeated with a sweet smell of pipe smoke that reminded him of visiting his grandfather's office as a little boy when his grandfather was a law professor at Georgetown University.

At the far end of the room was a roaring fire in a stone fireplace—where the smoke went in this mountain, he had no idea—and a beautiful working grandfather clock that had to be at least a hundred years old, a huge wooden desk with a banker's lamp, and a big green leather chair. In it sat the president of the United States with two Secret Service agents standing nearby.

"Come in, Jon—come, have a seat," said MacPherson, his voice soft but sincere.

It was only as Bennett got closer that he realized how much worse the president's condition really was than had been reported in the press. Yes, the president had briefly addressed the nation last night. But he had done so by audio—not by video—Bennett learned from Black upon landing at Peterson. Yes, the president had given several interviews to AP and major newspapers for Thanksgiving-morning editions. But they had been done by telephone, not in person, citing "security concerns." Security, indeed. If the country could see what Bennett now saw, whatever the Dow was about to lose Monday morning would be three times as bad.

Bennett couldn't believe how frail his friend and mentor looked.

Already a trim man, it seemed like he'd lost twenty or thirty pounds in the past twenty-four hours. MacPherson's face was bruised and scarred. His eyes were black and blue. His head was wrapped in bandages. His left arm was broken and in a cast. His right arm was fractured and in a sling. He was on two IVs, and Bennett now noticed he was sitting in a wheelchair. Could both of his legs be broken as well?

Bennett didn't have the heart to ask. His eyes darted from the long scratches on the president's hands and face to the quiet confidence in his eyes. "Mr. President . . ."

"Jon, I'm okay."

"But I . . ."

"Really, I'm okay. I lived. Don't worry about me. I want to talk about you. Please have a seat."

Bennett quietly took a seat across the desk from the president.

"Jon . . . I . . . I want you to know . . . well, I'm sorry."

"Mr. President, please . . ."

"Jon, I'm serious. I can't even begin to tell you how sorry I am. . . . I know that's not enough . . . but I really don't know how to . . ."

"There's no need, Mr. President."

"No, Jon, there is, really. You're a colleague. You're a friend. You've always been . . . loyal . . . and . . . well, you're practically family to Julie and the girls and me. And I feel terrible about all this . . . but I do take full responsibility."

"Sir . . ."

"It was my decision. And honestly, I'd do it over again if I had to."

What was he supposed to say? Bennett had trouble even looking at the president, not really out of anger or resentment but just out of sheer pain at seeing him in such terrible condition and knowing how close the man had come to dying in that attack. It was some kind of miracle that he had survived, and it seemed to make the trauma Bennett had just gone through somewhat more bearable.

"Julie and the girls baked you a pumpkin pie." The president nodded to the corner of his desk and the plastic-wrapped pie tin with a little note with his name on the envelope and a smiley face.

Bennett nodded, but said nothing.

"Deek and I spoke by telephone while you were sleeping on the plane."

"You know him?"

"His brother and I flew jets in Vietnam."

"I didn't know that."

"Did you know he was tailing you in Israel?"

"No."

"Did you know he had agents within twenty feet of you every step you took from the moment you got off the plane at Ben Gurion to the moment you reentered the airport to come home?"

Bennett shook his head quietly.

"Did you know that I spoke to the prime minister of Israel before you left to go over there, requesting his personal assurance that no harm would come to you while you were in the country? Did you know that Barshevsky works for us?"

Bennett shook his head again.

"Did Deek tell you that he and the CIA have been vetting Sa'id and Galishnikov for the past six months?"

"Not exactly."

"Every phone call. Every associate. Every meeting. Every letter. Every e-mail."

"Why?"

"I think you know why."

Bennett nodded.

"Jon, I've talked to every person involved in this operation, every single one of them . . . and . . ."

This was not a side to MacPherson Bennett had ever seen, and he could see the president struggling to find the words.

MacPherson winced. ". . . every single one of them . . . they tell me you never gave in . . . never broke on the oil deal . . . never gave up your friends. . . ." His eyes were now red and moist.

Bennett's bottom lip began to quiver. Both were restrained and careful men. They were not given to displays of emotion, in public or private, and the events of the past twenty-four hours or so had done nothing to change that.

"Well . . . I just wanted . . . you know . . . I just wanted to say thanks."

Bennett glanced at Sanchez, who stared at him but showed no emotion. The other agents all stared at him as well. Was that suspicion in their eyes? Or sympathy? Or both? It didn't really matter. But he was curious.

"I don't know what to say, Mr. President. I'm just glad you're okay." Bennett was completely confused. His still-fuzzy mind was swirling with emotions and thoughts and reactions he didn't begin to have the strength to identify, sort out, or understand. Not yet. So he said nothing.

The room was silent, but for the crackling of the fire beside them and the lulling *tick-tock, tick-tock, tick-tock* of the grandfather clock in the corner.

"I am. I'm okay. Thanks," said the president.

Bennett suddenly snapped back, back to his old self. "Good—because you look terrible."

Startled, the president just stared at him for a moment, then burst out laughing. Bennett quickly joined him.

"You want a drink?"

"I thought you'd never ask."

"Good man. Sanchez, get your men to rustle us up two glasses and some brandy or whiskey. Something old. Something expensive."

"Yes, sir, Mr. President."

"I'm not kidding, Sanchez. Call the commander. Ask him what he has stashed away in case he ever finds out the birds are flying and heading straight for him. Then tell him to get his butt down here and break it open for us."

"You got it, sir. I'll check with your doctor as well."

"Oh, Sanchez, now don't go ruin it for us. Be a sport, would ya?"

Sanchez smiled and moved to the far end of the room where she picked up a phone.

The president turned back to Bennett. "Jon, I've got a National Security Council conference call in a little while. And we may be interrupted by some phone calls. But I wanted to talk to you heart-to-heart for a bit. And I've got a surprise for you."

"Please, no more surprises."

"No, this is a good one." The president picked up the phone. "Hi . . . would you send in Kojak? . . . No, right now. . . . Well, I guess. . . . All right. . . . That's fine . . . okay . . . thanks."

He hung up the phone.

"Kojak?" Bennett asked.

"It's a code name."

"You don't have Telly Savalas stashed away someplace?" quipped Bennett.

"Very funny."

"Really. Who is it?"

"Your partner in crime."

"My what?"

"Your partner. You've got a lot of work ahead of you, Jon. Can't do it alone."

"Sir, I don't know what you're talking about."

The president just looked at him for a moment. "Jon, why do you think I just put you through all this?"

"How should I know? I have no idea."

"Sure you do."

"I do?"

"Of course."

Bennett looked over at the flickering fire. It felt warm and peaceful and safe. "Well . . . I mean . . . I guess you wanted to make sure I was loyal . . . honest . . . not some kind of security threat."

"What else?"

"Sir, really . . . I . . ."

"Jon—listen to me."

Bennett turned back and looked the president in the eye.

"I need you on my team, Jon. Not on Wall Street. Not in Denver. I need you on *my* team."

"What are you saying, sir?"

"I want you to work for me."

"Full-time?"

"Of course."

"At the White House?"

"Where else?"

"Sir, with all due respect, I . . ."

"All due respect? Jon, you just told me how terrible I look."

Bennett had to laugh. The man might have almost been killed, but he still had his sense of humor. "Well, yes, that's true, sir, but I . . ."

"But what?"

Bennett scrambled to put a coherent sentence together. "I . . . sir, I . . . in case you didn't notice, I've just negotiated a billion-dollar deal."

"Believe me, I've noticed."

"Well, you know, I mean, the White House sounds fun, but, sir, I'm on track to become a billionaire over the next few years. A billionaire, sir. I mean, I . . ."

"No, you're not."

"I'm not."

"I know those drugs in you haven't completely worn off yet. But I don't think you've fully grasped what's going on here. You and I are at NORAD. NORAD, Jon. I was just attacked by terrorists. Terrorists just bombed Buckingham Palace. Bombed Paris. Attacked the Canadian prime minister. They just flew a fully loaded 747 into the palace of the Saudi Arabian royal family. Jon, it's over. The world the way you and I knew it twenty-four hours ago is over."

MacPherson at heart was a mentor, always trying to help Bennett discover the bigger picture, the story behind the story.

"Unless . . . ," added the president.

Rattled by his own lack of instincts, Bennett took the bait. "Unless what, sir?"

"Unless, Jon, you and I rebuild it."

"Rebuild it?"

"That's right."

"How, sir?"

"We'll get to that."

"But first I need to join the White House staff?"

"Exactly."

Bennett leaned back in his chair and rubbed his eyes. Where was that drink Sanchez was fetching? "Sir, I . . . I don't know what to say."

"Say yes."

"Sir, what would I do? I don't know anything about Washington, about politics, about terrorism," Bennett protested. "I've spent my whole life thinking about investment strategy, not . . . you know . . . not . . . well, whatever."

"You're wrong."

"Beg your pardon?"

"Jon, your expertise is deal-making, research, analysis, assessing leaders and companies and industries for opportunities and signs of trouble. You have a knack for reading the tea leaves and convincing people to buy the tea company. That's exactly what I need right now."

Bennett just sat quietly.

"Jon, unless I act—and act fast—the markets are going to tank. The world is going to slip into a recession. Maybe a depression. But we're going to act. And when we do, we need a strategy for peace, not just for war. That's where you come in."

"What, some kind of twenty-first-century Marshall Plan? Mr. President, you know—"

"No, no, no. Come on, Jon. Think. I guarantee you when the dust settles, we're going to find Saddam Hussein behind all this. And if we have to go to war with Iraq, when we win, who benefits, besides us?"

"Well, sir, it depends. . . ."

"Come on, Jon. If you woke up a few months from now and Iraq was no longer a threat—just suppose—who benefits?"

"Israel, I guess."

"Exactly. Now think about it. If we do this right, your oil deal is going to happen. We can defang the biggest geopolitical threat in the Middle East—the epicenter of evil—and then help Israel and Palestine become two of the wealthiest countries in the history of mankind. We can wipe out terrorism and bring peace and prosperity to the modern Middle East. We can do what people have been thinking about and dreaming about and praying about for five thousand years, Jon. Next year in Jerusalem. Peace in the Middle East. And your deal has to be the centerpiece."

"You think so?"

"I've been thinking about this for months. For quite some time now, I've been meaning to talk with you about turning your oil deal into a historic peace deal. But it wasn't really until I woke up here—at NORAD— that I understood precisely what I really needed to do."

"So why don't I stay where I am?"

"Because I need you where I am. Jon, forget it. You're not going to be a billionaire. It's not going to happen. And the problem is, if you stay with GSX, then I can't use your deal as the centerpiece of my peace strategy."

"Why not?"

"It's a conflict of interest, and you know it."

"What about Stu?"

"Stu sold off everything to become treasury secretary. I made him do it. Of course, he could have made a fortune. But hey, he's already loaded. So he is my right-hand man at Treasury. But on this deal, I want you working with me to oversee it day-to-day, to help me navigate this baby and pull it off."

"Sir, I just don't exactly see where you're going. I mean . . ."

"Jon, look, it'll all be clear soon. But first—first, I need an answer from you."

Bennett leaned back in his chair and looked up at the ceiling. "Leave GSX and move to Washington?"

"Senior advisor to the president."

"And join the White House staff?"

"I know just the guy I'm going to kick out and give you his office."

Bennett laughed. "Bob?"

Now the president laughed. "No—not that I wouldn't like to sometimes, but . . ."

Bennett pondered the whole thing. Yet again, his life was about to change radically. He didn't like it, but there was obviously nothing he could do about it either. "Well, I guess I owe you for not having me killed off, right?"

The president smiled and slid a black leather folder with the gold presidential seal across his desk. "That's the spirit, Jon. Now sign here."

"What am I signing?"

"The top one is your resignation from GSX, effective immediately. The next one is your acceptance of my job offer. Senior advisor to the president. Ninety a year, plus all the government benefits."

"Bob makes one-forty."

"Don't push it, Bennett. I didn't make Bob a millionaire at GSX."

"Oh, and he didn't have a cut of all the ad buys during the campaign?"

The president smiled again. "Okay, I *did* make him a millionaire—but not at GSX."

"Whatever."

"Jon, look. First of all, you can afford a pay cut. Second, the whole point is that you need to be incognito. If you make more than a hundred, you're going to pop up on everybody's radar screen. The press is going to be all over it, and that's something I just can't afford right now."

"You always were a pretty good salesman."

"Son, you ain't seen nothin' yet."

Bennett began to look over the documents in the folder. "So who's Kojak?" he asked, pulling out his Montblanc pen to sign.

"Oh, that's right. Sanchez?"

The agent picked up a phone to find out what the delay was.

"It's Black, isn't it?" Bennett asked.

"No, but I do want him on your team. I want you to set up a small team inside the White House that can coordinate with me and the NSC. Publicly, you won't exist. Privately, while I run the war, you guys will run point on turning this oil deal into a peace deal. You'll report directly to me and Marsha Kirkpatrick."

"Captain Kirk?"

"You've got good sources, Bennett. I like your spunk."

"So why do you call this guy Kojak? I mean, you know, I just figured it was Black, 'cause he's bald."

"Yeah, well, nice guess—but wrong."

"All right, well, what then?"

"Kojak's been with CIA for five years. Top-secret security clearances. Top assistant to the director. Knows everybody. Knows me. Knows this oil deal. Been working as a field agent the past two years—keeping an eye on you, as a matter of fact."

Bennett was lost. *It sure better not be that sick, demented, deranged CIA guy in Israel, the one with the yo-yo,* he thought. He'd rather retire and join Greenpeace than work with that lunatic.

The door at the far end of the room opened, the same door Bennett had come through earlier. Bennett couldn't believe it. He felt like the wind had just been knocked out him.

Kojak wasn't a he. He was a she. His new "partner in crime" was Erin McCoy.

8

★ ★
★

"HEY, JON," said McCoy with a smile, a grape lollypop in her mouth. "Heard you took a bullet for the president."

Bennett just sat there bewildered as McCoy slowly walked over to the two of them and sat down in the other green leather chair. Her sea green eyes sparkled with amusement.

"I think you two have been introduced," said the president, savoring the moment.

"Very funny," Bennett quipped. "CIA?"

"Yep."

"Not GSX?"

"Well, both."

"Both?"

"Yep."

"What are you, like an analyst?" asked Bennett, with an edge of derision.

"What are you, like a moron?" McCoy shot back, never losing her smile.

"What's that supposed to mean?"

"No, I'm not an analyst. I'm an agent. Operations."

"*Operations?*"

"You got it, friend."

"What are you talking about?"

McCoy laughed.

"No, I'm serious. I was paying you two hundred thousand a year—plus options, plus health care, plus profit sharing—and you were really working for the CIA? In *operations*? I mean, come on. What's going on?"

"Hey, it's good work, if you can get it."

"Well . . . well . . . I mean, isn't that *illegal* or something?" he snapped, turning to the president for an ally.

"No, it's not illegal," replied the president, bemused by Bennett's reaction. "In fact, I think it's kinda cool."

Bennett turned back to McCoy.

"Cool? What are you, Jane Bond—double-O, you know, whatever?"

McCoy glanced at the president.

"I told you, sir," she said. "That guy in Israel should've finished the job."

* * *

It was known in Iraq as *Al Nida*, the German camel of the Middle East.

Of course, this Daimler-Benz tractor-trailer looked like any other U.N. truck that delivers humanitarian food and medical supplies from Jordan to the ancient homeland of King Nebuchadnezzar. It was large and long and white, with big pale blue *U.N.* block letters painted on every side and on the top of the truck to prevent any mistakes in identification by Iraqi military forces or U.S. spy satellites orbiting overhead.

Like the handful of other trucks traveling back and forth week after week, month after month, along the lonely, seemingly godforsaken Highway 10 from Amman to Baghdad, this one always traveled in a small caravan of four other white vehicles—British Range Rovers, actually—all with U.N. markings.

Few things were worse than breaking down, finding yourself stranded and alone in the western deserts of Iraq where blinding, suffocating sandstorms can descend upon you without a moment's notice, and where daytime temperatures can easily top 120 degrees. Traveling in teams, therefore, with more-than-adequate supplies of water, food, and fuel was not the exception but the rule.

An hour and a half after leaving the outskirts of Baghdad, the caravan known to Iraqi officials as Q17 was flagged down by police officers and diverted to *Al Habbaniyah*, a military compound and air force base heavily guarded by elite forces of the Republican Guard, where it disappeared into hangar number five.

The entire detour lasted just shy of ninety minutes, after which the caravan was allowed to resume its trek to Jordan—one Range Rover leading the way, followed by Al Nida, followed by three more Range Rovers.

The twenty-five men comprising Q17 passed through Toliahah and Ar Rutbah, maintaining the strictest code of silence. No two-way radios. No cell phones. No AM/FM radios. No tapes or CDs. Not even conversations were allowed. Now they pulled off to the side of the road, just before the fork in Highway 10 where one must make a decision between heading northwest to At Tanf, Syria, or southwest to Trebil, Jordan.

Using hand signals, most of the men broke out food and drinks. Four others quickly unloaded large cans of fuel and poured them into each of the Range Rovers, not caring apparently that the vehicles were still running or that each of them was smoking a cigarette.

* * *

Under the circumstances, the president was grateful to laugh a little.

His next NSC briefing was just minutes away. Then he'd once again focus on the crisis at hand. But getting Bennett and McCoy comfortable working with each other in a new way was important too. Especially given the mission he was giving them.

"Look, Jon," he said. "You're like a son to me. That's why I told Stu to hire Erin a few years ago. I asked her to keep an eye on you. To watch your back. To check out Sa'id and Galishnikov. All I can tell you is she's good. Very good."

"Stu knows she works for CIA?"

"No, he doesn't. But he will. All in due time. Now, look, you've got one more paper to sign," said the president, sliding him another black leather folder.

"What's this for?"

"It says everything that we've discussed here—and will discuss in the future—is privileged and confidential, subject to all relevant federal laws governing confidential presidential communications. You can read all the fine print if you want. But the bottom line is, none of what we're going to do can be discussed with anyone without my express permission. Understood?"

"I haven't passed my 'loose lips sink ships' test yet?"

"Erin?" the president asked.

"I guess we can trust him." She smiled.

"Well, thanks for the vote of confidence."

"My pleasure."

"Just sign, Bennett," said the president matter-of-factly.

And he did.

"So, Mr. President," Bennett continued, "how do you guys know each other—I mean, obviously through GSX. But this seems to predate all that, doesn't it?"

"See, Erin, I told you he's a smart guy."

"You did, you said that."

"You weren't so sure."

"Well, you know, I've worked with him a little more closely in recent years than you have."

"That's true."

The president looked at Bennett, then back to McCoy, then back to Bennett. "Wait a minute. You've got stories."

"What? No," she demurred.

"No, no, no. Don't give me that. You've got stories, McCoy."

"Mr. President, please, she doesn't have any—"

"Oh yes she does. Spill 'em, McCoy."

"No, sir, I . . ."

"Spill 'em."

"Well, sir, you know . . . all right, maybe just one."

"Erin," Bennett protested.

McCoy just laughed. "What?"

"Don't tell him any stories."

"Jon, I have to. He's my boss."

"*I'm* your boss."

McCoy took his cheek and pinched it like a grandmother. "Yeah, but you're not the president."

"I don't believe this."

Sanchez stepped back into the room with a very old, very expensive-looking bottle of brandy and three glasses and set them on the president's desk.

"Good work, Sanchez," shouted the president. "Way to go."

"I'm just the delivery boy, here, sir."

"Hardly."

Bennett took charge and poured everyone a glass, including one for McCoy, even though he knew she didn't drink. "Sir, I'd like to propose a toast."

"Sounds good. Fire away, Bennett."

All three now raised their glasses.

"To my friend the president, may you find those who did this—and nuke 'em."

They all laughed, clinked glasses, and watched McCoy drink hers dry in one long sip.

"Erin, I thought you didn't drink."

"You've just got a lot to learn, don't you?"

"All right, McCoy, start talking," the president ordered.

So she did.

"Okay, well, here's one. Last year, Jon and I were invited to the Super Bowl in Miami as personal guests of former Treasury Secretary Murphy and his wife, Elaine."

"Oh, come on, Erin, you can't tell the president that story."

"This must be good," said MacPherson, taking another sip of brandy.

"You haven't heard this already, Mr. President?" asked McCoy.

"No, I don't think so."

"I have," said Sanchez.

"What?"

Bennett was mortified. Now Sanchez smiled.

"Okay, so we fly the GSX Learjet to Miami, right, and we get picked up in this stretch limousine and arrive at Joe Robbi Stadium—you know, VIPs, the whole thing."

"Nothing but the best for Jon."

"Absolutely, sir. We're ushered upstairs to the secretary's private box, and it's him and his wife and his security detail and a few CEOs. You know the drill."

"Sure do."

"So, everything's been a lot of fun—the Murphys are great people— and it's just about the end of the fourth quarter and the secretary is at the door, saying good-bye, you know, to all of the CEOs who are getting out early. Off to someone else's party, I'm sure."

"Ingrates."

"Exactly."

McCoy glanced over at Bennett, whose face was buried in his hands. "So, the secretary is at the door saying good-bye, and it's just me and Jon and the secretary's wife and the security guys."

"Okay."

"And, you know, Mrs. Murphy is getting up there a bit in age, and she doesn't hear so well, right?"

"Right. Has those two huge hearing aids."

"Exactly. But—" McCoy started to laugh a little as Bennett shook his head—"but Jon is like totally engrossed in the last few minutes of the game—we all are, no one's saying anything."

"It was a good game."

"It was . . . and Jon's munching away on this, I don't know, some kind of Tex-Mex platter—nachos and cheese and salsa and guacamole and re-fried beans. So, anyway, somebody kicks a field goal with like two minutes to go and Jon . . . well, how shall I put this delicately?"

"Please don't."

"And Jon, well, he just . . . ."

"Spit it out, Erin," ordered the president.

". . . well . . . let's just say he could have used some Beano."

The president began to laugh.

"And this wasn't, you know, muted or anything—this was really loud."

"I can't believe you just said that to the president of the United States," groaned Bennett, totally dying now.

Both the president and McCoy were cracking up, especially as Bennett was obviously so completely mortified.

"Why don't you just shoot me now."

"The agents are just doing everything they can not to burst out laughing hysterically, and I glance over to Mrs. Murphy and she's expressionless—I mean, completely stone-faced."

The president was laughing even harder now.

"But, sir, that's not the best part."

"There's more?"

"Well, see, two minutes later, the game is over and Mrs. Murphy walks out into the hallway with her husband. And the minute she steps out of the room, we all start howling and Jon is turning all red and we're all just dying."

Everyone in the room was laughing now, even Sanchez and her agents.

"So what happened next?"

"Well, the lead agent goes over to Jon and says, 'You know, that was pretty rude. You gotta go over and apologize to the lady.' And Jon's just looking at him like he's crazy. The agent says, 'No, I'm serious. You know, she's a cabinet secretary's wife. You need to go out there and apologize.'"

"He didn't."

"He did—I kid you not."

"Jon, Jon, Jon."

Bennett didn't say a word, and McCoy continued.

"Well, he looks at me and I'm like, there's no way I'm getting in the middle of this, so I say, 'Hey, it's their call, not mine.' So Jon gets up and looks back at all of us, and he goes out the door. And we all just start breaking up. I mean, I'm on the floor at this point."

"It wasn't enough to try to kill me. You guys have to humiliate me too."

"Oh, lighten up, Francis," said the president.

"So, wait, wait, it's not over. The best part was a few moments later. Jon comes back into the suite and the lead agent said, 'So, did you apologize?' And Jon goes, 'I tried to. I went out there and told her I was really sorry and it was rude and I didn't mean it and it'll never happen again.' And she goes, 'Sorry for what, Jon?' She never heard it."

"She never heard it?"

"So, she goes, 'What are you talking about, Jon? What was so rude?' And, Mr. President, Mr. President, Jon actually told her. . . ."

"No."

"I'm not making this up, sir. True story. True story."

Suddenly, Agent Sanchez piped up. "He did, sir. In fact, that story's been told by every agent in the country by now."

"You're so dead, McCoy," Bennett laughed. "When you least expect it, expect it."

That just made everyone howl all the more.

✯   ✯   ✯

The rapid refueling and equally quick meal were now complete.

Everyone piled back into their vehicles and waited for the lead four-wheel drive to move. But it didn't. Inside, the three men were frantically poring over their maps and using binoculars to look in every direction, all the while sweating profusely despite having the air-conditioning turned up full blast. The small dirt road they were looking for was supposed to be right here—or close by, anyway—but it wasn't. Worse, time was running short. So were tempers.

Ali Kamal, twenty-six and hand-chosen by General Khalid Azziz to be the leader of this team, stared off into the sizzling sunset before him. It would be dark soon, and if he was not where he was supposed to be within the hour, he might as well put a bullet in his own head or it would certainly be done for him by the sleeper agent in one of the vehicles behind him. He didn't know which one to worry about. There might even be more than one. But someone would be gunning for him if he failed this mission. Of this he had no doubt.

Kamal took a final drag on his cigarette and looked around him. It really was a beautiful, luxurious car, this Range Rover, even if it was painted white. He would have much preferred jet-black, but "U.N." staff could not be so picky.

The three behind him were standard models. But his was a gem. A big chassis and powerful V-8 diesel engine that purred because he personally cared for it day and night. A longer wheelbase than earlier models, and electronically controlled air suspension that made even a hundred-mile-per-hour drive through this ugly desert smooth and comfortable. Power windows. Power antilock brakes. Power steering. Air bags. Even a state-of-the-art global-positioning-satellite navigation system that he had personally installed in Amman after returning from a brief trip to London, where he'd rented a car with a GPS system.

With a mission, a team, this car, and a bright future ahead of him, Ali Kamal had everything he wanted, except for a lover. That would change soon too. But for now he could not afford to be distracted by such primal pleasures. He needed to focus on this task, and Allah would bless him. If not now, then with seventy virgins upon arriving in paradise.

Kamal lowered his passenger-side power window for a split second to toss his cigarette butt outside. *Forget the maps*, he silently screamed. He had a job to do, and no room for error. Kamal reached for the Range Rover's GPS system and pressed a few buttons. It took just a fraction of a second, and in that instant all of his anger and frustration melted away.

He laughed out loud. Remarkable. How simple, yet how brilliant. He now knew where he was. He knew where he was going. And he knew how to get there. He flashed a smile at his driver and held up three fingers on his left hand. Three more kilometers on the left.

Back in business, the caravan moved out.

* * *

"Gotcha," he shouted in Hebrew.

The young intelligence officer couldn't believe it. His adrenaline started pumping. His heart started racing. He doubled-checked his electronics to rule out the possibility of a malfunction, then grabbed the red phone in front of him and punched 212.

The call was picked up instantly. *"Ken?"*

"Acshav."

"Tov."

Now it was Captain Jonah Yarkon's turn to grab a phone and relay the message, and he did just that. A split second later, a red phone rang inside the IDF operations bunker eight stories underneath the Ministry of Defense in downtown Jerusalem.

Defense Minister Chaim Modine picked it up and listened carefully.

"Tov. Fire up the birds and stand by." The accent was as thick as the tone was urgent.

Modine put the phone on hold and turned quickly to Prime Minister David Doron, standing beside a large conference table with Mossad chief Avi Zadok, Shin Bet chief Yossi Ben Ramon, Aman head Brigadier General Yoni Barak, and General Uri "The Wolf" Ze'ev, chief of staff of the Israeli Defense Forces.

"That's Yarkon. We just picked up a signal close to the Jordanian border."

"Can we be sure?" asked the prime minister.

"No, sir. But we can't afford to be wrong."

"Uri?"

"I agree, sir. We've got to move quickly."

Zadok and Ben Ramon both nodded.

The prime minister didn't hesitate. "Do it."

Modine took the phone off hold. "Captain, you have clearance. Operation Ghost Lightning is a go."

* * *

Bennett was settling down now, pouring everyone another glass of brandy and stoking the fire. "Okay, so really," he pressed. "How do you guys know each other?"

"Well, actually, Jon, I knew Erin's dad," said the president, quieting down and getting serious. "Sean McCoy was a Navy SEAL in Vietnam when I first met him. When we got out, I went to Wall Street, and he joined the CIA and worked his way up over time to become the DDO, first under Nixon and later under Carter."

"Really?" Bennett could sense the president's changing demeanor.

"Besides Julie, Erin's dad was my best friend. I've never met anyone else like him."

"Was?"

"Sean was killed on an undercover mission—in Afghanistan, actually, after the Soviets invaded in '79."

"Oh . . . I'm so sorry. . . ." He looked at Erin. She wasn't smiling anymore.

"Thanks," she said. "It's okay. Mr. President, you really don't need to . . ."

"I know," the president continued, "but it's important he know a little background here if you guys are going to work together."

McCoy nodded her reluctant assent, and the president continued.

"So, anyway, when I was at Fidelity, I helped set up an account for Erin and her mom, you know, just to help them through it all."

"You're an only child?" Bennett asked.

McCoy nodded.

"In fact," the president continued, "when I started GSX, Erin's mom, Janet, worked for us for, what, two years, I think."

"That's right, sir," McCoy added.

"The problem was, and I didn't even know it at the time—not right away, at least—but, it turns out Janet had a very severe case of ovarian cancer and she . . . she was a trooper. Except for Julie and Sean, I don't think I've really ever met anyone like her in my life. She just had incredible strength and optimism. She was amazing."

"I had no idea."

"It's not something that comes up a lot," McCoy offered quietly.

"Julie and I knew she had something we didn't," said the president, pausing a moment to look into the flickering fire. "I don't think I even believed in God before I met her. But she had an incredible story. Christ had really changed her life, and I think that's what started Julie and me asking a lot of spiritual questions for ourselves. Janet was at total peace about dying and where she was going when she died. And Julie and I knew we certainly didn't have that kind of certainty. I don't know. She just really got us thinking."

The room fell silent again.

Bennett had no idea what to say. "When was all this?"

"It was the year before you came, I think. In fact, Erin ended up living with us and our girls that year, right?"

"Right. About ten months, I think."

"So we all got to know each other pretty well during that time. My girls fell in love with her. Personally, I couldn't stand her."

"Very funny, sir," said McCoy. She appreciated the president's playful, personal banter. It had been a long time since she'd seen him last—and more than a decade since she'd seen his family.

When she'd gotten the call in London to come to Colorado ASAP on an air force jet to see the president, she wasn't exactly sure what would happen when she got there. But after spending a fitful night trying to sleep in a bunk room on the Peterson base, she'd spent nearly an hour with the president at breakfast, being briefed by him in between calls from the vice president and various foreign leaders. Then he'd sent her off for a few hours to wait for her "reintroduction" to Bennett.

It seemed strange, but McCoy was suddenly beginning to feel at home again. The idea of being at the epicenter of a high-priority mission for the president of the United States would have made her mom and dad very proud. She tried hard to steady herself and not concede to the powerful emotions roiling inside her. But it wasn't easy.

"Julie and I have known little Erin—not so little anymore—since . . . well, since before she was born. Julie even threw a baby shower for Janet at our old house in Cherry Creek way back, I don't know, whenever that was."

"I loved that house," said McCoy, staring into the fire.

"Me too," said the president. "Me too."

★ ★ ★

IDF Unit 212— *Sayeret Maglan*—was one of Israel's most highly trained and secretive special forces teams.

Three of its pilots and eight special ops commandos were already in place. The two American-built AH-64 Apache helicopter gunships and accompanying Sikorsky Blackhawk helicopter were already fully powered and ready for takeoff.

The largely underground and ultra-top-secret air base in the Negev desert was on full alert. So by the time Captain Yarkon burst out of the command center door with his orders, his team was ready to move. Yarkon jumped into the back of the Sikorsky and gave the thumbs-up sign. Within moments, the whole package had lifted off and disappeared without a trace.

Flying without lights, without radio communications, and flying low—at times just fifty feet above the desert blurring below them—would be terrifying to most men. But not to Unit 212. They had practiced such operations in the dark, foreboding, shadowy mountains and wadis of the Negev for years, and they were confident.

In a certain sense, in fact, the three pilots weren't piloting at all. They were just monitoring the computer as it did most of the work. The Israelis, after all, had nearly perfected the art of flying by autopilot, precisely for such a time as this.

Every few months—at night—the IDF secretly flew highly sophisticated computerized drones—essentially tiny unmanned reconnaissance planes—across their borders at incredibly low levels and steered them by remote control to predetermined rendezvous points inside hostile countries.

The drones gathered a wealth of data every inch of the way. They videotaped the entire journey with night-vision equipment so IDF pilots could later watch and rewatch and rewatch again the very routes they may one day fly. The strategy allowed the pilots to learn every crack and crevice and rock and boulder and tree and snake they would encounter along the way, until they could fly such routes with their eyes closed or in their sleep. Just as important, the drones recorded every ascent, every descent, every turn, and every increase and decrease in airspeed.

The data was then washed through IDF computers and recalculated to account for the differing weights and response times of other IDF aircraft, all of which were heavier and "stiffer" than the tiny drones. What spit out on the other side were highly classified CDs that could precisely replay the "musical score" of a trip across enemy lines to certain preselected destinations. These CDs could then be loaded at a moment's notice into an aircraft's computers for a proprietary software program to read and replicate.

Tonight, all three superquiet Unit 212 choppers were flying by CD, across the Red Sea and through the rugged, unforgiving mountains of Saudi Arabia. And this was no exercise. This was the real thing.

* * *

Ali Kamal was ecstatic.

He'd found his destination not far from Highway 10, the shadowy base of a massive sand dune perhaps sixty feet high. He arrived on time . . . three minutes under the wire, but on time. And his team was moving quickly to get ready.

The first order of business was to unload the German camel. This was the most difficult, labor-intensive, and time-consuming of their tasks. Nothing else mattered if it wasn't done right. But Kamal wasn't worried.

The average team took thirty-four minutes and eighteen seconds, followed by another four minutes and six seconds to complete their other procedures. The record had been set back in 1991—thirty-one minutes and twelve seconds.

Three days ago, Kamal's team had done it in twenty-eight minutes, forty-seven seconds—a new record, and the reason they'd been selected by General Azziz for this very mission.

* * *

"Any word?" asked the prime minister.

He stepped back into the blastproof war-room bunker after making a series of phone calls to various cabinet members from the bunker next door.

"Not yet, sir," replied the defense minister, calmly sipping an icy glass of freshly squeezed orange juice. "But don't worry. It won't be long."

The seventy-six-year-old prime minister sat down, pulled out his reading glasses, and began glancing over the newly received intelligence reports from Washington, London, and Paris. A nightmare was unfolding, and if the Americans didn't or wouldn't act, he just might have to.

* * *

Maybe it was the cold night air.

It was now the middle of the night in Iraq, and the desert temperatures kept sinking. Maybe it was the fatigue of such a long day of driving from Baghdad. That had not been part of his team's training, and perhaps it should have been.

Maybe it was the fact that the new warheads they'd been given were significantly heavier than the ones they'd always used and trained on in the past. This seemed to have created an unusually high level of anxiety among his men, and they were taking extra time and moving too slowly.

Or maybe it was the fact that this was their first real mission and the stakes were so much higher. All of them had been too young during the previous Gulf War.

Whatever it was, they were finally done. But they would win no awards. It had taken them thirty-nine minutes and twenty-one seconds. A complete failure.

Ali Kamal raced back to his Range Rover and powered up his cell phone. Ten seconds later, he speed-dialed a phone number in Berlin. That was automatically forwarded to a phone number in Johannesburg, South Africa. From there it was forwarded to a phone number in Sao

Paolo, Brazil. That was digitally forwarded to a number just outside of Moscow, where it was forwarded to Tangiers, Morocco.

At that point, it was intercepted by Gibraltar Station—an Echelon listening post run by the U.S. National Security Agency on the British-controlled Rock of Gibraltar—on its way to the Iraqi Defense Ministry, where it was fed down into Saddam Hussein's personal war room, deep under Baghdad.

"The letter is stamped and ready for the post office," Kamal said in Farsi, though his native tongue was Arabic.

"Praise be to Allah," responded the voice at the other end, also in Farsi. "Go ahead and mail the letter."

Kamal quickly turned off the phone and threw it back in his precious Range Rover. All eyes were on him now and he gave his team his full attention, flashing them five fingers. They had five minutes to warm up their R-17 *Al Hussein* rocket—a Soviet-designed ballistic missile known in the West as the Scud B—and wait for his signal to launch.

This was no humanitarian mission, and Kamal and his team didn't work for the U.N. Indeed, they had murdered an entire U.N. relief team a few days earlier, dumped their bodies in a lake, and taken over their vehicles precisely for this moment.

Kamal and his top lieutenant scrambled up the sand dune to use their night-vision goggles and make sure all was clear. But they were hardly worried. Since the Gulf War, America and her allies had launched more than twenty-eight thousand air sorties over these deserts but had never found, much less destroyed, an Iraqi mobile missile launcher. How could they? Western Iraq alone was more than twenty-nine thousand square miles of raw, ugly desert. It would be easier to find a specific drop of water in the Indian Ocean than to find them, particularly at night.

Sure, the Americans and British had found and destroyed a few fixed-site missile launchers. But not a single mobile launcher. Nor would they. Especially not one hidden inside an official U.N. food-and-medical transport. Especially not at night.

The young platoon leader couldn't help but smile as he approached the top of the dune, even though his eyes and face were now completely covered with sand and stinging horribly. Maybe he would be personally given a medal of honor by President Hussein himself.

A shudder of excitement rippled through his body. He looked back once more to see his lieutenant about twenty yards behind him, taking a swig from a canteen of water and trying to get the sand out of his mouth. He looked down below and saw his team lit up by the headlights of their Range Rovers. They gave him the go sign. The missile was ready. They were ready.

Let history begin.

Kamal adjusted his night-vision goggles and fell flat on his stomach against the dune. He carefully inched his way to the top, just five feet away. On the other side would be the Jordan Valley, Jordan herself, Palestine, Israel, and the sea. His heart raced with joy and pride.

And then he heard it.

Kamal carefully peeked over the dune and turned on his goggles.

The shock of what he saw froze him in place.

Had he been standing, his head would have been chopped clean off by the Israeli Apache now slicing the air just a few feet above him.

Kamal instinctively ducked, looked down at his team, and tried to scream. But he couldn't. And it wouldn't have mattered if he had. No one could have ever heard him over the roar of the chopper. He could see the blank expressions on the faces of his team. It wasn't fear. It was total disbelief. And now it was death.

The Apache's 30 mm guns began blazing away. Fire and smoke poured out of them as tracer bullets shredded Kamal's men into tiny bits of bloody vapor. Two laser-guided Hellfire missiles penetrated his precious Range Rover and the one beside it, causing both to erupt in a massive fireball that left Kamal screaming and writhing in pain and trying desperately to remove the night-vision goggles from his eyes.

Another Apache suddenly emerged out of nowhere. Two more Hellfire missiles exploded in two more Range Rovers. Then two missiles struck the Daimler-Benz truck and it, too, exploded in a deafening fireball, fed by hundreds of gallons of reserve diesel fuel.

With every man on Kamal's team dead or dying, the Sikorsky quickly landed nearby, and eight Israeli commandos and Captain Jonah Yarkon burst out the side door. They moved to secure the Scud missile and remove its warhead.

Kamal was still screaming in pain, but none of the commandos could hear him over the ongoing explosions and the roar of three choppers. He tried blindly to reach for his sidearm, but it was then that the lead Apache pilot whirled his chopper around—constantly looking for an enemy—and saw the twenty-six-year-old leader thrashing about wildly on the sand dune.

With a flick of a switch and a press of his thumb, the IDF pilot put Ali Kamal out of his misery, though he seriously doubted the man was now in the arms of seventy virgins in paradise.

The two Apaches moved away, enlarging the perimeter of security for the commandos and switching on their high-powered radar to see if there were any other mobile Scud launchers—or aircraft—in the vicinity. But they saw nothing. All was clear.

Six minutes later, the commandos—each wearing hazmat clothing and protective goggles, headgear, and gloves—had the warhead detached from the rest of the missile, secure in a heavily insulated and hermetically sealed safe box, and piled back into the Sikorsky.

The chopper lifted off, joined the Apaches, and began their race back home, leaving timed explosive charges to detonate and destroy the rest of the Scud B rocket and its launcher just seconds after the Israeli strike force had cleared the area.

"The snow cone is on ice," said Captain Yarkon into a digitally encrypted radiotelephone, his only communication of the night.

Now the question was, what flavor was the snow cone?

9
* *
*

THE TRAIN RIDE from Vienna to Moscow normally takes about fifty-two hours.

But it is more than merely a slow, plodding, and quiet journey through snow-covered fields and hamlets and villages and the Carpathian Mountains. It is a journey back through the heart of darkness.

With a glass mug of hot Russian *chai* in your cold hands and some warm black bread and a plate of steaming *kasha-varnishka*, you can sit at the small table in your sleeping car and play cards and smoke cigarettes, or get lost in a novel, or just stare up at the ceiling and think about nothing or everything or a little bit of both. But if you care to peek out through the smudgy, filthy windows of your claustrophobic compartment, you will find a sad and war-weary land, scarred by German occupation and Soviet suffocation.

You will snake your way through Bratislava, the poor but proud capital of Slovakia, a city of trade and learning and history, born of Romans and Celts and eventually settled by Slavs in the eighth century and now almost half a million people strong.

It was here that a good peace was once found when Napoleon and Francis II signed the Treaty of Pressburg in 1805, following the Battle of Austerlitz.

Yet it was here, too, that a great rescue was once narrowly and tragically lost. In 1942, the Nazis—perhaps cynically, perhaps not—offered a rabbi named Weissmandl and a woman named Gisi Fleischmann a deal to trade one million imprisoned Jews headed for the gas chambers for two million dollars. But the rabbi and Fleischmann and their colleagues couldn't persuade anyone in the West to come up with the cash. It may have been the West's callous indifference. It may have been the fear that the Germans would renege on the deal and use the money to help defeat the Allies. It may have been something else entirely. But the money never came in, and a million souls never came out.

Along your journey to Moscow, you will also wind your way through L'viv, the largest city in Western Ukraine. With its sprawling open-air market and crumbling Russian Orthodox churches that barely survived the age of atheism, L'viv can seem like a city somehow trapped in a time gone by.

In warmer weather, in genuinely lovely, tree-lined parks, *babushkas* play with their grandchildren. Young mothers stroll their infants. Old men play chess and dominoes. There is a sense of family and faith that has been the glue holding this seven-century-old society together. But the fashions are drab and colorless and seem right out of the American thirties. The cars and trucks are old and styleless, like a black-and-white scene from Mayberry. The storefronts are simple and unattractive—no neon, little advertising, few brand names, just signs like Bakery and Drugstore and Butcher, though the racks are sparse and the cupboards nearly bare.

Somehow, the whole city has the feel of a Hollywood back lot amid the filming of a Depression-era period piece. And L'viv, like most cities and towns in the region, has a sad story and a wounded spirit.

It, too, was occupied by the Nazis, from 1941 through 1944. It, too, saw thousands of Jews rounded up into concentration camps, wherein the SS and the Gestapo proceeded to murder nearly the entire Jewish population. And as if that weren't enough, the Soviet Red Army then rolled in to "liberate" the city for Communism, killing, maiming, and enslaving the already traumatized citizens and plunging everyone into a new war, a Cold War, a new age of ghettos and gulags. So often has the city been in different hands that it actually has four different names—L'viv in Ukrainian, L'vov in Russian, Lwów in Polish, and Lemberg in German.

Eventually, your journey by train will bring you to the end of German- and Soviet-ravaged Ukraine, and you will arrive at the Russian border. A huge guard tower, barbed-wire fences, and searchlights will welcome you. A few dozen soldiers, all wearing green wool uniforms and green caps with red bands and gold badges around them, toting machine guns and walking German shepherds, look like a scene straight out of *All Quiet on the Western Front.*

The soldiers step aboard the train to check passports and visas, as well as to check every compartment from top to bottom and every passenger from head to toe, and even the engines and wiring underneath the cars, looking for contraband and drugs and guns and bombs and more recently for anthrax and other weapons du jour.

Satisfied that all is well, the soldiers direct everyone to a fairly large customs building across the border, hot and stuffy and crowded. It is the last chance to buy a newspaper and make a phone call, get some food and drinks and use a slightly cleaner bathroom, though *cleaner* is a distinctly relative term in Russia. Then, eventually, it is time to board the train once again and cross the three hundred or so kilometers of the great Russian "bread basket" to the capital on the turbid Moskva River.

What's different about entering Russia by rail rather than by air is the remarkably lax security at the borders in the post–Cold War era, a loophole the four horsemen now exploited with a vengeance.

Soviet borders were once impenetrable. Russian borders are now Swiss cheese.

Traveling through airports east or west meant traveling past video cameras and high-tech surveillance equipment such as state-of-the-art facial recognition software, and counterterrorism experts on a heightened state of alert, painstakingly checking passengers against watch lists developed by the FBI, FSB, and Interpol, updated daily, sometimes hourly. But slipping incognito across distant Russian borders spanning eleven time zones, manned by ill-clothed and poorly paid soldiers more interested in getting drunk than monitoring every loser who couldn't afford to fly into Moscow, was fairly easy.

Getting weapons into the country wasn't easy. But getting people trained and willing to use them was, and the country had more than enough weapons within its borders to get the job done. That's all that really mattered.

After all, the Russian Federation comprised nearly 11 million square miles of territory, almost twice the size of the U.S. And in a time of near famine and starvation, few if any of the nearly 150 million citizens cared to think much about who wanted to get into their country, at least by car, truck, or train. Most, instead, thought several times a day about how to afford getting out. And this was one of those days.

☆　☆　☆

"Mr. President, we need to move you immediately," said Agent Sanchez.

"Why? What's going on?"

"Checkmate's on the phone. He's got the NSC team in place and events are moving rapidly," answered Sanchez as she and the other agents maneuvered his wheelchair out of the commander's private office and into the adjoining conference room. Corsetti, Iverson, and Black were already waiting for them, as was General David Schwartz, the NORAD commander.

"Bennett, McCoy, get your butts in here," shouted the president as Sanchez positioned him behind the oak table at the head of the room.

All evidence of a Thanksgiving meal was long gone. Instead, the previously plain and unadorned walls were lowering to reveal video screens, computer monitors, and a high-tech ThreatCon map of the world, the likes of which Bennett had never seen before. Even the top of the conference table was rapidly removed by NORAD staff to reveal four banks of secure phones—one for each side of the table—and networked laptops allowing each person to simultaneously read real-time threat condition information and type each other instant messages without having to speak out loud if they were in the middle of a conference call.

Bennett glanced up at the wall over the major video screen to the twelve digital clocks, one from every major time zone. It was now 7:13 p.m. at NORAD—9:13 p.m. in Washington, 4:13 the next morning in Jerusalem.

"This is amazing," whispered Bennett to McCoy as the two got seated next to Black. "You ever see anything like it?"

"Where do you think I got the idea for our little war room in London?" McCoy whispered back.

Bennett looked at her for a moment. "I just thought you'd watched too many James Bond movies."

Everyone was ready.

Except for the president and Secretary Iverson, the entire National Security Council was physically gathered and assembled in the Presidential Emergency Operations Center underneath the White House. Present and accounted for were the vice president; National Security Advisor Marsha Kirkpatrick; Defense Secretary Burt Trainor; Secretary of State Tucker Paine; CIA Director Jack Mitchell; Attorney General Neil Wittimore; four-star general Ed Mutschler, chairman of the Joint Chiefs of Staff; and a top aide for each. Unlike the Counterterrorism Task Force, the FBI and Secret Service directors were not present, but both were on standby in their offices.

The vice president began immediately. "Mr. President, first of all, how are you?"

"Fine. You all got my medical summary?"

"We did, sir. Chuck wants to know if we should release it to the media."

"Absolutely. People need to know the facts if they're going to understand exactly how hard we're about to hit back. Marsha, you there?"

"Yes, sir," said Kirkpatrick.

"Call Marcus Jackson at the *Times*. Give him a briefing on my condition and a copy of the summary exclusively—on background—as a 'high-level government source.' I want it to look like a deliberate, calculated leak, a message to the world that we regard these terrorist attacks as a prelude to war."

"Yes, sir."

"Good. Make sure Jackson has the story and it's big, front-page news. The *Times* puts it up on the Web around midnight your time. The moment the story goes up on the Web, have Chuck page the White House press corps staying over at Peterson and alert them that he'll do a full background briefing at 4 a.m.—6 eastern. I want every TV morning show, plus radio, talking tomorrow morning about how serious the president's condition really is and that high-level government sources say a massive retaliation is coming."

"Sir, this is Tucker."

"Yes, Tuck."

"Is that really wise? We need to be careful not to inflame the situation."

"Mr. Secretary, can you see me? Am I on your video screen right now?"

"Yes, sir."

"Then with all due respect, what in the world are you talking about?"

"Sir—sir, we cannot make this personal. This is not about you, sir."

"No, you're right, Tucker," the president replied, making an extra effort, Bennett could see, to remain calm. "It's not about me. It's about the American presidency. It's about the security of our government and our people. It's about the British royal family. It's about the Canadian prime minister. It's about the royal family of Saudi Arabia."

"My point, sir, is—"

"I know what you're saying, Tucker. And I couldn't disagree more. We are not inflaming the situation, Mr. Secretary. The situation *is* inflamed. We're simply responding to a war that has been forced upon us. And make no mistake about it: this is war. We are at war. It's not a war on terrorism anymore. It's a war against the country or countries that did this. We are going to strike. And we're going to strike hard. Am I clear?"

Everyone but the secretary of state nodded quietly.

Tucker Paine looked like he'd just been punched in the stomach. He was mortified at the way he'd just been dismissed by the president. But he didn't dare walk out. In his judgment, things were disintegrating rapidly now. Cooler heads were not prevailing. Emotion was winning the day.

"Now, Jack, what've you got?" the president continued.

Kirkpatrick slipped out of the room for a moment to call Marcus Jackson with the *New York Times* in Colorado.

"Sir, we at CIA are now convinced that the events of the past thirty-six hours are not acts of terrorism," said Mitchell. "They are, in fact, acts of war."

The CIA director had everyone's undivided attention, and he began methodically going through the evidence his team had gathered.

"In the past thirty-six hours, the Iraqis have shot down three of our reconnaissance planes. They're readying several mechanized units. They're readying their Republican Guard forces. They're sending recon units to the borders of Kuwait and Saudi Arabia. They've put their bombers on standby. The streets of Baghdad are like a ghost town. No car or truck has left the city—except for a U.N. relief team headed back to Jordan—in the past twelve hours.

"And Saddam just delivered a real humdinger of a speech. Allow me to quote: 'My Arab brothers. If we cannot recapture the glory of Palestine from the river to the sea, and from the sea to the river, with its crown Al Quds, then we shall erase the Zionist invaders from the face of the earth. We will make the blood of the criminal Zionist invaders and occupiers run cold, then cease to run at all. I have no intention but to do whatever pleases Allah and bestows glory onto our Arab nation. Allah will not disappoint the Arab nation, and we will triumph. Allah is the greatest. . . . Allah is the greatest. . . . Allah is the greatest . . . Let the imperialist and Zionist enemies of our nation be debased. . . . May Allah damn the Jews.' End quote."

"Jack, you're sure about that translation?"

"Absolutely, sir. Just got it from NSA. The scary thing is that the language is almost exactly the same as Saddam has used in speeches to the Arab League in the past. The critical difference my guys point out is that in the past, Saddam talked about 'liberating' Palestine. Now he's talking about erasing Zionism from the face of the planet."

"And?"

"Well, sir, we're not quite sure yet. We need more time to analyze it. But there's no question Saddam's rhetoric is hotter than it's ever been. He seems to be getting an itchy trigger finger. That's not good. And the fear my team has is that Saddam is becoming desperate and irrational."

"How would one know?" the president quipped.

"Fair enough, sir. But there is some disturbing circumstantial evidence to consider. About eighteen months ago, British intelligence intercepted a phone call between Saddam Hussein's personal physician and the physician's father. The call was cryptic, but seemed to suggest that Saddam may have just been diagnosed with terminal prostate cancer. Then, about nine months ago, Saddam's eldest son, Uday, was killed in a car crash outside of Tikrit. We don't think it was foul play or anything. The kid— well, he was forty-five—did have a long history of fast cars and fast women. But we're not sure. The bottom line, however, is that our analysts believe the death hit Saddam incredibly hard. He'd been grooming Uday to succeed him and he may very well blame us, or the Israelis, for trying to take him out. Back in 1996, you may recall, someone—we don't know who, it wasn't us, we think it may have been the Iranians—did try to assassinate Uday. They failed, but eight bullets left the young man permanently disabled."

"Go on."

"Well, Mr. President, you may reacall that two and a half months later, Saddam's younger son, Qusay, was killed in a car bomb explosion in downtown Baghdad. We believe that was the work of a Kurdish rebel faction. But it doesn't really matter. We're certain that regardless of who was really responsible, Saddam blames you and Prime Minister Doron. The bottom line, sir, is that Saddam Hussein is now seventy-three. He is dying. He has no sons. No direct offspring. No direct line of succession. No one to pass on his power to. If he really believes time is running out, there's no telling what he might do."

The president was quiet, sober, distant. "What about the G4?" he asked, abruptly changing the subject. "Is there any evidence Iraq was connected to that?"

"Actually, there is, sir," Mitchell responded. "The Canadians just found the two pilots who were supposed to be flying the Gulfstream IV that attacked you. They were bound, gagged, and double-tapped to the head, then left in a Dumpster outside of a Toronto hotel, near the airport."

"Good God."

"We also found the three oil executives who were supposed to be on that flight. Same thing: double-tapped to the head and dumped in some woods beyond the perimeter of the airport."

"So it wasn't actually hijacked in flight?"

"Not exactly."

"Any idea who took the plane?"

"Yes, sir, we do," added Mitchell. "We have the thugs on a security tape."

"Who?"

"Two men, dressed as pilot and copilot of the G4. The images are as clear as a sunny day in Houston—one from a camera aimed at the front door of the private terminal and one behind the counter as they signed a credit card receipt—stolen, of course—paying for their fuel."

"Names, Jack, names."

"We checked the tapes against our database. You won't believe who popped up."

"Who?"

"Daoud Maleek and Ahmed Jafar. Both are members of Al-Nakbah—which translated into English means 'The Disaster.' It's a Shi'ite group set up originally by the Iranians to help fight in the war in Chechnya. Run by a guy named Mohammed Jibril."

"The guy who seems to be trying to take the place of bin Laden?" asked the vice president.

"Exactly."

"Okay, keep going," pressed the president.

Bennett couldn't believe what he was hearing. He was a long way from Wall Street, riveted by the discussion and increasingly anxious about where it might lead. He poured himself a glass of water and silently offered to do the same for others. All but McCoy turned him down.

"We've been hunting Maleek and Jafar for the last several years. We had a pretty solid report that they were hiding out at a training camp in the Ural Mountains outside of Moscow. Obviously, we haven't caught them yet."

"Obviously."

"But we do know Saddam Hussein has been funding Mohammed Jibril."

"I thought you said the Iranians were funding him," said Kirkpatrick.

"The Iranians did give Al-Nakbah some initial seed money to wage war against the Russians in Chechnya. Al-Nakbah has also received some funding from Yuri Gogolov's ultranationalist faction in Russia."

"Ultranationalist? Try Fascist fanatics," said the attorney general.

"True."

"God help us if Gogolov ever becomes the next czar of Russia," added the AG.

"Amen to that," said Kirkpatrick.

"Why's Gogolov involved?" asked the president.

"Well, sir, it's complicated. Gogolov is Russian. But he hates the current Russian government, led by President Vadim. He thinks Vadim's a traitor. Too cozy with the West. Too nice to Israel. Too soft on Russian Jews immigrating to Israel. Gogolov's furious that you and Vadim have gotten so close in the last few years, and particularly that we worked so closely to destroy Al-Qaeda and the Taliban. He's been willing to fund any rebel or terrorist group that might weaken Vadim, including Al-Nakbah."

"Okay, Jack. So tie it all together. What does this all mean?"

"Sir, Mohammed Jibril and Al-Nakbah have gotten help from several sources, including the Iranians and Gogolov. But in the past few years, the bulk of Jibril's money—about six million dollars—has come from Iraq. Specifically from Saddam Hussein's right-hand man, General Khalid Azziz, head of the Republican Guard. That ties the Iraqis in directly with this attack on you."

"We know all that for sure?" asked Kirkpatrick.

"Well, ma'am, I wouldn't take it to court. Not yet. But it's pretty solid. We photographed Maleek and Jafar in Berlin eighteen months ago."

Pictures of the two now flashed on the video screen before them.

"They hadn't done anything yet. But they were meeting with an Iraqi intel guy in Prague for more than four hours inside a local hotel."

More pictures flashed on the screen.

"We were kind of curious about them. So we trailed them to Madrid, where they set up shop for two months. They kept getting wire transfers from Berlin and Prague, money washed through a Swiss bank in Basel. But it was all coming from payments made for Iraqi oil sold illegally on the black market, despite the U.N. embargo. We've got all the paperwork on this. That's where the six million figure comes from. Then Maleek and Jafar left Madrid for Cairo. We believed the two were heading back to Baghdad. That's when we had the Egyptians nab them."

"Why didn't we nab them ourselves?"

"We didn't have enough to hold them, sir. But you'd just threatened Egypt's foreign aid and they happened to be in a mood to help us out."

"So how did they escape?" asked the president.

"Honestly, sir?"

"Jack."

"Sir, you're not going to be happy."

"I'm not happy now."

"Maleek and Jafar were released the day the latest U.S. foreign aid wire transfer was deposited in the Cairo account."

"You've got to be kidding me."

"No, sir. On a hunch, I had my station chief in Cairo make some calls the day before the wire was authorized. You know, just to let them know we were watching."

"And?"

"And he didn't get a call back till the next day—the next night actually. By that time, the two were gone. Of course, the Egyptians said they felt terrible."

"I bet they did."

"So where'd these Maleek and Jafar characters go?"

"Well, sir, we're not positive. But we believe they headed back to Baghdad via Khartoum. We have photos of a Gulfstream jet that landed in Khartoum the next day, refueled and headed for Baghdad."

These pictures, too, were on one of the screens for the NSC team to see.

"A Gulfstream, huh?"

"Yes, sir. We didn't actually see anyone on the plane—no one got on or off—they just refueled. We didn't have enough guys on the ground to do anything about it, much less authorization to do anything if we had."

The president leaned back in his wheelchair and tried to get comfortable. "What about London and Paris and Riyadh? What do we know about those operations?"

"Nothing—not yet, sir. We're lucky to have as much as we do already."

The president nodded, looked over his notes, and took a sip of water. "So let me get this straight, Jack. We have positive ID on the two guys that tried to kill me?"

"Check."

"And we're positive these guys were top lieutenants of Jibril and Al-Nakbah?"

"Check."

"And we're convinced that Al-Nakbah was begun with seed money from the Iranians and some Russian ultranationalists, but has been receiving most of its money in the past two years or so from Iraq?"

"Check."

"And Maleek and Jafar were in Baghdad a few months ago?"

"Check."

"Anything else?"

"Mr. President, we're concerned about a new intercept NSA just picked up."

"What intercept?"

"NSA picked up a phone call through its Echelon facility on Gibraltar. We're pretty sure it came out of the desert of western Iraq."

"Who's making cell phone calls in the middle of the night in the desert?"

"Well, sir, that's just the thing. It doesn't make any sense. Plus, about an hour or so before we intercepted that call, one of our military satellites got a GPS request in western Iraq. From a vehicle on Highway 10 to Amman. The only thing we know was on that road was a U.N. relief convoy—a large truck and four Range Rovers. But the convoy has now disappeared without a trace."

"What was said on the call?"

"We'll have that in a few minutes, sir."

"What do you think is going on?"

"Honestly, Mr. President, I don't know yet. But given all the rest that the Iraqis are up to, I've got a bad feeling about this. We're trying to track it all down. I'll get you more just as soon as I can."

The president was in serious and increasing pain. He whispered something to Agent Sanchez, then addressed the group. "Guys, I apologize. I'm really getting uncomfortable up here. I think my pain medications are wearing off. Let's take a break. I'll huddle with my doctors. Then we'll pick this thing back up in a few minutes. Okay?"

"No problem, Mr. President," said the VP. "Let's reconvene in fifteen minutes."

☆　☆　☆

Fourteen minutes later, Marsha Kirkpatrick reentered the PEOC.

A moment later, Agent Sanchez wheeled the president back into the conference room at NORAD. The president's punctuality was legendary and consistent, even if he was on heavy medication. The NSC meeting was back in progress.

"Marsha, let me start with you for a moment," the president began promptly. "What've you got?"

Kirkpatrick poured herself a fresh cup of coffee. "Mr. President, I just got off the phone with Marcus Jackson at the *Times*. He's salivating. The story's running front page, top of the fold, banner headline."

"What's it say?"

"He wouldn't say. But I think you'll be happy."

The president glanced over at the vice president. "Bill, when was the last time I was happy with a story by Marcus Jackson?"

"I have no idea."

"The profile of you after the Gulf War for the *Denver Post*," noted Bennett.

Everyone looked at him like he'd just sworn to the pope's face. Black and McCoy winced. For a moment, no one said a word, until Kirkpatrick broke the silence.

"Mr. Bennett, you're here as a courtesy, not as a participant," she said, with a tone of voice that made Bennett feel like his father had just grounded him for a month.

"That's true—but he's right," said the president. "Jackson was nice to me once. Since then he's been a total . . . well, a total idiot."

"Big time," added the VP.

"This conference call is completely secure, isn't it?" asked the president.

"It better be," said the VP.

Everyone laughed.

Bennett crawled back into his shell. Better to be seen than heard, he told himself. This was the big leagues and he was a rookie.

"All right. Back to business. Jack, let's pick up with that intercepted call."

"Yes, sir. We've got the transcription of the intercepted Iraqi cell-phone call."

"Good. What is it?"

"It was in Farsi."

"What did they say?"

"The caller says, 'The letter is stamped and ready for the post office.' That's it. Then the receiver says, 'Praise be to Allah. Go ahead and mail the letter.' Then there's some static, and that's it."

"That's it?" asked the president. "So? What does that tell us?"

"On a normal day, sir, nothing," said Mitchell. "On a normal day, we wouldn't have even noted or transcribed—much less interpreted—that three-second call for a couple of weeks, at best. Today, we're watching things a lot more closely."

"And?"

"And, sir, I'm concerned a new operation is under way someplace."

"Iraqi or Iranian?"

"Iraqi."

"Then what's the deal with the Farsi?"

"That's partly why I think it's an operation. Sir, the Iraqis aren't sure about our intercept capability. Not exactly. And we believe that they believe that even if a quick call like that is picked up and recorded—which is highly doubtful, but thank God it happened—that even if we got it, we couldn't precisely trace it. We might think it's coming from Jordan or Saudi Arabia or Syria—but not Iraq. And even if we could trace it precisely, the Farsi would confuse us and cause us to suspect the Iranians."

"Okay. But . . . ?"

"But, because of the GPS intercept an hour before, our analysts are sure the call was made by one of the U.N. Range Rovers we lost along Highway 10."

"Meaning what?"

"Meaning the U.N. vehicles could actually be part of an Iraqi military or intelligence operation, not a relief convoy."

"Burt, what do you think?" asked the president.

"My gut tells me it's military in nature," said Secretary Trainor.

"Why?"

"The Jordanian military sealed its border minutes after the attack on you, Mr. President. Nothing's come over from the Iraqi border, and they haven't even seen anything come that way."

"One of those roads splits off to Syria, doesn't it, Burt?" asked Kirkpatrick.

"It does. But the Syrians insist nothing's come their way either."

"Do we believe them?"

"We checked with the Israelis," answered Mitchell. "They've got . . . well, let's just say they've got assets nearby, and they say no convoy has come through there."

"What about the U.N.? What are they saying?" asked Paine.

"The U.N. mission in Amman says they haven't heard a peep from their team in the last few days. They put in an inquiry, but haven't heard back yet from the Iraqi Foreign Ministry. And none of their team speaks Farsi."

"What are you guys trying to say?" asked the president.

Bennett could tell the president was genuinely worried now.

"Sir, there are a couple of possibilities," said Mitchell. "The first is that the Iraqis are sending another covert terrorist team into the desert to secretly cross into Jordan somewhere, either to attack the Hashemite kingdom—the king and queen themselves, perhaps—or onto the West Bank and then Israel to make a move on Prime Minister Doron."

"What do the Jordanians say?"

"Honestly, my call to their intelligence chief was the first he'd heard of it."

"What about the Israelis?" the president pressed.

"Well, sir, now that's a horse of a different color. Three military helicopters lifted off one of their secret bases in the Negev several hours ago. One of our satellites picked up the liftoff. Originally we thought they were heading on a recon mission into Saudi Arabia. They do it all the time, so we didn't think much of it. But then one of our experts looked at the image more carefully. Barry, can y'all put the image up on the screen?"

The president looked up to the video screen on the wall and strained to see what was coming into focus, as did Bennett. "Holy . . ."

"I don't believe this," added the VP.

"Tell me for sure what I'm looking at, Jack," insisted the president. "I don't want to jump to conclusions—but that sure looks like a helicopter full of commandos."

"You got it, sir. You're looking at the top of two American-built Apaches and one Sikorsky heading across the Gulf of Eilat at about a hundred feet off the water."

"Why?"

"One Apache and I'd say they're doing recon. Two Apaches and I'd say they're taking someone or something out."

"And the Sikorsky, Jack?"

"Well, sir. That's what makes it interesting. I think they're planning on bringing something or someone back home with them. That's what worries me."

"So what does that mean?"

Mitchell took a deep breath.

Bennett glanced at McCoy, who looked as grim as he'd ever seen her.

The president rubbed his chin and made eye contact with the VP, then Kirkpatrick. Then he turned back to Mitchell. "Well, Jack?"

"Sir, I don't think we're looking at Iraqi terrorists. Mr. President, I believe we're looking at some kinda Iraqi missile operation, under the cover of a U.N. relief truck."

"So—assuming that's true for a moment—why wouldn't the Israelis run in a Scud-busting mission? You know, just send in a couple of jets or Apaches to blow them to smithereens?"

Mitchell said nothing.

Bennett looked at Black, then around the room, not understanding what was happening.

The president leaned forward, waiting for Mitchell to answer. "Jack?"

"Mr. President?"

It was Kirkpatrick. The president looked over at her screen. "What? Why don't they just take out the Scud—or whatever it is?"

"There's only one possible explanation, Mr. President," Kirkpatrick said slowly.

The president waited. Bennett looked at Tucker Paine. He obviously hadn't a clue. Neither did the AG, for that matter. But from the looks of things, Burt Trainor knew. Mitchell obviously knew, as did Kirkpatrick. McCoy gently squeezed Bennett's hand under the table. She knew too. Surprised but grateful, Bennett squeezed back.

"Sir, the Israelis must believe that whatever it is, it's too risky to destroy."

Just the way Kirkpatrick said it made the color instantly drain from Bennett's exhausted face. He suddenly felt cold and clammy and scared—like the moment he'd looked into the eyes of the scar-faced man in that cell in the Israeli airport and seen the foreshadowing of his own imminent death.

"Too risky?" pressed the president. "What are you trying . . . no . . . you don't think . . . ?"

The president froze. He looked pale and nauseated.

What? Bennett silently screamed. *What are they talking about?* Now the president had figured it out. *Was someone going to say it?* He didn't dare ask. Not now. Not after Kirkpatrick lowered the boom on him. Desperate, he looked at the vice president—his worn and aging face now ashen. The vice president was looking straight into the haunted, frozen eyes of his mentor and friend, President James Michael MacPherson. And a shudder ran through Bennett's body.

"The Israelis," the vice president of the United States said quietly, "now believe Iraq is about to use a weapon of mass destruction."

Bennett contemplated the horror of that statement for a moment, as did they all.

"What's the worst-case scenario?" asked the president. "Lay it out for me."

No one wanted to take that question, and it hung there in the air for a moment while they all processed the nightmare unfolding before them.

"Could be chemical," the VP added. "Could be biological—anthrax . . . Sarin . . . mustard gas . . . Ebola . . . or . . ." His voice trailed off. Each was too hideous to truly imagine.

Then all eyes suddenly shifted back to MacPherson.

"Or," said the president, "it could be worse. . . ."

He didn't finish his sentence, but he didn't have to. The entire National Security Council team knew what he was thinking and were thinking it themselves. Even Bennett got it now.

Iraq was about to go nuclear.

10

★ ★
★

THE FOUR HORSEMEN of the apocalypse had arrived.

They came in by way of Kievsky Station, one of eight major train stations in Moscow, handling more than two and a half million people arriving daily. Each took a separate cab as they left from the Square of Kievsky Terminal—*Ploshchad Kievskogo Vokzala*—on the banks of the Moskva River, near the Ministry of Foreign Affairs. But sure enough, they all wound up at the same place, in this case the Hotel National.

Constructed in 1903 by the renowned Russian architect Alexander Ivanov at a then-staggering cost of one million rubles, the historic landmark could boast of having been home both to the first Soviet government, in 1918, and to Vladimir Lenin. Lenin actually resided for a time in room 107 until he moved into the Kremlin itself, just across the boulevard on Red Square.

Completely renovated between 1991 and 1995 when Royal Meridien purchased the property, the Hotel National was now one of the city's most luxurious and expensive hotels. Four massive white marble statues of Greek gods greeted guests in the foyer. The sumptuous Moscovsky Restaurant offered the best borscht and beef Stroganoff in town. And wonderful live piano music seemed to perpetually emanate from the Alexandrovsky Bar—a gorgeous greenhouse structure with a pitched, tentlike glass ceiling, natural light, and lush trees and bushes inside and out—often packed with businessmen and tourists until the wee hours of the morning.

But the four horsemen didn't care about the hotel's look. They cared about its location, overlooking Tverskaya Boulevard and the pale yellow Kremlin buildings. They quickly checked into four adjoining suites reserved months before, then seemed to do nothing but leave CNN on, all day, every day. They didn't make calls. They didn't order room service. They never even ventured out into the hotel's public areas, much less outside the building. They seemed content to settle in. And they forced those trailing them to do the same.

The problem for their tails was that they were at a severe disadvantage. All of the eavesdropping equipment once built into the hotel's walls by the KGB had been removed by the new owners. And with high-paying guests occupying all 224 rooms, the best the surveillance team could do was play the parts of room-service waiters, housekeepers, and fellow tourists. So the agents discreetly infiltrated the building while their team leader took up residence in the management's state-of-the art security center in the basement and called back to Langley for instructions. They had these guys surrounded and in their sights. Now all they needed was clearance to take them down.

☆　☆　☆

It had better not be them again.

Marcus Jackson's SkyTel satellite pager went off with an infuriating series of high-pitched squeals just as he'd finally fallen asleep. He cursed and fumbled in the darkness for his glasses and his stupid pager, the bane of his existence, the omnipresent electronic leash that tied him 24/7/365 to his editors in New York.

It was almost three o'clock Friday morning back on the East Coast. Two of his editors had already wrestled with him over this story most of the night before finally putting the paper—and him—to bed. Couldn't everyone just let him get a few measly hours of sleep? There were other reporters on the payroll. Let them show a little elbow grease. He'd just scooped the world on the biggest story since the attacks, and the banner headlines in this morning's New York Times would reflect his coup: "U.S. Prepares for Massive, Imminent Retaliation; Sources Finger Saddam As Iraq Shoots Down 3 U.S. Planes; President's Injuries Far Worse Than Previously Known."

There's no rest for the wicked, Jackson concluded.

After the events of the past few days, the White House correspondent was physically and emotionally spent, bone tired, and desperately missing his wife and twin girls. He had actually just crawled into bed and turned out the lights several hours earlier—shortly after nine o'clock Colorado time—when the president's national security advisor called him with the scoop.

Then came the urgent page from White House Press Secretary Chuck Murray. Followed by a brief call from the president's personal physician. Followed by a fax from the White House Situation Room. Followed by a call from a high-ranking source at CIA—a top aide to Mitchell—arranged by Kirkpatrick, giving him deep background on the administration's latest thinking on Iraq's apparent involvement in the attacks.

Jackson finally found his glasses and silenced his pager. It wasn't New York. It was Murray—"911." He fumbled for the light switch, then stumbled into the bathroom, where his two cell phones were turned off and recharging. He grabbed one, powered it up, and speed-dialed Murray's personal cell phone. Murray picked up instantly.

"Chuck, it's Marcus," Jackson said mechanically, his body, mind, and soul still essentially asleep.

"Gambit's moving—you've got ten minutes."

"What? Why? Where we going?" asked Jackson, suddenly alert with a burst of adrenaline.

"Can't say. Just get packed and get to the lobby—ASAP."

"Why? What's the rush?"

"I can't, Marcus. Not now. Meet the press pool out front. Bus leaves in ten minutes. *Air Force One* leaves in fifteen. No exceptions."

☆   ☆   ☆

Officially, they didn't exist.

For nearly six years, this crack team had trained for this exact moment. Along the way they'd been code-named GhostCom. If they made the slightest mistake, that would actually be true. Thus the nickname, Ghost Commandos, given to them by the prime minister himself.

Phase One of the special-forces mission was now complete. Operation Ghost Lightning was a smashing success. The Iraqi Scud missile operators were neutralized and the missile—the snow cone, as it was called—had been "iced," carefully secured and delivered back to the top-secret Israeli military base known affectionately as the Carnival.

Now Phase Two—Operation Ghost Buster—was about to begin, and its success was far from assured. An elite team of twenty-seven Israeli missile designers, bomb-squad specialists, nuclear scientists, and chemical- and biological-weapons experts huddled nervously in a specially designed "operating room" several hundred feet under the Negev desert. They had one mission, and ten more minutes to complete it. Then the prime minister would call, and all hell would break loose.

* * *

General Azziz struggled not to hyperventilate.

Things weren't going as planned, and he needed hard, accurate intelligence immediately. It was almost eleven in the morning in Baghdad. An entire night and most of the morning were gone, and Saddam Hussein had expected to hear of a successful attack on Tel Aviv by now.

Moreover, he was demanding the personal presence of General Azziz to explain what was going wrong. There was just one problem. Azziz had no idea what was going wrong. Nor was he entirely sure something *had* gone wrong.

True, as of yet, no attack on Israel had transpired. True, Kamal and his men had not checked in. But Azziz was loath to phone his team—Q17—or send planes or helicopters out to find them. Not yet. It was too big a risk. What if they were just having some technical problems with the rocket, easily and quickly fixed? What if they were hiding from a Jordanian or Israeli or U.S. recon scouting expedition? What if the tractor-trailer had broken down and they were in the midst of repairing it? Many things could have gone wrong and many things could still go right. This mission was too valuable—too decisive—to not succeed or pull the plug now.

Azziz knew he had more rockets, including his "crown jewel." But how quickly should he deploy them? It was daylight. The strategic element of surprise was lost for another ten hours or so. Worse, it might have been lost forever. Tel Aviv was supposed to be reeling. The world was supposed to be gasping. The Israelis and Americans were supposed to be thinking twice about retaliating. Now what?

His real problem, however, was far more immediate. For Azziz knew that neither an Israeli nor an American attack was the most immediate threat to his own personal survival. Saddam Hussein was. He needed solutions—and he needed them fast.

✫ ✫ ✫

It was cold and wet and nasty.

The gleaming green-and-white *Marine One* helicopter, illuminated by floodlights, was ready to go on one of three pads outside the tunnel from Cheyenne Mountain. Two other Marine transport choppers were ready and waiting as six Apaches circled and F-16s streaked by overhead. Air force MPs in full battle gear created a perimeter around the helipads and nearby parking lot, and Agent Sanchez radioed each of her team members for one final check. All systems go.

"All clear, Mr. President," shouted Sanchez above the deafening roar of the choppers. *"You ready, sir?"*

"I am. You, Football, Jon, Erin, and Deek come with me," the president shouted back from the confines of his wheelchair. *"Put my medical team and the rest of your guys in choppers two and three."*

"You got it, sir," Sanchez responded. *"Let's do it."*

Sanchez and her agents moved the president first, carefully lifting him off the ground, locking his wheelchair where his usual seat had been removed, and rapidly closing the bulletproof side door. With Gambit secure and Sanchez sitting in the seat behind him, another agent came back and quickly led Bennett, McCoy, and the military aide nicknamed Football—the one carrying the briefcase with the nuclear launch codes—to the other side door, where they all quickly piled in.

Bob Corsetti and Secretary Iverson had already left for Peterson on another chopper a few minutes earlier. No sooner had the door closed than they were off the ground.

Neither Bennett nor McCoy had ever been in *Marine One*, nor had Black for that matter, and it was far more cramped than they'd expected. But it would all be over in a moment. It was just a quick hop to the tarmac at Peterson AFB, where *Air Force One*, two C-130 transports filled with the remains of the presidential motorcade, and six F-16s armed with Sidewinder air-to-air missiles were revved up and ready to rock.

But what struck Bennett most looking out the window as they came in low and hovered briefly was the sheer number of soldiers and security personnel standing guard. He could see Secret Service sharpshooters on the roofs of the nearby hangars, Secret Service SWAT teams ringing the president's plane, and tanks, Humvees, and armored personnel carriers lining the runway.

None of the men and women down there knew what the future held. None of them knew if another attack was imminent, nor what form it might take.

Had any of them really signed up for this? Were they really prepared to lay down their lives? Why? Why was it worth it to them when these smart, strong, savvy Americans could be doing anything else, anything they wanted?

They clearly were part of something important, something they loved and believed in very deeply. They were willing to die, if necessary, to protect the president of the United States and the principles he and their country represented, even if they hadn't voted for him or even liked him.

Bennett honestly didn't understand any of it. Not really. He'd been raised in a family that despised guns and distrusted anyone with one. He wasn't exactly a pacifist, but he was sympathetic to those who were. He believed a lot of money and a good stiff drink could solve most problems. And he was terrified of dying. He didn't know why, but he didn't think much about it either. He just couldn't fathom what motivated a person to be willing to die for a stranger or a colleague, much less a country or a cause.

Yet, for the first time in his life, he found himself humbled and grateful and moved by the simple patriotism of these soldiers and Secret Service agents, patriotism he had often thought trite and unsophisticated. In high school and college he remembered feeling superior to buddies who'd gone off to wallow in the mud and "play war." After all, he was going to become a Wall Street big shot and make the big bucks. He was a going to become a Harvard globe-trotter, jetting from London and Davos to Hong Kong and Tokyo. Sitting around watching NASCAR and eating hot dogs (which he called "fat sticks") and chugging beer and singing Lee Greenwood's "I'm Proud to Be An American" had all seemed so hokey and blue collar to him. He'd never wanted any of it.

He always wanted to get his MBA, work on the Street, pick up a copy of the *Journal* and the *Times* every morning, and smell the reassuring leather of his briefcase as he stepped on the elevator and rode up a tower of steel and glass and stepped out on the top of the world. And he'd done just that.

He believed a "new world order" was possible. He believed in a "twenty-first-century global financial architecture," about which he'd waxed so eloquent to colleagues around the world. He truly believed that fiber-optic networks and digital capital were making nation states obsolete. Why not one giant global free-trade zone, rather than all these trade barriers and complications? Why not do away with all these exchange rates and friction and all these currency speculators making fortunes and wreaking havoc and causing ulcers?

Now Bennett didn't know what to believe. The men and women on the ground below him had something he didn't, and though he didn't dare admit it to anyone, it was something attractive. So did the president, come to think of it. So did McCoy. He didn't quite know what it was. Not yet anyway. But as *Marine One* touched down on this military base at war, he knew he needed to find out.

The world was changing so fast. The constants in his life suddenly didn't seem so constant anymore. Here he was, sitting next to the most powerful man in the world. Yet never had Bennett felt so powerless.

Ten minutes later, *Air Force One*—flanked by fighter jets—roared down the runway and headed for Washington.

* * *

Air Force One and its flying armada leveled out at forty-five thousand feet.

They were far above the clouds, far above any visual reference points that would allow anyone inside—anyone without classified information—to figure out where they were going.

The president and his family were in their personal quarters with an air force medical team.

The reporters in the traveling pool were in the back of the plane, confined to their seats and prevented from making or taking any phone calls. As journalists, they were eager to know what was going on. But as corralled sheep in a safe and comfortable pen—and assured by Chuck Murray that they weren't going to get any information for several hours at best—

most of them were just as eager to get some sleep. They had no idea what lay ahead. Why not be rested?

Corsetti came back to the senior staff seats and pointed at Bennett, McCoy, and Black. "You three, get your butts up to the conference room."

"What's up?" asked Bennett.

"The president's getting the NSC back together by video-conference."

"What about me?" asked Murray.

"Chuck, you get some sleep," counseled Corsetti.

"I need to be there, Bob," insisted Murray.

"No, really, Chuck, you need your beauty sleep." Corsetti smiled.

Murray didn't. "What's going on, Bob?" he whispered.

"You don't want to know."

* * *

Nine stood on the left end, nine stood on the right.

The eighteen young, rugged, clean-shaven, unarmed but elite war-riors—Q18 and Q19—wore green fatigues and black berets and stood ramrod straight, hands at their sides, in the sparse, barren, concrete-block barracks behind the Presidential Palace.

Decked out in his full military dress uniform, General Azziz sat in a large, ornate, and magnificently painted chair—more of a throne, really—along the far center wall. Beside him stood his four heavily armed personal guards. The moment Azziz stood, all eighteen commandos dropped to their knees and bowed their heads down to the dusty cement floor. Azziz observed the worship, then barked a command in Arabic and the men were again instantly on their feet, ramrod straight.

"O mighty warriors of our savior and lord, the king most high, the redeemer of our blessed people," Azziz shouted. "O mighty warriors of the one true hope of our people, the president and direct descendant of the great King Nebuchadnezzar who ruled our land with an iron fist and a heart of gold. O mighty warriors of His Excellency Saddam Hussein."

"Praise His Excellency," shouted all the men in perfect unison, includ-ing the general's personal security detail. "Praise his most excellent name."

"Mighty warriors, you have been chosen by our redeemer, our protector, for the most glorious of missions—and you shall not fail His Excellency."

"We shall never fail His Excellency," the young commandos shouted. "We shall never fail His Excellency."

"Mighty warriors, those who have gone before you have failed. They have failed and been destroyed by the filthy, wicked Zionists, the infidels who desecrate and pollute and poison the earth and all that belongs within it."

The men said nothing, but as Azziz glanced to his right, he could see the eyes of his men widen and their hands stiffen.

"Such men swore to me, to Allah, and to His Excellency, that they would never fail. Yet they did. And their payment to the most high has only yet begun."

The barracks were silent, but for the booming, echoing voice of the general.

"Such weak, filthy men are dead. My only regret is not to have killed them myself. Now their women shall die. Now their children shall die. Now their parents shall die. Now their cousins and uncles and grandparents shall die, die at the hands of the terrible swift sword of the executioner— the defender of His Excellency."

"Praise His Excellency," all the men shouted in one accord.

"Colonel Shastak," the general shouted.

"Yes, sir."

"Present yourself."

"Yes, sir." Colonel Shastak, commander of Q18, rushed forward to the center of the room and bowed low before the general.

"Stand."

The commander stood, stiff, straight, and proud. The general was calling upon him. The general was showing him the honor of leading new forces into the ultimate battle against the Zionists. He would not fail as those filthy men who had gone before him, the filthy men he had called comrades and friends just twenty-four hours before. He would do his country proud. He would do his beautiful wife and four young daughters proud. And he would not fail.

Actually, he would never have the chance. The general drew his .45

caliber gold-plated sidearm—a gift just a year ago from His Excellency—and aimed it at Colonel Shastak's face, no more than four feet in front of him. The man's eyes widened—then exploded in a cloud of blood and smoke.

"Mighty warriors, let this be a lesson to each one of you," said the general as each man saw their lifeless comrade slump to the ground in a quickly growing pool of his own blood. "Let Colonel Shastak's death be an inspiration for your life. *You shall not fail. Am I understood?*"

* * *

"Mr. President, we've got the whole team here," said the vice president.

Bennett, McCoy, Black, and the official White House photographer sat on one side of the oak table. Corsetti and Iverson sat on the other. The president sat in his wheelchair at the head of the table. Agent Sanchez stood just behind him. But all eyes were on the video screens at the far end of the small airborne conference room.

"Good, let's begin. Jack, anything new?"

"Afraid so, sir," replied Mitchell. "Couple things. First, I just took an urgent call from Chaim Modine, Israeli defense minister."

"What's Chaim got?"

"It's not good, sir."

"Let me have it."

"We were right. The Israelis sent a strike force into western Iraq a few hours ago. Attacked a Scud B team and captured the missile—well, the warhead, actually. They blew up the rocket itself. Chaim even uplinked some footage."

"Really?" asked the president, taken aback. "All right. Let's see it."

Corsetti dimmed the lights with a remote control on the conference table. What unfolded on screen two before him chilled Bennett to his bones, both for its imagery and the incredible technology that made it possible. Eerie green-and-black night-vision thermal photography from the lead Israeli Apache showed the entire strike unfolding, including the brutal death of Ali Kamal, though no one in the U.S., of course, actually knew his name.

"Well, Chaim Modine isn't in the habit of showing us videotape of his commando missions," said the president. "What's he got, Jack, and what's he want?"

Bennett could see Jack Mitchell shift uncomfortably on the video screen in front of him. It wasn't like the CIA director to hold back.

"Sir, they've examined the warhead," Mitchell began carefully.

"Please tell me it's conventional."

Mitchell shook his head.

"Chemical?"

Mitchell shook his head again.

"Biological?"

Mitchell shook his head a third time.

The room quietly but collectively gasped. Out of the corner of his eye, Bennett caught a glimpse of Sanchez's hand moving to her mouth in horror. The president seemed unwilling to speak, as though by not saying the word it would somehow not be true. But it was, and he knew it. They all knew it.

"The Iraqis have developed nuclear warheads," the president said finally.

"Sir, the Israelis are faxing all the data their team has developed on the warhead. They're sending photos and Geiger counter readings—anything we need. They're even willing to let our ambassador and defense attaché see it if we want them to. But we'd have to move fast."

"Bottom line?" asked the president.

"Fairly sophisticated, actually, and very deadly. The Israeli scientists say it would have worked. Had it hit Tel Aviv—say, Dizengoff Center, downtown . . ."

"The shopping mall?"

"Yes, sir. The Mossad calculates over one million people would have been incinerated in a millisecond. Another two to three million could have died over the next few months."

"Lord have mercy," whispered the president.

"The real question is, are there more?" asked the vice president.

"Honestly, they've got no idea," said Mitchell. "But all of the Mossad analysts and their military intel guys agree: Saddam Hussein wouldn't play ball with just one nuke. He has more and he's prepared to use 'em or lose 'em—and not just against Tel Aviv but against Washington and New York if he has the chance. Remember, we're talking about a guy who has already used weapons of mass destruction. He used chemical weapons to kill about one hundred thousand of his own people during the 1980s and 1990s. We've got to be ready for him to do anything."

"So what's Modine want?" the president asked again.

"It's not just Modine, sir. The entire Israeli Security Cabinet just voted in emergency session."

"And?"

"Sir, we've got one hour. Either we go nuclear against Baghdad . . ." Mitchell paused abruptly.

"Or what?" the president asked, his eyes as bloodshot and weary and anxious as Bennett had ever seen them.

"Either we go nuclear, or Israel does."

Bennett was numb. His mind raced to put the pieces together. The Israelis had just thwarted an imminent nuclear attack from Iraq. Now they were prepared to attack Baghdad with their own nuclear weapons, weapons never before officially acknowledged. But they clearly understood the consequences. They would have very little proof to show the outside world, and very little sympathy as well. They hadn't actually been attacked. Not yet. They hadn't actually lost a million people in a millisecond. Not yet.

But if Iraq had more of such terrifying weapons, the Israelis were facing an imminent nuclear holocaust on the order of all of the Nazi horrors combined, if not worse. Some six million Jews had died during World War II inside the Nazi death camps and gas chambers. Now some six million Jews lived in the entire State of Israel. Every single one of them was in grave danger. Thus, the Israelis were now asking the United States of America to launch its own nuclear strike against Saddam Hussein—within the hour.

After all, thought Bennett, *we have cause. We have standing.*

It was our president who was just nearly killed by Iraqi terrorists.

It was our planes that were just shot down by Iraqi surface-to-air missiles.

It was our Twin Towers and Pentagon that were once viciously and suddenly attacked.

It was our White House and Capitol Building that were targeted.

It was the U.S. that was leading the global coalition to eradicate terror from the face of the earth.

And it is our president who could certainly make the most persuasive case to the world that Iraq is a lethal, existential threat to world peace and prosperity.

We already told the world Iraq was part of an "axis of evil," together with Iran and North Korea. But for a host of reasons—some political, some strategic— we've never actually taken decisive military action to neutralize that axis.

Would the president really order such a strike? How could he? Then again, how could he not?

✳ ✳ ✳

The black phone rang only once.

The CIA agents in the basement security office of the Hotel National answered in English. "Check your e-mail," came the message, and the line went dead. The e-mail was checked, read, and immediately discarded by the lead agent. The team had clearance to secure the help of Russian special forces, and to move when the moment was right.

The agent quietly passed word to his men: "Be ready in fifteen minutes."

✳ ✳ ✳

This was it.

Prime Minister David Doron sat across from his top military advisors. His defense minister had just spoken to the U.S. CIA director and defense secretary and expected word from the president any minute. But he could not wait. He needed to be ready to strike, and do so at a moment's notice—even before the hour was up—if necessary. Doron turned to Defense Minister Modine and General Uri Ze'ev, the IDF chief of staff, and nodded.

Ze'ev picked up a phone, pressed four numbers, and slowly read the first nine numbers of the Israeli nuclear launch code, authorizing the immediate fueling of their missiles, but not yet their firing.

"Commence Operation Cosmic Justice—*now.*"

✳ ✳ ✳

The secretary of state finally broke the silence.

"Sir, it's Tucker."

"Yes, Tuck."

"Is it possible that the Israelis are bluffing?"

"What do you mean?"

"Sir, they have nuclear weapons themselves. Is it possible they are feeding us bad information to provoke an attack that would neutralize the Iraqi threat forever?"

"Are you kidding?" the president asked, incredulous. "No, no, I don't think so. Jack? I mean, is that possible?"

"Sir, it's possible, but highly unlikely. We've just confirmed their attack on the Scud site. I'll have satellite photos for you in the next few minutes. But we know they hit a Scud site. We know they recovered something. And our analysts think Modine is playing it straight. I had four of my best guys listening in on the call and sifting through the data. Given everything else that's going on in the world right now, it feels real."

"Burt? What about you?"

Defense Secretary Burt Trainor didn't hesitate. "Sir, I was on the call with Jack and his team, and I'm afraid I have to agree. My team and I think it's legit—and serious."

"Marsha?"

"Well, honestly, sir, I don't believe the Israelis would play games with us. As for what we do about it . . . ."

"Sir, it's Tucker again."

"Hold on a second. Bill, what do you make of it?"

"The whole thing is unreal, sir, a nightmare," said the VP. "But I agree with Marsha. It's not a game. Saddam has been trying to develop nuclear weapons for the better part of the last thirty years. We know that. We know he came close just before invading Kuwait in 1990. We know UNSCOM found evidence of a very aggressive program to develop weapons of mass destruction—chemical, biological and nuclear. Jack even helped two of their top nuclear scientists defect, even if one of them went back. So we've known for a long time this moment was coming.

"Maybe Jack's guys and Burt's guys were right a couple of years ago. Maybe we should have gone after Saddam from the beginning of this whole war on terrorism. I don't know. That's water under the bridge now. But there's no question we've got to do something now. The problem is, how many nukes does Saddam have? We have no idea. What will he do next? Is he really dying? Is he really desperate? We have no idea. What we do know is that we don't have much time, and the Israelis will strike if we don't act fast."

"Osirik?"

"Absolutely, sir. The Israelis attacked and destroyed the Iraqi nuclear reactor at Osirik back in 1981—without, I might add, giving us a heads-up. And, for my part, I say thank God they did. There's absolutely no reason to believe Prime Minister Doron won't order a strike in the next hour if we don't. The bigger question is whether or not he's really willing to wait that long given the imminent holocaust his people are facing."

"Bill, are you saying we should do it?" the president queried. "Do we go first?"

"Mr. President," shouted Paine. "Tell me you are not seriously considering for one moment the possibility of firing a nuclear intercontinental ballistic missile at Baghdad."

Everyone in the *Air Force One* conference room and back at the Presidential Emergency Operations Center under the White House seemed to recoil. The thought of using a U.S. nuclear weapon for the first time since Hiroshima and Nagasaki in 1945 was almost too unreal to contemplate. But, Bennett thought, that's precisely what they were doing. And quickly running out of time in the process.

"Well, given that we don't exactly have a lot of options right now, what do you have in mind, Mr. Secretary?" asked the president.

"Sir, I beg you, take a deep breath. Step back. Don't even let the thought cross your mind."

"Mr. Secretary, I don't believe I have that luxury."

"It is *not* a luxury, sir. We are talking about life as we know it. Sir, *think*. More than forty-five thousand people died in Hiroshima on the first day alone. Twenty thousand more over the next few months. That was a quarter of the population of the city at the time, sir. In Nagasaki, if I remember correctly, there were more than twenty-two thousand people who died in the first day, and another twenty thousand over the next few months. And those were small cities, sir. Baghdad is something else entirely. We're talking about . . ."

"About five million residents," said Secretary Trainor.

"Five million people, sir. Five million souls. You cannot hold them responsible for the acts of a madman." The secretary of state's pasty white face was bright red now. This was no longer about policy. It was personal.

"Tucker, I hear you loud and clear. I have no animus toward the Iraqi people themselves. Indeed, I pity them for what Saddam has done. But what do I tell the prime minister of Israel? What do I tell him? He's got six million people to protect. He himself is a Holocaust survivor. He's a former prisoner of war in Lebanon. I can guarantee you he's not going to sit back and do nothing. And what about me? How many Holocaust memorials and religious conferences have I spoken at where I've said, 'Never again'?"

"No," Paine shouted. "No. We can run some bombing campaigns. We can send weapons inspectors back in there. We can make him pay. But we do not, under any circumstances, attack a foreign power, even Iraq, with weapons of mass destruction. That is not who we are as a people, sir. That is not what God put this great country on the earth to do."

Bennett watched the president mull his options. They weren't good, and everyone knew it. The minutes ticked by. No one dared say anything. But everyone knew if the president didn't make a decision soon, the Israelis would. For his part, Bennett was sympathetic to the secretary of state's argument. The thought of using a nuclear weapon—particularly against a capital city—was abhorrent. Paine might be pretentious, but that didn't mean he was wrong. Aggressive conventional-warfare options were available. But was the president fully considering them, or was he being swept along by the horrifying emotions of the moment? Saddam Hussein clearly had just crossed a Rubicon and declared war. But was it really true that the nuclear option was the *only* option?

"Stu, what do you think?" the president asked, turning to Iverson.

"Honestly, sir, I don't think you have much choice. I don't like it. But I still think you need to do it."

"How will the Russians react?"

"I think if you explain the situation to President Vadim before you strike, you'll find him reluctant, but understanding."

"Jack, how about you?"

"Well, sir, I think we need to do it. But if we do, we've got to do it right."

"What do you mean?"

"I mean we've got to do what Harry Truman did. Mr. President, when it came time to shut down the Japanese in World War II and end their mortal threat to our people and our interests once and for all, Truman didn't hit just one enemy city with the bomb. He hit two. Iraq is the most deadly regime on the planet right now. Personally, I'd include Iran in that assessment, but they really haven't been directly implicated in any of these particular events. They'll be a very serious future problem; I guarantee that. Especially if we keep taking actions against their neighbors. But, that said, we need to focus on the immediate problem in front of us: Iraq. It's the epicenter of evil in the modern age. It's a breeding ground for terrorism. They've been doing everything they possibly can to buy, build, or steal nukes, not to mention chemical and biological weapons. They're recruiting Russian scientists. They're threatening to incinerate Israel. We need to take out Saddam and his stockpile of weapons once and for all. The world needs to know the price of going to war with us. You try stunts like this, and we will melt you down. If you're going to do it, Mr. President, do it all the way. Like Truman. A one-two punch."

"Where else would you hit, Jack?"

"Tikrit, a small city about a hundred and fifty kilometers north of Baghdad on the Tigris River. It's Saddam's hometown. He has a presidential palace there. He kicked UNSCOM out of there when they were hunting down his weapons of mass destruction. We believe he's got huge underground storehouses of chemical, biological, and nuclear materials there. There's also a site near there called *Al Alam*, where he's been known to be building missile engines. We hit Baghdad and Tikrit, and the world will know we mean business."

Paine was beside himself but tried to hold his fire.

The president listened carefully, chewed on that for a moment, then addressed Defense Secretary Trainor. "Burt, how long would it take for one of our ICBMs to hit Baghdad and Tikrit?"

"Mr. President, I beg you not to go there," insisted Paine. "This is total insanity."

That didn't sit well, but the president tried not to be sidetracked. "Burt?" he persisted.

Bennett could see the president was fast moving from annoyance with Paine to outright anger, not because of the secretary's position so much as his smug, self-righteous attitude. That worried Bennett, mainly because he found himself agreeing with—or at least strongly leaning toward—Paine's position. If Paine blew his credibility now, as Bennett guessed the secretary already had or was close to doing, a critically important viewpoint would be lost and a serious vacuum would be created.

"A Minuteman launch out of one of our underground silos?" continued Trainor. "About twenty-five to thirty minutes."

"And from a sub?"

"Sir, we have several Sea Wolf nuclear attack subs in the Indian Ocean right now. I'd say maybe eight or nine minutes, to either or both cities," replied Trainor.

"And the impact?"

"Well, sir, Iraq is a country of forty million people. As I said, there're about five million in and around Baghdad. Tikrit's fairly small. Big strategically, as Jack says, as Saddam's birthplace, hometown, and home of several of his most secure underground bunkers. But it's not much of a population center. So, a strike at both cities? Depending on the size and type of weapon used, I think we're talking about upward of one to three million dead by the end of the first week. Minimum."

"Good God," said Paine.

"Minimum?" asked the president.

"I'm afraid so, sir."

Tucker Paine was now on his feet. "Mr. President, I cannot be part of . . ."

"Mr. Secretary, *sit down*—or you *will* be relieved of your duties," snapped the president. "I appreciate your dissent and I welcome it—and that of others if they share it. But I need your advice, not your hysterics, Mr. Secretary. And I will tolerate nothing less. Do I make myself clear?"

"Mr. President, I—"

"Do I make myself clear?" MacPherson demanded again with fire in his eyes.

Secretary Paine remained standing, but said nothing.

"Mr. Vice President?" MacPherson called out.

"Yes, sir, Mr. President?"

"I want two more Secret Service agents in that room with you right now. The secretary *will* sit down. He *will* listen. And he *will* participate—

peacefully. Or he will be removed, locked up, and face federal charges. Am I clear?"

"Crystal, sir."

Bennett watched the monitor as two new agents moved into the room and took up positions near the secretary of state. Stunned, Paine slowly backed down and settled into his seat, beet red and fighting to contain his emotions.

☆   ☆   ☆

Each wore a bulletproof Kevlar vest.

Two dozen U.S. and Russian commandos took up positions on the fifth floor and the roof of the Hotel National. Each was dressed in black from head to toe. Each was equipped with enough firepower to start a small war. But starting a war was not what they had in mind. Preventing one was.

The U.S. and Russian team leaders checked and synchronized their watches. It was time. Huddled in a stairwell just a few yards from the doors they were about to bust down, they gave each other the thumbs-up sign and whispered commands in English and Russian into their headsets.

Instantly, eight commandos rappelled down the front of the hotel and tossed stun grenades through every window of all four suites. The deafening explosions rocked the building and terrified passersby.

"*Go, go, go,*" the American team leader shouted.

He and his Russian counterpart burst into the hallway with a dozen commandos. Seconds later, they'd crashed down all four doors and plunged into the smoke-filled rooms with more stun grenades and guns blazing. Their orders were explicit. Take down the four horsemen dead or alive. Given the murderous, barbaric histories of these demons, it was decided to neutralize them immediately, rather than take any chances.

There was just one problem. When the smoke cleared, the team leaders found themselves sick to their stomachs. The lights were on, but no one was home.

CNN was still playing. But the four horsemen were gone.

11

"WHAT DO YOU MEAN you lost them?"

Mitchell was pacing and screaming into his headset in the Global Op Center deep under CIA headquarters in Langley, Virginia.

"Sir, we stormed the rooms—and they weren't in there," said the American team leader on a secure satellite phone from the fifth-floor hallway of the Hotel National.

"Well, where did they go?"

"Sir, we have no idea."

"So I'm supposed to call the president and tell him my guys just lost the four most dangerous terrorists left on the face of the planet?"

"Well, sir, I . . ."

"Find them. You wake up President Vadim. You get him to mobilize the Red Army and you tear that city apart until you find them. Got it?"

"Yes, sir."

"Then do it—now."

★ ★ ★

Bennett splashed cold water on his face and stared into the bathroom mirror.

The president was in his personal airborne office, on the phone with the Israeli prime minister. Corsetti and the rest of the National Security team were also on the phones, gathering more information and discussing their various options. Bennett rubbed his neck and discreetly popped a

Valium. His heart was racing. His head was pounding. His neck and back were aching. His eyes were bloodshot. And he was beginning to feel feverish. He just wanted to find someplace to curl up and fall asleep.

A few minutes later, he stepped back into the in-flight conference room and poured himself a mug of coffee, two creams, two sugars. A steward brought in a large plate of sandwiches, a tray of vegetables and dip, small bags of Ruffles and Fritos, and a large plate of oatmeal-raisin cookies. Suddenly, Bennett felt famished.

He felt a twinge of guilt for wanting to eat at a time like this. But that didn't stop him from grabbing and wolfing down a ham and Swiss cheese on whole wheat with lettuce, tomato, and Grey Poupon, and a big, thick, warm cookie.

Black quickly joined him, taking not one but two such sandwiches and snagging two Diet Cokes and cookies as well.

McCoy sat in the corner, munching on carrots and celery and quietly sipping a bottle of Evian.

☆   ☆   ☆

"Bob, it's Jack," said the CIA director. "It's not good."

The White House chief of staff pressed the secure satellite phone—just handed to him by an air force communications specialist—close to his ear as he glanced over at the president.

"What've you got, Jack?"

"I need the president."

"Why? What's going on?"

"We lost them."

"Who?"

"What do you mean, 'who'? Take a guess, Bob."

It took a moment, but suddenly Corsetti snapped out of his fatigue induced haze and realized what was going on. "You lost the four horsemen?"

"I need to talk to the president—now."

☆   ☆   ☆

Ten minutes later, the president, Iverson, and Corsetti reentered the conference room.

The president was wheeled back into position at the head of the table, and he didn't look happy. They all took their seats again and reconnected with the PEOC.

"I just talked with Doron," the president began. "He briefed me on what they know. They've got several agents on the ground looking for any sign that Scuds are being moved into position. Nothing yet. And now Jack tells me they've just lost the four horsemen somewhere in Moscow."

Everyone winced. Things were quickly going from bad to worse.

Corsetti locked eyes with Bennett for a moment. The two had never been close. Corsetti had always been way too conservative for Bennett's taste, and Bennett had always been way too unwilling to raise money for the president or the party for Corsetti's taste.

Imagine what Corsetti would do if I ever told him I voted for Dukakis, for Clinton twice, and for Gore? thought Bennett. *He'd personally throw me off this plane—midflight.* The Denver Don didn't do dissenters well. It was just as well, thought Bennett. He knew Wall Street. Corsetti knew Washington. They were both loyal to the president. A match made in heaven. Who said diversity was a bad thing?

"Marsha?"

"Yes, Mr. President," responded Kirkpatrick.

"Get NSA on the line. Tell them I want saturation satellite coverage of every square inch of Iraq starting immediately. I want them snapping pictures of every Iraqi hangar, house, and hut—every tank, truck, and tricycle—every minute of every hour of every day until we know where they're hiding their missiles and we can target them and take them out. You got it?"

"Yes, sir."

"I don't care what they have to do. If they need to retask their birds, then do it. If they need air force assets—U-2s, SR-71 Blackbirds, Predators, and Global Hawk drones, whatever—make it happen. Doron is very nervous, as you can imagine. He's ready to strike Baghdad right now. He flat-out told me they're fueling their missiles as we speak. I all but begged him not to move. I said we're prepared to act—decisively—and we're moving our forces into position. I told him our National Security Council was meeting right now and we'd let him know precisely what we would do within the hour."

"What did he say, sir?" asked the vice president.

"He was pretty concise. He said I have fifty-three minutes, twenty-seven seconds—not one second more."

*   *   *

Iverson couldn't believe he was here.

For many reasons, the idea of being on *Air Force One*, with the president of the United States, in the midst of this global nuclear crisis was the last thing he wanted to be doing. He hadn't been on this job for long, and it now seemed everything was falling apart.

That said, however, no matter how he sliced it, Iverson couldn't shake the thought of how much he hated the man he'd helped elect president. Everything he'd been working for, planning for, strategizing for over the past few years had just been robbed from him.

He'd never wanted to be treasury secretary. He wanted to be a billionaire, on the Forbes 400 list—at the top of it, if possible.

Now his best-laid plans lay smoldering in ruins. The president had forced him to accept the position by first leaking the news of his impending nomination to the *Wall Street Journal* and then having Corsetti fan the flames of public and political approval until Iverson couldn't possibly say no. But he'd wanted to say no. He should've said no. Becoming treasury secretary meant having to divest all of his GSX and Joshua Fund holdings, just when they were about to make him richer than he'd ever known.

Sure, he was already wealthy. But the Medexco deal would have multiplied that wealth exponentially. And now—in just a matter of months—it was all gone. All of it. Neither the president nor Corsetti had any idea of the rage Iverson felt. But it was real, and it was smoldering, and it couldn't be bottled up for long.

Suddenly, Iverson felt his BlackBerry vibrate on his hip. He glanced down to check the latest e-mail and couldn't believe his eyes.

It was them. They weren't happy. They wanted answers. But how dare they e-mail him here, now.

He quickly hit *Delete* and turned off the BlackBerry, fought to regain his composure, and tried to reenter the National Security Council's discussion midstream.

* * *

"Secretary Trainor," the president said firmly.

"Yes, sir."

"I need a recommendation, quickly."

"Well, Mr. President, let me first say that if you do decide to do this, I would not recommend that you order the use of an ICBM."

The president was visibly taken aback. "Why not?"

The secretary of defense spoke calmly and carefully, especially in light of the confrontation that had just ensued with the secretary of state. "Sir, I believe that all of our strategic nuclear forces are top of the line. But . . ."

"But what?"

"But I offer you this scenario. What if we try to launch a Minuteman or a Peacemaker and it doesn't work? What if it blows up in its silo? or blows up heading into the atmosphere, like the space shuttle *Challenger*? or disintegrates in the stratosphere? Or, sir, what if the ICBM works just perfectly—but misses and hits another country?"

"Burt, what are you trying to say? You're telling me our strategic nuclear missile forces are unreliable?"

"No, sir. I'm telling you I don't want to find out. And I don't want the rest of the world to find out. I believe they work just fine. But I, for one, am not interested in being wrong on a matter of this magnitude. The consequences could be catastrophic, both in terms of lives lost and the complete loss of our strategic nuclear deterrence. Besides, even if everything works perfectly—as I'm sure it would—it's just too much firepower."

The president took a deep breath, then nodded to Corsetti, who quickly poured him a glass of water. "So you agree with the secretary of state. You wouldn't fire a nuclear weapon at Baghdad?"

"No, sir, I didn't say that."

"Then what are you saying?"

"I'm saying I wouldn't fire an ICBM."

"What would you do?"

"*If* you choose to launch such a nuclear strike—and I repeat, *if*—I would recommend the use of a tactical nuclear weapon. A cruise missile."

"Spell it out for me, Mr. Secretary."

"Sir, on your command, we can launch B-2 stealth bombers out of Whiteman Air Force Base near Kansas City. They could be armed with conventional cruise missiles, but also with AGM-129As. These are air-to-ground cruise missiles that fly at over five hundred miles per hour with a range of some two thousand nautical miles and can deliver a W-80-1 nuclear warhead with pinpoint precision."

"Walk me through the W-80."

"Well, sir, the W-80 is actually a nuclear warhead for sub-based ballistic missiles. The W-80-1 is a nuclear warhead designed for use on ALCMs—air-launched cruise missiles. It's a two-stage radiation implosion weapon. Three feet long, about three hundred pounds each. Delivers a yield of about one hundred and fifty kilotons. Mr. President, that's essentially the equivalent of detonating three hundred million pounds of dynamite in one location."

Bennett suddenly felt nauseated.

Secretary Trainor continued. "First designed in '76 at Los Alamos. First deployed in '81. Production completed in '90. We built about seventeen hundred of them. After the START II talks, we've got about, what, maybe four hundred of them in stock right now."

"Mr. President?"

It was National Security Advisor Marsha Kirkpatrick.

"Yes, Marsha?"

"Let's just say for a moment that you order such a strike. You can't do it unilaterally. You'll need to consult the leadership of Congress. The allies. Russia."

"And Doron," added Mitchell with an air of urgency in his voice. "The prime minister is waiting."

"I know, I know—Bill, talk to me. What do you think?"

"Sir, it's not just that. The real question is, what would we do next? I mean, this would be an unprecedented chapter in human history. I think we'd need to have—and explain to Congress and our allies—some sense of how the next chapter might read."

"Okay, one moment on that. But, Bill, what do you recommend we do?"

The vice president was a good man. Bennett respected him enormously. He had far more government experience—particularly federal experience and national security experience—than MacPherson. And he was always calm, cool, and collected in a crisis.

Even more attractive to Bennett, this vice president was a strategist. In the 1980s, he'd been a key Senate ally to President Reagan in helping outflank and outfox the Evil Empire. In the 1990s he'd been a staunch and unwavering voice for strategic missile defenses as well as modernizing U.S. nuclear forces. He'd also applied his impressive intellectual heft to the rethinking of the U.S. role in a post-Soviet world.

This man had the ability to play three-dimensional chess, thought Bennett, the ability to calculate and assess each possible move and counter-move and countercountermove when it came to domestic politics and global affairs. And win. No wonder the Secret Service had code-named the man Checkmate. The shoe fit snugly.

"One to three million people?" The vice president shook his head slowly. "Most of whom are innocent civilians? Baghdad and Tikrit unin-habitable for decades?"

"Bill, I get it. I know it's unthinkable. I'm asking you this simple ques-tion: Does it decisively shut down the threat of state-sponsored Iraqi ter-rorism and the imminent threat of the use of weapons of mass destruction by Saddam Hussein, or doesn't it?"

"It does, sir."

"Does it send a message to other nations that are even remotely consid-ering an attack on the U.S. or our allies with such weapons of mass murder that we have the means and the will to obliterate them once and for all?"

"Yes, sir. It does."

"In your estimation, does it buy the world fifty or a hundred years of peace?"

"I'm not entirely sure. But, basically, yes, my instinct is that it would."

"Do we have any other immediate, viable, effective options?"

The VP pondered that for a moment. That was, of course, the heart of the matter. Bennett found himself silently imploring this man to come up with something better.

"In the next half hour? No."

Bennett could feel the train leaving the station, and he wanted to jump off.

"Could we invade western Iraq and move toward Baghdad and occupy the city and find Saddam and shut him down? Given six to nine months? Yes. Given the willingness to lose upward of ten thousand to twenty thousand American soldiers, at least, maybe many more? Probably. Would U.S. public opinion support that? Doubtful. Would our alliance hold, particularly in the Arab world? Absolutely not. Could it become our next Vietnam? Absolutely. You were there, Jim—Mr. President. You know what it was like. You want to go back?"

"So what are you saying, Bill?" the president pressed. "Give me a bottom line."

"We're in one heck of a mess."

"I noticed."

"Sir, I'm saying that I am not in favor of a nuclear strike. Not under any circumstances . . ."

Everyone's eyes were riveted on the vice president. McCoy bit her lip. Bennett held his breath. The president visibly tightened.

". . . not under any circumstances, that is, but these."

Bennett could feel the oxygen get sucked out of his body. He was winded and scared and cold.

"In the abstract, it's ugly and grotesque and bordering on the barbaric," the vice president continued. "But in terms of our immediate military options and the threat to U.S. national security and that of our allies? It's instant. It's overwhelming. It's decisive. And yes, I believe it buys us fifty or a hundred years of world peace, at the very least."

"Does that make it worth it?" the president asked.

"Well, sir, it might. But again, I go back to my previous question. What next? Where would we go from here?"

"Ecclesiastes."

"I beg your pardon, sir?"

"There's 'a time to kill and a time to heal, a time to tear down and a time to build . . . a time to love and a time to hate, a time for war . . .' "

The words hung in the air for a moment.

" ' . . . and a time for peace.' "

"Yes, sir. That might be a good way to put it. We can't just think about how to destroy our enemy. We need to think about how to rebuild a new world, a world of peace and prosperity."

Bennett could tell the president wanted to get up and pace. That's what he used to do in GSX strategy meetings when he was trying to get his hands around how to approach a new deal.

But now he was trapped in a wheelchair, deprived of sleep, forced to decide about the use of nuclear weapons in the middle of the night at forty-five thousand feet and a thousand miles away from his top national-security advisors.

Unable to pace, however, the president suddenly chose to pray. Without saying anything to anyone, he simply bowed his head, closed his eyes, and folded his hands.

Bennett just stared at him.

The next few moments felt like an eternity, and Bennett found himself seething inside, furious with his friend and mentor for wasting such valuable time when there was so little of it to begin with. This was no time for fairy tales. This was the time for rational thinking and logical decisions. The fate of the world hung in the balance.

☆　☆　☆

Carrie Downing was smart, stylish, and thirty-two.

She had been a rising star at Excite@Home, once the world's leading broadband Internet provider. That is, until the company filed for Chapter 11 bankruptcy protection in October of 2001.

Downing's dream of riding the wave to dot-com millionaire status had been sunk faster than the *Titanic*. She and more than thirteen hundred other employees got dumped overboard just as the Al-Qaeda terrorists struck the Pentagon and the World Trade Center and the U.S. economy was sinking fast into a serious recession.

So Downing did what any aspiring e-mail software writer might do when her boatload of stock options plummeted in value from $100 a share in April of 1999 to a mere thirteen cents a share two and a half years later. She joined the FBI.

Trained in short order as a specialist in electronic counterintelligence and counterterrorism, she was fast making an impression on her superiors. She'd been assigned to an elite team and a highly classified project known to the outside world only as Magic Lantern.

The state-of-the-art and highly controversial software was part of what the bureau called the Enhanced Carnivore Project Plan.

It was designed to gobble up as many meaty morsels of e-mail as possible. It could be secretly installed onto the hard drive of the computer of a potential enemy of the United States or sent incognito as a virus to such a person, attached to a seemingly innocuous e-mail note or advertisement.

Once installed, it allowed the FBI to read encrypted files and even capture individual keystrokes, like passwords, thus unlocking the most sensitive financial and organizational details of the most elusive criminals and crime syndicates. And it could evade even the most sophisticated antivirus software on the market, so far.

But even the best technology is only as good as the people who make use of it. It fell to people like Downing to invade a target's computer, steal its data, and sift it rapidly and without detection for the kind of information that could help her fellow agents in the field break the toughest of cases. And Downing was good. Very good. She'd helped blow open so many cases in the last several years that she'd landed on FBI Director Scott Harris's radar screen and been dubbed The Carnivore Queen.

That didn't mean she got to avoid the night shift, of course. It was, after all, the busiest and most productive time of day for the Magic Lantern team. But what did it matter? Despite her striking good looks, dazzling blue eyes, and feisty, infectious laugh, she hadn't been out on a date since she'd first joined the Home team. Working twelve to fourteen hours a day might have something to do with that, her roommates kept telling her. But the lack of a social life was getting old, and it just made her work all the more.

Carrie Downing now froze. Any trace of fatigue or self-pity suddenly and instantly evaporated. She stared at the freshly intercepted e-mail but had no idea what to do with it. She knew who'd received it. The target— Stuart Iverson, the U.S. treasury secretary, and his private AOL account— was one of sixty-three e-mail accounts of top administration officials personally authorized by the FBI director himself to be monitored. But it wasn't Iverson per se that caught her attention. Not at the moment. It was the sender's name that made her blood run cold.

She quickly ran a trace and a systems check, then triple-checked her results. An involuntary shudder rippled through Downing's body. Everything she'd been doing for the FBI had been fun and cool and clandestine—until now. This was different, and she knew it. She could feel her heart racing and the beads of perspiration forming on her upper lip. She quickly picked up the phone in front of her and speed-dialed the watch commander in the Counterterrorism Op Center downstairs.

This one was hot—and way above her pay grade.

* * *

The president lifted his head again and began to speak calmly and confidently.

"All right. Hear me out. I'm not saying this is what we're going to do. But try this on for size for a moment."

Bennett glanced at the monitor trained on Tucker Paine. He couldn't help but feel for him. The man looked stricken.

The president gathered his thoughts, then continued. "Let's say I call Prime Minister Doron back again when we're done with this meeting. I refuse to acknowledge his request. I simply say that I'm calling to inform him that I am launching a massive air strike against Iraq immediately. Moreover, I tell him that based on rapidly developing and very disturbing new intelligence, the United States is immediately declaring war on Iraq. We will be unleashing the full fury of our military might on Saddam Hussein's regime. And I tell him that in the course of the next few days, we may—I repeat, *may*—be forced to use one or more weapons of mass destruction against Iraq. Would his government and country support the United States if such a series of actions were to ensue?"

Now Bob Corsetti broke in for the first time. "Right. Pledge war, but hedge on one-hundred-percent commitment to going nuclear. Start an air campaign immediately. Bomb Baghdad and Tikrit back to the Stone Age and send the 82nd into the western deserts of Iraq to hunt for any mobile Scud missile launchers. That will buy us time. If you need to go all the way, you can make that decision. Hopefully, that won't be necessary. But in no way can we acknowledge that we've been asked by Israel to do this. If we do this, we'll need to do it without Israeli fingerprints."

"Absolutely," echoed Kirkpatrick. "But you have Jack or Burt or me— probably Jack—call Defense Minister Modine back immediately after the president's call to the Israeli prime minister and personally insist that the Israelis neither strike first nor ever allow word of their commando action to leak out. And he can tell them we need the warhead in our possession in Washington by seven o'clock eastern tonight."

Now the vice president jumped in.

"Exactly. You address the nation at nine tonight. You explain that the United States has just foiled an Iraqi effort to launch a nuclear missile at the State of Israel. You announce that you consider such an act an attack against the United States of America. You explain that our actions to date have wiped out most of the world's terrorist cells. But you help people understand that this has moved beyond a war on terrorists, that the government of Iraq has declared war on us and put us in existential danger. You tell the world our forces—no, *American-made Apaches*—went in and took out an Iraqi Scud team and captured this warhead. You show photographs to the world; explain the Iraqi biological, chemical, and nuclear threat; and explain that if decisive action is not taken immediately, no one will be safe from Saddam Hussein's weapons of mass destruction."

"Then, Mr. President," added Kirkpatrick, "you declare war. You say that the 'full and courageous forces of freedom will prevail against the cowardly forces of evil' and that Americans and 'all freedom-loving people the world over must now prepare for the darkest moment in our history as a civilization.' You prepare people for what we're going to do and why, and you ask them to pray with you and for our armed forces during this moment of grave national peril."

"Then you end," Corsetti added, "by telling the Iraqis, 'May God have mercy on your souls. For we will have none.'"

"No," said the president, raising his hand in opposition to Corsetti's remark. "We're not going to end on a note of vengeance, however well deserved."

"Mr. President, I—"

"No, Bob, I know what you mean. But the answer is no. Look, I need to lay out the case against Iraq. It will be clear and concise and convincing. But we also need to start talking about a new case, a case for peace and prosperity, beginning in the Middle East. Not in the speech tonight. But among ourselves, and with the Israelis and Palestinians."

"Sir, what are you talking about?" asked Secretary Paine.

"I'm talking about a post-Saddam world. I'm talking about ending the threat of war and violence in the Middle East once and for all. I'm talking about bringing the Israelis and Palestinians together here at the White House. I'm talking about a peace treaty and the oil deal Bennett's been working on. Why? To allow every single Jew and every single Arab to personally profit and prosper if they agree to live together in peace. To offer the world a future and a hope, plans for good and not for evil."

A wave of intense anxiety mixed with gnawing curiosity washed over everyone, including Secretary Paine. They were fast running out of time, and they didn't quite know where the president was headed.

"Okay, I know time is limited—but follow me here for a few moments," MacPherson continued. "We need an endgame, right? Okay. So think about it. If the world is about to live through a nightmare, let's be ready to offer it a dream as well. The dream of true Arab-Israeli peace—not because they all will love each other but because the price of war is too high and the profits of peace are too lucrative."

"What would that mean, sir?" pressed Paine.

"Well, here's what I'm thinking . . ." The president paused a moment to sip some water and clarify his thoughts. "The moment the war with Iraq is over, we immediately begin working with the Israelis and Palestinians to turn Medexco into a publicly traded company. Officers of the company will be rich beyond their wildest dreams. But we basically insist that every Israeli and Palestinian be given shares in the company from the beginning, from the IPO."

"The way Thatcher did in Britain," Bennett interjected, fortunately without being shot down by Kirkpatrick or anyone else.

"Sort of," replied the president. "Every Israeli and Palestinian would own shares of the company. The Joshua Fund would supply the billion dollars in venture capital. That deal's already done. All the Joshua Fund investors retain their shares—but by going public, Israelis and Palestinians could become instantly, miraculously wealthy."

"You're really talking about co-opting Bennett's deal?" asked Kirkpatrick.

"Absolutely," said the president. "You've all been briefed on the basic details, right?"

"We have, sir," responded Kirkpatrick. "But I'm not sure how it applies here, sir."

Bennett's heart was racing and his mind was whirling. But he felt clearer than ever in his life.

The president glanced at him and smiled, then continued. "Most people have no idea what the Israelis and Palestinians are sitting on in terms of oil and gas. That may include some of you, even if you've read the file. But it's unreal, almost unimaginable. At first we thought it was just natural gas. But last year they discovered oil. Unbelievable amounts of oil. To put it in context, you need to compare it with Saudi Arabia, which of course is the world's largest oil producer, with about a quarter of the world's known petroleum reserves. The Saudis pump about eight and half million barrels a day, right? So when oil is between twenty-five and thirty dollars a barrel, they gross well over two hundred million dollars a day—nearly eighty to ninety *billion* dollars a year, at current prices. Now Bennett and McCoy and their team believe that once all the drilling and refinery equipment is in place and everything is running at full speed, Medexco could rapidly become one of the largest petroleum companies in the world. It could eventually pump between five and six million barrels a day, grossing—conservatively—about fifty to sixty *billion* dollars a year, just from raw oil and gas sales alone, to say nothing of all the other refined products and retail sales they could have."

"There's really that much oil and gas there?" asked the vice president.

"There is," said the president. "In fact, when you factor in all the other potential products and sources of revenue for which we—well, not me anymore—for which GSX and the Joshua Fund have developed a detailed business plan, Medexco could, before too long, do gross annual sales of somewhere on the order of $180 billion to $220 billion a year."

"That's more than Israel's entire GDP right now," noted the VP.

"That's right. That's the magnitude we're talking about. Israel's GDP is about $120 billion a year at the moment. This oil deal would absolutely change everything. And that's not all. All this would make Medexco one of the largest oil companies in the world, on the order of, say, Exxon-Mobil, which does about a quarter of a trillion dollars a year in gross sales."

"The company will be worth a bloody fortune," Secretary Paine gasped, previously unclear about what Bennett had been cooking up.

"Now, of course," continued MacPherson, "all of these figures were best-case scenarios based on low-intensity violence in the region, but no war. Obviously, these massive oil and gas drilling platforms and refinery facilities would be incredibly vulnerable to attack, making the investment practically worthless to most investors if the region were to see continually aggressive terrorism or plunge into a war."

"That's how Bennett got in so cheap?" asked the VP.

Bennett looked back at the president, who nodded assent for him to speak.

"That's true, sir," said Bennett. "Remember John D. Rockefeller's little investment in Standard Oil back in 1862? He invested just four thousand dollars at the time. But seven years later . . ."

". . . he owned about ninety percent of the company," finished the VP, "and was sitting on a gold mine."

"Exactly," said Bennett. "And the rest is history. That's why GSX so strongly recommended that the Joshua Fund invest a billion dollars in this project immediately. Because few others would take the risk in such an environment. Now, of course, if we had peace . . ."

"You mean if Iraq was essentially eliminated from the face of the planet," Secretary Paine corrected.

Bennett refused to take the bait. ". . . if we had peace—real peace, lasting peace of some sort—all these calculations become moot, or conservative at best. The real value of the company could be many times higher, virtually overnight."

"Where would you go from there?" asked the VP.

Bennett looked back for guidance, but the president didn't stop him.

"My sense is that we'd be able to leverage our initial investment into an IPO and raise hundreds of billions of dollars in capital to complete all the necessary facilities much faster than expected. We'd see the creation of huge shipping ports in Gaza. We'd see the Egyptians involved very quickly. I imagine they'd be interested in building huge refineries in the Sinai desert."

"What about Jordan?" asked Paine.

"I think Jordan's going to absolutely love this," said Bennett, smiling. "Erin?"

"Absolutely," McCoy jumped in. "Jon and I war-gamed this out. We believe the Jordanians could either invest in Medexco directly—or build refinery facilities and the like on their own land—or, Jon and I think more likely, they'd move quickly to develop high-end housing communities, resorts, golf courses. Their competitive advantage is they've got land and space and a good workforce. You put some serious capital in that country and look out. Our projection is that Gaza, the West Bank, and the Sinai would likely become the new Saudi Arabias, focusing on the actual drilling, refining, and industrial development of the petroleum. We believe Israel would become the new Silicon Valley and Switzerland of the region, emerging as one of the world's great high-tech banking, financial services, and health-care capitals. Jordan, we suspect, could become the Palm Springs or Phoenix of the region—you know, tourists, trade, resorts, luxury spas . . ."

"A world of Biltmores and Ritz-Carltons?" asked the VP.

"Something like that," McCoy agreed.

Now MacPherson stepped back into the conversation. "The opportunities would be extraordinary. Israel and any Palestinian entity or state that emerged from a final peace negotiation could both potentially become wealthier and more powerful economically than most of the other OPEC countries—combined."

Bennett noticed that the secretary of state, among others, was clearly intrigued by what he was hearing.

"And a publicly traded Medexco," Bennett interjected, "with the vast majority of shares held, at least initially, by Israeli and Palestinian citizens—unless they chose to sell off—would be a godsend to the people there, particularly Arab families, many of whom are absolutely destitute and poverty-stricken."

"Best guess, Jon?" asked the president.

Bennett turned to McCoy. "Erin?"

"Mr. President, our projections suggest that every Israeli and Palestinian could, one year from an IPO, be holding stock worth somewhere between a half a million and a million dollars per family."

"Are you serious?" asked the vice president.

"A couple of years from now," McCoy added, "if things stay peaceful and on track—and if people keep their stocks rather than sell out after the IPO and the subsequent holding period—they could very well be sitting on several multiples of that."

"Just to put it in perspective," Bennett added, "the average Palestinian family today earns less than fifteen hundred dollars a year. We'd be turning most of them into multimillionaires essentially overnight."

"Unbelievable," remarked Kirkpatrick, rapidly calculating the cost-benefit analysis as well. "The incentives for peace—real peace, lasting peace, a secure peace—would be extraordinary."

"What are the implications for the U.S. in your estimation, Jon?" asked the VP.

"Well, sir, I think I'd better defer to the president on that," Bennett said, turning to MacPherson.

"Thanks, Jon," said the president, already formulating his reply. "I guess, Bill, what I'd say is that this could seriously jump-start the global economy and avoid the total collapse in consumer and investor confidence we could see soon if we don't move decisively on a series of fronts. I'd say that the pure psychic shock of neutralizing the planet's greatest evil, and then—in fairly short order—announcing the discovery and development of oil and gas in the Holy Land, followed by a major peace treaty ceremony on the South Lawn of the White House, would absolutely electrify investors and consumers all over the world. Suddenly, anything and everything would seem possible. Peace and prosperity would be seen as the defining charter of the new millennium. I think consumer confidence would come roaring back instantly. It could be unlike anything we've ever seen before."

"Or not," added Mitchell.

"Right," agreed the president. "Or not. We have one opportunity to make all this work. If we get it right, the rest of the world will have a chance to get it right. But if we blow it, we and the rest of the world will be in very, very serious trouble."

Everyone now contemplated the enormity of the decisions about to be made. But clearly the mood and momentum were changing dramatically.

"Now, obviously, I could be totally wrong about this," MacPherson added. "But, you know, my gut instincts have served me well over the years."

"So they have, Mr. President," said the VP.

"But, sir," interrupted Secretary Paine, "we are still talking about having to use nuclear weapons to achieve all this."

"That's true."

"Then, Mr. President, I must repeat once again that it is not worth it. I beg you. I implore you. Please don't do this."

"Mr. Secretary, I hear what you're saying. I do."

"How can you even begin to consider incinerating several million souls with the push of a button, in the blink of an eye? We cannot become the barbarians we've been forced to fight. The end never justifies the means. Never. That was the lesson of Hiroshima and Nagasaki. That was the lesson of Vietnam. And that was the lesson of the Soviet experience in Afghanistan. How can you—?"

"Mr. Secretary, that's absolutely not true," the president shot back, firmly but fiercely. "That is not true. It just isn't. The lesson of Vietnam was never fight a just war—a war against an evil empire and its proxies who seek to enslave mankind—unless you intend to win. The lesson of Afghanistan was don't fight a war you have no business winning. And the lesson of Hiroshima and Nagasaki, Mr. Secretary, was that a president must never—*never*—flinch from using any and all means necessary to prevent the wholesale slaughter of American citizens and our allies."

"Sir, this is repaying evil for evil. It's becoming the very essence of what we hope to defeat."

"No, no, no—it's not. It's not. It's stopping evil once and for all."

"How? By using the instruments of evil, the instruments of war?"

"The instruments of war are not evil, Mr. Secretary. Not in and of themselves. Not unless they are in the hands of those who use them for evil. Preventing the slaughter of innocent Americans is not evil. It is profoundly moral and inherently just."

"Mr. President? Do you hear yourself? Do you? Let's say we invade Iraq. Maybe—*maybe*—we'll lose fifty thousand Americans. Maybe. But maybe not. It's a worst-case scenario. But you're talking about murdering fifty times that number, guaranteed, and civilians at that."

"Whose side are you on here, Tucker?"

Paine looked stunned. "I resent that, sir."

"So do I," the president continued. "My oath was to uphold the U.S. Constitution and protect and defend the American people from all threats, foreign and domestic—*not* to protect and defend every man, woman, and child on the face of the earth. I am not God. I am not responsible for everyone. I am responsible to make sure our innocents—American innocents—are not slaughtered. Not by Saddam Hussein. Not by Mohammed Jibril. Not by the next Osama bin Laden. Nobody. Ever. Period. End of story. I didn't bring us to the point of nuclear war, Mr. Secretary. Saddam did. But I am not sending ten thousand or twenty thousand or fifty thousand or even five hundred Americans to their certain deaths in a protracted ground war in Iraq—not when I know that Saddam has nuclear weapons and anthrax and Sarin gas and VX . . . not when I know Saddam is dying, desperate, hates us, and might think he has nothing to lose . . . not when I know that our people could be slaughtered by the Butcher of Baghdad. *That*, Mr. Secretary, would be evil. I won't be part of it, and you shouldn't be either."

For the first time, Bennett was glad these two men were not in the same room. It might have come to blows, no matter how badly injured the president was. Nevertheless, as much as he loved the president and thought he made sense, Bennett found himself internally siding with Paine.

He didn't know what the president should do beyond launching air strikes. But he knew that under no circumstances should he resort to nuclear weapons. And in the end, Bennett was convinced that no matter how powerful and passionate an argument MacPherson was making now, in a few hours he would cool down and change course. Of this he had no doubt.

"It is this that I won't be part of," the secretary responded, just as passionately. "You are talking about pushing the button and then drilling for oil and making everyone in Israel and Palestine fat and happy. You're talking about your little pipe dream, Medexco. And I agree, it *is* compelling. It *is* attractive. And under other circumstances it might be perfect. But right here, right now, it does not wash. You cannot kill millions of innocent Iraqis with a nuclear weapon and then hold an IPO. It is wrong, Mr. President. Profoundly wrong. And it is conduct unbecoming of you and the American people."

"You are out of line, Mr. Secretary," said the president. "Let me be perfectly clear. If the United States decides to use nuclear weapons against murderous enemies, it will not be in order to bring peace and prosperity to Israel and the Palestinians. No. It will be to protect the lives and vital national interests of our people and our allies—and to rid civilization of a mortal threat to its very survival. Period. What I was asked, Mr. Secretary, is what might come next. What I was asked was where we might go next after making such a dreadful and horrible decision. And what I'm saying is that this is one answer. Not the only answer. It's not a panacea. But it is one answer among many. Yes, the world will still have problems. Yes, we'll still have to deal with North Korea and China and the Sudan and AIDS and cancer and poverty and racism and all the other sins and ills and plagues that existed last week and last month. But I'm saying this could be one of many silver linings to a very dark cloud. This could be the dream of a sunny day after a terrible gathering storm. *That's* what I'm talking about, Mr. Secretary. And I deeply resent your implications to the contrary."

★ ★ ★

Bennett's back and necked ached terribly.

He found himself hunched over, clenched up, deeply anxious about where this was leading.

"Mr. President, we only have eighteen minutes."

It was Mitchell. Time was running out.

"Ladies and gentlemen," said the president, "we need to begin to set things in motion. There will be time to make a final decision. But there are some things we need to do immediately."

Bennett instinctively reached for McCoy's hand under the table and squeezed gently. She glanced over at him and squeezed back.

"Secretary Trainor."

"Yes, sir."

"I hereby direct you to commence Operation Imminent Cyclone immediately. Begin massive bombing runs against Baghdad, Tikrit, and all Iraqi air bases. Use conventional munitions only. Flush the bombers—the B-52s, F-18s, F-111s, the whole team. Use conventional cruise missiles and Tomahawks off the carriers to begin with—and make it hurt."

"Yes, sir, Mr. President."

"Get the 82nd and Delta Force on the ground immediately, hunting down those Scuds. How far away are they right now?"

"Almost there, sir. They've been flying from the U.S. all night."

"Good. Get SEAL Team Six and the guys from the Nuclear Emergency Search Team on a chopper headed toward Baghdad. I want them in
the theater as fast as possible. The minute we get any whiff of another
possible nuclear launch, we'll send them in like the Israelis' GhostCom
force to disable the missile and recover the warhead. But look—we don't
have much time and we've got to keep the Israelis and the Saudis out of
this war. You got that?"

"Yes, sir."

"Okay. Then launch B-2s out of Whiteman and get them to Incirlik,
Turkey, as fast as you can. Have them each locked and loaded with those
tactical nuclear missiles. And get their targeting packages ready for Baghdad and Tikrit, just in case. This goes without saying, but I want it said to
those pilots anyway, by you personally, Mr. Secretary: those pilots may not
release those nuclear missiles except on my direct command and with the
appropriate nuclear launch authorization codes. I have not made my final
decision. But I want them to be in place if necessary. Let's just pray to God
it doesn't come to that."

"Yes, sir." The defense secretary picked up a secure line back to the
Joint Chiefs at the Pentagon and set things in motion.

"Sanchez?"

"Yes, Mr. President."

"Get Football in here and at my side ASAP—and have him call back to
the National Military Command Center at the Pentagon and get briefed."

"I'll do it right now, sir."

"Good. Bill, get on the horn with all the congressional leadership.
I know they're scattered all over the country, but I need them on a conference call as fast as you possibly can get it arranged."

"Yes, sir."

"Bob, get me Prime Minister Doron on the phone immediately. Then
get me Chairman Arafat on a separate line. And go get Chuck Murray.
Have him line up the networks for tonight and begin to coordinate some
leaks. Make them work, Bill. We can't afford to blow it now."

"Yes, sir."

"Then call Shakespeare back at the White House. Get him working
on a draft speech for tonight. And check with Public Liaison. I want the
details of the memorial service, and make sure the First Lady has them,

too. I'd like to see if Franklin Graham could come and speak. Call him yourself, Bob. Let him know I'll call him the moment I can."

"You got it, sir." Corsetti moved to the other end of the conference room, grabbed a secure phone, and got a White House operator on the line to begin making things happen.

"Marsha, get all the allies on the phone. Start with London. Then President Vadim in Moscow."

"Mr. President?"

It was Secretary Paine. He was clearly being left out of the loop, but he no longer seemed enraged.

Nevertheless, the president continued to be very formal with him. "Yes, Mr. Secretary?"

"One question."

"What?"

"Mr. President, you are unleashing the power of the gods, and with it the law of unintended consequences. Who's to say what will happen next? What if Moscow decides it needs to use nuclear weapons someday? Or Beijing or Pyongyang or India or Pakistan? What if Tehran ever decides to go nuclear against Israel? What then? What would we do? What could we possibly say when they look us in the eye and say, 'Hey, you did it first'?"

The silence was almost eerie.

"Mr. Secretary, I've got less than fifteen minutes. We don't live in a perfect world, and I guess I'll just have to cross those bridges when I come to them. For now, I've got a job to do. And I'm going to do it."

The president nodded to Corsetti and the transmission was cut. The videoconference call was over. The debate was finished. Now it was time for the hard part—shutting down Saddam before Iraq could actually launch a nuclear missile. And time was running out.

* * *

David Doron stared at his colleagues, took a deep breath, and picked up the call.

"Mr. President, I trust you have an answer."

"Mr. Prime Minister, I am calling to inform you that the United States has just launched full-scale war on the Republic of Iraq."

The exhausted Israeli prime minister exhaled with relief.

"Our cruise missiles are in the air," MacPherson continued. "Our bombers are taking off as we speak. We're deploying ground forces as quickly as we can. You have my word: we are going to take down Saddam Hussein and neutralize his military machine no matter what it takes."

"That is welcome news, my friend."

"At 9 p.m. eastern I will make a televised address from the Oval Office, explaining the events that led up to this moment. I will explain why our national security, our vital interests, and our friends and allies are in grave danger. And I will describe our course of action. But David, as a friend, I need to know one thing."

"Yes, Mr. President?"

"If I find it necessary to order the use of a weapon of mass destruction against Iraq, finding no other course of action effective in neutralizing Saddam's forces quickly enough, would your government back us publicly and at the U.N.?"

"We would," Doron replied instantly. "How else can we help?"

"You can stand down your nuclear forces, David," MacPherson said softly but firmly.

There was a long pause.

"Please don't ask that of me," Doron replied.

"I must. It would be bad enough for the U.S. to use such weapons. But make no mistake—there will be terrible international repercussions if your country were to use them. That I can assure you."

"Mr. President, I am well aware of the risks we face in terms of international opinion. Even international trade. But we are on the brink, sir. We are talking about the very survival of the Jewish race as we know it. My government wishes you well in this military campaign. But let me be clear—if we see the slightest indication that Iraq is again prepared to use such catastrophic force, we will act. We will act decisively. We will act with cataclysmic force. And we will act without warning."

"I urge you to reconsider," MacPherson responded, his mind scrambling to find a coherent argument—any argument—to dissuade the Israeli leader.

"That I cannot do."

"Then I guess my country better get the job done, so you won't have to take matters into your own hands."

12

⋆ ⋆
⋆

IT WAS A KILLER STORM—in the wrong place at the wrong time.

It was daytime in the Middle East. But it looked and felt like the dead of night. The winds were gusting over the Mediterranean—as well as over Lebanon, northern Syria, and northern Iraq—at upward of forty to fifty knots.

Massive sheets of rain were moving horizontally. Bolts of lightning lit up the dark and ominous sky, allowing anyone brave enough or stupid enough to be on the pitching, heaving decks of the two American nuclear-powered aircraft carriers to see monstrous waves cresting at thirty to forty feet.

It was no time to go to war. But then soldiers, sailors, and airmen never get to choose when they go into battle.

The flash-traffic e-mail arrived from CENTCOM, and it was red-hot. The message was quickly decoded, printed, shoved in a black folder marked "Top Secret," and rushed to the captains of each ship. Minutes later—despite the raging storm—dozens of fighter jets began catapulting off the decks of the USS *Theodore Roosevelt* and the USS *Ronald Reagan*, the newest ninety-seven-thousand-ton, state-of-the-art, Nimitz-class American aircraft carrier patrolling the Med.

The commander in chief had spoken. America was going to war— now. And the man in the gunsights was Saddam Hussein.

⋆　⋆　⋆

"Downing, don't mess with me."

Sam Maxwell—the counterterrorism watch commander sitting

behind a bank of sixteen computers and five giant TV screens in the FBI's fifth-floor OPS2 center—couldn't believe what he was hearing over the phone. "I'm in no mood for a joke."

"No joke, sir. I'm telling you, I just got it. I triple-checked it. It's real."

"You're telling me Treasury Secretary Iverson just got an e-mail from Yuri Gogolov?"

"Yes, sir."

"And he opened it?"

"Yes. It was forwarded from his personal AOL account to his Black-Berry—*and he opened it right on Air Force One.* Then deleted it. It's a weird note, too. I don't get it. And I don't know what to do. I thought you and the director should see it right away."

"Got that right, Downing. Okay. Sit tight. Don't tell anyone. I'm coming to you."

* * *

The president finished his call with Doron and turned back to Bennett.

"Jon, the minute we get to Andrews, I want you and Erin and Deek to get on a plane and head back to Israel immediately. I'll brief you guys in the air. But when you land, you'll need to huddle with Galishnikov and Sa'id and let them know what I want to do with this peace plan. Then you all need to meet personally—but separately—with Doron and Arafat. Walk them through this peace-plan scenario. Step by step. Piece by piece. Doron is trigger-happy right now. I don't blame him. But we need to get him and his team thinking about life *after* we take out Saddam—about the endgame. Arafat is another story. He may only be an honorary figurehead leader now, not the actual duly elected leader of the Palestinian Authority anymore, but don't kid yourself. He and his loyalists still effectively run the place. He's the man you need to persuade. And the key with Arafat, Jon, is to make one thing crystal clear. He either signs on to this deal—a deal that will make him and the Palestinian people richer than they've ever hoped for, dreamed of, or imagined—or he and his cronies are finished."

The ominous words just hung in the air. Ultimatums weren't Mac-Pherson's style, thought Bennett. But then again, neither was nuclear war.

"I *will* cut off all U.S. aid to him," the president continued. "I *will* send in the rangers and Delta Force to hunt down his terrorists. And then we'll go after him. Personally, I've had it with Arafat and his whole corrupt bunch. It's time for them to lead, follow, or get out of the way. If I have to wipe out Iraq, then believe me, we're going to knock heads together and get peace throughout the region or there are going to be serious consequences for the Palestinian leadership. Got it?"

Bennett just stared at his friend the president in disbelief.

"You got a problem with that, Jon?"

"No, Mr. President, I just . . ."

"You just what?"

"I'm sorry . . . I mean . . . an hour ago I worked on Wall Street. Now you want me to go to Israel to negotiate a peace plan with Yasser Arafat while Saddam Hussein rains nuclear missiles down on our heads?"

"First of all, Iraq isn't going to get a second chance to fire any missiles, nuclear or otherwise. Second of all, who am I going to send, Tucker Paine? You know the situation. You know this oil deal. And you know me. You're it, Jon. You do your part and I guarantee you I'll do mine. I'm not going to let Iraq nuke Israel. Period."

The president's case wasn't all that convincing, much less comforting, thought Bennett. The prospect of dying in a nuclear holocaust in a country he knew so little about—and cared about even less—nearly paralyzed the normally unflappable Bennett. But what choice did he have? Those were the cards he'd been dealt. And one thing was for sure: he couldn't afford to lose.

★ ★ ★

Daylight is no time to fly into the heart of darkness.

But they had no choice.

In Saudi Arabia, the issue at the moment wasn't a raging electrical storm. It was a blinding sandstorm that dangerously reduced visibility. But America was at DefCon One, sandstorm or no sandstorm.

So, without warning, twenty-two F-15E Strike Eagles—part of the 48th Fighter Wing (dubbed the Liberty Wing during the Eisenhower administration)—roared out of Prince Sultan Air Base near Al Kharj, Saudi Arabia, about an hour southeast of Riyadh, and shot hard, fast, and low over the desert, heading north into Iraq.

Their orders were straight from CENTCOM in Tampa: take out

Iraq's air defense installations, establish 100 percent American air superiority, and then hunt down and destroy Iraq's mobile missile launchers.

Scud hunting was like a finding a needle in a haystack at five thousand feet going Mach 2. But first they needed to dominate the skies. That's what each pilot and his weapon-systems officer were trained to do. But it took time. And time was one thing of which they had very little.

It was going to be a supersonic game of cat and mouse, with one little twist.

The mice might be nuclear.

★　★　★

He'd lost the element of surprise.

But he still had cards to play.

General Azziz, sitting alone in his private command center—staring at a bank of computer screens providing him the latest updates on the mobilization of his elite Republican Guard forces and his agents overseas—knew he could still deliver a knockout punch. The only question was when.

He quickly tapped out three cryptic e-mail messages. The first was to the four horsemen, now racing out of Russia to get into position as quickly as possible. Their mission: assassinate Dmitri Galishnikov ("the dirty Jew," barked Saddam) and Ibrahim Sa'id ("that filthy traitor to his people," the Iraqi leader had added), then launch a bloody suicide-bombing campaign in Jerusalem, Tel Aviv, Haifa, and Eilat. The second e-mail was to his "assets" outside of Moscow—Gogolov and Jibril—activating another phase of the terror campaign. The third was to his fail-safe, "Mr. C," deep inside the U.S.

Next Azziz picked up a phone and barked commands in Arabic to his senior deputy in the larger command-and-control center down the hall.

"Send out the general alarm. We should be expecting American planes within the hour. All forces prepare for battle. And seal up the bunker. The battle is about to begin."

★　★　★

Air Force One finally landed at Andrews at four-thirty Friday morning.

Only two days had elapsed since the initial kamikaze attack on the president and his motorcade in Denver. Yet everything had changed.

The president, Corsetti, Football, and a team of Secret Service agents—led by Jackie Sanchez—flew *Marine One* and a backup helicopter back to the White House to get an update on the first air strikes. Iverson directed his security detail to take him home. He needed to shower, shave, change his clothes, and take care of some urgent business before he headed back to Treasury to work the phones and help manage the crisis.

Bennett, Black, and McCoy, meanwhile, grabbed their luggage and crashed in an officers' lounge until their G4—trailing *Air Force One* all night—was refueled, restocked, and ready to whisk them back to Israel.

A long day's journey into night was about to get much longer.

★　★　★

By 5 a.m., Iverson was back at his newly purchased sprawling Georgetown mansion.

His Secret Service detail took up their standard positions around the house and inside the front and back doors. Iverson immediately headed upstairs to his bedroom, flipped on CNN's breaking news coverage of the mushrooming military crisis in the Middle East, and booted up his personal laptop on the desk beside his antique canopy bed. By the time he finished taking a quick hot shower and donning a freshly dry-cleaned Brooks Brothers suit, his computer was already logged on to AOL and downloading his e-mails. It had been a while since he'd even had time to check this account.

"You've got mail," said the pleasant voice, heard more than 40 million times a day, more than twenty-seven thousand times a minute, by AOL subscribers worldwide.

Most of his e-mails were junk. Except one. The last one. It had arrived just a few minutes before, as though the sender knew he'd be coming home, though he couldn't possibly have. Iverson was afraid to open it. It was marked inconspicuously *Special offer/rush order.* But he knew immediately what it was, whom it was from, whom it had been forwarded from, and what it would say.

```
Mr. I—you must RESPOND NOW to our SPECIAL OFFER. Send
us your entry and CLAIM YOUR PRIZE. Reminder: if we
don't hear from you within twenty-four hours, the offer
```

```
will be null and void. And Mr. C—next on the list—will
win. Don't let that happen. ACT TODAY.
```

Iverson knew what it was, all right. He'd even fully expected it. Never-theless, now that it had arrived, he just stared in disbelief. Evidence of the horror yet to come. Unless he sent back his own brilliantly conceived plan by Saturday morning, someone—he didn't know who—was going to set into motion their plan to assassinate the president of the United States. And soon. Especially if the U.S. started bombing Baghdad back into the Stone Age.

He had no idea who this sleeper agent—this "Mr. C."—was. Nor had he any way to contact him. Especially not as the new secretary of the Treasury. Not now that he oversaw the U.S. Secret Service, responsible for the protection of the president. No one had expected that to happen. Least of all him. But here he was. If he wanted to go through with the plan, it should be even easier, given the new role fate had given him to play.

But what if he wanted to call it off? That would be tougher. How could he actually inform Secret Service director Bud Norris about a sleeper agent he knew nothing about? And how would he explain exactly how he knew a hit on the president was imminent without implicating himself?

Everything was happening too fast. When he'd met Gogolov years before, he'd had no idea what he was getting into or where that relation-ship would lead. How could he have?

Iverson stopped and thought about that for a moment. Was that really true? Was this really such a surprise? Maybe not.

Born January 23, 1940, in a tiny hamlet in the Swiss Alps, Iverson was the only child of a powerful banking family. Iverson's mother, also an only child, forced a bitter, painful divorce in the spring of 1948 after finding her husband in a vault with his secretary. The ensuing custody battle was a particularly nasty affair, a shrill, demeaning bid by both parents to force their son to take sides.

Eventually securing sole custody, Iverson's mother rapidly set about using her contacts and her own considerable personal fortune—nearly $69 million, left to her after the death of her parents—to immigrate to the

U.S. and set up a new life in New York. Refusing him the chance to ever see his father again, she immediately sent Stuart off to a series of boarding schools in Delaware and Massachusetts, preparing him to eventually attend and graduate from Harvard with both a BS and an MBA and hopefully go back into banking, where her parents and their parents and their parents had made their fortunes.

The problem was that Stuart had no interest in banking. Not as a career, at least. Fluent in French, German, and Russian, he joined the State Department's foreign service division and headed overseas after leaving Harvard, variously posted in Hong Kong, Prague, Paris, and Bonn before arriving in Moscow as an economic attaché in the summer of 1973. It was then that he was introduced to Yuri Gogolov, a former *Spetznatz* commander who'd become the director of security at Russia's central bank, and his career began to take a radical, unexpected turn.

Perhaps U.S. counterintelligence officials should have seen it coming. Rich, restless, and devoid of deep personal, professional, or financial ties in the U.S., Iverson was, perhaps, a classic Soviet espionage recruit. Except that he was never recruited by the KGB to spy against the U.S. He was recruited by Gogolov to spy against the Soviet Union.

As the two slowly became friends between 1973 and 1979, Iverson—who did two tours of duty in Moscow as an economic attaché, then was transferred back to the State Department to monitor Soviet economic affairs until he later became the U.S. ambassador to Moscow in 1989—slowly came to learn that Gogolov was actually a mole inside the Bank of Russia. But he wasn't working for a foreign intelligence service. He was working for himself. A fierce Russian nationalist, Gogolov was intensely opposed to the presence of the Soviet Communist regime in his homeland, and deeply angered by the rampant corruption of the politburo, which he saw up close and personal every day in his position at the Bank of Russia.

Gogolov's dream—indeed, his mission in life—was to undermine the Kremlin from inside, to recruit and raise up an enormous underground cadre of nationalist insurgents, dedicated to reclaiming "Russia for the Russians" and to burying the Communists as Nikita Sergeyevich Khrushchev had once threatened to bury the West.

When the Soviet Union invaded Afghanistan in 1979, Gogolov—then responsible for the security of all Russian central banking officials in

Moscow—believed he could see the beginning of the end. Afghanistan would become the Soviets' Vietnam. Kabul would become Moscow's Hanoi. The more eighteen- and nineteen-year-old Russian-born soldiers who died at the hands of the *mujahedin*, the more support Gogolov found for his cause.

That's where Iverson came in. In the summer of 1981, at a Black Sea resort where the two both vacationed, Gogolov made his move. He asked Iverson to begin investing a small portion of his personal funds—safe and out of the sight of the FBI in an anonymous account in a bank in Basel, Switzerland—in a complicated but fascinating scheme.

First, together, they would start buying the loyalties of junior up-and-coming Soviet military and political officers posted throughout the various Soviet republics. Then, they would begin funding a new paramilitary unit Gogolov was developing, run by a shadowy operative from Tehran by the name of Mohammed Jibril. Gogolov's *Spetznatz* connections were already identifying men who could be trusted to sign up. But they needed at least small amounts of cash to seal the deals and provide incentives for each new recruit to recruit still more members.

The goal, Gogolov made clear, was not to harm U.S. interests, but to further them—to use a little venture capitalism to destabilize the Soviet empire from within and leave the U.S. the only true superpower on the planet. Of this outcome—and Gogolov's motives—Iverson wasn't wholly convinced. But it didn't really matter. The game sounded fun—a whole lot more exciting than the life of a bureaucrat, much less a banker.

On August 2, 1981, Iverson signed on, asking only one thing of his new business partner in return. Iverson wanted to be supplied the latest and most accurate economic and political intelligence on the real state of the Soviet Union developed by this new clandestine network Gogolov was wiring.

The more Iverson knew about the inner workings of the Soviet empire—particularly its economic strengths and weaknesses, and particularly in the area of natural resources such as gas and oil—the more valuable he would be to his superiors in the State Department and to his friends in the White House.

Iverson could see the handwriting on the wall as well. He knew the Soviet Union's days were numbered. And he saw a strategic opportunity to call it first and set himself apart from the hacks all around him who believed Reagan was a lunatic for predicting that the Soviet Union would soon wind up on the ash heap of history. He could scratch Gogolov's back and Gogolov could scratch his. It was the oldest business deal in the book, and though the stakes were high, Iverson concluded the price was right.

What he should have predicted, however, but hadn't, was that a chess player of Yuri Gogolov's caliber would not be satisfied by making friends only of an American like him. He would harbor other ambitions. Bigger ambitions. Deadly ambitions.

Gogolov and Jibril, for example, believed they could eventually build a new Russian-Persian strategic alliance, combining Moscow's nuclear might with Tehran's gas and oil reserves and strategically critical warm-water ports on the Persian Gulf and Indian Ocean. A Russian-Iranian alliance would create the wealthiest and most powerful north-south alliance on the planet, and Gogolov was offering Iverson an opportunity to buy in early.

There was just one obstacle in the way: Iraq.

If Iraq could be neutralized—wiped off the face of the planet forever would be preferable—Gogolov's and Jibril's dream of their Russian-Persian alliance could actually be within striking distance of reality.

The question was, how do you neutralize Iraq? An eight-year war between Baghdad and Tehran had left millions dead, but no winner. So war between the two countries would not be an option. Iraq was a Russian client state. So there was no possibility of inciting a war of Moscow against Baghdad. That left only two nations capable of reducing Iraq to rubble: the U.S. and Israel. How, then, could such nations be prodded into going nuclear against Iraq?

And then came America's "war on terrorism."

In January of 2002, then-president George W. Bush named Iraq, Iran, and North Korea an "Axis of Evil." And Gogolov and Jibril got an idea. It would take time. Careful planning. A lot of money. And some luck. But if they played their chess pieces shrewdly, they could actually buy their way into the good graces of Saddam Hussein, become his putative allies, and offer to help him destroy the U.S., the "Great Satan," and Israel, the "Little Satan."

They would offer Saddam nuclear scientists and nuclear weapons–grade materials. They would offer Saddam the latest intelligence from

Tel Aviv, Jerusalem, London, and Washington. Eventually, to seal the deal, they would actually offer Saddam the assistance of Stuart Iverson, the American president's best friend and closest confidant.

Then, when Saddam least expected it, they would tip off the Israelis and the Americans and set in motion Iraq's ultimate demise. When Iraq was gone, a new Russian-Iranian alliance would be the most powerful player remaining on the geopolitical chessboard. And the real fun would begin.

That, at least, was the theory. Anything could go wrong. But at the moment—as far as Gogolov and Jibril were concerned—all systems were go. And for the moment, they didn't know half of what Iverson knew. The American president was, in fact, poised to go nuclear against Saddam Hussein, and Iverson was gently egging him on.

Becoming treasury secretary, however, had never been part of Iverson's personal plan. Gogolov and Jibril had been ecstatic when they'd heard the news. But Iverson hated the idea. He knew full well that it would bring new and nearly untenable risks—exhaustive background checks, Senate confirmation hearings, constant Secret Service protection, neverending media coverage. It would also deny him what he wanted most: a piece of the financial action from the megadeals he was helping engineer in the shadows.

But there was no turning back now, thought Iverson. He'd sealed his fate long ago.

In 1981, when he first began secretly diverting funds to Gogolov and his inner circle.

In 1995, when he helped Gogolov narrowly escape a frantic Yeltsin mole hunt.

In 1999, when he reconnected with Gogolov at a hotel in Prague and began discussing how much better the Clinton-Gore administration was for Gogolov's purposes than a new, tough, no-nonsense Republican administration.

And certainly by last month, when he'd agreed, however reluctantly, to commit treason and help assassinate the president of the United States. All to become a player in a world of pawns. If he got away with it.

Iverson quickly deleted the e-mail, without responding. He deleted all the e-mails from his AOL account and from his MSN account using

Microsoft Outlook. He then went to *Tools*, scrolled down to *Empty Deleted Items Folder*, and got rid of his trash. Then he logged off, shut down his laptop, and headed back outside to the waiting Lincoln Town Car. He wasn't ready to reply to Gogolov, who would then reply to Azziz. He wasn't ready to give them an answer. Not yet, anyway.

Time was running out. But he needed to be sure. He was tired, hungry, and his head was splitting. And he could hardly afford to make a mistake now.

☆　☆　☆

Maxwell and Downing didn't spend much time here.

Especially not in the wee hours of the morning. But destiny has a strange way of bringing men and women skilled in their work before those who hold power and the wisdom to use it. The two young agents stood on the thick blue carpeting in the seventh-floor executive suite, looking over portraits of Teddy Roosevelt and Bobby Kennedy and Martin Luther King Jr. before a bleary-eyed and none-too-happy Scott Harris.

Unshowered and unshaven, the director wore jeans and a gray sweatshirt sporting the FBI logo and a navy blue baseball cap with *FBI* in white letters stitched across the front.

They watched silently as he read two intercepted e-mails from Gogolov to Treasury Secretary Iverson. The first one Iverson had received and deleted aboard *Air Force One*, and the second he'd received and deleted at his home less than twenty minutes ago. Harris flipped through the sheaf of additional papers in the newly created and highly confidential file on his desk.

Reaching for his bureau mug, topped off with freshly brewed black Gevalia coffee, Harris took several sips before looking up and addressing the two directly. "You're absolutely sure both of these e-mails are from Gogolov?"

"Yes, sir," Downing said quickly, fully cognizant of the chilling implications.

"Agent Maxwell, you concur?"

"Yes, sir. I triple-checked her work. It's solid."

"Have you guys told anyone else about this?"

"No, sir," Downing replied.

"What about these other e-mails?" Harris asked Downing.

"Sir, once I intercepted the first, I considered the possibility that previous e-mails had been sent or received from the secretary's personal home computer before we launched Magic Lantern. Based on the search warrant you gave us after the president's directive, I immediately went into the secretary's hard drive and began reconstructing all of his incoming and outgoing e-mails for the past several years."

"And you found these nine, plus the one that just came in?"

"Yes, sir. Seven from Gogolov. Three sent to him. You can see the dates on each one, sir. The one on the top of the file was transmitted by Mr. Iverson to Gogolov precisely one month to the day before the airborne attack on the president. He received a reply from Gogolov three days later. The next one Mr. Iverson received arrived the day after the attack. And so forth."

"So Iverson initiated the contact."

"Well, sir, I'm not sure we can conclude that. They obviously knew each other before the e-mails began. And they knew each other's personal e-mail addresses. But yes, the text of Mr. Iverson's recent e-mails does suggest he is not a passive player in this whole thing."

"And you don't think he replied to these last two e-mails from Gogolov?"

"Not from his personal computer, at least. Mr. Iverson trashed them both immediately, then tried to get rid of any trace that they had ever arrived."

"What about this one, Max?" asked Harris, picking one particular e-mail out of the pile. "It mentions a trip. Have you cross-checked the dates to see if Iverson really went?"

"Yes, sir. It all checks out. Gogolov says he'll meet Iverson in a café in Prague on August 2, 1999. We've confirmed that Iverson booked a flight on British Airways, leaving Denver, Colorado, on August 1 of that year, arriving in London, transferring to a flight to Prague, and returning to Denver via Basel, Switzerland, on August 4."

Harris leaned back and rubbed the sleep out of his eyes. "So, just to be clear, Max. I need a no-holds-barred assessment. Is it your belief that Secretary Iverson and Yuri Gogolov are complicit in this attack on the president?"

"Yes, sir. It appears that way. Though I would add that they are probably not alone, of course. As you know, sir, Gogolov is known to work closely with Mohammed Jibril. Both have been heavily funding Iraqi intelligence operations, including those of the four horsemen over the past decade."

"How do you assess this newest e-mail?"

"That's what worries me most, sir. I think we're possibly looking at another hit on the president within the next week or so, especially now that we're at war with Iraq. What really troubles me is this reference to a Mr. C."

"Yeah, what do you make of that?" asked Harris, taking a quick sip of coffee.

"I doubt Secretary Iverson knows who Mr. C is. But the implication is that he's some kind of sleeper agent, already positioned here in the U.S., ready to strike at a moment's notice if the secretary doesn't provide his own assassination plan."

Harris was afraid he was right. He grabbed the phone and called down to see if Doug Reed, the head of the FBI's Counterterrorism Division, had made it in yet. It turned out he'd just sat down at his desk.

"Reed, get up here. *Now.*"

☆　☆　☆

Corsetti's phone rang just before six. It was Chuck Murray.

"Chuck, what have you got?"

"Drudge has it already."

"What?"

"Pull it up. See for yourself."

"What are you talking about?"

"Drudge is reporting that we're at war. He's got the story already, and I'm getting killed with calls. The press is furious. Not only didn't they know we were going to war this morning, they also got scooped by Drudge. They're past their deadlines. They've got no information. They're out of control, Bob. And I need to know what to say—fast."

"All right. All right. Calm down. Get the word out that there will be a backgrounder in the pressroom at seven. Tell them a senior official will be briefing."

"Who?"

"I don't know who. If I knew who, I'd tell you who. Just tell them it will be somebody senior. I'll figure it out. And start leaking the word that the president will address the country at 9 p.m. Don't spill all the beans yet, Chuck. But let people know this is the real thing. It's bad. And it's getting worse very, very quickly."

Corsetti slammed down the phone, fired up his computer, and pulled up the Drudge Report.

Sure enough.

There it was.

How did this guy do it—from a little place in Palm Beach, no less?

★ ★ ★

DRUDGE REPORT

XXXX DRUDGE REPORT XXXXX NOV. 26 2010 XXXX
05:49:59 AM ET XXXX

NYT JACKSON: CIA Fingers Saddam Regime
for Assassination Attempts

WP Woodward: President Plots War on Air Force One

WSJ: Israelis and Palestinians Strike Oil;
Huge Find Threatens OPEC

WAR!
DEFCON ONE
U.S. WARPLANES ATTACK IRAQ

** WORLD EXCLUSIVE **
[CREDIT DRUDGE REPORT WHEN QUOTING]

President James MacPherson overnight ordered U.S.
forces to Defense Condition One—war—and authorized

MORE

a massive air strike against Iraq, government sources
tell **THE DRUDGE REPORT**. American airplanes began
pounding Iraqi military bases, radar sites, and SAM
(surface-to-air missile) sites at approximately 4:30
a.m. eastern time. U.S. troops are also headed to the
region.

"Forget surgical strikes," said one senior official.
"The Iraqis tried to kill the president. We're
responding. This is war. And Saddam is finished.
Period."

DEVELOPING . . .

Filed by Matt Drudge
Reports are moved when circumstances warrant
http://www.drudgereport.com for updates

☆   ☆   ☆

Doug Reed was an eighteen-year veteran of the FBI.

Former deputy chief of the bureau's counterintelligence section, he'd also once served as chief of the bureau's international-terrorism section and as head of the Iraq unit of the counterterrorism section. He was also Dietrich Black's direct supervisor and mentor, though they rarely saw much of each other these days.

Reed closed the file and looked up. "Sir, the good news is it looks like you just bagged yourself the highest-ranking spy in American history."

"And?"

"And a definite coconspirator in the assassination attempt against the president."

"So what's the bad news?"

"The bad news is the guy who wants to kill the president is the head of the Secret Service. We don't know whom he's working with. He may not be the only mole inside the highest levels of the U.S. government. There's a killer out there named Mr. C who's apparently planning to finish the job if Iverson doesn't. My guess would be that Iverson probably doesn't have the foggiest idea who Mr. C is. And we don't have much time to figure it out ourselves. Nor do we really know where to begin looking. And to top it all off, we don't know whom we can trust. Mr. C could be anyone, beginning with the White House chief of staff."

"Corsetti?"

"Or the White House press secretary."

"Murray?"

"*Chuck* Murray. I mean, the list goes on and on."

"I need a plan," pressed Harris. "And I need it yesterday."

* * *

At forty thousand feet, the skies are sunny and blue and cloudless.

Even if the world is at war seven miles down.

With Colonel Frank Oakland and his copilot, Lieutenant Colonel Nick Brindisi—dubbed by Bennett as his team's "designated drivers"—at the controls, the G4 streaked toward Tel Aviv at nearly the speed of sound. McCoy uploaded the latest intel from Langley as Black worked the phones to nail down ground transportation and all their security arrangements. Bennett gulped down his third cup of coffee and waited for the call from Washington.

* * *

The statutes were crystal clear.

Like Title 18: Part I: Chapter 37: Section 794: "Whoever, with intent or reason to believe that it is to be used to the injury of the United States or to the advantage of a foreign nation . . ."

That wouldn't be tough to prove. Iverson's actions clearly intended to injure—read: *kill*—the leader of the United States to the advantage of Iraq.

". . . communicates, delivers, or transmits, or attempts to communicate, deliver, or transmit . . ."

Harris now had the damning e-mails—true smoking guns.

". . . to any foreign government, or to any faction or party or military or naval force within a foreign country, whether recognized or unrecognized by the United States, or to any representative, officer, agent, employee, subject, or citizen thereof, either directly or indirectly . . ."

This would be a bit tougher. But here Mitchell at CIA would be helpful. He needed to be able to prove that at the time the e-mails were written, Gogolov was somehow operating as a faction of—operating in concert with—Iraqi military intelligence and/or the Iraqi president himself. Harris didn't have that intelligence on hand at the moment. But he was sure the CIA would have what he needed when it was safe to ask for it.

". . . any document, writing, code book, signal book, sketch, photograph, photographic negative, blueprint, plan, map, model, note, instrument, appliance, or information relating to the national defense . . ."

Would details of how to foil the Secret Service's protection of the president of the United States—the country's commander in chief—qualify under this statute? The FBI director was pretty confident it would.

". . . shall be punished by death."

Technically, life imprisonment was also a possibility. But Harris could think of only one reasonable solution for a man who attempts to kill not only the president of the United States, but one of his best friends as well.

Drop the pellets.

☆　☆　☆

"Mr. Bennett, this is the White House operator."

"Go ahead."

"This is a secure line. Please stand by for the president."

Bennett waited a moment, then heard the familiar voice of his friend and mentor—and now boss, yet again.

"Hello? Jon? That you?"

"Yes, Mr. President. I'm here."

"Good. Hey, look, we've got the air war under way. Cruise missiles. F-15s. F-16s. F-111s. The whole thing. Plus we've got boots on the ground in western Iraq hunting down Scuds. I just got off the phone with Doron again. We talked for almost twenty minutes. He's willing to hold back and not go nuclear for a while—so long as we get results. Now, I told him you guys were coming. I told him we had some ideas for how we might get some lasting peace and prosperity on the other side of all this. And he's open to listening. But I got to tell you—right now, he's frankly not all that interested in next month or next year. He's trying to defend his country hour by hour. I can't say I blame him, so we talked mostly about military details—not oil deals and peace treaties."

"Mr. President, that makes sense and I totally agree. But, you know, that just begs the question—what role can I really play in all this? I mean, should we even be going over there at all right now?"

"No, no, you've got to go, Jon—for two reasons. Listen, first of all, I've got to persuade him that we are committed to Israel's security and prosperity for the long haul. That we're in this thing together. That they don't have to feel isolated and alone. That we've got a serious stake in their survival. The moment they conclude they're all alone in the world, that's when they're going to strike on their own, and that, I fear, would be catastrophic. By you going over there—with the initial outlines of an endgame strategy for a real, lasting, enduring peace—that's got to be part of my overall strategic concept to keep the Israelis out of this war and to not go nuclear. You with me?"

"I think so, sir."

"You're my ambassador on this thing, Jon. You're proof that I'm dead serious about working with them for the long haul—and, frankly, that the U.S. no longer believes that hammering Israel to make more and more concessions to Arafat is the right policy. I totally believe—and I know you do too—that an Israeli-Palestinian peace has to bring serious, tangible benefits to everybody. It can't be seen as a series of concessions. It has to be seen as an investment with a big payoff. And not a payoff of billions of dollars of American and European aid. But the payoff of real wealth generated by Israelis and Palestinians cooperating on this oil-and-gas venture. I've got to make that real to Doron and his team somehow, so they see a real upside potential in not going nuclear. Does that make sense?"

"It does. But you mentioned you had two key reasons for me going. That's the first. What's the second?"

"I've got to be blunt, Jon."

"Okay . . ." Bennett was wary. He had no idea what the president was going to say next, and he wasn't sure he wanted to know.

"I need to give Israel a hostage."

"What?"

"A hostage, Jon. I need to give Doron and his team someone close to me who will be on the ground in Israel in harm's way for the next few days or weeks until this thing is resolved. They've got to believe that, even more than the prospect of peace, I've got a real-life tangible stake in whether they all live or die."

"And I'm it."

"Well, you and Erin and Deek."

Bennett didn't know what to say. "Did the Israelis ask for that?"

"No. I offered."

"You offered to put us in Iraq's crosshairs to keep Israel out of the war?"

"Essentially, yes."

Bennett just stared out the window of the G4 into the brilliant blue skies and the fields of white clouds below them. He'd basically just been given a death sentence by the president of the United States. He could feel the blood rising up the back of his neck and his ears. His face was flushed and hot, and he fought to control his voice. "Okay then. Anything else, sir?"

"Jon?"

He took a deep breath. "Yes, sir?"

"I'm not going to let anything happen to you guys. I promise. But I've got to go. Harris is on the other line from the FBI. Call me when you guys touch down."

With that, the line went dead.

* * *

Harris considered his options—and he wasn't pleased.

The only thing more difficult than tracking and capturing a mafioso or terrorist—surrounded by bodyguards trained to kill—had to be tracking and capturing the U.S. treasury secretary, surrounded by Secret Service agents trained to protect him. Nevertheless, the hunt was on, and the noose was tightening. Stuart Morris Iverson was now number one on the FBI's Most Wanted List. Wanted for multiple counts of murder. Multiple counts of attempted murder. Multiple counts of conspiracy. Multiple counts of espionage. And treason.

The world didn't know that, of course. Nor did Iverson. Or his protective detail. Only twelve people on the face of the earth knew. But one more was about to find out.

* * *

Black thanked Mitchell at CIA and hung up the phone.

"The director wants Galishnikov and Sa'id to meet us at the home of Dr. Eliezer Mordechai in Jerusalem," he told his colleagues.

"Who's he?" asked Bennett.

"Dr. M's a good man. Former director of the Mossad. Knows Saddam Hussein better than almost anyone else on the planet. He's also close to Doron and has worked as a back channel to Arafat for President MacPherson over the last few years. He and the president are very close. It's a long story. But let's just say they see the world the same way. The good thing is that he doesn't really work for the Israeli government anymore. So he can help us figure out our strategy to hold Doron's hand while also helping us navigate how best to have a conversation with Arafat and his team."

"Okay," said Bennett, not really in a mood to talk but privately grateful for any help he could get.

"By the way," Black added, "when we arrive, we'll be met by an armored Chevy Suburban from the embassy. I've got one of my counterterrorism teams sweeping Dr. M's house for any potential problems. We're also running background checks on his housekeeping staff and his neighbors, and we're cross-checking everything with Shin Bet and Mossad, just in case."

Black was paid to be suspicious. So he was.

"Dr. M?" asked McCoy. "You guys close?"

The three of them now gathered around the conference table with their laptops and coffee. McCoy helped Bennett log on to the secure, satellite- enabled CIA computer network, allowing him—and all of them—to access files and share them with one another during their discussion.

"I've gotten to know him fairly well over the years I've been in Israel," Black told them. "He's been somewhat of a mentor of mine."

"What can you tell us about him?" McCoy continued.

Black opened up a top-secret FBI computer file called DEMTRACK and e-mailed it to Bennett and McCoy. It contained an updated photo of DEM—Dr. Eliezer Mordechai—along with basic biographical history and a TRACK report of his involvement in Israeli intelligence over the last several decades.

Bennett and McCoy opened the file on each of their computers and took a moment to read the highlights.

Eliezer Samuel Mordechai, PhD. Only child. Born May 28, 1930, in a little city in Siberia known as Tobolsk. Family escaped in the spring of

1941 through central Asia, Afghanistan, Iran, and Iraq, finally arriving in Palestine in the fall of 1945. Father, Vladimir, fought in the Israeli War of Independence in 1948 and went on to become a professor of Russian studies at Hebrew University. Mother, Miriam, was a nurse. Both died in a terrorist bombing of a Jerusalem restaurant while Eliezer was away in IDF boot camp. Eliezer went on to become an intelligence officer, first in the military intelligence organization called Aman, then later in the Mossad. Graduated from Hebrew University with two undergraduate degrees—one in Russian language studies, one in Soviet studies—and a master's degree *and* doctorate in Near Eastern Studies.

Worked his way up through the Mossad, first as an operative, then becoming an analyst, specializing in Soviet foreign policy. Fluent in Russian, Arabic, Farsi, and English, as well as his native tongue, Hebrew.

Director of the Mossad's Arab Desk from 1976 to 1984.

Director of the Mossad's Nuclear Desk from 1985 to 1987.

Full director of the Mossad from 1988 to 1996. Helped develop the plan to rescue Israeli hostages held in Entebbe, Uganda, in 1976. Helped develop the plan to bomb the nuclear reactor in Osirik, Iraq, in 1981. Helped develop the plan to assassinate Khalil al-Wazir (aka Abu Jihad)— a major PLO figure responsible for numerous terrorist attacks on Israelis—in Tunis on April 16, 1988. And so forth. The brief went on page after page.

"Bottom line," McCoy concluded, "this guy was Israel's top spook."

"Still is, as far as I'm concerned," said Black. "One of the best in the world. Maybe *the* best. When he retired, he got into the stock market and apparently hit the jackpot. I've always suspected he picked up some good intel on Intel during his Mossad days, but don't quote me on that. Anyway, he built a huge home on this gorgeous plot of land in the hills overlooking Jerusalem. Never been there, but it's supposed to be spectacular."

"What kind of guy is he personally?" asked McCoy.

"Quiet. Gentle. You'd never know he was head of the Mossad. I mean, he looks kind of bookish, like an old English professor at Oxford. Gray. Balding. Thick spectacles. Cardigan sweaters. Smokes a pipe."

"We should have brought him some good tobacco."

"Who says we didn't?" said Black, producing a small package from his briefcase.

"Hey, nice work."

"That's why I make the big bucks," Black added.

"You said you've worked with him pretty closely, right?"

"We get along pretty well. And he's been invaluable to me as I've tried to build an effective counterterrorism team and strategy over there. I first met Dr. Mordechai at a party at the U.S. ambassador's home in Herzliya back in the summer of 1990—June or July, I think—right before Saddam made his move on Kuwait. I hadn't really done any work in Israel to that point. Only been there once on a vacation with my wife. But Iraq was doing a lot of saber rattling—that was the catchphrase everybody seemed to be using at the time—and the bureau thought we'd better beef up our work in Israel and spend more time with the guys from Shin Bet and Mossad. Our specific mission, though we didn't tell the Israelis this at the time, was to develop an evacuation plan. In case war broke out and the president gave the word, we needed to know where every American citizen living, working, or visiting in Israel was at a given moment, how to round them up, how to get them to one of six different extraction points, and what resources we'd need from the Sixth Fleet out there in the Med to get them out and home safely. As it turned out of course, war did break out, and Saddam did start lobbing missiles. But we never had to make good on the evacuation plan."

Bennett was staring out the window. Black wasn't sure he was really paying attention. But he continued anyway.

"Anyway, I met with Dr. Mordechai at this party, and then we had lunch the next day. We talked a lot about Saddam and Iraq and the prospect of something going down. And I'll never forget something he said."

"Why? What was it?" asked McCoy.

"He said, and I quote: 'The problem with you Americans is that you don't believe in evil.'"

"What's that supposed to mean?"

"That's what I said. So he went on to explain that in his opinion, the CIA and FBI and definitely the guys at State don't properly anticipate horrible, catastrophic events because we don't really believe in the presence of evil, the presence of a dark and wicked and nefarious spiritual dimension that drives some men to do the unthinkable. So I say, 'I don't know what you're talking about.' And he goes, 'Exactly. A man like

Saddam Hussein, for example. Saddam tells the world for years that he has a territorial claim on Kuwait. Builds up his armed forces. Develops weapons of mass destruction. Moves troops to the border. Signals everyone he's going in. But all the boys and girls at the CIA and DIA say Saddam won't do it. Just wants to drive up the price of oil. Just saber rattling. Just flexing his muscles. Couldn't possibly invade. Why would he? It would make no sense. It would be irrational. No Arab nation has ever invaded another Arab nation. Why start now?'"

"And the good doctor thought our guys were wrong?" asked Bennett, apparently listening more closely than Black had realized.

"They *were* wrong."

"Well, obviously. But we couldn't have known that at the time."

"No, we could have. That's what he was saying. Saddam was drawing us a road map, and we simply didn't believe he'd start the car and take the trip."

"Nobody did, Deek. You'd have needed a crystal ball to get inside the mind of Saddam Hussein and divine what he was going to do next. The guy's a lunatic."

"No, no, no," said Black. "You're missing the point. That's exactly what Dr. Mordechai was trying to say. On the one hand, we tell ourselves that Saddam is a rational person but a liar. He says he'll invade Kuwait, but we say he doesn't mean it. He's just lying. He's just bluffing. He's just playing with our heads. But then when he did invade, we decided he was a lunatic—crazy, unpredictable, irrational, a nutcase."

"So what's your point? Or his?"

"Dr. M's point is that there's a third option—Saddam Hussein is not a lunatic and, in that case, he wasn't a liar. He was rational and calculating and evil. So he told the world what he was going to do—commit an act of evil, not an act of madness—and then he did it. It took a bunch of highly paid analysts with Harvard degrees to completely miss the simplicity of the moment."

"Hey, I resemble that remark," deadpanned Bennett, with his MBA from the Harvard Business School.

"Hey, so do I, brother," Black, another Harvard alum, reminded him.

"That's why I went to Wharton, boys." McCoy smiled. "But seriously, he thinks he could have done better?"

"He did do better. We were having lunch at an outdoor cafe in the Old City, and he told me point-blank that Saddam was going in, even told me the day—August 5. He was only off by three days."

"Did he have some inside info?"

"No. He said he didn't need any. He said everything a person needed to know in terms of basic intelligence, basic fact-finding, could be found in the newspapers. But he stressed that intelligence is about more than simply finding out facts. It's about properly analyzing those facts. It's about drawing the right conclusions, even based on incomplete evidence. In this case, the only difference between Dr. Eliezer Mordechai and the top leadership of the U.S. government was that Mordechai took Saddam Hussein at his word, and we didn't. Or, to put it in his words: 'I believe Saddam Hussein is both capable of and prone to acts of unspeakable evil, and you don't. I'm right, and you're wrong. It's not because I know more than your government. I don't. I know less. But I believe that evil forces make evil men do evil things. That's how I anticipate what can and will happen next in life. That's how I got to be the head of the Mossad, young man. And why I'm good at it. It's going to be a horrible August, and my country is going to suffer very badly because your country doesn't believe in evil, and mine was born out of the ashes of the Holocaust.'"

The three were silent for a moment.

"What happened then?" McCoy asked finally.

"He got up, paid his bill, and left."

Bennett leaned back in his leather executive swivel chair, ran his hand through his hair, then reached for a crystal dish of red and green candies. "Hmm, well, can't wait to find out his next prophecy," he said quietly, staring out the window of the G4 at a brilliant blue sky, not quite sure what else to say.

"M&M's anyone?"

☆   ☆   ☆

General Azziz knew he was gambling with his life, but he was ready to die.

He knew full well that he breathed only at the pleasure of Saddam Hussein. He was wholly devoted to the regime. He was a widower with no children. And he was willing—even eager—to sacrifice himself and his countrymen to inflict vengeance on Israel and the U.S. It was the right thing to do—the ultimate suicide-bombing mission—and a tremor of energy rippled through him in anticipation of all that was waiting for him.

He knew, of course, that Saddam wanted results. And there were results to be had. But his gut told him to wait. He needed just a little more time to orchestrate this final concerto of his career.

The only question was, could he and his colleagues survive this brutal, relentless American bombing campaign until everything was ready and the moment of eternal glorification had arrived?

As the proud architect of this incredible bunker complex, Azziz knew beyond the shadow of a doubt that the answer was yes. He would wait until he was good and ready.

☆　☆　☆

The president hung up the phone and stared at the ceiling.

Two Secret Service agents stood post outside the French doors. The First Lady was sound asleep. He'd been asleep for only fifteen or twenty minutes—trying to catch a few hours' rest upon his doctors' orders—when the call had come in. Now his mind raced. This couldn't be true. It wasn't possible. He had to know for sure. But how?

MacPherson picked up the phone again and got Corsetti on the second ring. "Bob, I need you to do something for me."

"Yes, Mr. President?"

"Call Stu. Tell him to meet me at Camp David at noon. I have a little project I need done just right. And I think he might be the right guy to help me."

"Yes, sir."

"How's Shakespeare doing with my speech for tonight?"

"Not bad. Marsha and I are meeting with him at noon to go over it."

"Good. Now call Stu. Make sure he's at Camp David at twelve sharp."

"High noon it is."

☆　☆　☆

Bennett's BlackBerry started beeping.

He leaned back in his seat and quickly checked the incoming e-mail. It was his mother in Florida, and it was urgent—911. He called her cell phone immediately.

"Mom, it's Jon. What's going on?"

She was hysterical. "Jon . . . it's your father, Jon. . . ." She could barely get the words out.

"What? What happened?"

"He's . . . he's had a massive heart attack. . . ."

"Oh no."

"They don't think he's going to make it. . . . They're giving him twenty-four hours to live—at the most. . . ."

He didn't know what to say.

"Where are you, Jon? . . . You've got get here right away. I need you. . . ."

Bennett was in shock. He couldn't go home. He couldn't tell her where he was. And worst of all, he couldn't say why.

✲   ✲   ✲

Marine One landed at Camp David just before 11 a.m. Friday morning.

A storm was moving in, and the wind and rains were picking up. Only MacPherson, Special Agent Jackie Sanchez, and the flight crew were on board. Waiting for the president at Camp David were FBI Director Scott Harris, Special Agent Doug Reed, three members of Reed's team, and computer specialist Carrie Downing. They huddled in the Aspen Lodge and reviewed the plan. The president kept asking if it would work. It better, thought Harris and Reed; there was no Plan B.

Reed's earpiece crackled with the voice of one of his agents.

"Sierra One to Romeo. Swiss Cheese is on the ground. Sixty seconds out."

"Copy that, Sierra One. Mr. President, he's here."

Reed's deputies took up positions around the room, checked their weapons, and waited, hearts pounding. Reed slipped behind the door while Harris stepped in front of the president. Downing moved to the far side of the room, as Reed had instructed. She had no weapon, no place to hide, and no desire to get caught in a cross fire.

"Sierra One, Swiss Cheese is ten seconds out."

Reed didn't respond. He could hear the outer doors of the lodge opening and the secretary and his chief of staff, Linda Bowles. Iverson's agents were being asked by Sanchez's team to wait outside until the meeting was over.

Then it came. Two hard, sharp knocks.

"Stu, that you?" shouted the president. "Come on in."

"Mr. President, Scott, gentlemen," Iverson said calmly. "Some storm, huh?"

The words had barely tumbled from his lips when he heard the distinctive metal click. The cocking of a Smith & Wesson .45 ACP revolver directly behind his left ear.

Iverson's blood ran cold. The game was up.

13

IT WAS DARK, MOONLESS, and well after eight o'clock Friday night, Israel time.

The white Chevy Suburban finally wound its way up the narrow road, passed through the massive stone-and-steel gates, and pulled into the secluded driveway.

Dr. Eliezer Mordechai's home was built into the top of one of the hills on the northern edge of Jerusalem. And with Israel entering the darkest hour of her existence, Dietrich Black took comfort in seeing the two security vans from the U.S. Embassy waiting for them, just as he'd requested. It was his job to expect the unexpected. It was his job to make sure nothing happened to Jonathan Meyers Bennett, the newly appointed architect of the president's secret Middle East peace plan. And it was a job he took seriously.

A Marine guard immediately recognized and greeted Black, but carefully checked the photo IDs of each person in the Suburban anyway, beginning with Bennett. Security agents combed the perimeter with M16s and bomb-sniffing dogs. Every *i* had been dotted. Every *t* had been crossed. And that was all that could be expected.

Bennett knew from the dossier Black had put together for him that Dr. Mordechai had designed this home himself. With a Frank Lloyd Wright feel to it—sort of a Fallingwater without the water—the structure itself seemed nearly indistinguishable from the hill into which it was built. A cobblestone path—lit on each side by small, discreet ground lamps— snaked authorized visitors up a labyrinth of outdoor stone staircases.

Eventually, these arrived under an immense, thick, jagged limestone cantilever. The cantilever jutted out like a large cliff over a spectacular view of the Old City to the right, and into the home's shadowy, arched, cavelike entrance to the left. The front door rightfully belonged in some museum, not here where so few people could admire it. A massive slab of Lebanese cedar, it had hand-whittled carvings depicting the history of Jerusalem adorning the exterior, gently lit by miniature overhead lamps recessed into the dark stone above.

From the moment McCoy announced their arrival by ringing the doorbell and heard the echo of chimes as beautiful as those in the Church of the Holy Sepulchre in the valley below, the three Americans suddenly knew how little they really knew. Dr. Mordechai's cloak-and-dagger past already intrigued them no end. But now they began to sense that his home was somehow a reflection of the man inside, a man shrouded in mystery and murkiness and a hint of magic.

*　*　*

Everybody on board was already puking their guts out.

But the SH-60B Seahawk helicopter—the navy's version of the army's Blackhawk—lifted off from the *Reagan* anyway and headed into the raging storm.

Their cargo: SEAL Team Six and three counterterrorism specialists from the Lawrence Livermore National Labs, each part of the U.S. government's top-secret Nuclear Emergency Search Team.

Their mission: to make sure Saddam Hussein never got a second chance at firing a nuclear missile at Israel or her neighbors.

Their probability of success: limited, at best. Preventing any missile attack—much less a nuclear attack—from a mobile missile launcher was a million-to-one shot. And since the Israelis had just successfully done it once, no one on this chopper was optimistic they could beat the odds.

*　*　*

The wooden door opened.

The two Mossad agents who greeted them were backlit and it was hard to see their faces. But the Uzis hanging at their sides were unmistakable.

For the second time in less than five minutes, Bennett, McCoy, and Black were asked to show their photo IDs. They were required to put their thumbs down on an electronic touch pad, tethered to a powerful notebook computer whose superthin screen glowed eerily in the dark.

As they waited a few moments for their Social Security numbers and fingerprints to clear, a tiny, barely visible security camera mounted in the ceiling took rapid-fire snapshots of each visitor. All three faces were instantly digitized and processed simultaneously through high-speed databases.

The face-recognition software quickly conducted a "feature extraction." The computer measured pixels on their eyes and lips. It scanned eighty different facial landmarks. It analyzed their cheekbones and skull structures. It then cross-checked their three-dimensional "faceprints" against the photos of thousands of known criminals and terrorists worldwide.

A moment later, one of the Israelis' cell phones rang. It was Dr. Mordechai. From some other room deep inside this house, he was watching them. Once the computer gave its clearance, so did he. One of the Israeli agents threaded thin metal chains through three visitors' passes, handed them over, and instructed that they be worn at all times in the house and on the surrounding property. He also asked the guests to remove their wet coats and shoes and put them in a small hall closet, which they proceeded to do.

On the left and the right, there were long, unlit hallways projecting east and west. But rather than proceed down either of these, the three were directed down the dimly lit hallway straight ahead. It was almost like a tunnel—covered by the limestone cantilever that came right through the external wall—and ended where a wide, circular staircase began.

It was here, finally, as they began to slowly spiral upward to the second floor—the main floor—that they experienced an explosion of light and color and sound and aromas that swept them away into a world so different from their own.

* * *

Several e-mails arrived just before dinner—and they brought welcome news.

His forces were taking a beating. But Azziz wasn't worried. Wasn't this what boxers in the West called "rope a dope"? Iraq would look quiet and weak and wounded amid the U.S. pummeling—then strike when the Americans least expected it.

Q19 e-mail said they were ready to go the moment Azziz gave the word. The e-mail from the four horsemen confirmed that they were making excellent time to their target. And then, of course, hidden in a children's hospital in downtown Baghdad, there was the crown jewel of the mission President Hussein now dubbed "The Last Jihad," history's final holy war against the Western and Zionist infidels.

*　*　*

Bennett, Black, and McCoy climbed the spiral staircase.

As they did, they found themselves staring into a magnificent glass dome instead of a ceiling, a dome that allowed for a spectacular view of the moon and the stars above. It was clear and captivating and certainly unexpected. But in truth it was not the dome but the warm and gentle interior light from lamps scattered about the great room that seemed to beckon them from the dark tunnel below.

As their eyes gradually adjusted to the light, they could see a home filled with precious treasures. Thick, rich, gorgeous purple-and-gold-and-maroon Persian rugs covered the polished brown hardwood floors. Lush, green young palm trees—at least half a dozen of them—rose out of huge reddish clay pots positioned here and there.

Large brown Italian-leather couches and chairs surrounded a glass-and-wrought-iron coffee table, adorned with ancient archeological knick-knacks from all over the Near East and the latest newsmagazines from Israel, Europe, and the U.S.

A sleek, black baby grand piano sat quiet and unused in one corner of the room. Beside it stood a full-size stuffed camel whose glassy, haunting eyes seemed to follow them as they walked. A mahogany dining table set for four with china and silver and crystal—but easily able to accommodate at least a dozen guests—occupied another corner. In the center of the table sat a huge vase of freshly cut roses.

Behind the table, above an antique chest of drawers covered with family photos, on the curved, carved, chalky limestone wall that seemed to be the actual interior of the mountain, hung a painting.

It was no ordinary painting. It was a sweeping, larger-than-life canvas of royal blues, vivid yellows, and smudgy reddish orange brushstrokes that immediately captured the imagination but seemed completely indecipherable. A small plaque underneath it read simply: "Jackson Pollock: *Blue (Moby Dick)*, 1943."

That was followed by a typically cryptic Pollock quote: "When I am in my painting, I'm not aware of what I'm doing. It's only after a sort of 'get acquainted' period that I see what I have been about. I have no fear of making changes, destroying the image, because the painting has a life of its own."

Abstract art didn't do anything for Dietrich Black. What struck him most was that he couldn't see a kitchen anywhere. But he could smell it. Ginger and turmeric and cumin and coriander hit him first, followed by tomato and onions and chili powder and roast lamb. A succulent, mouth-watering Indian curry was stewing somewhere close by, and surely great pots of yellow basmati rice were steaming there as well.

McCoy closed her eyes for a moment and listened. She could hear the tinkle of a fountain. She could hear the crackling of a roaring fire in the great stone fireplace. And, as she listened more carefully, she began to hear the gentle strains of a Bach violin concerto seeping from small Bose speakers hidden all over the house. It was one of her favorite CDs, performed by Itzhak Perlman, the Israeli-born violinist on whom President Reagan had bestowed America's Medal of Liberty back in 1986.

McCoy had briefly taken violin lessons as a young girl and hated them. But in 1993 she had met Perlman at the U.S. Embassy in Prague, and nearly fell in love. He had come to the romantic Czech capital to perform a concert with the cellist Yo-Yo Ma, and she was hooked. When she wasn't jet-setting around the world with Jon Bennett, crafting billion-dollar oil deals, she was usually home at night in London in her Notting Hill town house, curled up under an old wool afghan, reading one of her favorite books and falling asleep to the sounds of the great Itzhak Perlman.

Bennett scanned the cavernous room. He found himself uninterested in, but not unaware of, the curry and the concerto. He had other things on his mind, like the Iraqi missiles pointed at their heads. The room was warm, but not overly so. Occasionally a cool breeze seemed to emanate from somewhere, and now he knew where. He left Black and McCoy and began walking toward the huge plate-glass windows and the sliding glass door that led to the veranda. Sitting atop the limestone cantilever, the veranda gave him a breathtaking view of the Old City. But more than that, it now brought him face-to-face with Dr. Eliezer Mordechai, who seemed to appear out of nowhere.

* * *

The Skyhawk helicopter shot into Iraqi airspace hard, fast, and under radar.

Following Iraq's Highway 10 toward Baghdad, the team flew just fifty feet above the pavement at over 180 knots, and the crew was fully prepared to unleash its two 7.62 mm front-mounted machine guns on any military vehicle it came across in their hunt for mobile Scud missile launchers.

"Striker One Six, Striker One Six, this is Sky Ranch. Do you copy?"

It was the senior controller on an E-3 AWACS some twenty-two thousand feet above them.

"Sky Ranch, this is Striker One Six. We read you five by five."

"You've requested refueling. We can have a tanker to you in about—"

Suddenly warning lights and buzzers filled the Seahawk's cockpit.

"What the—Sky Ranch, Sky Ranch—some bogey just locked onto me."

Someone out there in the storm had just acquired tone and was preparing to fire.

"Striker One Six, say again. We don't have anyone on radar."

"Well, some bogey's got me, Sky Ranch. Get me cover—now—or we're history." Lt. Col. Curtis Ruiz, the Seahawk pilot, scanned his instruments, desperately trying to figure out what was going on, before it was too late.

"Striker One Six, this is Sky Ranch. We see it now. You've got an Iraqi MiG-29 hugging the highway behind you at Mach 2. He's twenty miles back and gaining fast. We're directing two F-14s to your location. Stand by."

Stand by? thought the lead Seahawk pilot. *What the heck was that supposed to mean? Two minutes from now, they'd all be history.*

* * *

Downing answered on the first ring.

It was Harris, desperately seeking good news. Downing was back at

FBI headquarters, but she had none. Not yet. Whether she'd have any at all remained to be seen. But she promised to keep guzzling the bureau's bad black coffee in the hopes that something would turn up. Soon.

✯ ✯ ✯

No sooner were they finished introducing one another than the doorbell rang.

"That must be them," Dr. Mordechai said. "Come, follow me."

He led Bennett, McCoy, and Black back down the spiral staircase to the front door. Glancing at the security monitor, he immediately recognized the faces at the door without all the fancy high-tech equipment and brushed by the antsy Mossad agents to open the door and welcome Dmitri Galishnikov and Ibrahim Sa'id.

"You're late," he quipped, greeting the two men with traditional Middle Eastern hugs and kisses and reacquainting them with Bennett and his team.

As the two men entered, Dr. Mordechai instructed the Mossad agents to take up positions in front of the house, then quickly closed and deadbolted the door behind them. But then, rather than head for the stairs, the old man turned down one of the darkened hallways, proceeded to the end, opened what looked like a closet door, and bid them to follow him inside.

"Ladies and gentlemen, let me show you something I designed into this house to have a little fun," Dr. Mordechai said with a smile. "I think you'll get a kick out of it."

Is this guy nuts? thought Bennett.

But, curious, they all packed themselves into the closet and then—at their host's bizarre request—closed the door behind them. The minute they did, they could hear the hydraulics kick in. This was no coat closet. It was an elevator, and they were headed up. Moments later, the door opened into the walk-in closet of Dr. Mordechai's office, on the west wing of the sprawling house. They all then followed the old man through his private office, past his bedroom, past the kitchen, down the hall, and into the living room, under the gorgeous glass dome in the ceiling.

Sure enough, thought Bennett, this place was as mysterious as the man who owned it.

★ ★ ★

Ruiz took evasive action.

With the SEAL and NEST teams holding on for their lives, he banked hard to the left, then pulled up, climbing to three thousand feet, then dove back toward the deck and banked hard right.

Beep, beep, beep, beep.

"He's fired. Sky Ranch, we are under attack. I repeat—*we are under attack.*"

Ruiz took the chopper up again sharply, then banked hard left. Just then a Russian AA-10 air-to-air missile swiped by his face at Mach 4, missing the Seahawk by inches.

"Sky Ranch, Sky Ranch, we are under attack. We are under attack. *Where is our cover?*"

"Striker One Six, this is Lone Ranger and Tonto. We are inbound at Mach 2. Ready to trash a bandit."

Beep, beep, beep, beep.

Another missile was in the air. Every warning tone in the cockpit seemed to be screaming for help.

"He's fired again. Fired again. Lone Ranger, *where are you?*"

The Seahawk now shot toward the heavens—a thousand feet, two thousand, three thousand—then Ruiz again plunged the chopper toward the ground, away from the incoming missile.

Suddenly his copilot screamed bloody murder. *"Break left, break left—go, go, go—now, now, now."*

The lead pilot yanked so hard on the yoke he practically tore it out of the floor—and just in time. Bodies slammed against the left side of the chopper, but all heads turned right—only to see another heat-seeking AA-10 missile come slicing past the window, hit the ground and explode into a massive fireball below them, engulfing the entire chopper in flames, smoke, and sand.

Warning buzzers and flashing lights suddenly filled the chopper.

"We're hit. We're hit. Sky Ranch, we are on fire. I repeat—*we are on fire.*"

Ruiz instinctively pulled back on the yoke to gain altitude and get away from the fireball below. It was a risk. It would give the Russian MiG a clearer shot. If the bogey on their tail was in fact a MiG-29, it no doubt had four more AA-10s ready to blow them to kingdom come. But Ruiz didn't have much choice. Moreover, if he could get the Seahawk turned around, perhaps he could fire off a couple of his own Hellfire missiles and take this guy out. It might be their only chance, and they weren't ready to go down without a fight. If they were going to die, they were going to take this Iraqi with them.

Suddenly two F-14 Tomcats screamed past overhead, missing the rising Seahawk by less than a hundred yards. They were flying low, hard, and fast, and right into the MiG.

"*Look out,*" screamed the copilot.

"*What was that?*" yelled Ruiz.

"Hi ho, Silver, boys," the lead Tomcat pilot declared. "The good guys are here."

"Tonto, too," yelled his wingman. "Me get bad guys, Kemosabe."

"You got him?"

"I've got tone."

"*Take him, Tonto.*"

"*Fox two, fox two.*"

Two AIM-9 Sidewinder missiles exploded from the side of Tonto's F-14.

The two planes jerked back into a vertical climb as the Sidewinders sizzled toward their prey. Everyone in the Seahawk was glued to the radar screen in front of them, indicating the MiG on their tail, the Tomcats above them.

Then they saw it happen.

The two Sidewinders tore through the cockpit of the MiG, erupting in an incredible explosion that lit up the sky and could be seen for miles.

"You da man, Tonto."

"Who da man?"

"You da man."

"Great job, guys—and thanks," shouted Ruiz, breathing a quick sigh of relief while simultaneously trying to assess the damage to his chopper.

"Who was that masked man?" whooped the Lone Ranger.

"Keep it focused, boys," yelled the controller on the E-3.

"Roger that, Sky Ranch," Tonto responded. "We are scannin' our radar. Nothing yet, but we'll keep looking."

"Striker One Six, this is Sky Ranch. What's your condition?"

"Sky Ranch, this is Striker One Six. Looks like we're not hit. Repeat, not hit. Close call but we're okay. Proceeding with mission as directed."

"Roger that. And Godspeed, boys."

★   ★   ★

Everyone in this room knew the danger they all were in.

In a few hours—the middle of the night, Israeli time—the president of the United States would explain to the entire world the threat Iraq now posed to her allies and the West. But for now, there was business to be done and questions to be answered.

At eighty, Dr. Mordechai was gray, balding, slight, and frail. But behind the thick, bushy beard and round, wiry gold spectacles were warm eyes and a quick mind.

As the night wore on, Bennett grew more and more intrigued with this sharp, insightful old man and his two comrades–in–arms. They covered Doron's background and Arafat's and the possible contours of an oil-for-peace deal.

But what Bennett really wanted to know was this: how was it possible that a secular Russian Jew and a moderate Ramallah Muslim found themselves in a joint business venture for which an evangelical American president was suddenly prepared to wage both war and peace?

The unassuming, owlish Sa'id took that one, in his distinct Palestinian Arab accent, as thick as his mustache. "Jon, Vaclav Havel once said, 'The real test of a man is not when he plays the role that he wants for himself, but when he plays the role destiny has for him.' I believe that. It was not my choice as a Palestinian Arab to go into business with a Russian Jew. Far from it. But I believe that something larger than myself is at work here. Maybe it is fate. Or destiny. Or God. I don't know. But I truly believe that something great and wonderful and lasting is about to be born here—peace and prosperity that will stun the world and dazzle even our own cynical selves."

Sa'id looked away from Bennett and stared out the window at the Dome of the Rock, all lit up and glistening like gold. "Jon, I grew up a stranger in a strange land—my own. Occupied at various times by the Bab-

ylonians and the Persians, the Egyptians and the Ottomans, the British and
the Jordanians and now the Israelis. My father was a real-estate agent.
What can I say? He was right. Real estate is about three key factors—location, location, location. Until a few years ago, I always wondered, what's
the big fuss about? Why are we all fighting about land that has so little
intrinsic value? If you want to fight about something, you know, fight about
the Gulf. Where there's gas. Where there's oil. Where there's wealth. To
me, that makes sense. But, of course, the battle has always been the hottest
here—in *this* place, on *this* land, in *these* hills, in *this* city—even before we
discovered oil and gas. Why? I've never been able to explain it.

"But I've come to believe that there's something supernatural at work
here, Jon. Unseen forces are at work—angels and demons, powers of
darkness and light—that move quietly and mysteriously, like the wind.
You can't see wind. You can't hear it. You can't taste it. But it's real. You
can see its effects. And so it is with these unseen forces battling for control
of the Holy Land. They're real. They're alive. They're shaping events
here, turning some men into heroes and others into fanatics. And I believe
they're locked in some kind of cosmic, winner-take-all battle that is yet to
be decided. I don't pretend to understand it. But I believe it. Because I live
here. And I know this is not a normal place."

The room was completely silent, save for the crackling of the fire in
the fireplace.

"Somehow—don't ask me how—I guess I just believe deep down inside of me that somehow good will triumph over evil. That this oil deal is
going to go through. That we're going to help people become richer than
they've ever imagined. That we're going to help people see the value of
working together in a common market, for the sake of their children, even
if they and their parents and their parents' parents have been at war for
generations. Look at the French and the Germans. Look at the Japanese
and the Koreans. They've made it work. There's no reason we can't do it.
And I just have this little dream that the time to do it is now."

Bennett thought about that for a moment, then looked straight into
the warm brown eyes of his friend Ibrahim Sa'id. "And if we are all incinerated in a nuclear inferno? What will you say then?"

McCoy winced at Bennett's bluntness. But Sa'id didn't blink.

"At least I died on the side of the angels, not the demons."

* * *

"Reed—go."

"Sir, it's Maxwell."

"Talk to me."

"There's more."

"Like what?"

"We've been scrubbing Secretary Iverson's phone and bank records for the last ten years. It's not pretty."

"Let me guess—offshore accounts in the Caribbean."

"You got it. Five of them, actually. All in the Cayman Islands. All routed to banks in Basel and Zurich."

"How much did he send the monsters?"

"It's gonna take more time, sir."

"Ballpark. Millions?"

"No, sir. Looks like tens of millions."

* * *

Stuart Iverson was under house arrest.

He was subject to almost round-the-clock interrogation by the FBI at an undisclosed location near Camp David. But almost no one knew it. Not even the national security advisor. Or the White House chief of staff. Or the vice president.

Most of the White House and Treasury Department staff believed the secretary was doing a top-secret assignment for the president, related to the showdown with Russia, and must not be disturbed under any circumstances. Which wasn't entirely untrue.

For the time being, the deputy treasury secretary was handling all other issues and had direct access to Corsetti and the president if necessary. Communication by Iverson or anyone but the lead FBI agent with him was strictly forbidden by a freshly signed and aggressively enforced executive order.

* * *

At midnight, Dr. Mordechai declared a verbal cease-fire.

Breakfast was at 8 a.m. sharp. Their discussions would resume then.

They all packed up their notes and headed to guest rooms in the east wing of this incredible house.

Black called home—a local call, his house being just a few blocks from the Tel Aviv University campus—to check in with his wife, Katrina, and his three little girls. He hadn't seen them for more than a week. They were scared. And they didn't know the half of it. He couldn't tell them the magnitude of the threat Israel now faced. He wouldn't even if he could. Katrina understood war. She had gas masks and water and flashlights and supplies. But there was no way he would tell her that she and the kids might really be obliterated by an Iraqi nuclear missile. It was just too horrible to contemplate. And they needed their rest.

They missed him. He missed them more. The good news, at least, was that in January—less than two months away—they were all leaving Israel to head back to the States for a long-overdue, two-week vacation at the Polynesian Resort in Disney World. Black promised himself right then and there that if they all lived through this nightmare, he would let nothing come in the way of his family and the Magic Kingdom.

He was getting too old for this job, and he knew it. There'd been a time when saving the world from terrorism was his sole ambition. Now he just wanted some sand, some sun, some piña coladas, and some time to tickle his kids and have a quiet candlelight dinner with his beautiful, patient, long-suffering wife.

Bennett, meanwhile, shut down his laptop, went back to his room, and dashed off a quick e-mail to his mom. He asked for an update on his dad and apologized—again—for being out of the country and unable to come home. For one of the few times in his life, he actually missed his parents. And the thought of losing his father and never being able to say good-bye to him made him sick.

In no mood to sleep, and in serious need of some fresh air to clear his head, Bennett ambled back down the hall, through the living room, and out onto the limestone veranda overlooking the Old City. McCoy was sitting out there, wrapped in a thick wool sweater, cleaning the 9 mm Beretta she kept in her pocketbook.

"You really know how to use that thing?" Bennett quipped.

She raised her right eyebrow. "You want a demonstration?"

"I'll just take your word for it."

Thunder rumbled overhead. Bennett leaned against the wrought-iron railing and stared out at the twinkling lights of the Old City and the gleaming Dome of the Rock.

"I never even took a tour," he said quietly, almost to himself.

McCoy snapped in a fresh clip, then put the Beretta away. "You will."

"I don't know."

"Jon, you think the president's really going to just let us die out here?"

"I don't think it's really up to him."

McCoy looked over at her friend, at the little flecks of prematurely gray hair around his temples and the crinkly little lines around his grayish green eyes. He seemed a million miles away. She didn't quite know what to say. So she said nothing at all.

"I just keep thinking about those Secret Service guys," Bennett said softly. "And I don't get it. What makes a person give up his life to save someone else's?"

The question hung in the air for a few minutes.

"That's not what I signed up for, Erin. You know? I mean, I'm not a Secret Service agent. I don't work for the FBI or the CIA. You and Deek, you guys chose this life. That's fine. That's cool. But I'm not—I don't know—I'm just a Wall Street guy. I'm not James Bond. I'm not a hero. I'm just a simple guy trying to become a billionaire. That's all."

McCoy couldn't help but laugh gently. At least he still had a sense of humor.

It was quiet for a while—just some wooden wind chimes and distant claps of thunder and a pitter-patter of light rain beginning to come down.

Then, again, Bennett broke the silence. "I don't think my dad's going to make it."

McCoy had never seen Bennett like this, unsettled and unsure. "I'm so sorry, Jon."

He nodded. "I miss him. I've never missed him in my whole life. And now I miss him."

A bolt of lightning crackled on the horizon.

"You've been there, done that, haven't you?" he asked her.

"Twice."

"Does it get any easier?"

"No."

"How old were you?"

"I was pretty young when I lost my dad. It was actually harder when my mom passed away, because then I knew I was going to be all alone in the world. And it scared me. Anyway, I was a different person back then. Insecure. Angry. Bitter about things. And my mom and I were really close. . . ."

She and Bennett had never been really candid with each other about personal things, and she wasn't entirely sure now was the time to start.

"How'd you handle it? Losing your mom, I mean."

"I don't know. The only good thing was we both *knew* she was dying. We *knew* she only had a few months left. She really wanted to prepare me for it. We did her will together. We picked out songs for her funeral. Flowers. The whole thing.

"I remember she once heard a sermon about a woman who'd also died of cancer. The woman had come to her pastor and told him exactly what she wanted at her funeral and what Bible verses to read and everything. Then, when she was all done, she told him that she wanted to be laid out in an open casket with a fork in her right hand. The pastor says, 'A fork? Why a fork?' And she says, 'When I was a little girl, I used to love church suppers. When the meal was done and people were clearing the dishes, one of the older women in the church would always come over and lean down and whisper to me, *save your fork*. I loved that. Because I knew it meant something better was coming—apple pie or chocolate cake or blueberry cobbler or something. And pastor,' she said, 'when I die, I want people to come by and see me and then ask you, *Why's she got a fork in her hand?* I want you to tell them my little story, and then tell them the good news—that when you know Christ, you know there's something better coming. There's something better coming.' "

Bennett could see McCoy holding back her emotions.

"My mom loved that story. She had a tape of that sermon and she played it over and over. So she asked me to make sure she had a fork in her hand at her funeral. She wanted her friends to know—she wanted *me* to know—that when you know Jesus Christ in a real and personal way, there's something better coming."

McCoy turned and looked Bennett straight in the eye. "That's how I deal with it, Jon. I know there's something better coming."

Bennett looked at the drops of rain beginning to streak down her soft cheeks and her large green eyes. "You really are a Jesus freak, aren't you, McCoy?" he said softly, smiling.

She smiled back at him. "You don't know the first thing about me, Jon Bennett."

"That's true," he admitted. "But I'd like to."

* * *

Back in Washington, it was just after 6 p.m.

Reed and Downing were gathering in Harris's office when the president called during a break from his NSC meeting. He was due to address the nation in three hours, and he wanted the latest update from the FBI.

"Where are we?" MacPherson asked.

It fell to Harris to bear the bad news. "Nothing's happened. Not yet, Mr. President."

"Scott, we don't have much time. The Secret Service has got to know. Right now only Sanchez knows. But we obviously can't keep up this charade for long."

"Mr. President, I understand. I really do. But we talked about this already. We have no idea who Mr. C is. We're pretty sure he's inside the government. Perhaps inside the White House. Especially if he was complicit in the last attack on you at DIA. So we may have a sleeper agent—working for Saddam—on the inside. It could be anybody. We just don't know. But until we do, we can't risk telling anyone else."

That didn't sit well with the president. The world was rapidly sliding toward nuclear war. One of his oldest friends—the head of the Secret Service, for crying out loud—was under arrest for trying to kill him. Now the FBI believed his chief of staff or press secretary or any one of several hundred other people who worked for him could be about to take him out. And to top it all off, he couldn't tell his own protective detail, for fear that the sleeper agent might be one of them.

"So what do we do?"

"We stick with the plan, sir. Ten minutes after we arrested the secretary, Agent Downing here sent an e-mail back to Gogolov. She sent it from the secretary's personal AOL account, in Iverson's name, written just like Iverson wrote all the others. It told Gogolov he had a perfect plan all worked out. All he needed was a way to contact Mr. C to give him the details and finalize the plans."

"What happens when people realize Iverson isn't around? Won't Gogolov and Saddam and everybody get suspicious?"

"Sir, look, we've been over—"

"Don't give me that. Just answer the question."

Harris was startled by the president's anger, but he certainly understood the pressure the man was under. "Yes, sir. We sent out a press release this afternoon in the secretary's name praising the British and French central banks for lowering their interest rates during this time of crisis and insisting that Germany do the same immediately. It made all the business wires and will be on the front page of the *Wall Street Journal* Monday morning. We booked a major address for the secretary at the National Press Club for next month on 'The Future of the U.S.-Israeli Economic Relationship.' That's making waves as well. And *Meet the Press* called tonight. Russert wants the secretary on ASAP."

"Good. So Saddam and his people must think Iverson's still alive and kicking."

"We hope so. It doesn't seem prudent to do more than that."

"No, you're right. So we just wait and hope Gogolov writes back?"

"That's the plan, sir."

There was a brief pause as the president gathered his thoughts.

"And what does the secretary have to say for himself?" he finally asked.

"You really want to know, Mr. President? It's pretty complicated."

"I assume you guys are putting together a report for me?"

"We are, sir."

"Give me the executive summary. How much were they paying him to sell out?"

"Well, Mr. President, that's just the thing—they weren't paying him."

"What do you mean? Stu's never done anything in his life that wasn't for money."

"Sir, we can't find any record that Gogolov or Jibril or the Iraqis themselves ever paid him a dime to do any of this."

"What? What are you talking about?"

"Well, Mr. President, it appears that Iverson . . ."

"What? Just spit it out."

"Mr. President, it appears that Mr. Iverson was paying them."

✷ ✷ ✷

Bennett woke up suddenly—startled and scared and in a cold sweat.

He could see the man and the pistol pointing at his head. He could hear the explosion. He could feel the flash of fire and smell the acrid powder and smoke. But it was just a nightmare, he told himself again and again. It was just a nightmare.

Exhausted and rattled and disoriented, he checked his watch—six thirty in the morning—reached for his glasses on the nightstand beside him, and sat up in bed, trying to turn off the whole brutal scene replaying in his mind over and over. He fought to remember where he was.

Israel. Jerusalem. The mansion on the mountain. East wing. Second door on the right. In between Black's room to the left and Sa'id's room on the right. Straight across from McCoy's room and Galishnikov's beside it. With a nuclear missile—not a pistol—aimed at his head.

His was a fairly spacious and well-appointed VIP guest suite. It came with a queen-size canopy bed, a ceiling fan, a spacious worktable for his laptop and files, and a color TV hooked up to a newly installed satellite dish. It also came with a spectacular view of the Old City of Jerusalem through custom-made plantation shutters and slightly tinted bulletproof windows.

When he retired for the night, he'd found his garment bag waiting for him on a small luggage rack, apparently put there by one of the security aides. Two fresh terry-cloth towels and matching washcloths were set out at the end of his bed, along with a large, thick, comfortable, white terry-cloth bathrobe. Next to these were two small wicker baskets filled with bars of orange-scented soaps, shampoo, mouthwash, toothpaste, and a new toothbrush.

It was as good as staying at the King David, maybe better. Just cheaper.

✷ ✷ ✷

The president's stunning televised speech was over.

People were scared. Churches, synagogues, and mosques around the globe were packed. And tens of thousands of Washingtonians gathered outside the White House perimeter to hold a candlelight vigil and pray for the peace of Jerusalem and the peace of the world.

✶　✶　✶

Bennett's BlackBerry began to beep.

It was Black. He'd been up most of the night. But not because he couldn't sleep. He hadn't been allowed. Just after 2 a.m. he'd been awakened by the op centers at FBI and Langley. Operation Black Stallion had gone south.

Bennett felt a shot of adrenaline fire through his veins. That was not good. The four horsemen were neither dead nor captured. The four most dangerous terrorists left on the planet were on the loose despite a global manhunt to track them down and take them out.

Bennett quickly typed a note back to his colleague in the next room:

deek—best guess . . . why were they in moscow?

A moment later, the reply came back:

jon—best-case scenario? a little winter getaway. worst case? . . . they went to hook up with gogolov—perhaps to get new orders and new money . . . that's the way it's worked in the past.

where do you think they're headed now? Bennett fired back.

no idea—not for sure—but my fear . . . they're heading to washington to take another shot at POTUS . . . but don't quote me on that—deek.

Bennett pondered that for a moment. Someone—apparently the Iraqis—had come awfully close to assassinating the president. They'd been trying for years, including the foiled attempt to kill Bush senior in Kuwait after the Gulf War. Clinton had done nothing to seriously punish Saddam. Now the Iraqis were at it again, and they'd no doubt keep at it until they got it right.

An e-mail came in from McCoy across the hall. *Jon—good morning . . . hey, did you see the headlines this morning? . . . the speech rocked . . . i actually got up early to see a replay on CNN . . . POTUS did an incredible job . . . it was spooky . . . but now the whole world knows what the stakes are . . . NYT headline: "President Unveils Dramatic Evidence Iraq Tried to Nuke Israel; Special Ops Foil Attack; U.S. Promises 'Full-Scale Retaliation'; Won't Rule Out Nuclear Option" . . . btw—heads up: langley says our meetings with doron and arafat are set up for monday . . . will get back to us on more details soon—erin—PS: you sleep ok? how are you feeling? PPS—love this place! . . . wish we could stay longer—just to explore—fifty bucks says there's more to this house than meets the eye.*

Bennett couldn't help but smile. McCoy was sharp, smart—a good agent and, the more he thought about it, an increasingly good friend. Always thinking ahead. Always looking out for him. And she was right. There was something about this house that was as captivating as it was mysterious. The same was true about her, thought Bennett.

Morning, he wrote back. *how'd I sleep? don't ask . . . haven't read the papers yet . . . or seen the speech . . . will do by eight . . . as for your bet—no way—are you kidding? . . . of course there's more here than meets the eye . . . the guy's a spook—that elevator thing was unbelievable . . . there's probably a secret passageway to Jordan or Syria or China in the basement . . . see you at breakfast—jon.*

He tried to sound upbeat. But it was mostly a facade. And he knew she'd see right through him. But, too tired to care, he simply punched *Send* and jumped in the shower.

✶ ✶ ✶

The building shook mildly.

The lights occasionally flickered. But General Azziz knew that he and his men—and their esteemed leader—were perfectly safe from the barrage of American cruise missiles decimating their Defense Ministry headquarters up above.

Finally, the general picked up the phone. He speed-dialed the young and terrified but still alive and loyal captain of Q19, one of the elite missile-launching teams under his command.

"Captain, this is General Azziz. You have authorization. Deploy immediately to Sector Six. Then wait until you have instructions from me."

"Yes, sir."

"Praise be to Allah."

✶ ✶ ✶

Bennett appreciated the intensity.

Dr. Mordechai launched in at breakfast, giving Bennett and his team a play-by-play analysis of how best to approach Israeli prime minister David Doron and now-honorary Palestinian chairman Yasser Arafat on Monday.

Galishnikov and Sa'id chimed in with color commentary, specifically offering suggestions on how best to formulate a final peace settlement between the Israelis and Palestinians with the Medexco-PPG oil deal as the centerpiece.

Bennett appreciated the help. Somehow he found being mentored by these older, wiser, more experienced men as comforting as it was instructive. He still felt flashes of fear, but at least he wasn't in this thing alone. Others understood the dangers far better than he did. And they were oddly optimistic.

"Dr. Mordechai," Bennett finally said, "may I ask you a question?"

"Certainly," came the quick reply.

"Why do you seem so sure this is all going to turn out all right?"

The old man cocked his head back and looked Bennett in the eye, sizing him up, gauging the seriousness of his question. After a moment, he answered cryptically, "I don't believe God is quite done with us yet."

"Done with whom?"

"With Israel. With the Jewish people. I think He's got some big plans for us yet. I also think He's got some plans for the Iraqis, as well."

☆   ☆   ☆

The results from the highly confidential overnight White House polls were in.

Corsetti scanned the numbers. They were unbelievable. Ninety-one percent of Americans backed the president's declaration of war on Iraq. Ninety percent believed Saddam Hussein had tried to use a nuclear weapon against Israel. Eighty-five percent believed Saddam would try to use weapons of mass destruction again. And a stunning 81 percent supported the use of nuclear weapons if the president felt it was necessary to protect the national security of the United States.

Not that he necessarily would, thought Corsetti. But he could. That couldn't be more clear.

☆   ☆   ☆

They didn't have much time.

It was two in the morning in Washington. The Saturday memorial service was just twelve hours away. Bud Norris and his team gathered to go over last-minute details, triple-check the motorcade routes, and review the latest intel from the FBI, the CIA, and the Secret Service's Protective Intelligence Division.

Norris's big concern was the threat of new airborne-attack scenarios. So all airspace over Maryland, Virginia, and Washington, D.C., would shut down from noon to four, including Reagan National, Dulles, and BWI. F-15 Strike Eagles would fly combat air patrols, and AWACs would help Norris coordinate all air activity.

But that wasn't enough. Not today.

Norris picked up the phone and ordered in two more Stinger missile operators. They'd ride in the motorcade, in one of the Suburbans behind the president, while Norris would put Cupid—his best Stinger operator—in the cathedral's bell tower along with two sharpshooters. The cathedral was, after all, the highest point in the city. From there his special-ops guys could see anything and everything—and hunt it down if need be.

14

THE PRESIDENT slept like a baby.

He knew the stakes. He knew he might have to order a nuclear strike, the first since Truman. And now the world knew too. But he also knew something the rest of the world didn't. People were gunning for him. Possibly someone on his own staff. Yet, somehow, he didn't feel plagued by fear. Instead, he could feel the prayers of a billion souls lifting him up and a peace that seemed to pass all understanding.

The alarm went off. It was a few minutes after 6 a.m. eastern—time to put the finishing touches on the eulogy he'd deliver in a few hours. He called Corsetti—catnapping on the couch in his office—and asked him to bring Shakespeare's latest draft up to the residence.

★ ★ ★

The call snapped Corsetti awake.

Yes, sir, Mr. President. Right away, Mr. President. How high? Mr. President? It was time to quit this job and go make some real money, thought Corsetti. Growing up, he'd never dreamed he'd make $140,000 a year. It would have sounded unreal in the sixties. Now it felt like slave wages. Recently, he'd done the math. Sixteen-hour days. Seven days a week. Fifty-two weeks a year. That was 5,824 hours a year. At that pace, he was making only twenty-four dollars an hour. Not horrible. But if Iverson hooked him up with some Wall Street firm, he could be making five

266 . . . . JOEL C. ROSENBERG

hundred an hour. He could cut back to only four thousand hours a year, only seventy-seven hours a week—a vacation, by Corsetti's standards—and still clear a cool $2 million a year. Not a bad gig for a plumber's kid from Fort Collins.

So that was it. When World War III was over, Corsetti knew his mission: get out of Washington and get a real job. For now, rather than hoof this speech all the way up to the president, he'd simply fax it upstairs.

Work smarter, Corsetti told himself, *not harder*.

★ ★ ★

The clock was ticking.

D.C. Metro cops began blocking streets, towing unauthorized vehicles, and diverting traffic away from the motorcade route, though there wasn't really that much traffic to divert. Most Washingtonians anticipated the security headache the memorial service would cause and made sure to steer clear of it. And if that weren't enough, an intense electrical storm was descending upon the capital, driving even the homeless indoors.

Helicopters circled overhead, carrying surveillance agents sporting high-powered binoculars and looking for any signs of trouble. Local hospitals were double-checked to make sure they had ready stocks of the president's blood type on hand. Just in case. D.C. police headquarters were again checked for any signs of missing uniforms, badges, or patrol cars. Meanwhile, Secret Service technical teams carted off mailboxes and trash cans along the route, checked underground tunnels for terrorists and explosives, and sealed manhole covers. They also swept the National Cathedral buildings and grounds yet again for unauthorized people, weapons, explosives, and biological and chemical weapons. Just in case.

Around eleven, the sharpshooter and Stinger teams arrived and began taking up positions in the bell tower as well as on rooftops across the street, facing the cathedral. Weapons were loaded, checked, and rechecked. Scopes adjusted and glass cleaned.

Finally, the fifteen-vehicle motorcade was assembled in the driveway and loaded with the necessary weapons and portable communications equipment. A white tent was set up between the back door of the White House and the two identical limousines so the president couldn't be seen, shot at, or—more likely—drenched.

Bud Norris was thinking of everything. Everything, that is, except what the FBI still hadn't told him.

* * *

Downing grabbed the phone on the first ring.

"Downing—go."

"It's Reed. Talk to me. What've you got?"

"Nothing, sir. Zero."

"Nothing? Come on. Is it possible he's using a different e-mail system?"

"It's possible. We're tracking everything digital coming out of Russia and Iraq right now. We've got all the phone trunk lines tapped. NSA's watching the satellite communications. But so far, nothing."

Reed slammed down the phone. He nervously ran his hands through his thinning hair. Maybe Mr. C didn't exist. Maybe he'd somehow gotten wind of Iverson's arrest. Maybe Gogolov and the Iraqis had been spooked off for some other reason. Maybe, thought Reed. Or maybe they'd just missed him.

* * *

Harris moved into position.

He entered the FBI's Strategic Information Operations Center on the fifth floor of the Robert F. Kennedy Building and took his seat. He scanned the ThreatCon board and the banks of computer screens tracking every facet of the president's imminent departure from the White House. He also kept track of the five large-screen video monitors above him, tracking the latest coverage of the war against Iraq.

He was taking no chances. He had part of the FBI Hostage Rescue Team pre-positioned on the helicopter pad at the Pentagon, fully briefed on the delicate situation, on standby and ready to move at a moment's notice. And unbeknownst to Bud Norris, the Secret Service, or anyone else, Harris also had teams of HRT snipers hidden strategically along the motorcade route, shadowing every move the Secret Service made—just in case. Doug Reed and his team—including Maxwell and Downing—were also on standby, just a speed-dial away.

Now there was nothing else to do but worry and wait.

✴ ✴ ✴

At 1:45 p.m., the president still sat in the Oval Office.

He was finishing the ninth and final draft, and he liked what he saw. Shakespeare—his chief speechwriter—had finally gotten it right. And not a moment too soon. Doron would be watching. Saddam would be watching. The world would be watching. It had to be right. And now it was.

Corsetti poked his head in the door and told the president it was time to go. Sanchez radioed the driver of the newest addition to the Secret Service fleet: a specially built, armor-plated, top-of-the-line Cadillac limousine known as Bull Market, which had arrived just in time to replace the recently totaled Stagecoach.

MacPherson needed a few minutes more. He asked Corsetti for his BlackBerry, typed in a quick note, and hit *Send*.

Now he was ready. It was showtime.

✴ ✴ ✴

"Blowtorch to Sierra One, copy?"

Ed Burdett, in HRT sniper position one—an apartment building across from the cathedral—immediately radioed back. "Copy, Blowtorch," he whispered.

"Status check."

"Read you five by five. In position. All clear. Over."

"Copy that, Sierra One. Blowtorch to Sierra Two, copy?"

Daryl Knight, in sniper position two—high up in another apartment complex across from the cathedral—quickly responded as well. "Copy, Blowtorch."

"Status check."

"Same here, Blowtorch. I read you five by five. In position. All clear. Over."

Harris continued with all seven FBI snipers along the route. Everyone was in position, and everyone was giving the all-clear sign. No signs of trouble. Not yet, at least.

✴ ✴ ✴

"Gambit is moving. I repeat, Gambit is moving."

The president left the Oval Office and headed toward the motorcade, with Agent Sanchez and a dozen other agents at his side. Word came in that Saddam Hussein was about to make a radio address to the people of Iraq. But MacPherson would have to hear it later, or listen to it on the car radio. He had his own speech to give. If he didn't leave now for the memorial he'd be late, and like his predecessor in the Oval Office, Gambit was never late.

"Copy that, Gambit is moving," Norris confirmed. "Status on Checkmate?"

"Checkmate is secure in the Bunkhouse," replied the VP's body man.

"Copy that, Checkmate secure. All sectors, give me your status. Cupid, do you copy? Status check."

"Roger that, Home Plate. This is Cupid. I read you five by five. The heavens are clear. The lawn is dry. We are good to go."

A blinding flash of lightning lit up the bell tower momentarily as thunder rumbled ever closer and rain soaked every sharpshooter in the area. The heavens definitely weren't clear and the lawn was anything but dry. But codes are codes, and the airborne environment was secure.

Norris moved on. "Home Plate to Crossbow leader. Status check."

"Roger that, Home Plate," the SWAT team commander responded. "Crossbow team good to go."

"Home Plate to Candlestick. Status check."

The mobile communications command center replied instantaneously. "Roger that, Home Plate. Candlestick good to go."

"Home Plate to Nighthawk," Norris radioed to the pilot of *Marine One*, fully powered and ready to lift off from Bolling Air Force Base at a moment's notice, should the call come in. "Status check."

"Roger that, Home Plate. Nighthawk is in position and good to go. Let's just hope this is business as usual today, boss."

"Roger that, Nighthawk. Home Plate to Blueprint. Status check."

Silence. No response, just the crackle of radio static. The technical team leader inside the cathedral wasn't responding. Norris checked his radio and frequency and repeated himself. "Home Plate to Blueprint. I repeat. Status check."

Norris winced and held his breath. Then, finally . . .

"This is Blueprint. Sorry about that. Yep, I'm here. Just cleared through the last of the guests, sir. We are good to go."

Norris breathed a sigh of relief. He was in no mood for anything but precision. Not today. But he quickly reminded himself that he needed to be careful not to betray the rising anxiety he felt in the pit of his stomach. Everyone needed him to set the pace and keep communications clear and confident. And that's what he intended to do.

"Home Plate to Halfback. Status check."

"A-OK, Home Plate. Halfback good to go, boss."

The president's follow car—packed with six heavily armed agents in full Kevlar and combat gear—was in place and ready to roll.

"Home Plate to Dodgeball. Status check."

"Roger that, Home Plate. Dodgeball locked and loaded. Let's do it, sir."

"Home Plate to Bull Market. Status check."

"Roger that, Home Plate. Gambit is secure. Bull Market is good to go."

That was it, thought Norris. There was nothing more to be done now than drive fast and pray hard.

"Bamboo Pincer, this is Home Plate. Package is wrapped. You are clear to roll."

The heavy, black-steel White House gates now unlocked electronically and swung open slowly. The massive metal road barriers—designed to stop the kind of truck bombs Islamic extremists once used to kill 241 Marines in Beirut in 1983—retracted into the ground, and the motorcade began to move through into the storm.

★   ★   ★

Bennett was transfixed by Sky News when the e-mail came in.

Everyone in Dr. Mordechai's home was huddled around the television, watching the breaking news coverage as both President MacPherson and Saddam Hussein prepared to make major addresses.

The world was still in shock from the speech MacPherson had given the night before, laying out the case against Iraq while sitting next to the remains of an Iraqi nuclear warhead. Now the Butcher of Baghdad was about to speak publicly for the first time since the U.S. bombing campaign had begun.

Bennett grabbed the BlackBerry off his belt and began reading the new message. It was sent from Corsetti's BlackBerry, but it was written by the president.

> jon—you guys ok? . . . i'm about to head to the
> memorial service . . . have to admit, don't feel quite
> worthy for the task . . . it's a humbling thing to
> know a man has freely given up his own life—the most
> precious gift he could possibly give—that you might
> live . . . the worst thing is, i know how unworthy of
> that gift i really am . . . the best i can do, i guess,
> is be grateful, and try to live a life worthy of that
> sacrifice . . . but how can that be easy?
>
> hey, we could sure use your good humor around
> here right now . . . we miss you guys—you, mccoy, deek
> . . . julie and the girls and i are praying for all of
> you . . . you have no idea all that burt, jack, marsha,
> and the team are doing to keep you guys safe . . . in
> time you will . . . but for now, please try to trust
> me . . . i know it's not easy . . . but you're doing
> a great job, jon—you're making a difference—don't get
> weary in well-doing, all right?
>
> thought you might be interested in the two verses
> i've chosen for my eulogy for the agents who died for
> me—matthew 16:26—Jesus asks: "what good will it be for
> a man if he gains the whole world, yet loses his soul?"
> —and john 15:13—Jesus tells his disciples: "greater
> love has no one than this, that he lay down his life
> for his friends." my dad used to call this VOSA—the
> "voice of sound advice" . . . chew on these, young man
> . . . they'll serve you well—your friend, mac.

* * *

The motorcade snaked its way through streets gushing with rivers of rain.

The president sat in the back of Bull Market, listening to a live broadcast from Baghdad, a bloodcurdling speech by Saddam Hussein, hunkered in some bunker.

"It is said we are part of some 'axis of evil'—but the world can plainly see that America and Israel are evil personified—they are the sons of Satan—and they

must be destroyed," fumed the Iraqi leader. *"The MacPherson and Doron regimes are terrorist regimes—seeking to eat our flesh, drink our blood, annihilate our sons, and destroy our way of life. These cancerous tumors will kill us unless they are removed. They threaten the Arab world, the world of Islam. But their reign of terror is almost over. Allah, we beseech thee, please destroy them with your wrath, which is like a sword. Make their blood flow like a river of justice through your holy city of Al Quds."*

✷ ✷ ✷

That was the signal.

Azziz lit a new cigar. He let the smoke slowly fill his lungs and curl around his head and drift toward the ceiling. Then he reached for his computer and began typing.

It was time.

✷ ✷ ✷

An involuntary shudder rippled through his body.

The president quickly considered scrapping his own remarks and responding directly to Saddam. The problem was that those inside the cathedral weren't listening to Saddam's speech.

The discreet "little" memorial service had swelled to more than eight hundred mourners, including the agents' families, friends, and colleagues, congressmen, senators, and international dignitaries. At the moment, the audience was listening to a guitar solo. They were expecting a tribute to some of America's bravest public servants. And they deserved nothing less. Yet how could he not respond when the rest of the world was right now listening to Saddam, translated and simulcast around the globe?

As the motorcade headed north on Massachusetts Avenue, then turned right on Wisconsin, he picked up the phone and called the vice president, secure in the Presidential Emergency Operations Center underneath the White House. He had only a few minutes, but he desperately needed Checkmate's advice.

✷ ✷ ✷

The U-2 streaked across the night sky at eighty thousand feet.
Click. Click. Click. Click. Click.

American warplanes were pulverizing Saddam's military assets far below. But the president's orders were crystal clear. Photograph every square inch of Iraq over and over and over again in a feverish hunt to find weapons of mass destruction.

Downtown Baghdad was an unlikely place to find them. But it wasn't this pilot's place to question the orders. His mission was to get in, snap those shutters, and get out before an Iraqi SAM site could lock onto him and fire its missiles.

So far, so good.

* * *

"Bull Market approaching. Secure the perimeter."

The motorcade pulled onto the cathedral grounds as another flash of lightning lit up the black and stormy sky.

"Snapshot, this is Peso. Prepare for arrival."

The lead advance agent moved to the front door and alerted his team inside.

"Roger that, Peso. We are in position. Choirboys, stand by one. Gambit is pulling up. I repeat, Gambit is pulling up. Stand by one."

* * *

"You've got mail."

Downing gasped. She quickly checked her diagnostics and ran a trace. This was it. They had a hit. She grabbed her phone and speed-dialed Harris. *"Pick up. Pick up."*

"Harris—go."

"We got him. He just transmitted."

"What's he say?"

"It's coming through now, sir. Hold on."

"Downing, come on. Move it."

"Hold on. Almost."

"Downing."

"Here . . . here it comes—*'take him out.'* It says, *'take him out.'* "

"Who's it to, Downing? Who's it to?"

"Hold on, sir. I don't have it yet."

"Downing . . ."

"I know. I know. I'm . . . here . . . hold on . . . here it comes. Got it."

"A name, Downing. Give me a name."

* * *

Sanchez signaled to the president.

It was time to move. But the president waved her off and continued talking to the vice president, Kirkpatrick, and Corsetti in the PEOC. Kirkpatrick and the VP insisted the president should stick with his script, stay on message, and ignore Saddam.

"The United States Air Force is responding even as we speak," said the VP. "You've got a great speech to give. It's strong. It's eloquent. It's spiritual. And no one's going to miss the moral clarity of the contrast."

Kirkpatrick agreed. "Stay the course, Mr. President. Let us worry about the rest."

Corsetti went nuts. He argued it was political and strategic suicide not to respond immediately. To sidestep Saddam Hussein's direct threats would look weak and out of touch with reality to the entire world. The death of several Secret Service agents was a terrible thing. But the world was watching a nuclear holocaust unfold. It needed to hear the president give them some kind of assurance—any assurance—that there was at least a ray of light at the end of this long, dark tunnel. This was the moment. Use it or lose it.

* * *

"It's coming, sir. Hold on. AOL account. Washington. Northeast—transmitted from Moscow, but forwarded from Baghdad."

"Give me the name, Downing."

"Here it is—Gary Sestanovich."

"Spell it."

"G-a—"

"No, the last name."

"Sorry, sir. S-e-s-t-a-n-o-v-i-c-h."

As Downing spelled, Harris relayed the name to Agent Maxwell, who typed it into the FBI's massive computer system and hit return.

"Come on. Come on. Who is this guy?" shouted Harris, hoping against hope that the name was somewhere within the billion-dollar database.

"I-I don't believe this," Maxwell stammered at the other end of the Op Center.

"What? Who is it?"

"He's an agent."

"One of ours?"

"No."

"Then whose?"

"Secret Service—former CIA, special ops."

"What'd he do?"

"You're not going to believe it, sir."

"Maxwell, I don't have time . . ."

"Sir, he taught *mujahedin* how to kill the Russians."

⁂ ⁂ ⁂

The four settled on a compromise.

Corsetti dictated a few lines to add to the beginning of the speech. The vice president and Kirkpatrick insisted on modifications. The president took notes as fast as he could.

All the networks were cutting away from the Baghdad transmission and now focused on the president's storm-battered limousine, parked in front of the National Cathedral. But the president was still inside.

Around the globe, people couldn't help but wonder: Why wasn't the president getting out? What was wrong?

⁂ ⁂ ⁂

Harris speed-dialed Bud Norris at the Secret Service Op Center.

"Norris—go."

"Bud, it's Scott. Gary Sestanovich. Who is he?"

"Why? What are you—?"

"Bud, just tell me—now."

"One of my best guys—you know, code-named Cupid—the guy who helped save the president in Denver. Remember?"

Harris froze. Cupid was Mr. C? The guy was standing in the bell tower with a Stinger missile aimed at the president's head. How was that possible? Why?

Harris didn't have time to think.

"Scott? What's this all about?"

"Can't say—I'll get right back to you."

But that was a lie. Norris hadn't been briefed. He had no idea that Iverson was in federal custody or the subject of a high-tech sting operation the president had set into motion. But Harris didn't have time to brief him or argue with him. At best, he had a few seconds to save Gambit's life.

Harris punched the mute button so Norris couldn't hear him. Then he picked up the other line, with Downing at the other end.

"Downing."

"Yes, sir."

"Has this guy read his e-mail yet? I mean, do we know if he's even received the thing yet?"

"He just did, sir. I was trying to tell you but you had me on hold."

"Tell me what?"

"That the e-mail went to his personal computer—at his home—but was then forwarded to his wireless, probably a BlackBerry. I'm actually watching him open it right now."

Harris's mind raced. There wasn't time to tell Norris. And what would he do, anyway? True, Norris had two other sharpshooters in the bell tower. But if he said anything over any of the Secret Service radio frequencies, Cupid would hear it and could fire before he could be stopped.

Harris grabbed his handset and punched a button on the console before him. "Blowtorch to Sierra One. Copy?"

"Sierra One, copy," replied Burdett.

"Sierra One, suspect is the Stinger missile operator in bell tower. Can you see him?"

Burdett could barely believe what he was hearing. "Copy that. Which one, sir?"

"Cupid—you know him?"

Know him? Cupid? Of course he knew him. Their daughters went to the same school. They'd trained together at Quantico every three months for the last ten years.

"Sir, I . . ."

"Sierra One—*can you see him?*"

Burdett quickly opened the apartment window, aimed the forty-power Burris scope atop his Remington Model 700 sniper rifle, and put Cupid in his crosshairs.

"I've got him, sir. But—"

"Do you have a shot?"

"I do. But, sir . . ." Through his sights, Burdett could see his friend and colleague pressing the IFF challenge switch on his Stinger missile launcher, and pushing the actuator button forward and downward, warming the battery coolant unit to make the weapon go live. "Oh no."

"Sierra One, what is it?"

"He's preparing to fire at the president."

"Sierra One, take him out. I repeat—take him out."

Burdett clicked off the safety, took a deep breath, and tried to adjust for the whipping winds.

Suddenly glass exploded all around him. Burdett dove for cover, but more gunfire came blazing through the window.

☆ ☆ ☆

What were these guys doing?

The gunfire erupting from the two sharpshooters to his left and right stunned Cupid, jarring his concentration.

"*Code Red. Code Red. Sniper at one o'clock,*" shouted one of the sharpshooters, instantly turning all of the Secret Service's ferocious firepower on the apartment complex Burdett was hiding in.

Cupid's colleagues had seen the barrel of Burdett's rifle emerging from the window. Not knowing FBI snipers were shadowing them, they'd obviously read it as hostile and begun firing.

But who else was out there, preparing to take a shot at Gambit? Cupid wondered. *Did Gogolov, Jibril, and/or Azziz have another sleeper agent in place?*

Poor soul, Cupid thought . *Whoever that guy in the apartment building was, he'd never be an Islamic hero. At best he was about to become a new martyr.*

☆ ☆ ☆

"*Blowtorch, Blowtorch. Sierra One taking fire. I repeat, Sierra One taking fire.*"

A hail of bullets, shattering glass, and exploding concrete now poured into the sniper's lair, filling the room with fire and smoke and dust.

"No shot. I have no shot. Abort. Abort. Abort." Burdett scrambled for the door, trying to get out in the hallway, trying to stay alive.

✳   ✳   ✳

Sestanovich—aka Cupid—found himself oddly mesmerized by the firefight.

So was the rest of the world. The entire gun battle was being broadcast live by local and international TV news crews to a worldwide audience of more than 2 billion people.

Suddenly a flash of lightning and crash of thunder startled him back to reality. He glanced down at the BlackBerry attached to his belt, wiped away the rain fogging up the display, and reread the message, just to be sure. The three-word message—and its origin—were unmistakable: *Take him out.*

This was it. Yuri Gogolov, the financier of his partner, Mohammed Jibril—the man he'd met and trained so long ago in the mountains of Afghanistan, the man who'd become his leader into the Way of Islam—had a mission for him. The fact that it originated from inside Saddam Hussein's bunker made no difference. And he was not about to fail.

He quickly reengaged, only to see the president's limousine roaring out of the driveway in an evasive maneuver. Cupid checked his Stinger, flipped off the safety, recharged the BCU, and took aim. This was it. One shot, and it was over.

✳   ✳   ✳

"Sierra Two, Sierra Two. This is Blowtorch. Do you copy?"

"Roger that, Blowtorch."

"Sierra Two—do you have a shot? Repeat—do you have a shot?"

Special Agent Daryl Knight, high up in the second apartment complex, could barely see through the raging electrical storm outside. But at least his window was already open a crack, and the Secret Service's attention—and firepower—was concentrated elsewhere. Even if it was on his colleague Burdett.

"Stand by, Blowtorch—hold on . . ."

Harris—his head pounding and heart racing—could see the president's limousine peeling out onto Wisconsin Avenue on the video monitors in front of him. *"Sierra Two."*

In the crosshairs of his Remington, Knight lined up Sestanovich's head . . .

"There's no time," Harris screamed.

. . . covered in the black ski mask that had become Cupid's trademark. . . .

"Take him out."

He adjusted for the gale-force winds . . .

"Now."

. . . and squeezed the trigger.

The .308 caliber hollow-point bullet flew straight and true.

It was the last image Knight remembered—Sestanovich's head exploding in a spray of blood and bone.

15

BENNETT AND HIS TEAM stared at the TV screen.

They could not believe the horror unfolding in Washington. Then—without warning—the living room was plunged into darkness. The television shut down. As did all the lights in Dr. Mordechai's home. Something wicked was here—something evil, deadly, and dark.

Dr. Mordechai's Mossad training kicked in instantly. "Follow me," he shouted, hitting the deck and beginning to crawl on his belly toward the west wing.

Galishnikov and Sa'id immediately dropped to the ground and scrambled after Mordechai.

Bennett hesitated. He was sure he could find his own way back to his room. But then what? What good would it do him to be separated and alone, unarmed and unprepared for what might happen next?

Against his natural instincts, he turned around, joined Galishnikov and Sa'id, and followed the sound of Mordechai's voice as he led them quickly across the living room, down the hallway, past the kitchen, through his office, and into the only sure escape route the house had to offer.

"Quick, through that door," Mordechai yelled.

Amid an almost blinding flash of lightning, Bennett could see Mordechai pointing to the elevator door he'd shown them earlier.

"*But there's no power,*" Bennett shouted back as he brought up the rear.

"*Don't worry. It works on a separate power system. But hurry.*"

* * *

Black and McCoy stayed back, guns drawn.

A powerful storm had been building over Jerusalem for hours. But their instincts told these two that this was no weather-related blackout.

"Erin, this way," Black whispered.

They began moving the other direction, away from Mordechai, Bennett, and the others, down the hall through to the east wing, to the bedroom Black had been using.

"You got your goggles?" McCoy whispered—the pair of night-vision goggles Black kept with him wherever he went, standard operating procedure for the counterterrorism specialist he was.

"In my bag—hold on a second."

* * *

"This way. Stay down."

Mordechai and the three men with him stayed low, crawled through the walk-in closet, and piled into the elevator. Sure enough, it had a different power system and was fully operational. Mordechai punched in his own personal seven-digit access code, and in the blink of an eye, a heavy steel door slammed closed behind them. They were immediately plunged deep inside the mountain, far below the mysterious house above.

Bennett couldn't believe what he saw when the elevator door finally opened. It was like another world—a series of interconnected, state-of-the-art, high-tech, computerized war rooms worthy of the best NORAD or the CIA had ever designed. Sleeping quarters. A fully stocked kitchen. Bathrooms and showers. Independent communications, power, water, and HVAC systems. It was remarkable. And Bennett figured the bunker could hold a dozen or more people for several weeks, at least.

ThreatCon maps equal to those in the White House Situation Room displayed the latest Israeli and enemy movements on land, at sea, and in the air, all updated in real time. A bank of computers tracked the latest intelligence assessments from Mossad, Shin Bet, and Aman.

Five large-screen TVs displayed the latest satellite feeds, while a dozen smaller black-and-white monitors showed the images from tiny security cameras positioned all over the house and grounds. The images were as startling as they were brutal—the bodies of the U.S. and Israeli security force, all shot dead.

Bennett's mind reeled. *What was going on upstairs? Who was trying to kill them and why? Moreover, where was he now? How had Mordechai done all this? How had he financed it? How long had it taken to prepare?*

Bennett's thoughts were consumed by questions. But there wasn't time to ask. Not now.

There was only one question that mattered to him now: how could he find his friends and get them down here to safety?

* * *

"Man down. Man down. Cupid hit. I repeat—Cupid hit."

Sanchez could hear the furious chatter over the emergency frequencies as the president's limousine raced back for the White House.

At the cathedral, an Apache helicopter gunship—battered by wind and rain—began unleashing its 30 mm front-mounted machine guns into the apartment identified by a Secret Service surveillance team as the one from which a sniper's gun barrel had emerged.

It was a devastating response, and Bud Norris had no idea what was going on.

Then Norris's phone rang. It was Scott Harris at the FBI Op Center—with some semblance of an explanation for all this madness.

* * *

Black slipped quickly and quietly into his room, the first on the right.

He lay on his stomach, careful to keep his head down lest enemy eyes be watching through the plantation shutters. Suddenly a massive explosion rocked the house. McCoy—still out in the hallway—went flying, stunned by the deafening roar of the blast. Fire, smoke, and glass were raining down everywhere.

And then she heard it—men shouting in Arabic.

"Go, go, go."

Black heard them too. Unlike McCoy, he didn't understand what they were saying, but it didn't really matter. He grabbed his night-vision goggles, pulled them over his head, grabbed a spare set, ducked his head into the hall, and looked left. He could see two men in black helmets and black jumpsuits rappelling down from the gaping hole in the roof over the circular stairwell, where Mordechai's gorgeous glass dome had been. Wooden beams from the roof were now burning in the middle of the living room, providing some light but not much protection.

His head snapped to the right, and he saw McCoy, crumpled in the corner at the end of the hall—exposed. She immediately caught Black's eye, though, and he quickly tossed her his spare set of goggles and motioned for her to get into Sai'd's bedroom at the end of the hall on the right. He had no idea where Bennett, Mordechai, and the others were. But at least he and McCoy were alive . . . and armed.

*　　*　　*

They could hear the ferocious blast up above.

Dr. Mordechai rapidly closed the three-foot-thick steel door behind them and sealed off the elevator shaft, preventing whoever was upstairs from descending, even if they could somehow bypass the elevator's security code. Next he directed Galishnikov and Sa'id to park themselves in two cushioned swivel chairs in front of the bank of computers and television monitors.

To Galishnikov he gave a set of headphones and told him to provide constant updates on what was happening in Washington. They could all see the gun battle going on around the National Cathedral and the images of the presidential limousine racing back to the safety of the White House complex, and they needed to keep a close eye on the unfolding drama.

To Sa'id he gave the job of scanning the security monitors and providing him and Bennett continuous updates of what was going on upstairs. Top priority: locating Black and McCoy and finding some way to help them if they possibly could.

Next Mordechai grabbed Bennett, pulled him into a side room, flipped on the light, and unlocked a cabinet full of automatic weapons, gas masks, Kevlar vests, and radio headgear.

"There's two of them up there, both with AK-47s and night-vision goggles," Sa'id shouted, the tension in his voice thick and real. "They've just dropped down through the dome and are spreading out through the living room."

"Looking for you, no doubt, Eli," said Galishnikov.

"Where's Black and McCoy?" Bennett shouted.

"I don't see them. I can't see them."

"Jon, take this stuff," ordered Dr. Mordechai, handing Bennett weapons and several boxes of ammunition.

"Me?" asked Bennett, hardly a card-carrying member of the NRA.

"Who's supposed to go up there, me?" the old man shot back. "We can't leave those two up there by themselves. If they don't get more firepower fast, they're going to be dead inside of five minutes."

* * *

Black crawled inside his tiny closet.

The night before, bored and poking around, he'd found a hatch against the back wall of the closet, sort of like the hatch some houses have leading to the attic. But rather than up to an attic, this led through to the next guest room. Why? He had no idea. Nor did he care.

He opened it and quickly climbed through, into Bennett's room. He then raced across that room and found a similar hatch in the back of the closet. Climbing through this time, however, Black found himself staring directly into McCoy's loaded Beretta.

"It's me," he blurted, not thinking, then quickly lowered his voice. "It's just me."

McCoy exhaled, then heard someone shout in Arabic.

"We've got them. Down the hall. Cover me."

"Quick, follow me," she ordered Black.

She dove into the walk-in closet. Black followed suit, and sure enough, her instinct was right. There was another hidden elevator on this side of the house, just like the one they'd come up inside Dr. Mordechai's closet. They got in, slammed the door, pushed a button, and descended out of sight. Just then, the two terrorists burst into the room, machine guns blazing, drowning out the sound of the retreating elevator.

* * *

"They're in the east elevator," Sa'id shouted.

"Where are they headed?" asked Bennett.

"First floor. They'll come out at the end of the hallway leading to the front door."

Bennett raced back into the main war room, an Uzi now in his hand, two more slung over his back. His eyes scanned the bank of monitors and spotted two masked men, dressed in black from head to foot, racing up to a door.

"Two more terrorists," Bennett shouted to Mordechai. "Where is that?"

"They're attaching explosives to the front door."

The four men could see Black and McCoy on one of the TV monitors, inside their elevator. In a moment, their door would open and they'd go racing down a darkened hallway into two pounds of C-4, ready to blow them to kingdom come.

"Black and McCoy are going to run right into them," screamed Bennett. "Is there any way we can warn them?"

"There's no audio link to the elevator," said Dr. Mordechai.

They could only watch in horror.

*　　*　　*

The elevator came to a stop.

Another massive explosion rocked the house, sending Black and McCoy crashing into each other, alive but shaken. Their door opened.

Gagging on the smoke, Black pulled himself up, popped his head and .45 out into the hallway, and saw two more terrorists heading through the "tunnel" for the circular stairway. He raced forward, pivoted out of the hallway, took aim, and fired off four quick rounds.

One missed by inches, but three ripped into the base of one terrorist's skull, virtually ripping it from his shoulders. The man crumpled in a pool of gurgling blood.

Black quickly ducked back inside his darkened hallway as McCoy raced up behind him. Just in time. The second terrorist whipped around, fired three bursts from his AK-47, then scrambled upstairs.

*　　*　　*

"The president's secure."

Galishnikov shouted the good news as he watched the TV coverage.

Thank God, thought Bennett. He just wished he could say the same about Black and McCoy.

★ ★ ★

Black poked his head into the hallway again, but saw nothing.

He raced across to the other side, into the hallway leading to the west-wing elevator Dr. Mordechai had used earlier.

Seconds later, the hallway still clear, McCoy raced across to join him. "What's the plan?" she asked, trying to calm her breathing.

"Okay, we've killed one and now we've got three more upstairs, right?" Black asked, reloading his Smith & Wesson.

"I think so."

"Okay, I'll head upstairs. You wait here. If they come through the east elevator, blow them away. If anybody comes down those main stairs, blow them away. Anybody comes in through the front door, blow them away. Get it?"

"Got it."

"Good."

★ ★ ★

Bennett couldn't hear what the two were saying.

All he could see on the monitor was Black taking off and leaving McCoy by herself. He didn't like it. He punched the button and waited for the east elevator to come down to him. The least he could do was bring her an Uzi and some ammo.

★ ★ ★

Black opened the door as quietly as he could.

He dropped to his stomach and crawled along the floor, through Dr. Mordechai's office, using his night-vision goggles to figure out the way. At the door, he carefully snuck a peek and saw one of the terrorists with his back to him, down the hallway. Should he shoot? That would leave two more. It would also unleash the wrath of hell. Two AK-47s against his .45? Not exactly good odds.

Forget it, he thought. *Take the shot.* He raised his revolver, took aim— and suddenly another terrorist came around the corner and looked straight at him.

"*Gun*," the man screamed in Arabic.

Black didn't know what the guy was saying. Nor did he care. He pulled the trigger hard. The bullet went high.

He squeezed off two more rounds. Again, both missed. He fired again. This time the bullet ricocheted off the wall as the standing terrorist raised his machine gun and moved to pull the trigger.

Black pumped out his last two rounds and froze. As if in slow motion, he watched these two bullets flash out of the barrel of his gun, streak through the air, and explode through the beady, black, lifeless eyes of the terrorist glaring at him. A blaze of machine-gun bullets began spraying everywhere as the man went down. But he was down all right. And down for good.

Black took no time to inspect his handiwork, though. He quickly ducked into the elevator, slammed the door, and headed back down to McCoy.

* * *

"*Yes, yes,*" cheered the men in the bunker down below.

Two down.

Two to go.

* * *

The sound startled her.

Down the darkened hall across from her, she could see and hear the east elevator door beginning to open. McCoy could hear the gunfire upstairs, and her heart was racing. She had no idea who might be coming through that door. But Black had been clear. It wouldn't be him. So blow them away.

She waited a split second for the elevator door to open just a little more, then saw a shadowy figure holding a machine gun. It certainly wasn't Black. She opened fire—cool, smooth, just like she'd been trained. Double-tap to the torso. The man crashed to the floor, barely knowing what hit him.

Now the elevator behind her began to open as well. McCoy wheeled around and aimed her Beretta at the door. She hoped it was Black.

"*McCoy. It's me—Deek.*"

"*Hands! Hands!*" she shouted back, her adrenaline racing.

The door opened, and Black came out with his hands up. Both breathed a quick sigh of relief as Black hurried to her side.

"*Look out,*" Black suddenly screamed. "*Get down.*"

McCoy, already down on one knee, flattened herself to the floor.

The bloody man in the elevator began lifting his machine gun.

Black raised his revolver, took aim, and squeezed the trigger. But nothing fired. His weapon was empty, and the bloody, shadowy man was still raising his weapon.

"*McCoy—I'm out,*" Black screamed.

McCoy looked up and saw the machine gun barrel aiming at her face. She instinctively emptied her Beretta 9 mm into the shadows. The man's machine gun dropped to the floor as she heard him scream and collapse, limp and lifeless.

It was over. But it had been close. Black just stood and stared. It took a second for him to get his bearings again. But he did, rapidly reloading as McCoy did the same.

"How many left?" she whispered, popping in a fresh clip and watching nervously for any signs of movement in the dark hallway.

"Let's see," he answered, taking a fast accounting of their work. "We got two in this hallway. One up in the kitchen. That should leave just one more, I think. Upstairs."

"What do you want to do?"

"It's too risky to take the stairs. If he's in the living room, he'll see us before we see him. But he obviously knows about the elevators. He could be waiting at either one." Black looked around. "Where did everyone else go?" he whispered.

"I have no idea," McCoy responded. "They just disappeared."

"I know. It's weird."

"Come on, Deek, man. We need a plan."

"Okay. You go up the west elevator here," Black said, motioning to the one behind him, the one he'd just come down. "I'll go up the other side. When the doors open, if you see movement, just start firing. If not, try to work your way toward the living room. Make sure to check all the beds, the closets, whatever. Don't take any chances, okay?"

"Don't worry."

"Good. Let's do it."

"And Deek?" asked McCoy. "Are you thinking what I'm thinking?"

"The four horsemen?" responded Black.

"Exactly."

"We'll know soon enough. Let's just get this last guy before he gets us."

Black quickly checked the hallway. It was clear. He raced across to the east elevator, grabbed the dead man's AK-47, and ripped off his black mask. Then he dragged him back into the hallway and left him under the security cameras.

* * *

Sanchez and the president burst into the safety of the Presidential Emergency Operations Center underneath the White House.

The vice president and Kirkpatrick—already assured that the president was safe—were on a videoconference with Mitchell at CIA and Secretary Trainor and General Mutschler at the Pentagon.

"Jim, thank God," said the First Lady, giving him a big hug, getting him seated, and holding his hand.

"Mr. President, thank God you're okay," echoed the VP.

"Have you talked to Harris?" the president responded.

"We just did, sir. Told us the whole thing."

"Cupid?"

"Unbelievable. I can't believe you didn't tell us earlier."

"How could I?"

* * *

The cameras focused on the face of the dead man in the hallway.

It was instantly digitized and processed through a high-speed database. A few seconds later, Dr. Mordechai saw the Interpol record come up on one of his computer screens. Sure enough, he was Iraqi. The four horsemen had come gunning for them.

* * *

"Sir, I have more bad news," said Kirkpatrick.

"What now?" asked the president, shaken and livid.

"There's been an explosion inside Dr. Mordechai's house."

"What happened? What about Bennett and his team?"

"They're in the house right now, sir. We don't know what's happened, or their status. Not yet. I immediately retasked a satellite to move over the house to let us see what's going on inside. We should be in range in the next sixty seconds."

"Get me Doron on the line."

"We've been trying, sir," Kirkpatrick told him. "For the last fifteen minutes. We can't get through. Not since the gun battle at the cathedral. We think they've gone into an emergency session. Our fear is that they are weighing a first strike against Iraq."

"Keep trying. Try every number we've got."

The president seethed. It was everything he could do not to explode at someone right now. One of his own Secret Service agents had just tried to kill him. Three of his best people were pinned down—possibly dead—inside Israel. And Israel and Iraq were on the brink of going nuclear.

"SEAL Team Six—are they still on the *Reagan*?" MacPherson demanded.

"No, sir," said Kirkpatrick. "They're heading to Baghdad with the NEST guys."

"Well, send someone in to rescue Bennett's team— *now.*"

* * *

The west elevator door opened in Dr. Mordechai's room.

McCoy peered out anxiously, her fully loaded Beretta leading the way. There was no one in the closet. She inched forward. No one in the office.

* * *

Black pushed the up button, but the east elevator started going down.

Down? Why was it going down?

Black tried not to panic, aimed his .45, and prepared to fire.

* * *

McCoy scanned the hallway—clear.

She darted across into Dr. Mordechai's bedroom—clear. Then she plunged her Beretta through the bathroom door, scanning for signs of life. Nothing. She darted back into the office and hugged the wall, trying to plot out her next move.

* * *

The elevator clanged to a stop—but the door didn't open.

This is it, thought Black. *I'm about to die.*

"Black," Bennett whispered. "Can you hear me?"

Black was stunned.

"Jon? Is that you?"

"Yeah, it's me."

"Where are you?"

"I'm going to open the door. Just don't shoot."

"I won't if you won't."

Black still had his sense of humor, even under fire. The elevator door opened. Now Black saw what Bennett and the others had seen some thirty minutes before: a spectacular underground bunker where Mordechai could track two battles at once—one for his country and one for his home.

"We can't leave McCoy up there by herself," said Bennett, triple-checking his Uzi and getting into the elevator.

"You really know how to use one of these things?" asked Black.

"Hey, just aim and shoot."

"Good grief, Jon. It's an Uzi. Not a Polaroid."

* * *

McCoy quickly—carefully—peered around the corner.

She still saw no one in the hallway to the kitchen. But where was Black? He'd have a much better view of the living room and the kitchen coming from the east wing than she had from this office.

She held her Beretta close to her face, her mind racing for options. She looked down on the floor and saw something small and black. What was it? It was bigger than a clip. A wallet, maybe? She glanced down the hallway again, then quickly grabbed it.

It was Deek's BlackBerry. She switched it to mute/vibrate to make sure it didn't suddenly make a sound. Then she typed in a quick message:

jon—where are you?—seen black?—erin

* * *

Bennett suddenly felt his BlackBerry vibrating.

It was from McCoy.

"Deek, look," Bennett whispered.

The two glanced at the message as Black realized his BlackBerry was gone.

"Where is she?" Black whispered back.

The elevator stopped, and the door opened. Black thrust his AK-47 out into the guest room and scanned for any sign of life or movement. Nothing.

He moved forward carefully, covering Bennett as he typed a note back to McCoy: *Where are you? Wait there. We'll come to you.* When he was done, Black pointed to the hatch into his bedroom closet, instructing Bennett to go through it, then quietly explained that he'd cross the hallway and work his way down through the bedrooms on the other side of the hall. When he knocked twice on the wall, they should both burst into the living room, guns blazing.

Black took off his night-vision goggles and put them on Bennett. They only had one set between them, and Black certainly had a lot more experience at this than Bennett. Confident they were as ready as they were going to be, Black glanced out the hallway door, drew his head back in, double-checked his machine gun, then sprinted across.

The hall erupted with gunfire, the distinctive tinkling of spent metal shells dropping to the hardwood floor. Bennett dropped to his knees, shivering with fear. His back against the wall, he huddled in the corner by the hatch, but didn't dare go through it. What if this monster was on the other side?

The house suddenly became eerily quiet. Bennett strained to hear something, anything. Where was this guy? Had Black been hit?

His BlackBerry vibrated again. It was McCoy. She was in Dr. Mordechai's private office. He typed a quick note: *i'm fine—not sure about deek.*

She wrote back: *i'm praying for you guys.*

Strangely enough, it actually did make him feel better. He tried to muster some courage, settled his breathing, adjusted the night-vision goggles, and carefully lifted the hatch. He aimed the Uzi inside and peered through, not moving a millimeter, not making a sound. He saw nothing. No movement. No signs of a human presence of any kind.

Now what? His BlackBerry went off again. He grabbed it, hoping it was McCoy. It wasn't. It was from the White House, half a world away.

Jon—POTUS requests status check . . . you guys okay? . . . intel says explosions, gunfire in house . . . seal team three in route . . . thirty minutes . . . stand by—K.

It was Kirkpatrick. The president was sending in a Navy SEAL Team to rescue them. *Thank God*, he thought. Maybe McCoy's prayers really were working. *Then again*, he thought, *we might not be alive in thirty minutes.*

* * *

Black was hit.

He was bleeding heavily from the fiery gash in his right elbow and thought the bone might be shattered. True or not, he could barely hold his weapon and wasn't much of a shot as a lefty.

Slowly, painfully, he worked his way through the bedrooms, leaving a trail of blood as he went. He made it to the final bedroom and crouched by the door. His eyes were blurring. His head was swimming. He was losing blood fast. If something didn't happen soon, he'd be unconscious in less than five minutes.

* * *

"The satellite's in place, Mr. President," Kirkpatrick shouted.

The president and vice president were huddled in the corner, on the phone with the Joint Chiefs, considering their options. At the sound of Kirkpatrick's voice, however, the two whipped around and stared up at the video screen on the far wall. The lights were dimmed. The static cleared up. Now the president and his NSC team found themselves looking down into Dr. Mordechai's house via high-resolution thermal imagery.

"Who's that?" asked the president

Mitchell, via videoconference—but watching the same image in the CIA Op Center at Langley—answered quickly. "The person on the far left, Mr. President—I think that's McCoy."

"How about the two on the right side of the house?"

"The one on the upper part of the screen, in the northern bedroom of the east wing, looks a little larger, taller—probably Black. The one crawling through one of the walls—my guess is that's Bennett."

"The rest of those bodies look dead."

"They do, sir."

"And that guy—the one crouching in the stairwell—is that Dr. Mordechai?"

"Doubt it, sir. Looks like a bandit. In fact, looks like the guy's surrounded, but the good guys don't know it."

The president's combat instincts began kicking in. "Marsha, are you able to send them all an e-mail simultaneously?"

"Absolutely, sir."

"Good. Tell them what we're seeing. Have McCoy move into the kitchen. Then around the corner behind that wall there. Tell her when we see her in position, we'll tell Black and Bennett to throw their doors open and lay down fire on the stairwell. When the bandit ducks down, have McCoy pop out and put a full clip in the back of his head."

"You got it, Mr. President."

* * *

A moment later, Bennett got the message.

So did McCoy, twice—on her BlackBerry and Black's.

Black got nothing. And he was fading fast.

* * *

Israeli prime minister David Doron huddled with his team.

"This is it, gentlemen. I'm afraid the fate of Israel rests with us. We all agree the latest attack on the American president is Saddam's doing. We know what he tried to do to us. We know he is desperate and may very well feel he has nothing left to lose. Despite a relentless U.S. air attack, Saddam is still playing some scary strategic cards. And my fear is that he's got at least one left. With our names on it. The question is, what do we do now? Do we sit back and wait? wait to be slaughtered? Or do we strike first? We've got to make a decision—and we've got to do it right now."

Doron scanned the room. Every heart was heavy with the burden of this devastating moment in the long, tragic, extraordinary history of the Jewish people.

"This is our moment, gentlemen. Let us be worthy of it."

* * *

Azziz sat in the control room with a phone in his hand.

At the other end of the line was his maximum leader, Saddam Hussein. And his orders were clear. It was time to unleash the Last Jihad.

* * *

McCoy double-checked her Beretta.

Then—in stocking feet—slowly, carefully, quietly, she inched her way into the kitchen, then back into the hallway, just behind the archway into the living room.

* * *

The president and his team watched McCoy's image move into position. Kirkpatrick then sent an e-mail to Black and Bennett to get ready. When they received the next e-mail, they should both burst out of their doors, guns blazing.

* * *

Mordechai, Galishnikov, and Sa'id could see everything that was happening.

But they could do nothing about it. Mordechai's impressive array of equipment was even able to pick up the wireless transmissions coming into the house. They could, therefore, intercept and read all of the White House's e-mail communications with Bennett, Black, and McCoy, since they weren't encrypted. But what could they do to help?

Galishnikov proposed taking one of the elevators up to ground level and sneaking up on the last remaining terrorist through the "tunnel." But Mordechai vetoed the idea. The president had his plan, and it was in play. Any sound or disturbance could confuse an already dangerous situation.

* * *

Bennett's heart was racing.

He was breathing hard. His legs felt weak. He wiped the sweat off his palms, then set his BlackBerry down on the carpet in front of him where he could see its screen glowing in the dark, and could see it vibrate when the message from the White House came in. He pulled the Uzi tight to his side, clicked off the safety, and put one hand on the door handle. This was it. There was no turning back now.

Five, four, three, two, one—there it was, thought Bennett.

He could see the little machine shake in the dark. Instinctively, he stood, pulled the door handle down, and opened the door. *Click.*

But something made him hesitate. He glanced down quickly at the new e-mail. It wasn't from the White House. It was from his mother—from the hospital. His father had just died.

Bennett froze in disbelief. He couldn't think. Couldn't speak. Couldn't move.

But standing still and exposed, twenty paces from the fourth horseman, was not a smart move—whatever the reason. The Iraqi heard the door click open, popped up, saw Bennett's shadowy figure, and opened fire. The bedroom exploded with bullets and smoke.

Bennett snapped to. He'd never fired a gun in his life. He'd never even held one before. But now—seething with rage—he wheeled around and opened fire before three bullets ripped through his upper body, sending him crashing to the floor in a spray of blood.

Deek had no BlackBerry. He had no way of knowing of the president's plan. But he could hear his friend Bennett's terrifying scream, and when he did, he instinctively jumped to his feet and burst into the hallway, his AK-47 roaring with bullets and smoke. One of Black's rounds hit the Iraqi in the shoulder, sending him crashing down the stairs. But not before Black, too, was hit in the chest.

McCoy now played her part. Pivoting around through the archway, she saw the Iraqi plunging down the circular stairs and quickly emptied all twelve rounds into his twitching, clawing, contorted body.

Then the shooting stopped. And it grew quiet. Too quiet.

★　★　★

"*What happened?*" demanded the president.

"I don't know," Kirkpatrick responded. "I never sent the next e-mail."

"Why did Bennett move?"

But there was no answer.

✩   ✩   ✩

Mordechai, Galishnikov, and Sa'id burst off the elevator with Uzis in their hands.

They shouted to McCoy not to shoot and came racing up behind her. That's when they saw the entire battle scene for the first time, in living color, not on some black-and-white TV monitor. They stopped cold, in total shock.

McCoy ejected the spent clip in her Beretta, popped in her last full clip, and handed it quickly to Galishnikov and Sa'id. "Make sure they're all dead, and round up their weapons—all of them," she ordered, then raced over to Bennett and Black.

She came upon Black first, in a pool of blood at the head of the east hallway. She knelt at his side and put her right fingers on his neck, checking for his pulse. *Oh, God,* she thought, her left hand reflexively covering her mouth. *Oh, God, no.* It was too late. Black was dead.

McCoy scrambled over to Bennett, slumped against the bedroom wall near the doorway. *Please—please don't let him be dead too,* she silently pleaded.

He certainly looked dead. Blood was everywhere, pouring from his right and left shoulders and from his right forearm. But he'd actually been quite lucky. None of his vital organs had been hit, nor had he been hit in the face. She quickly checked his pulse.

"Jon's alive," McCoy shouted to the others. *"Help me move him."*

"Let's get him downstairs," said Dr. Mordechai. "I've got a whole medical room down there. Blood. Drugs. Surgical supplies. Everything."

"Good," said McCoy. *"Let's do it!"*

✩   ✩   ✩

"Burt, we've got a problem."

Defense Secretary Burt Trainor monitored the air war over Iraq from the National Military Command Center under the Pentagon. It had been going quite well—until now.

"What've you got, Jack?"

"One of my birds just picked up some unusual activity in a building that's supposedly a children's hospital in downtown Baghdad. I'm cross-linking the live feed to you right now."

The image crackled to life on the main screen in front of Trainor, downloaded from a Keyhole photo-electronic spy satellite, in this case the USA-116. Among the most sophisticated spy satellites ever built, its imagery was so vivid that it allowed American intelligence officials and military commanders to read a person's license plate or the logo on a baseball cap. It could even take a picture of a man holding a cup of coffee and practically determine whether he was drinking regular or decaf.

The instant he saw the pictures, Trainor felt nauseated. This was more than "unusual activity."

The ten-story hospital before him had been completely gutted inside and turned into a state-of-the-art missile launch center. The roof of the building was completely opened up, the way some sports stadiums can mechanically slide back their domes and let their teams play in the great outdoors.

Mitchell and Trainor were now staring down the barrel of one massive gun—a gleaming, sixty-foot rocket. And this was no short- or medium-range Al-Hussein rocket, merely capable of hitting Israel. This was a full-blown intercontinental ballistic missile, capable of hitting Washington, New York, or any point in North America or Europe. And it was being fueled up and readied for liftoff.

"You concur, Burt?" asked Mitchell. "I don't want to call this on my own."

"I'm with you," said Trainor, staring at the screen in disbelief. "We're looking at an Iraqi ICBM—almost certainly with a nuclear warhead—and we can't have more than ten or fifteen minutes to take it out."

Trainor turned to a stunned Joint Chiefs chairman Mutschler, who nodded. Then he turned to an aide.

"Get me the president—*now.*"

＊　＊　＊

"Can the SEAL team take it out?" asked the president.

"There's not enough time, sir," Secretary Trainor responded.

The president then directed Trainor to relay the latest intel to CENTCOM, launch the B-2s, and order all other U.S. air and ground forces—including SEAL Team Six and the NEST guys—to evacuate the theater immediately. The only question now was, would it be enough, and would it be in time?

* * *

The Iraqi engineers raced to complete their mission.

They knew the consequences of failing. The rocket's fuel tanks were almost full. The targeting package was almost loaded into the computers. They needed only a few more minutes, and the Last Jihad would be airborne.

* * *

Two B-2 Spirits roared out of Incirlik, Turkey, locked and loaded.

The sixty-nine-foot lead bomber—designated Bravo Delta Foxtrot and piloted by Lieutenant Colonel Dave Kachinski—entered Iraqi airspace from the north at 49,400 feet. His backup—designated Bravo Delta Bravo—entered a split second later.

* * *

Bennett was quickly stabilized.

Secure in the medical suite in the underground bunker, he was hooked up to IVs, given plasma, and put on painkillers. But there was nothing else they could do here. They needed to get him to a trauma unit, and Black to a morgue.

The only good news: SEAL Team Three would be there soon to extract them and get them back to the USS *Reagan*.

* * *

Kachinski radioed the NORAD operations center.

He was patched through to the NMCC, the Strategic Air Command at Offutt Air Force Base, and the Presidential Emergency Operations Center under the White House.

"Crystal Palace, this is Bravo Delta Foxtrot. We are standing by for orders."

The entire National Security Council huddled with their commander in chief, waiting to see what the president would do.

☆ ☆ ☆

The missile was fueled.

The targeting program was loaded.

They were ready.

☆ ☆ ☆

At a cost of $2.1 billion, the B-2A is a marvel of modern warfare.

Better known as Stealth bombers—sleek, black, and virtually undetectable by radar—they were designed precisely for dropping The Bomb. But would they?

☆ ☆ ☆

"Dr. Mordechai," McCoy said softly.

Only now was she beginning to feel the shock of one dead and one gravely wounded friend. She sat in the center of the main war room, staring at all the video screens, glassy-eyed and distant.

"Yes, Erin," the old man replied gently.

"I think I should call the president."

"Sure. Use this phone here."

"Thank you." She sat there for a moment, trying to remember the phone number for the PEOC. But she couldn't. Her mind was a dizzying swirl of adrenaline and emotions, and she was having trouble focusing. Finally, she dialed the main White House number—202-456-1414—and told the switchboard operator who she was and where she was calling from.

☆ ☆ ☆

"Mr. President, the Iraqi missile is ready to fire," shouted Secretary Trainor.

"There's no time for any B-52 attacks. If you're going to fire nuclear weapons into Baghdad and Tikrit, you've got to do it now. And we've got to order the B-52s to turn around and get out of the way or they're history."

This was it. Decision time.

* * *

Marsha Kirkpatrick answered the phone.

It was McCoy. She wanted to explain what had happened. But there wasn't time.

"Erin, listen to me. Are you listening?" Kirkpatrick interrupted.

"Yes . . . ," McCoy replied, foggy and faraway.

Kirkpatrick hesitated. Should she really tell this brave young woman, especially after all that she'd already been through? Then again, McCoy had just explained she was calling from a war room bunker several hundred feet under hardened concrete and granite.

"Erin, the Iraqis are minutes away from launching a nuclear missile."

"What? At Israel?"

"We're not sure. Could be at you. Might be at us."

* * *

The PEOC was interrupted again by the crackle of the call from NORAD.

"Crystal Palace, again this is Bravo Delta Foxtrot. Repeat, we are high, clear, and awaiting orders. Please advise."

The president took a deep breath. He looked around the room. He was out of time.

* * *

Sweat poured from his face.

Azziz checked his computer console. T-minus three minutes. "*Come on,*" he screamed. "*Get it done.*"

* * *

McCoy was slipping into shock.

"Erin? What is it?" asked Dr. Mordechai as she hung up the phone.

She just looked at these three sweet old men. Her bottom lip was quivering. She tried to compose herself, tried to be strong like her mother had been at the end.

"The Iraqis . . ." She couldn't get through it.

"What? What about the Iraqis, Erin?" Sa'id pressed.

"They're about to launch an ICBM. . . ."
Galishnikov gasped.

* * *

The president's voice sounded more serene than anyone had expected.
"Secretary Trainor, order the B-52s to return to base."

* * *

The four of them—Mordechai, Galishnikov, Sa'id, and McCoy—turned
to the huge video screens positioned on the wall in front of them. One
was tuned to Sky News. Another to CNN. Another to BBC. Another to
Israel's Channel 2. And another to RTR in Moscow. There was still no
news of a possible imminent nuclear launch. But how could there be? No
one in his right mind would leak such horrifying news.

* * *

"Bravo Delta Foxtrot," MacPherson began. "This is the president of the
United States."
Everyone in the PEOC held his breath. They instinctively stood up,
though the president himself remained confined to his wheelchair.
"Yes, Mr. President," came the static-filled reply.
"Bravo Delta Foxtrot . . ." The president closed his eyes and bowed
his head.
"Did not copy that, Mr. President. Please repeat."
Precious seconds passed.
"Mr. President, did not copy that. I repeat, did not copy. Please
repeat. Over."
The president opened his eyes and looked down at a small plastic card,
no bigger than a credit card, that he held in his perspiring, trembling
hands. "Bravo Delta Foxtrot, the chairman of the Joint Chiefs has given
you an authentic launch code?"
"Yes, sir. Awaiting verification, sir."
The First Lady took a deep breath, folded her hands, and brought
them to her mouth. She stared into the president's eyes and tried to read
his inscrutable expression.
"Tango, Tango, Alpha, Zulu, Seven, Niner, Foxtrot, Niner."

Julie MacPherson gasped. Suddenly her head was throbbing. Her throat burned.

"Verifying, sir—Tango, Tango, Alpha, Zulu, Seven, Niner, Foxtrot, Niner."

"That is correct."

"I have verification, sir."

"Bravo Delta Foxtrot . . ."

"Yes, sir."

The White House photographer now snapped furiously, making it difficult for the president to hear. He held up his hand, and the autoadvance and flashbulbs stopped.

"You and your wingman are authorized to fire your weapons. Please acknowledge."

"Roger that, Mr. President. Bravo Delta Foxtrot acknowledges verified orders. We are authorized to fire our weapons."

"God be with you, airman."

"And you, sir."

* * *

Smoke began pouring out of the massive rocket engines.

The countdown was under way.

T-minus two minutes.

* * *

The B-2 pilots rapidly completed their final preparations.

They both double-checked their instruments, and each said a prayer. A split second later, each pulled the trigger.

Each twenty-foot, 3,500 pound, AGM-129A cruise missile and its W-80-1 nuclear warhead released cleanly and began hurtling toward its target at supersonic speed.

There was no turning back now.

* * *

Azziz picked up the secure phone and hit speed-dial one.

"T-minus one minute, Your Excellency."

"Praise be to Allah."

★ ★ ★

McCoy's head snapped to attention.

Someone was whispering her name.

"Erin . . ."

It was Bennett. She ran into the medical suite, moved to his side, and held his hand. She took a cloth and gently stroked the perspiration off his forehead and smiled at him as he lay trembling. "It's okay," she told him. "You're going to be okay."

Fortunately, it was true, and Bennett knew it was by the conviction in her voice. He was tired. He needed sleep. But he would live.

"I need to tell you something . . ."

His voice was raspy and faint.

"Hey, hey, quiet."

"No, no, I need to . . ."

"You need to rest right now, Jon. The president will kill me if you don't."

Bennett tried to smile, then again tried to speak. *"I need to tell you something . . . it's important. . . ."*

She leaned down close to him, and felt his weak breath on her cheek. "What is it, Jon?"

"I think I found some buried treasure . . . and I don't want to let it go."

Then he squeezed her hand and locked his eyes on hers.

★ ★ ★

All systems were go.

Azziz relayed the countdown over the phone.

"T-minus fifteen . . . fourteen . . . thirteen . . . twelve . . . eleven . . ."

★ ★ ★

The president lowered his head.

His team waited nervously.

The White House photographer snapped a few more pictures, then stopped. All was silent and surreal. All eyes shifted to a seismograph—connected to a highly sensitive monitor, pre-positioned by U.S. special forces in the desert outside Baghdad—set up in the middle of the table. It couldn't have been more than sixty degrees in the underground bunker, but the president could feel the perspiration beading on his forehead.

And then it happened.

The needlelike pen inside the seismograph machine started vibrating violently.

The president turned to the video screens on the wall. His eyes locked onto the live images being fed in from spy satellites in the stratosphere and from unmanned drones hovering over the Iraqi-Kuwaiti border. And what he saw was completely beyond his comprehension.

The flashes of brilliant white light. The two massive fireballs. The howling radioactive winds, surging to 160 miles per hour. The instant obliteration of large sections of two ancient cities. The twin signature mushroom clouds, rising mile after mile into the heavens.

In the blink of an eye—in the push of a button—it was all over.

And yet, in his heart, MacPherson knew it had really just begun.

IS IT TRUE?

★ ★ ★

To learn more about the research used for this book—and to track the latest political, economic, military, and archeological developments in Israel, Jordan, Iraq, and other countries described in *The Last Jihad*—please visit:

www.joelrosenberg.com

You can also sign up to receive Joel C. Rosenberg's
free e-mail newsletter,
>> FLASH TRAFFIC <<.

ACKNOWLEDGMENTS

Marry a girl who loves you enough to take big risks, who believes in you and is willing to ride the roller coaster of life together. I did, and I'm a better man for it.

Lynn—I thank God every day that He brought you into my life and that in some cosmic and counterintuitive moment I wasn't stupid enough to let you slip away. I cringe to think of what I would be if I hadn't married you. I cringe to think of how many jobs I would have been fired from if you hadn't patiently read and edited everything I've ever written—*before* I gave it to my editors. The fact that you are such a wise, discerning, and sensitive writer and editor, as well as a great wife, mom, daughter, sister, daughter-in-law, and friend, totally astounds me. I could never have written this book, or any other—nor would I have wanted to—without you. Thank you. I love you.

Caleb, Jacob, and Jonah—yes, you're the Ringling Brothers, a wild and wonderful three-ring circus, but nothing makes me happier than being your dad. Thanks for your love, your prayers, and your eagerness to go on big adventures together.

Dad and Mom Rosenberg—I can't tell you how blessed I am to be your son. Thanks so much for reading this manuscript umpteen times, and thank you even more for not naming me Lincoln. Em, Jim, Katie, and Luke—you've endured all my crazy projects through the years; what's one more? Thanks for rooting me on! The Meyers "fam"—Mom, Soonan, Muncle, Tia, little Michael, 'Fael, Dad, Carol, and "Great Gram"—thanks for welcoming me into your family.

To our kindred spirits from Syracuse—the Koshys, Akka, Dave and Barb Olson, Richie and Colleen Costello, Vince and Junko Salisbury, and Nick and Debbi DeCola—thanks so much for getting us started and keeping us going.

To our kindred spirits from McLean and Frontline—Dan and Elise Sutherland, "John Black John Black," Edward and Kailea Hunt, Daryl Gross, Amy Knapp, Lori Medanich, Julie Christou, Wendy Howard, John and Kelly Park, Jim and Sharon Supp, Kerri Boyer, Alan and Bethany Blomdahl, Tim and Carolyn Lugbill, Dave and Twee Ramos, Bob and Janice Lee, Brian and Christa Geno, Frank and Cindy Cofer, Ron and Gennene Johnson, and Lon Solomon and his team—what a thrill to be in the race with you guys. Thanks for doing fun, faith, and fiction with us!

To our kindred spirits in the political world—Rush, Steve and Sabina Forbes, Sean and Jill Hannity, David Limbaugh, Bill Dal Col, Diana Schneider, James "Bo Snerdley" Golden, Kit "H.R." Carson, Grace-Marie Turner, Marvin Olasky, Nick Eicher, Allen Roth, John McLaughlin, Nancy Merritt, Bill and Elaine Bennett, Pete Wehner, Burt Pines, Joe Loconte, Adam Meyerson, Ed Feulner, and Peggy Noonan—thank you so much for all your encouragement on this project and on so many others.

To my agent, Scott Miller, at Trident Media Group—why you took my first call I'll never know. But I'm so grateful you did. You've done an absolutely fabulous, relentless, tireless, brilliant job, and I am forever grateful. Thanks so much for your hard work, wise counsel, coolness under pressure, and your friendship. You da man! Let's hope this is just the start.

Finally, to Tom Doherty, Bob Gleason, Brian Callaghan, Jennifer Marcus, and the entire team at Tor/Forge Books—you guys rolled the dice and took a chance on a first-timer. . . . Then you all went absolutely above and beyond when the crisis with Iraq began to heat up to get this book locked, loaded, and fired into the marketplace *before* the war! I believed in miracles before I met you guys—but now I've seen one with my very eyes and I can't tell you how much I appreciate it! Thank you, thank you, thank you.

May 2002

JOEL C. ROSENBERG

Joel C. Rosenberg is the New York Times best-selling author of *The Last Jihad*, *The Last Days*, and *The Ezekiel Option*, with more than one million copies in print. As a communications strategist, he has worked with some of the world's most influential leaders in business, politics, and media, including Steve Forbes, Rush Limbaugh, and former Israeli prime minister Benjamin Netanyahu. As a novelist, he has been interviewed on hundreds of radio and TV programs, including ABC's *Nightline*, *CNN Headline News*, FOX News Channel, The History Channel, MSNBC, the *Rush Limbaugh Show*, and the *Sean Hannity Show*. He has been profiled by the *New York Times*, the *Washington Times*, and the *Jerusalem Post*, and was the subject of two cover stories in *World* magazine. He has addressed audiences all over the world, including Russia, Israel, Jordan, Egypt, Turkey, and Belgium, and has spoken at the White House.

The first page of his first novel—*The Last Jihad*—puts readers inside the cockpit of a hijacked jet, coming in on a kamikaze attack into an American city, which leads to a war with Saddam Hussein over weapons of mass destruction. Yet it was written before 9/11, and published before the actual war with Iraq. *The Last Jihad* spent eleven weeks on the *New York Times* hardcover fiction best-seller list, reaching as high as #7. It raced up the *USA Today* and *Publishers Weekly* best-seller lists, hit #4 on the *Wall Street Journal* list, and hit #1 on Amazon.com.

His second thriller—*The Last Days*—opens with the death of Yasser

Arafat and a U.S. diplomatic convoy ambushed in Gaza. Two weeks before *The Last Days* was published in hardcover, a U.S. diplomatic convoy was ambushed in Gaza. Thirteen months later, Yasser Arafat was dead. *The Last Days* spent four weeks on the *New York Times* hardcover fiction bestseller list, hit #5 on the *Denver Post* list, and hit #8 on the *Dallas Morning News* list. Both books have been optioned by a Hollywood producer.

The Ezekiel Option centers on a dictator rising in Russia who forms a military alliance with the leaders of Iran as they feverishly pursue nuclear weapons and threaten to wipe Israel off the face of the earth. On the very day it was published in June 2005, Iran elected a new leader who vowed to accelerate the country's nuclear program and later threatened to "wipe Israel off the map." Six months after it was published, Moscow signed a $1 billion arms deal with Tehran. *The Ezekiel Option* spent four weeks on the *New York Times* hardcover fiction best-seller list and five months on the Christian Bookseller Association best-seller list, reaching as high as #4.

www.joelrosenberg.com

ISRAEL DISCOVERS MASSIVE RESERVES OF OIL, GAS

In August 2005, while on *The Ezekiel Option* book tour, I had lunch in Dallas with Gene Soltero, the president and CEO of a company called Zion Oil. I had never heard of the MIT-trained economist and petroleum engineer before, but took a liking to him immediately. Balding, with short tufts of gray hair over each ear, and small, wire-rimmed glasses, Soltero was a soft-spoken man in his sixties who looked more like a professor of management at some college in the American Midwest than a treasure hunter in the Mideast. But he had quite a story to tell, and a lot of questions for me.

On a recent visit to Israel, an investor in his company had picked up a paperback copy of *The Last Jihad* in Ben Gurion International Airport, read it on the plane home, and gotten so excited about it that he had emailed Soltero and everyone else in the company urging that they read it too. Why? Because in the novel, an American company working with a team of geologists and petroleum engineers in Israel discover massive reserves of oil and natural gas in the Holy Land, making all of them rich and changing the geopolitics of the region forever. Except to Soltero and his colleagues it wasn't fiction. It was their lives.

As Soltero explained it, all the top executives in the company quickly read *Jihad* and *The Last Days*, in which a Wall Street strategist turned White House advisor puts together an "Oil for Peace" plan whereupon the U.S. will underwrite the billions of dollars necessary to develop the new petroleum find if the Israelis and Palestinians will stop the violence and find a way to work together. The more Soltero and his colleagues read, the more intrigued they got. *How had I come up with such an oil and gas storyline? Did I know about all the biblical prophecies that said Israel would, in fact, discover oil in "the last days"? More to the point, did I know just how close their company and others were to seeing these prophecies come to pass?*

We agreed I would tell my story and then he would tell me his.

THE PROSPERITY PREREQUISITES

When I began writing *The Last Jihad* series, I did base it on prophecies in the Book of Ezekiel which indicate that there are two things that must occur before Israel's "last days" showdown with Russia and Iran. The first "prerequisite," as it were, is that that there must be a period of calm and stability in Israel before the "war of Gog and Magog." The second is that Israel must build up significant wealth. But the truth is I had no idea at the time just how much detail the Scriptures contained with regards to the discovery of oil in the promised land, and thus I had no idea how close to reality my fiction was going to be.

The "prerequisites" come from Ezekiel 38:8 and Ezekiel 38:11-13, which read: "After many days, you [dictator of Russia] will be summoned; in the latter years you will come into the land that is restored from the sword, whose inhabitants have been gathered from many nations to the mountains of Israel which had been a continual waste; but its people were brought out from the nations, and they are living securely, all of them. . . . And you will say, 'I will go up against the land of unwalled villages. I will go against those who are at rest, that live securely, all of them living without walls and having no bars or gates, to capture spoil and to seize plunder, to turn your hand against the waste places which are now inhabited, and against the people who are gathered from the nations, who have acquired cattle and goods, who live at the center of the world.' Sheba and Dedan[1] and the merchants of Tarshish[2] with all its villages will say to you [the Russian dictator], 'Have you come to capture spoil? Have you assembled to seize plunder, to carry away silver and gold, to take away cattle and goods, to capture great spoil?'"

In the next chapter, I will discuss the "peace prerequisite." But as Soltero and I talked, I focused more on the "prosperity prerequisite."

Ezekiel 38 clearly indicates that prior to the Russian-Iranian attack:

The Jews have poured back into the land of Israel.

The Jews are settling and in the process rebuilding the ancient ruins and "waste places" of Israel—that is, there is a building boom under way.

The Israelis have become wealthy enough to acquire silver, gold, cattle and other material "goods."

Israel is so wealthy that even the Saudis and those who live in the Gulf states can see that Russia and her allies covet Israel's treasures.

A look at Ezekiel 36:11 provides yet another clue: "I will increase the number of men and animals upon you [land of Israel], and they will be fruitful and become numerous. I will settle people on you as in the past and will *make you prosper more than before*. Then you will know that I am the Lord." (New International Version, emphasis added) That would be quite a development, I thought. After all, when Solomon was king of Israel, he was one of the wealthiest men in the world. Yet Ezekiel was saying that modern Israel would be wealthier still.

In *The Coming Peace in the Middle East*, Dr. LaHaye had considered a number of ways that Israel could become so peaceful and prosperous. Among them: "Suppose that a pool of oil, greater than anything in Arabia . . . were discovered by the Jews in Palestine. This would change the course of history. Before long, Israel would be able independently

---

1 Ancient names for modern-day Saudi Arabia and the Gulf states.
2 Historically southern Spain, though it could refer more generally to Europe or the Mediterranean states.

to solve its economic woes, finance the resettlement of the Palestinians, and supply housing for Jews and Arabs in the West Bank, East Bank, or anywhere else they might choose to live. Even if something besides oil were discovered, it would have the same far-reaching effect if it were able to produce high revenues."[3]

When I first read that, I nearly laughed. *Oil in Israel?* Wouldn't that be nice? Israelis have long complained that if they are really the chosen people, why in the world didn't God resettle them in Saudi Arabia? As the late Prime Minister Golda Meir once put it: "Moses dragged us for forty years through the desert to bring us to the one place in the Middle East where there was no oil!"[4] But the more I thought about LaHaye's theory, the more it seemed just like something God would do—unveil a dramatic plot twist near the end of the story.

Interestingly enough, though, when LaHaye and Jerry Jenkins wrote the first *Left Behind* novel in 1995, they chose to make the Jews of Israel wealthy not through the discovery of oil, but through the discovery of a unique chemical that could make not just Israel's deserts bloom but help any country suffering from famines and other agricultural insufficiencies. When I read *Left Behind*, I was surprised. It was (and still is) certainly possible that God could use a stunning scientific discovery like the LaHaye-Jenkins character Dr. Chaim Rosenzweig invents to bring great wealth to Israel. But I couldn't help but think that it seemed more likely that the Lord would use oil than fertilizer.

And then in the fall of 2000, as I was working for Sharansky and Netanyahu, the *New York Times* published two headlines that riveted my attention:

GAS DEPOSITS OFF ISRAEL AND GAZA OPENING VISIONS OF JOINT VENTURES

New York Times, SEPTEMBER 15, 2000

ARAFAT HAILS BIG GAS FIND OFF THE COAST OF GAZA STRIP

New York Times, SEPTEMBER 28, 2000

---

3 LaHaye, p. 105.
4 Cited in "Moses' Oily Blessing," *The Economist,* June 18, 2005.

Wrote reporter Bill Orme: "Drilling deep below the seas off Israel and the Gaza Strip, foreign energy companies are discovering gas reserves that could lift the Palestinian economy and give Israel its first taste of energy independence. Industry experts, including those on this giant platform, say the Palestinians and Israelis will both profit if they can work together in a high-stakes partnership. They need each other for the efficient development of these offshore reserves, since neither side alone can fully afford the billion-dollar investment in pipelines and pumping facilities that is being sketched out, experts say."[5]

What's more, experts had calculated that Israel had "some three to five trillion cubic feet of proven gas reserves," and according to Yehezkeel (Ezekiel) Druckman, Israel's Petroleum Commissioner, "there may be more." At current prices, Orme reported, "the value of the strike was estimated [at between] $2 billion to $6 billion, depending on pressure, quantity and other variables."[6]

Ezekiel? Israel? Proven reserves? Billions? As I explained to Soltero, when I read those words the hair on the back of my neck stood up. True, the stories spoke "only" of natural gas, not a massive oil strike. But what if Druckman was right? What if this was only the beginning? What if there was more where that came from?

By the time I sat down to write *Jihad*, I had decided to add a fictional oil strike—discovered by a fictional American investment company working with a fictional Israeli company called Medexco, run by a fictional Russian Jewish petroleum engineer named Dmitri Galishnikov. I did so not because I believed that the Bible *specifically* predicted it, but because it suddenly seemed plausible, and I wanted this thriller to seem as realistic as humanly possible. Little did I know.

BLACK GOLD

Just days before *Jihad* was published in November 2002, a curious headline flashed across the news wires: "Israeli Geologist Drills for Oil

5 William A. Orme, Jr., "Gas Deposits Off Israel and Gaza Opening Vision of Joint Ventures," *New York Times*, September 15, 2000.
6 William A. Orme, Jr., "Arafat Hails Big Gas Find Off The Coast of Gaza Strip," *New York Times*, September 28, 2000.

Based on Biblical Guidance." The article told the story of Tovia Luskin, an Orthodox Jew born and raised in Russia who became so convinced by studying the Bible that there was black gold buried under the sands of the Jewish State that he moved to Israel, conducted extensive research, launched a limited partnership called Givot Olam, and came to the conclusion that "there are 65 million barrels of oil" in Central Israel alone.[7]

There was just one problem. Tovia Luskin was wrong. A year later, just before *The Last Days* was published, the news broke that Luskin and his colleagues had discovered oil reservoirs at their Meged-4 drilling site in Central Israel holding not 65 million barrels but 100 million barrels.[8] A few months later, came even more stunning news: new testing had revealed that the Givot Olam site contained not *100 million barrels* but upwards of *a billion barrels*, leading the Associated Press to report, "an Israeli oil company has made the largest oil find in the history of the country," and driving their shares on the Tel Aviv Stock Exchange up by thirty percent.[9]

People emailed me from all over the country to see if I had seen the stories and to ask me yet again if my novels were coming true. But the gusher of headlines about the activities of Givot Olam and Zion Oil had only just begun to flow.

NATURAL GAS, OIL FOUND IN DEAD SEA

Jerusalem Post, APRIL 1, 2004

ISRAEL STRIKES BLACK GOLD

ARUTZ SHEVA, MAY 4, 2004

OIL BARON SEEKS GUSHER FROM GOD IN ISRAEL

REUTERS, APRIL 4, 2005

---

[7] Ross Dunn, "Israeli Geologist Drills For Oil Based on Biblical Guidance," VOA/Israel Faxx, November 20, 2002.
[8] "Oil Traces Found East of Kfar Sava," *Haaretz*, September 12, 2003.
[9] "Israeli Oil Company Claims Oil Find Valued At US$6 Billion," Associated Press, May 4, 2004. Luskin told reporters that he believed "about 20 percent [of the reserves] are commercially exploitable," though he cautioned that much more testing had to be done and said "the company would need to raise between US$20 million and US$50 million to develop the find." See also Amiram Cohen, "Givot Olam Drills Afresh At Kfar Sava," *Haaretz*, November 23, 2004, which notes: "Based on rock properties of the Meged 4 site, Givot Olam calculated that each square kilometer of the oil structure contains approximately 5 million barrels of oil, which translates into a total of 980 million barrels of oil at the site."

IN ISRAEL, OIL QUEST IS BASED ON FAITH

Wall Street Journal, MAY 1, 2005

HIS MISSION: SEEK AND YE SHALL FIND OIL

USA Today, MAY 19, 2005

A VISION OF OIL IN THE HOLY LAND

Newsweek, JUNE 13, 2005

MOSES' OILY BLESSING: WILL ISRAEL FIND OIL?

The Economist, JUNE 18, 2005

SEARCHING FOR OIL IN ISRAEL

CBS NEWS, SEPTEMBER 20, 2005

IS ISRAEL SITTING ON AN ENORMOUS OIL RESERVE?

WorldNetDaily, SEPTEMBER 21, 2005

The story in the respected London-based *Economist* magazine particularly caught my eye. "In the 1980s, John Brown, a Catholic Texan cutting-tools executive, and Tovia Luskin, a Russian Jewish geophysicist and career oilman, both had religious epiphanies. Mr. Brown became a born-again Christian, while Mr. Luskin joined the Orthodox Jewish Lubavitch movement. Soon after, each found inspiration in chapter 33 of the Book of Deuteronomy, in which Moses, nearing death after guiding the tribes of Israel to the border of the promised land, leaves each tribe with a blessing."[10]

"The most lavish," the article continued, "goes to Ephraim and Manassah, the two tribes descended from Joseph (he of the technicolour coat). Their land, says Moses, will yield the 'precious fruits' of 'the deep lying beneath, of the 'ancient mountains' and of the 'everlasting hills.' In this text Mr. Luskin saw . . .'a classic description of an oil trap.' Where geological sediments are bent into an arch, the boundary at the top between an older layer (the 'ancient mountain') and a newer

---

10 "Moses' Oily Blessing," *The Economist,* June 18, 2005.

one can trap oil—the 'precious fruits.' Mr. Luskin named his company Givot Olam—'everlasting hills.' Mr. Brown had a more mystical revelation . . . that pointed to the same area: the biblical territories of Ephraim and Manassah, between today's Tel Aviv and Haifa. He registered his firm as Zion Oil."

Given my own Russian Jewish heritage and born-again Christian faith, I was intrigued. I tracked down Luskin at his office in Jerusalem and chatted with him by phone about all the headlines he was generating.

"Listen, news is not my profession," Luskin told me, clearly preferring science to public relations. "I'm a professional person looking for oil in a very professional way. . . . Since 1993, we've raised $50 million. We've drilled three wells and all three wells encountered oil. It's a big oil field. We're not producing yet . . . but we're on the way [and] we're learning more and more as we go."[11]

Luskin, a graduate of Moscow State University with a degree in geology and a love for oil exploration, told me he left Russia in 1976 and moved to Canada where he worked for Shell Oil and other petroleum companies. Later he worked for oil companies in Indonesia and Australia before emigrating to Israel with his family in 1990.

"Were you raised as a religious Jew in Russia?" I asked.

"Of course not," Luskin replied. "I became observant in Australia when my older kids went to [religious] school, I basically went, too. . . . Initially, I came to the idea of looking for oil in Israel from reading the *Chumash*, the first five books of Moses. This was the first thought [I had about it]. And then I came to Israel and started studying the geology here. . . . I collected a lot of data. I bought data with my own money, and also I had some information about oil exploration in [the mid-1980s] in Syria. When I got the Israeli geological data it was striking in that it was very similar to the Syrian Basin, which seemed to me to extend down to Israel, which turned out to be exactly right. And then before I came to Israel I wrote to the Lubavitcher Rabbi and asked for the blessing for the project, and he answered me, and I came."

"So how close are you to commercial production?" I asked him.

11 Interview with Tovia Luskin, March 22, 2006.

"We are about to start a new well," he said. "Hopefully this well will take us to production stage. . . . Eventually, we will probably need to drill around 40 wells."

OIL AT ARMAGEDDON?

Sitting with the president and CEO of Zion Oil, the man John Brown had hired to bring his "mystical revelation" to fruition, I began drilling him with my own questions.

What exactly had gotten him involved in such a risky and speculative hunt for oil in the Holy Land? What exactly were these prophecies upon which he and Brown and Luskin were basing their companies? And what did he believe the future held?

Soltero, who has worked in the oil and gas business for more than four decades and served on the board of the Independent Petroleum Refiners Association of America, explained that he joined Zion Oil not long after Brown had founded the company in 2000 because Brown had such a compelling way of looking at Israel through the third lens.

It seems that in 1981, Brown visited a church in Clawson, Michigan. There he heard a sermon by the Rev. James Spillman who had written a 79-page book called *The Great Treasure Hunt*. On the back cover of that book were printed three questions:

Would You Like to Know:
- Where the greatest treasure in the world is buried?
- Why will Russia attack Israel?
- The secret behind the battle of Armageddon?

Yes, Brown thought, *I'd like to know the answers to those questions,* and he listened carefully as Spillman made his case.

In his book, Spillman argued: "Biblical prophecy describes an event in which the armies of the world, led by Gog and Magog, would invade Israel 'to take a spoil.' What could Israel possibly possess in the last days that would make it such a prize for conquest that the world's armies would meet there to fight for the spoils? . . . Countries don't invade their neighbors for pomegranates and olive oil, but they do go to war over another kind of oil. Petroleum. . . . The problem, however, is that Israel is an oil poor country. Fifty years of oil exploration and production in Israel have produced about 20 million barrels total. That's a little over two days of the oil production coming out of Saudi Arabia. Armies will go to war over oil, but not two days worth. But what if a significant about of oil were discovered in Israel, a really significant amount?"[12]

That night, Spillman made a similar case to Brown and the rest of the assembled congregation, and then walked them through a series of Old Testament passages, describing God's ancient promise to unlock enormous wealth and treasures for the children of Israel in "the last days."

GENESIS 49:1—"And Jacob called unto his sons, and said, 'Gather yourselves together, that I may tell you that which shall befall you *in the last days*.'" (King James Version translation of the Bible, KJV)

GENESIS 49:22—"Joseph is a fruitful bough . . . *by a well*." (KJV)

GENESIS 49:25—"From the God of your father who helps you, and by the Almighty who blesses you with blessings of heaven above, *blessings of the deep that lies beneath*, blessings of the breasts and of the womb." (New American Standard Bible, NASB)

DEUTERONOMY 33:13—"Of Joseph he said, 'Blessed of the LORD be his land, with the choice things of heaven, with the dew, and from *the deep lying beneath* . . .'" (NASB)

DEUTERONOMY 33:19—"They will call peoples to the mountain; there they will offer righteous sacrifices; for they will draw out the abundance of the seas, *and the hidden treasures of the sand*." (NASB)

DEUTERONOMY 33:24—"Of Asher he said, '*More blessed than sons is Asher*; may he be favored by his brothers, and *may he dip his foot in oil*.'" (NASB)

---

12 Spillman's son, Steve, recently updated the book. See James R. Spillman and Steven M. Spillman, *Breaking The Treasure Code: The Hunt For Israel's Oil* (Medford, Oregon: True Potential Publishing), 2005 (original copyright 1981), p. 3-4.

DEUTERONOMY 32:12-13—*"The Lord alone guided him,* and there was no foreign god with him. He made him ride on the high places of the earth, and he ate the produce of the field; *and He made him suck honey from the rock, and oil from the flinty rock."* (NASB)

ISAIAH 45:3—"I will give you *the treasures of darkness and hidden wealth of secret places,* so that you may know that it is I, the Lord, the God of Israel, who calls you by your name."

As Soltero explained it, John Brown was electrified. He went home and carefully studied these Scriptures, and many others Spillman had laid out, asking God to help him understand them and know how, if at all, he could be involved in finding such a treasure. For the next two decades, Brown traveled back and forth to Israel, learning everything about the oil and gas business he possibly could, meeting everyone in the (tiny) industry that he could, studying maps, researching locations, cross-checking with the Scriptures, and praying for wisdom all the while. By April of 2000, he finally felt he knew just enough to begin a company, and launched Zion Oil with the help of an Israeli lawyer named Philip Mandelker, using the following mission statement:

> Zion Oil & Gas was ordained by G_d for the express purpose of discovering oil and gas in the land of Israel and to bless the Jewish people and the nation of Israel and the body of Christ (Isaiah 23:18) I believe that G_d has promised in the Bible to bless Israel with one of the world's largest oil and gas fields and this will be discovered in the last days before the Messiah returns.[13]

The company was soon awarded a license by the Government of Israel to explore for oil and gas on 28,800 acres in Northern Israel, and it was during this time that Brown turned to Soltero and Glen Perry, formerly with ExxonMobil, now Zion's Executive V.P.

13 Spillman, 2005 edition, p. 134-135.

"John had learned a lot about the oil and gas business," Soltero told me. "But he knew his understanding of the Bible was just the first step. He also needed experienced professionals well versed in the technical aspects of exploration to make this thing work."

"And how is it going?" I asked.

"We were recently awarded an expanded permit to explore some 219,000 acres in Northern Israel," Soltero told me. "We've been drilling for the past several months and the initial results are very exciting. For legal reasons, I can't say more right now. But let's just say it's possible that your novels have vastly understated how much oil is out there."

As he described where they were drilling, I realized it was just a few miles from the Jezreel Valley and the ancient city of Megiddo.

"Wait a minute," I said. "Are you telling me you think you've found oil under Armageddon?"

Soltero just smiled. "I wish I could say more, but right now I can't," he demurred.

In talking to other oil experts in Israel and the U.S. over the next few months I was able to confirm that there is, in fact, both oil and natural gas under the region known in the Bible as Armageddon, where the Scriptures say the final cataclysmic conflict of history will occur. Just how much is there remains unclear as I write this. There is more testing to do, and many technical challenges abound before any of it will be commercially viable to pump and refine, challenges that Tovia Luskin and his team are encountering as well, despite having already found a billion barrels of oil not far away.

Still, Soltero and Brown are clearly excited by the prospect that they are on the verge of something historic, and prophetic. What's more, former Israeli Petroleum Commissioner Ezekiel Druckman has joined Zion's board, and the company had gone public, filing on January 26, 2006 with the Securities and Exchange Commission for an Initial Public Offering to raise more money for more drilling and research.

What intrigues me is that they are not alone in their efforts to examine Israel's economy and geology through the third lens of Scripture.

"Zion is actually one of six companies to drill in Israel where the founder was originally inspired by Old Testament Biblical passages to take an initial look, and then turn the exploration management over to oil and gas professional," Mandelker, Zion's lawyer, told me when I met him and his colleague Glen Perry in Tel Aviv in the fall of 2005.[14] And several of them are beginning to see promising results.

Will one of these companies hit the big one? Will they all? Will someone else? The truth is we cannot know exactly who, or exactly when, because the Bible does not tell us. Nor does the Bible tell us for certain that the oil will be discovered in full before the rest of the Ezekiel 38 and 39 prophecies unfold. It does tell us that oil will be found in "the last days," and it says Israel will be wealthy before the Russian-Iranian coalition attacks. That much we can take to the bank. Thus, expect to read future headlines like this one, "Israel Discovers Massive Reserves of Oil, Gas."

Still skeptical about a small, resource-poor country suddenly finding "black gold, Texas tea" like an episode of *The Beverly Hillbillies*? Then consider the curious story of Equatorial Guinea. For centuries, the tiny country on the Western shores of Africa (tucked in between Gabon and Cameroon) was as poverty-stricken as one can possibly imagine. Until 1995, that is. That was when they discovered oil. Lots of oil.

The country's proven oil reserves have gone from virtually nothing to over 1.2 *billion* barrels. Production has shot from 17,000 barrels per day in 1996 to over 371,000 barrels per day in 2004. Foreign investment is pouring in. The economy has been averaging 15-20% growth per year. In 2005, the economy grew by over 25%, and little Equatorial Guinea is now the second richest country in the world on a per capita basis, after Luxembourg.

Not nearly enough of this oil wealth is actually winding up in the hands of the people. Much of it is winding up in the hands of the country's president and his elite circle of friends and advisors. But still, the

---

14 Author interview with Philip Mandelker, November 14, 2005. Among the other companies that recently have been pursuing oil and/or gas exploration (some with a Biblical perspective, but not all): Avner Oil Exploration, based in Israel; BG (formerly British Gas), based in Great Britain; Delek Group, based in Israel; Ginko Oil Exploration Ltd (which estimated in 2004 that there were some 20 billion barrels of oil in the Dead Sea basin), based in Israel; Isramco, based in Texas; Ness Energy, Inc., based in Texas; Lapidoth Israel Oil Prospectors, based in Israel; Modii Energy, based in Israel; and Sdot Neft, based in Israel.

whole little-country-hits-the-big-one scenario certainly has to make one stop and think. If miracles can happen in sub-Saharan Africa, could they not happen in the Holy Land, too?

ISRAEL, HOME OF MILLIONAIRES

That said, let's be clear: Israel has already become enormously wealthy over the last six decades, and far wealthier than her immediate neighbors. Finding oil would simply be icing on an already impressive cake.

Despite a population of only seven million people, for example, Israel is now home to more than 6,600 millionaires, defined as people with a liquid net worth of more than one million dollars. Of these, there are some seventy multimillionaires, individuals with liquid assets of $30 million or more. Of the top five hundred wealthiest people in the world, six are now Israeli, and all told, Israel's rich had assets in 2004 of more than $24 billion, up from $20 billion in 2003, according to a report published by Merrill Lynch.[15]

Today, Israel has become an economic powerhouse and one of the world's high-tech leaders and a magnet for foreign investment. "Israel is like part of Silicon Valley," Microsoft founder Bill Gates said on his first trip to the country in October 2005. "The quality of the people here is fantastic. . . . It's no exaggeration to say that the kind of innovation going on in Israel is critical to the future of the technology business. So many great companies have been started here."

No wonder, then, that foreign direct investment in Israel in 2005 alone hit a record $10 billion, up 67% from 2004, the second highest growth rate in the world. Or that more Israeli-based companies and companies started by Israelis are listed on NASDAQ than from any other country. Or that Intel, whose next-generation chip was designed in Israel, broke ground in February 2006 on a new $3.5 billion microchip factory and research and development facility in the town of Kiryat Gat, and reported that it now has more employees in Israel than

15 Shlomy Golovinski, "Israel, The Home of the Millionaire," *Haaretz*, June 15, 2005.

it does in Silicon Valley. Or that Google announced in 2005 it was opening new research and development facilities in Israel. Or that over the past decade, more than $8.7 billion has poured into Israeli venture capital funds. Or that an Israeli professor, Robert Aumann of Hebrew University in Jerusalem, won the 2005 Nobel Prize for Economics.[16]

And it is not just high-tech successes that Israelis are experiencing today. Israel now leads the world in exports of industrial oils, fertilizers and polished diamonds. In 2005, the tiny Jewish state placed 8th worldwide in per capita exports. Tourism, too, is surging since the end of the war in Iraq, climbing 26% in 2005, and up 78% in the number of first time visitors. Such a list of economic achievements could go on and on.[17]

That is not to say Israel does not still struggle with poverty, unemployment and underemployment. It certainly does and these are challenges her leaders must constantly and compassionately address. But Israel has made extraordinary—and some would say miraculous—economic gains since 1948 and has become dramatically wealthier than any of her immediate neighbors.

What's more, Israel is poised for explosive economic growth, quite apart from future oil and gas discoveries. Ben Gurion International Airport has been expanded and modernized. New highways and light railways are being built. Inflation, which raged at 100% or more a year in the early 1980s, was a mere 1.2% in 2004. Interest rates are historically low. The exchange rate has been stable. And after a serious recession in 2001-2002 due to the global economic downturn combined with the Al-Aksa intifada (a.k.a., "Arafat's War"), growth is surging again, hitting 4.4% in 2004 and 5% in 2005.

In June 2005, I attended a $1,000 a plate dinner with Benjamin Netanyahu at the St. Regis Hotel in New York. The evening was part of a fund-raising event for Israel's leading free market reform think tank, the Israel Center for Social and Economic Progress, run by Daniel Doron, who has been a friend and mentor of mine on all things Israel since the early 1990s. It was going to be held on the Monday night after the release of *The Ezekiel Option*.

---

16 See "Investing In Israel" and "Venture Capital In Israel," Updates, Israeli Ministry of Industry, Trade and Labor, www. moit.gov.il, accessed March 15, 2006.
17 Ibid.

That night, Netanyahu, who was then serving as Ariel Sharon's Finance Minister, talked about the sweeping changes enacted during his tenure—deep tax cuts, privatization of state-owned industries, banking deregulation, and so forth—and the remarkable economic growth that had resulted. But he insisted there was much more to come.

"In ten years, Israel could be one of the ten richest countries in the world," Netanyahu explained, noting that nine of the top ten wealthiest countries in the world are small countries with less than ten million people each, and that many of them were not on the list at all a decade or two or so ago.

Ireland, for example—a country roughly half of Israel's size, with about four million citizens—was barely a blip the global economic radar for most of the 20th century, Netanyahu observed. By 2005, however, the "Emerald Tiger" had a roaring, low-tax economy and was ranked the eighth richest country in the world in GDP per capita.

"There is absolutely no reason why Israel can't soon become one of the most successful countries in the world," Netanyahu concluded.[18]

Looking back, I am grateful for the opportunity to attend that night. For whether he meant to or not, Netanyahu had just confirmed that Ezekiel's promise of a dazzling economic future for Israel in the last days was rapidly coming to pass.

---

18 The Israel Center dinner was held on June 27, 2005. See www.iscep.org.il for details, accessed on March 15, 2006.